NO PLACE IS SAFE

Karen heard the front door slam.

She waited for Tom to call up to her from the hall as he usually did, but there was nothing more.

Imagined, as she got out of the tub, Tom standing down there at the hall table, going through his mail . . .

She wrapped herself in his white extra-large toweling robe and walked quickly around the bedroom, releasing the shades as she went, letting in the evening light.

Unless, oh Jesus—she stopped dead, staring at the sun crouched like a fiery red beast over Hoboken—he was checking out the contents of her pocketbook, which she'd been dumb enough to leave lying open on one of the hall chairs.

The key to the locker. . . .

She heard his footsteps on the stairs.

There was nothing she could do now.

"A great achievement—beautifully written, quite horrifying, and intriguing to the last page."

—Piers Paul Read

THE SILENCE

CHARLES MACLEAN

HarperPaperbacks
A Division of HarperCollins Publishers

![logo] **HarperPaperbacks**
A Division of HarperCollins*Publishers*
10 East 53rd Street, New York, N.Y. 10022-5299

This is a work of fiction. The characters, incidents, and
dialogues are products of the author's imagination and are not to
be construed as real. Any resemblance to actual events or
persons, living or dead, is entirely coincidental.

ISBN 0-06-101233-5

HarperCollins®, ![logo]®, and HarperPaperbacks™
are trademarks of HarperCollins*Publishers*, Inc.

Cover photo by Telegraph Color Library/FPG International

A hardcover edition of this book was published in 1996 by Viking in Great
Britain

First HarperPaperbacks printing: February 1997

Printed in the United States of America

┌───┐
│ Visit HarperPaperbacks on the World Wide Web at   │
│ http://www.harpercollins.com/paperbacks   │
└───┘

❖ 10 9 8 7 6 5 4 3 2 1

For Deborah

I
WATCHING

MONDAY

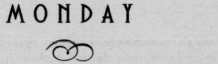

From the swimming pool end of the garden, still shrouded in early mist, came the dull rhythmic splashing that had roused Karen Welford from sleep: she had woken with a start, her forehead broken out in sweat, relieved when she reached a hand across to find herself alone in the bed.

She removed the damp, kidney-shaped mask and listened.

Tom . . . swimming laps. She recognized the signature of her husband's stroke. Short lull before a perfectly executed turn, then the slap of the backwash as he lunged forward again, briskly cleaving the water. It was almost eight thirty. Any other Monday, she couldn't help thinking, he'd have been at the office by now.

She pushed open the screen-door, shielding her eyes against the sudden brightness as she stepped out into the still, airless morning. On its green cliff overlooking Long Island Sound, the house was already in full sun, a sprawled offering to the oppressive heat the day promised. Wrapping herself in the sheet she'd swept up off the bed, Karen walked unsteadily to the edge of the balcony.

"Ned, honey, is nanny there?"

The boy was playing on the terrace below, crouched over a wooden truck he was busy loading with moss and pebbles, the tip of his tongue protruding, lost in concentration.

"Ned, honey?"

He gave no sign.

"Ned." She knew how to insist, only gently, avoiding the

note of supplication that could creep in when she spoke to her son. It was harder not to sound patient.

"Has anyone had breakfast yet?" As if she had every reason in the world to expect an answer.

He looked up at her and smiled, and it seemed so natural and unguarded a reaction—the angelic candor of those huge obsidian eyes squinting a little at the glare of the sky and taking on some of its confident blue cut directly to her heart—that for a moment she almost believed she would get her reply. Then his eyes clouded over, became solemn, watchful again. She felt their reproach. Knew how he longed to admit her to his hermetic world, his kingdom of little punishments, but that he could never let her off so lightly.

"I'll be down in two shakes of a lamb's tail," Karen said, the spirit of laughter in her voice. Noticing only now that the waters of the pool had fallen silent. "Look, here comes Bracken, honey." She had caught sight of Tom's elderly brown Labrador wandering up across the lower lawn.

Tom wouldn't be far behind.

Ned looked around for the dog, then returned to his solitary game and became instantly absorbed. The girl, Hazel, was calling to him now from somewhere inside the house. Karen waited to see whether he would respond or make her come out to look for him. When she appeared at the other end of the terrace, squatting down and holding out her arms to him, Ned ran to her. Bracken came padding up behind them and sniffed lugubriously around Hazel's bare legs.

Not wishing to be seen, Karen retreated into the shade of the balcony's green and white striped awning. She stood for a moment, letting her gaze wander out beyond the cliff edge and become lost at the indistinct horizon. In places, the sun had burned off the bank of haze that had rolled in over the Sound during the night, uncovering islands of dark blue water.

Leaning against the warm stone of the house, Karen closed her eyes, still seeing in outline a triangle of sail that stood off the Connecticut shore waiting for the first breeze.

. . .

"We should do this more often," Tom Welford announced from the head of the breakfast table, chair tilted back, hands clasped behind his neck.

He was a tall, slate-haired man of forty, with a thick boyish face, restless eyes and a delicate mouth that gave his bland Middle Western features an air of spoiled wholesomeness. To Karen, his corn-fed good looks and gravely benevolent manner had always suggested James Stewart in one of those movies—*Rear Window* or *Vertigo*—where the character he plays overcomes an unlikely handicap.

"Well, what do you say, Doc?"

The boy looked up from his cereal.

"Tom . . ." Karen began.

He waited for the maid to finish pouring his coffee, rocking gently in and out of the sun that streamed through the open french windows. "I mean, have breakfast together. What was that fifties sitcom about some perfectly ghastly suburban family? Thank you, Darlene."

"Don't, Tom."

"Whatever happened, they always had breakfast together. Waffles and syrup. The father was there . . . every morning. You'd like that, wouldn't you, Doc?"

"You don't mean it, why raise his hopes?"

"Wouldn't you, Doc?" Tom insisted. "Doc?"

The wide unblinking gaze.

"Hello? Is anyone in there? Anybody home?"

"Tom, no."

"Father Knows Best, Mr. Welford?" Darlene offered.

"Why thank you, Darlene—that was it. You're too young to remember, honey. *Father Knows Best*."

When the boy looked back down again, Karen saw how his eyes, reflecting in miniature the white linen tablecloth, gave nothing away. He began arranging rows of soggy Cheerio loops around the rabbit-infested border of his bowl.

The breakfast room was awash with light.

Karen said, "Ned understands. Don't you, sweetheart?

Daddy's the early bird who has to get to work before anyone else so that he can catch *all* the worms."

"I overslept," Tom said, stretching. Under his crisp Oxford blue shirt, a great pack of redundant muscle shifted lazily. "Slept right through the damned alarm. Never happened to me before."

"Did you call your office?"

"What do you think?" Tom's large head, still sleek from the pool, came forward suddenly out of the sunlight.

"We should have stayed at the apartment."

"The less said on *that* subject the better. What's on the agenda today, Doc? Kindergarten?" He pushed up off the table with both hands and stood, leaning on his knuckles, bearing over him.

Ned nodded, but didn't look up.

"How's the swimming coming along?"

God, why did he have to keep on with this?

"He's making truly excellent progress, Mr. Welford," Hazel volunteered, her spiny antipodean singsong somehow relieving the tension. "Yesterday he swam from one side of the pool to the other without arm-bands."

"Attaboy." Tom slipped on his jacket before bending down to kiss his son, looking over the top of his head at Karen when he said, "Tell you what, Saturday, we'll all go to the beach, spend the whole day together. Deal?"

The boy frowned and made a steeple of his milky fingers.

Karen managed a tight little smile.

"But you'd like that, Ned, wouldn't you?" Hazel coaxed. Only getting his attention when she added, slyly, "Maybe Mister Man could come too."

Ned shot her a fierce, pleading look.

"I bet you *he'll* want to swim in the ocean."

"Mister Man?" Karen heard herself echo.

The boy's hands flew up to cover his mouth.

"I've been meaning to tell you . . ."

"Tell us what, Hazel?"

"Ned's got a new friend—an imaginary friend."

Karen felt a tightening in her chest.

"Good Lord, how can that be possible?" Tom stopped at the door and came back slowly into the room. "Honey, do you know about this?"

Karen shook her head, no. She had to force herself to remain calm and say evenly to Hazel, "Did Ned tell you about this 'friend' of his? Has he talked to you?"

"Never to me. But he does talk, I mean he talks to him when I'm around, quite openly, Mrs. Welford." It was there for her, the hint of accusation behind the girl's smile. Or was it just her imagination? "He calls him Mister Man, or sometimes George—after the monkey in his Curious George books. Don't you, Ned? It's nothing to be ashamed of . . ." The boy was on the verge of tears. "They have conversations."

The tightness in Karen's chest rose up into her throat. She wanted to sweep Ned up in her arms and hurry him out of the room, but Tom was standing now behind his chair, a big warm grin spreading across his face.

"How long has this been going on?" he asked, his hands closing around the boy's shoulders. "This is just . . . I mean, it's *wonderful*."

Share the moment, Karen told herself, show him that you feel the same way he does. He could have arranged all this, the coincidence of his being late for work, Hazel choosing today of all days to make her revelation—testing her, because they knew? Share the moment.

She threw her hands in the air. "Yes, it is! Oh, Tom."

Knowing Ned would see right through her.

Hazel, glowing, said, "I overheard him in the bathroom one day chattering away to himself. I didn't tell anyone because—about two weeks, Mr. Welford—I don't think Ned wanted anyone else to know. It was our little secret. Only I felt it was my duty."

"Two weeks!"

"You did the right thing, nanny," Tom said. "Wait till that gloomy Dr. Miskin hears this bit of news."

Ned brightened, enjoying the attention now.

"I'll call her." Karen rose to her feet, flashing Tom a look. "Could we maybe discuss this later, in private? Hazel, would you take Ned up now to brush his teeth? We don't want him to be late for school."

But Tom had already picked his son out of his chair and, boosting him in the air—Ned chuckling, in spite of himself, laughing aloud for the first time in God knows when—was bearing him shoulder-high from the room like a trophy.

Karen hung back for a moment, watching Hazel busy herself with clearing up Ned's breakfast things. "When you've finished," she added, instead of what she wanted to say, which was more along the lines of you're fired.

Afraid of missing something, she went after them.

"Hey, Doc," she had heard Tom ask in a voice loud with bonhomie that resonated through the hall, "what do you and your Mister Man talk about, for Pete's sake?"

She understood the importance of doing things as usual.

There was a rhythm to her life at Edgewater; she had her chores, regular duties to perform, the little routines she must observe or, as Tom had warned, risk falling through the cracks. Always on a Monday she planned the week's menus with the cook, then talked to Dominic, the yardman, about new projects for the garden; there were the horses to water and feed, Bracken to be walked . . . Tom had taught her that correct form was after all only a matter of tidal repetition.

On the way to kindergarten Ned hadn't uttered a word.

A hazy photograph of Karen (one of a sequence taken that morning with a long lens from across the bay) shows her in blameless jodhpurs and navy shirt, her hair tied back in a simple knot, standing on the steps of the ivy-covered mansion; its weathered Beaux Arts façade, broken by white arches and verdigris guttering, rises shelteringly behind her. The image, enhanced by Karen's fragile loveliness, captures perfectly the aura of money and privilege that surrounds her at Edgewater, the melancholy enchantment of being suspended in a world that exists outside of time.

The worst part was the waiting.

Even before this happened, before Ned's breakthrough, if they wanted to call it that, the next twenty-four hours were going to be critical. But what was a day, two, three at the most, when you'd been waiting . . . Karen tried to recall the exact moment when she'd decided, months ago now, that she couldn't wait any longer.

She ran errands in the village, she saw a man about the flower arrangements for a dinner-party that was two weeks off, she kept a date to play tennis and then have lunch on the terrace at Piping Rock with the nice-but-dull wife of a friend of Tom. Her opponent, one of the few women members who didn't treat her as an interloper, annihilated her in straight sets.

The importance of not drawing attention to herself.

As they retired under the shade umbrellas to pick at salads and sip white wine with Perrier, Karen said what enormous fun it had been, how they should have a re-match when it wasn't so darned hot, savoring the knowledge that she was unlikely ever to set foot in the place again.

After she left the club, going home, the idea of spending the rest of the day sitting around the pool at Edgewater with Hazel and Ned—now that "our little secret" was out of the bag—suddenly seemed more than she could bear.

Instead of making the turn on Piping Rock Road, which would have taken her through Locust Valley and back out to the shore, she kept ahead, driving south, the radio tuned to a local station that was playing the hits of ten summers ago. She scanned the dial, paused for a traffic and weather update, then came back to the time machine, cranking up the volume on "London Calling" by the Clash, which made her think of the first sweltering August she spent in New York, when she didn't have the price of a train-ride to Jones Beach.

She resisted the undertow, the music's nostalgic power to draw her back. Hadn't Tom rescued her from all that? She saw her sense of obligation to him as the real danger. Afraid of weakening, she wanted to drive into the city right away to pick up the suitcase from Grand Central, just get on with it. The harsh jangling in her ears went to fade. It was way too risky middle of the day.

At the junction with 25A, relieved to have left behind the leafy enclaves of gated driveways, riding stables and plant nurseries that bounded her world, she pulled into the Sunoco station to pick up something cold to drink. Never imagining that having only once stopped there for gas—Thurston always saw to that—the pump attendant would recognize the car. Somehow it defeated her purpose to be greeted with a respectful "How are you today, Mrs. Welford?" The kid washed her windshield, stealing casual glances through the Volvo's sun-visor that made Karen wonder how soon news of her escape would get back, until she realized all he was trying to do was see up under the rucked hem of her tennis skirt.

Taking off with a little squeal of rubber, she rejoined the flow of eastbound traffic, sipping her Coke through a straw, letting her mind go with the unfurling blight of the strip that carried her out, light by light, on to the Northern State Parkway. She could feel the knot of pain between her shoulders slowly begin to dissolve.

She drove aimlessly, driving just to be driving, enjoying the solitude of the road, the rumble-hiss of hot tires on melting tarmac. In the city, until Tom made her stop because he feared for her safety, she'd liked to take long walks alone, to lose herself in crowds. She stopped at a roadside fruit-stand and bought a pound of black Moreno cherries, which she paid for with loose change. Her last dollar had gone on the Coke. As usual she was without money.

She could drive like this for ever.

The blue Buick had been sitting in her rearview mirror for less than a mile before it occurred to Karen that she was being followed.

She drove on a couple of miles, it was still there. Too far back to see the driver. A windshield that reflected blue sky but suggested stealth.

Then she was moving out into the fast lane, watching the

needle climb until she was doing seventy-five, not caring if she was pulled over for speeding. She saw the Buick drop back a couple of cars, stay out of sight, then reappear the far side of a U-Haul truck and take the exit for Lake Ronkonkoma.

Imagining things. She laughed at herself, adjusting the mirror to see if the relief she felt showed.

On the skyline a huge red letter billboard for "Toys 'Я' Us" loomed like a faith healer's promise. Ned, before he gave up talking, was always clamoring to be taken there. She felt a pang of remorse. Slowing, she waited for the U-Haul truck coming up now behind to pass her, and missed the first exit.

Across a waste land fringed by stunted pine trees and a few dilapidated frame houses lay the shopping mall, a gleaming white windowless city, where all roads—even the unpromising track she found herself on—seemed to lead. In the vast parking lot, half empty and shimmering like a Utah saltpan in the grotesque heat, Karen changed her mind.

Bringing back a present for Ned would look as if she was trying to reward him; or worse, salve her conscience.

She drove off slowly, planning her return by an indirect route along the shore, in no hurry to get home.

The hot briny smell of the sea was all through the house.

In the day-nursery, under a slow-turning ceiling fan, the table was laid for afternoon tea. Ned lay sprawled on the carpet, chin in his hands, playing a game of checkers with his nanny, who faced him in the same childish position, legs bent up over her behind and crossed at the ankles. An athletic blonde, twenty-two years old, Hazel had on loafers, an apple-green polo shirt and crisp white shorts.

Karen stood in the doorway, holding a finger to her lips so that the girl would know not to give her away. She wanted to surprise Ned—Dr. Miskin had once suggested they try to jolt him into talking—but the boy, who hadn't heard his mother coming along the hall, read the change in Hazel's expression and scrambled to his feet.

He made no sound as he trotted over.

She swept him up and waltzed him into the room under the supercilious gaze of Jeremy Fisher and friends, a pastel frieze of Beatrix Potter characters that Tom's first wife had put up all through the nursery wing. It still rankled with Karen that when she was pregnant with Ned she hadn't been allowed to redecorate the nursery. She didn't care about the rest of the house, which Tom wanted kept the same because "Helen had such marvelous taste," as he so cleverly put it, but the nursery, where Hazel, standing primly now at the tea table, was telling Bracken for no good reason to get down off the sofa—the nursery was her territory.

The dog, usually deaf to female commands, obeyed and, barely pausing to investigate Karen's ankles, slunk past her.

They never even had children.

"What's up, Bracken old buddy, did nobody take you for a walk?" She turned with Ned riding her hip and saw the grizzled Lab flop down on the carpet at the feet of his master.

Tom . . . sitting in an armchair behind the door.

In shirt-sleeves, loosened tie; his jacket and briefcase beside him on the floor; a fat wedge of papers on his knees.

Her grip on Ned tightened.

"Hi, babe," Tom said, smiling up at her. "I called the club, I got Nancy, but you'd already left."

She let the boy slide to the ground. "We didn't expect you home . . . this early."

The nursery windows, fitted with safety bars, were open wide to catch any cooling gust off the Sound. At her feet, a jalousie of shadows on the powder-blue carpet trembled with the faint reflections of the sea. But there wasn't any breath of wind. The house felt becalmed.

"Did we, Ned? I just felt like taking a drive, it was so unbearably hot. I couldn't . . ."

She faltered, unable to go on.

"Something came up at the office," Tom said. He stood facing them, feet planted importantly apart, doing his trick of rocking over and balancing on the outside edges of his shoes. "I have to be in Chicago, as from tonight. Just for a couple of days."

"Always something," she said. Brave smile.

Tom softened. "Hey, at least I get the chance to spend an afternoon at home with you and Doc."

"Great," she said.

The spore of paranoia multiplying.

"Would you like a cup of tea, Mrs. Welford?" Hazel asked.

"So, what happened?" Tom wanted to know, talking to her through the door to his dressing room while he packed.

"I told you," Karen called back, "I left the club around two, then I drove out to the mall, I . . ."

"About Ned and his 'friend,'" he said, patiently. "What did Miskin have to say?"

"She wasn't there." Karen closed her eyes, took a deep breath. "She's on vacation, some place in Europe. It's August, Tom. Every head doctor in Manhattan has gone to the beach. I wasn't even given a referral."

"You could have spoken to somebody, Jesus."

"Like who, for instance?" Karen stepped out of her tennis skirt and turned on the shower. "His nanny?"

"I couldn't get a word out of him," Tom said.

"What did you expect?"

Earlier, after tea, she'd watched them play ball together on the lawn, Tom making a rare happy fuss over the boy. It was only natural, she'd told herself, that he should want to be with him after Hazel's dramatic revelation. Although Tom never let it show, she knew how much Ned's reticence troubled him. As deeply, in a different way, as it troubled her.

"There's been nothing more from Mister Man."

"Is that a reason to celebrate?"

"Honey, it's just a phase," Karen said gently. "They call it 'elective' mutism because that's what it is. His choice. When Ned decides he's ready to talk again, he will."

She stood under the shower, an ancient nickel-plated fixture that looked like a birdcage, scrubbing at her skin with a loofa glove until it felt raw. But the queasiness, the clenched feeling at the pit of her stomach, wouldn't go away. Why hadn't Tom gone straight to the airport from their apartment as he usually did when he had to take an unexpected business trip? Because of Ned's "breakthrough"? Or was it because he really wanted to check on *her?*

"I don't get it," Tom said, coming into the bathroom. "Our son makes his first attempt to communicate with us in six months and you act as if you couldn't give a damn."

"I just don't want you to be disappointed."

"You're ducking the issue."

"Can we talk about something else?" She turned her face into the spray and held her breath a few seconds.

"Sure, why not? You want to discuss why you were an hour late for dinner last night?"

"I already told you."

"Everyone thought it extraordinarily rude."

"Maybe I should have explained about the subway being less than dependable on a Sunday night. I daresay your grand English friends would've been amused to hear I couldn't get a taxi because my pocket money ran out."

"Don't be ridiculous."

"Mrs. Tom Welford, stuck for a lousy cab fare."

"You've only had to ask," Tom snapped. "Did I ever deny you anything? It's for your own good, Karen."

"Well, I'm sick of living like this, having to account for every last cent I spend. It's too humiliating."

"You knew what time we were supposed to meet. I don't understand where that hour went. If, as you say, you left the apartment at six thirty . . ."

"I stopped at a bar on Lexington and got something to drink, all right?" She saw his eyes narrow. "Give me a break, Tom. I had a Coke, that's all. I must've lost track of the time. What is this, an interrogation?"

"You know what they told us at Silverlake. We have to think of Ned's safety. You agreed to the controls."

She stepped out of the shower, leaving the water running. "It's been a long time. Why won't you trust me?"

He was standing at the window with his back to her. "As I recall, it was your idea that I should keep an eye on things 'watch over me' is how you put it—until you were completely clear."

Karen gave a scornful laugh. "I still look dangerous to you? Well, do I?"

She stood in front of him, one hand defiantly cocked on her dripping hip.

"You could say I've been a little concerned, yes," Tom said quietly as he turned round, holding out a white mono-grammed towel.

"You're never going to let me forget, are you?"

He smiled at her. "What is so wrong with a woman being indebted to her husband? Does gratitude become a dirty word just because he happens to have saved her goddamned life?"

"That was five years ago," she said, knowing she'd gone too far now to retreat. "Don't try to drag me back to when I was someone else."

She was sitting at the vanity-table in the bedroom, drying her hair, when Tom came through carrying his briefcase and an overnight bag. He walked up behind her, and, stooping to kiss the back of her neck, asked if she'd like to ride with him out to the airport.

She turned off the hair dryer.

Tom said, "We can talk some more on the way."

"If that's what you want." She knew there was no question of refusing. Her earlier disastrous outburst, the last thing she intended, could only have strengthened his suspicions. "I mean, I'd love to come. Give me five minutes."

"Is anything the matter, babe?"

"No, I'm fine, really."

Their eyes briefly met, then slid past each other in the mirror, a silver-framed tryptich which also showed her Tom's unguarded profile. Something she saw there, some promise of indulgence, made Karen think for a moment that it wasn't too late to confide in him, tell him everything. There wouldn't be another chance.

"I want you to wear the same outfit you wore at dinner last night," Tom said in a voice she knew.

"To the airport?" She tried to sound light-hearted. "You don't think I'll be a little overdressed?" She'd put on a loose white T-shirt over her bra and panties; her jeans lay on the chaise longue.

He didn't smile. "The dress, the half-slip, the same shoes. Nothing else. You know the rules."

She felt a quick rush of fear. Was this the real reason he hadn't gone straight out to La Guardia, why he'd made the detour?

"Tom, please. I'm not feeling . . ."

"Didn't I hear you say a minute ago"—he took the hair dryer gently out of her hand—"that you felt fine? Here, you're not quite done yet. I can see a wet patch."

"It's just . . . it must be the heat." Karen closed her eyes. By the time he got back from Chicago, two days from now, she told herself, none of it would matter any more. She heard the hair dryer come to life and felt a sudden blast of hot air lift the damp hair off her nape.

"Nothing else."

It was like a door slamming shut.

TUESDAY

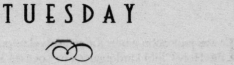

It was past noon when Karen arrived to pick up Ned from the Holy Child kindergarten in Locust Valley. A few minutes late, she found him playing alone on the swings in the yard. One of the teachers, who'd been keeping an eye on him, came out onto the porch and waved to her over the privet hedge, as if she needed to talk. Her beckoning stirred in Karen a childhood fear of having to give an account of herself: they knew, of course, someone must have overheard Ned talking to his imaginary friend, and now the woman was eager to discuss this miraculous event. But as soon as Karen opened the gate into the yard, Ned's teacher called out, "Just wanted to be sure it was you, Mrs. Welford. We can't be too careful these days."

Walking him to the parking lot (Ned trailing his security blanket, stopping to examine every other leaf and bug in his path), she had to suppress her impatience, the almost indecent sense of haste she felt. In the car, she started to tell him where they were going to spend the afternoon, but the boy already seemed to know—he always seemed to know. As she leaned over him, fumbling with the catch of his seat-belt, Ned's face suddenly lit up and she hugged him to her.

They drove out to the Wheatley Hills by an indirect route, crossing the Long Island Expressway at Old Westbury, then doubling back along the service road as far as Exit 39 South. After yesterday, even if she had only imagined that she was being followed, Karen knew that she couldn't afford to take chances. A mile further on, checking first in the rearview mir-

ror, she swung back across the expressway by an overpass that
took them into what Tom liked to call the first real country
east of New York.

Lately he'd taken to driving this way to and from the city,
retracing the old bluestone roads of the great mostly vanished
North Shore estates, because, he said, it relieved the mo-
notony. Karen mistrusted her husband's sudden enthusiasm
for scenic detours. These past weeks the small towns and villages of North Hempstead and Oyster Bay had lain crushed
and empty under the harsh leveling weight of the sun. Even
the shady compounds of the rich seemed to have lost their
seclusive charm to the long swelter of days without rain. The
last grand houses, no less than the encircling colonies of split-
level suburbia, had become rank, airless, insect-ridden places,
revealed beneath a wilting fringe of leaves to be primitive and
unsafe—as if this New World re-creation of some green and
pleasant corner of England had been transported to the
malarial shores of Belize or Zanzibar.

She thought of Tom, last night, on their way to the airport,
talking with vague, uncharacteristic melancholy about enjoying beautiful things while they were still there to enjoy—
and shuddered.

At the bottom of the hollow, after going through a stop
sign, she drove on at a crawl, searching the undergrowth to
her right for the derelict mailbox. She found it easily enough,
though it had lain all summer long under a thick green shawl
of weed; as always, when she saw that the flag was in the up
position, her heart quickened.

She pulled off the road under a bank of rhododendrons
and waited, asking Ned to help her count cars—a game he
could play on his fingers, holding up hands like starfish—letting twenty go by before she could feel reasonably certain that
they hadn't been followed.

Then another ten, just to be safe.

The soft classical music, like the tinted windows and the par-
tition that shut off the driver, helped insulate the tonneau of

the limousine from the outside world. In her own private darkness, enveloped by the skirt and black faille half-slip which Tom had bundled over her head and tied like a gunny sack with a rope around her wrists, Karen kneeled on the floor of the Mercedes. Her head had been pushed down next to the speaker under the jump seat. The music lulled her. She had a sense of her nakedness, complete below the waist except for a pair of shiny black court shoes, being left out for him like a tray, while he sat back deep in the leather upholstery and sometimes talked to her, sometimes conducted business on the phone, in a low confidential voice.

She had first to beg his forgiveness, mumbling into her suffocating hood, then, as he made a game of teasing her with the silver-chased handle of the flail, plead with him to begin.

She turned in the driveway, the steering wheel slick with sweat under her hands.

Halfway up the avenue that led to the main house, which lay just out of sight over the brow of the hill, she forked left and hurried across open meadow toward a cluster of white frame buildings on the edge of the wood. Under a widening circle of blue sky, her mild euphoria held in check by the fear of meeting someone who might recognize her or the Volvo, Karen felt like prey running for cover, only safe once she had gained the sanctuary of the compound.

She made a slowing sweep around the huge live-oak that stood in the middle of the gravel circle and nosed the station wagon in through the doors of the empty garage, which closed behind her, shutting out the harsh afternoon sunlight.

In the semi-darkness that temporarily blinded her, she heard the bolts go up on the heavy wooden doors. Joe was there. She leaned back and closed her eyes.

She wanted to tell him the good news first, right away, but his hand was on her mouth stopping her saying anything until she had kissed him, her face turned up to his through the open window. They hadn't seen each other for over a week. There was nothing that couldn't wait. The boy was forgotten while Joe helped her from the car and they stood entwined in the stifling gloom that smelled of grease and rotted leaves until Karen, feeling faint, started to pull away.

"It's going to be all right," she said.

"What is? Is anything wrong?"

"He's gone to Chicago."

"Well, hallelujah. How long for?" Joe laughed and held her at arm's length, trying to see all of her, swinging her around. He had on army shorts and moccasins, no socks, olive-drab tank top, his reading glasses; she thought he looked great— Joe always looked great.

"If he never came back it would be too soon. Two nights."

"We'll make the most of it."

"Joe, there's . . . nothing to stop us now."

"What do you mean?"

"Tom came through with the money."

She felt the slight hesitation.

"How about that," he said slowly, nodding his head. "I never thought it would happen."

Somehow she'd expected more from him.

She had to release Ned from his booster seat in the back of the Volvo, but she let Joe carry him up the narrow stairs that led from the garage directly into the apartment above. There was the usual resistance on Ned's part, an initial shyness that faded as soon as Joe set him down and he trotted ahead along the hall that ended in the surprisingly spacious living room of what had once been the estate chauffeur's cottage. Karen noted approvingly that Ned's favorite toys had been laid out ready for their visit.

Two years now since Joe had rented this place, at her insistence, so that they would have somewhere to meet beside motel rooms.

"What persuaded him to change his mind?" he asked.

"I told him that if I couldn't have money of my own, not an allowance but a small settlement, I'd leave him."

Joe looked at her.

She went in the kitchen and made them a sandwich, working around the pile of dirty dishes in the sink and the tops that hadn't been cleaned since she was last there. After they'd eaten and Ned had been sent out to play in the backyard, Karen came back and flopped down beside Joe on the couch.

"He just caved right in," she said, slipping an arm around his neck. "Since I was obviously well again, and in control of my life—those were his exact words—he was willing to admit I could handle the responsibility. Last night, he told me that as 'a token of his trust' he'd opened an account at Citibank in my name. No strings. I can make withdrawals whenever . . ."

She hesitated, pushing back a dark wing of hair that had fallen over her eyes, suddenly realizing she hadn't prepared what had to be said next.

"How much?"

"Everything I asked for, more."

"This calls for some kind of celebration."

She gave a little smile. "Don't it just."

Joe drew her slowly toward him, and her head fell back as he kissed down the long curve of her throat with an urgency Karen knew would become harder to resist. He whispered, close to her ear, "Go on in the bedroom. I'll get something cold for us to drink."

"No wait," she said, catching his hands as they slid under the backs of her knees. "I haven't told you everything."

She got up from the couch and stood above him, her legs under the washed-out blue cotton skirt still tangled up with his, reluctant to break off altogether. "I'm worried about Ned. Nothing's wrong. I just feel that maybe this is all getting to be too much for him."

He took a deep breath. "Do we have to discuss it now?"

"We can't afford to screw up, Joe. Not after all we've been through."

"Maybe you should have left him at home."

"It's the nanny's day off," she said, annoyed. "Anyway, I wanted to bring him. If we're going to be spending the rest of our lives together . . . Joe, he's started to talk again."

"An even better reason to celebrate."

"I'm scared he's going to give us away."

"You worry too much. Always did."

"This is different."

He let her explain, but it was as if Joe had to force himself to listen. She knew how touchy he could be on the subject of Ned. While she worried constantly that their relationship might be to blame for his troubles, Joe refused to even consider it a possibility. Nor did he share her guilt over how convenient they had found the boy's taking refuge in silence. He reacted calmly to the news of Ned's breakthrough. Mister Man.

"We've always known it was going to happen."

"The way things are now, he only has to say one word, make some innocent remark. I'm not even sure that he hasn't already. Let's leave, Joe."

"We don't want to rush things."

"No? What are we waiting for?"

"There's the job upstate. I can't just walk away from it, leave the man with half a house. I still work for a living. Remember?"

"Is this about money? We've got money. Don't you get it? Everything's falling in place."

"I guess so." Joe shifted uncomfortably.

"All I have to do is show up at the bank." She laughed, then added lightly, "With a suitcase."

"You think it'll be that easy?"

If she hadn't lost her nerve last night at Grand Central, they would have it now. There'd be no argument. She considered telling Joe about the locker, giving him the key and having him pick up the case that afternoon. But Karen decided it would be better to wait, let him come around to the idea.

Joe said, "I just need a little more time to straighten things out. I'm talking maybe a couple of weeks, that's all."

"We have two days. Not even. Tom gets back tomorrow night."

"You're over-reacting. An imaginary friend? It could be months before Ned really starts to talk. Who knows, maybe this is his way of saying we need to bring things out in the open. Find some other way for us to be together."

"We've been down that road before. You know it doesn't lead any place. We both agreed."

"I know what we agreed, but it was always going to be as a last resort. It can't hurt having another look at things from a legal point of view. I could talk to Herb again."

"And have him tell you there's not a judge or jury in New York that would grant me custody? Even if there was, do you have any idea what kind of fight Tom would put up?"

"If I came out and told Herb the whole story, he might be able to see a way through. One thing, he would never take you on as a client unless he thought there was a good chance of winning."

"Thanks," she said coldly. "Thanks a lot."

"I still think it's worth a shot."

"Why do I all of a sudden get the feeling that I'm talking to a complete fucking stranger? What are you trying to do, Joe?" She looked down at him, raking her hair back and holding it off her forehead with both hands; she turned away, then spun around to face him again. "You know damn well that what you call the last resort is our only hope, the only way out. Now that it's a reality, suddenly you get cold feet, you're backing off. Let go of me."

She began to struggle.

Joe relaxed his grip on her wrist. "That's not true."

"The hell it isn't!"

She broke away and went over to the screen-door, and stood staring out over the backyard. She could see Ned sitting cross-legged in the shade looking at a book with his hands clamped over his ears: she thought, God, what are we doing to the poor kid? She should have known Joe would try to weasel out of this. He'd done it before, he'd done it all his life. A breeze stirred the trees on the grassy mound behind the compound.

The light moved.

It was out beyond the curtilage of the white picket fence, something she had seen, some tiny disturbance. She peered into the tangle of underbrush. She moved her head this way, then that, chasing the source of the reflection, if that's what it had been. A bird flew out from the edge of the wood and banked along the sky, turning up the pale underparts of its wings.

The afternoon slipped sideways.

He kept her waiting, abjectly, until they were almost to La Guardia. Then Tom cracked open a window, letting in the roar of aircraft engines and the volatile smell of jet fuel on the warm night air. In darkness, her muffled cries went unheard; the pain, a tidy pain, was not excessive. Between rounds, she investigated with her tongue the inside of the gag, a silk handkerchief that tasted bitterly of his cologne. She felt numb with revulsion, but the authority over her flesh of Tom's delicate flail restored gradually her confidence in his judgment. She could accept that she was at fault and that she deserved to be punished, so long as she knew the pain was being inflicted in kindness and for her own improvement.

As long as there is trust, he said.

At the moment of his crisis, her joined hands projecting from the mouth of the dark bundle at her husband's feet opened and closed as if she was slowly applauding.

She shivered. "I think Tom already suspects."

Joe, coming up close behind her, put his arms around her shoulders. "All I'm saying is we should review our options."

"This is what you always do, sidle out of things."

"No, just try not to lose sight of what's important."

"All your life, Joe. How can you do this to me? To us?"

She turned inside his embrace, searching his eyes, which were blue and calm, not quite focused.

"We're here for each other. That's all that matters, and we're going to be together, soon, I swear to God."

"I just can't do this any more, coming here, living in that house, being near him. If only you . . . someone, something . . ." She took refuge in her own incoherence. "We have the money now, God's sake, let's just . . ."

"Don't say it."

Her mouth was almost touching his ear. "I hate him so much, Joe, you've no idea."

"But I do, I understand," Joe said.

Then she buried her face in his shoulder, letting him comfort her, surrendering to the inevitable. She no longer had the will to resist as he lowered her back against the cushions. She felt even a reckless urge to guide his hands, pulling them down, away from her breasts. When with the tips of his fingers he discovered raised areas of skin between her thighs, and formed little burning queries over each fine spray of cuts—the first time Tom had broken his promise to her never to leave a mark—she didn't want him to stop what he was doing even though it hurt, hurt like hell. She was ready now to tell Joe everything. She wanted him to know.

She felt him recoil, the sudden shaming absence of his hands, then they were pulling apart before she realized the phone was ringing.

They looked at each other.

Joe scrambled to his feet and walked over to the white telephone, which sat on top of a bookcase next to the TV. "It's for you," he said, letting it ring.

"Are you sure?"

"Line 2. Did you hook up before you left?"

She nodded. "He said he'd call, but not till this evening."

"You plan to answer it?"

Karen stood and deliberately smoothed her skirt over her hips, trying to get hold of herself. Concentrate. It's two thirty, an hour later than in Chicago. If he asks, you just came in from the garden, where you were watering the tubs—no, playing with Ned—when you heard the phone ring and ran inside, reason you're a little out of breath. It's been so darned hot here . . . if he asks.

She picked up.

"Hi, babe," Tom said before she had even opened her mouth. "Everything okay?"

She closed her eyes . . . She was speaking from the front hall at Edgewater, standing by the marble table with claw feet, with its vase of lilies, the Remington statuette, the green morocco visitors' book; looking up at that enormous equestrian painting over the stairs, *The Paddock at Belmont*, by . . . never mind who by, she could smell the goddamn lilies now, gracious, cloying . . . she was there.

"Tom! What a coincidence. We were just talking about you." She gave a gay laugh, turning her head so that Joe, who felt ambivalent about these Oscar-winning performances, couldn't catch her eye. "I was telling Ned all about Chicago and how you lived there when you were a little boy. And what was so cute, he puffed out his cheeks to show he knew people call it the Windy City, and when I told him that it has bears on its football team, honey, if you've got time tomorrow . . ."

"There's been a change of plan. The Goodrich thing, the deal I was working on, it fell through. We walked away with a whole skin, give or take a patch. I'm coming back tonight."

Her mouth dried. "You want me to have Thurston meet you?"

"It could be late. Let me call you back from O'Hare."

"You sound . . . tired."

"I'll be glad to get home. How's my boy? Any developments?"

"Nothing yet," she said brightly. "But we're having a good time. Just the two of us. Everyone's got the day off. I picked him up from kindergarten, then we . . . went for a drive."

"Let me have a word with him."

"With Ned?" She barely faltered. "He's out on the terrace, you want to hold, I'll go get him."

"I'll wait," Tom said.

He'd never asked to do this before.

Her hand shook as she put down the receiver. She could

not avoid looking at Joe now; they exchanged a short hard glance consciously pared of meaning, as if even their thoughts could betray them. She felt his eyes on her as she walked over to the screen-door, opening it carefully to avoid making any sound Tom wouldn't recognize. She waited until she was out in the yard, far enough from the house, before she called Ned over and told him his father wanted to speak to him on the phone.

When they came in together Joe had left the room.

She watched Ned climb on a chair and pick up the receiver and put it expertly to his ear, but the wrong way up. She was there to help him. "What's new, Doc?" she heard Tom say in Chicago. A brief smile of recognition crossed Ned's face; otherwise he didn't respond. His eyes grew big and serious as he listened. Karen waited, holding her breath, watching the boy's lips.

"As usual," Tom said, when she came back on, "nobody home."

A mosquito zeroed in on the sweaty scroll of flesh above Eddie Hendricks's collar. Resisting the urge to take a slap at it, he eased his hand up and rubbed his neck with the bundle of leaves he'd used to staunch the wound, then dabbed gingerly at his nose just to be sure the bleeding had stopped. He winced and his eyes began to water again. There was blood on his shirt, blood on the grass, blood on the hidden branch which had caught him with cruel precision under the septum as he crawled back from the edge of the bank, deeper into the shade.

His nose, starting to throb, felt about the size and shape of a dwarf pineapple. He threw away the compress, took a couple of snorts from his hip-flask, then retreated to a fall-back position behind the ruined shed overgrown with creeper where he'd set up the equipment.

It was maybe a hundred and fifty yards from the picket fence, but still gave him with the aid of binoculars a clear view of the back of the house. There was no movement now. Nor anything coming in over the headphones he was using to monitor the tape—except wind interference, the least gust sounding like a small tornado as it hit the wire-mesh snout of the directional mike aimed at the screen-door.

What he had so far was mostly noise, masking all but a few tantalizing fragments of an apparently heated exchange between the man and woman. He'd guessed as much from observing the kid, left out in the yard to amuse himself, suddenly jam his hands over his ears, as if he couldn't bear to listen to another word of what he himself was straining to hear. For a surveillance buff, Hendricks had a heretical dislike of gadgetry.

Leaning against a corner of the tumbledown shed, he picked up the smaller of his two recorders and flipped on the record button, holding the built-in mike close to his mouth.

"Two twenty-three. Continuing surveillance of 'Overbeck,' 1154 Wheatley Road. Five minutes ago subject came out into the yard and joined the boy over by the fence, and told him his father wanted to talk on the phone. Repeat, father. Which would indicate that Welford knows where his wife and son are spending the afternoon.

"For the record, sustained a slight injury while taking evasive action. Hazards of working out in the boondocks. There's a possibility also I got burned. The kid (who has on a red Mickey Mouse T-shirt and Yankees baseball cap) kept looking up at the trees, waving a skinny arm in my direction. The good news is he doesn't speak.

"Question: why, if she has nothing to hide, did the subject go to such lengths to cover her tracks earlier?"

He waited, thumb on pause.

"Two twenty-eight. No sign of movement. Correction. The kid just came back out, accompanied this time by white male, six two, one eighty pounds, around thirty-five; slim fucker, tan, wearing shorts; brown, semi-long hair, no facial growth, eyes . . . at a guess, asshole blue."

Tracking them with his binoculars, Hendricks watched the man follow Ned over to the shade tree and, squatting down beside him on the spread Navaho rug, try awkwardly to share his absorption in a video game. Only doing it to get the kid settled, obviously counting the minutes until he can go back inside. It made you wonder why Karen brought Ned along in the first place. Why she'd want to take the risk? Unless she was using him for camouflage.

Nothing to hide . . .

He exchanged binoculars for his Nikkon with the 200mm lens, focused and shot a couple of frames at 1/125th, but wasn't quick enough. The man, already on his feet—Ned didn't even look up—had turned away and was heading back toward the house. He needed one clear shot. Come on, turn around, look back at him, look back, jerk-off.

The screen-door banged shut.

Hendricks scanned the windows left of the doorway, wondering whether the bedroom gave on to the rear or front of the house. He lowered the camera into the grass. Sweat rolled down into his eyes, making them smart. The heat in the wood was something else. They had the opportunity now.

Under the tree, motionless, the shrunken figure of the boy was evidence enough.

At two forty-three, the detective duly noted, Karen Welford appeared within the house at the next window along from the kitchen. He watched her through the camera, shooting her vague outline as it moved restlessly back and forth across the screen, then stopped and bent forward with the gesture of someone slipping off clothes below the waist.

A few moments later, he heard over the headphones the man's voice, startlingly clear, exclaim angrily, "How could you let him *do* this to you?"

"He gets back tonight," Karen said.

Silence.

"You promise you won't ever bring up the subject . . ."

Hendricks saw the tall grass by the fence stir before he felt the breeze, and then a roar of surf rushed in behind it filling his ears.

". . . we never had this discussion, all right?"

She must have persuaded him to change his mind.

There was a long pause. Hendricks, waiting anxiously to play back the tape in case he could retrieve something of what had been lost, finally heard Karen say, "We don't have any choice."

Then a hand reached up and closed the window.

WEDNESDAY

She was early getting to the city. On the drive up from Locust Valley, she'd worried about fitting in a hair appointment, which in the event took up less of the afternoon than she'd allowed for. With time on her hands, two or more hours to kill before Tom was due back from his office, she decided to risk going downtown. As a pretext, she had Thurston drop her off at Brooks Brothers on Madison Avenue, and walked the last few blocks to Grand Central at a good clip, defying the heat.

She took a cab back to the apartment.

At the corner of 85th, loafing in her incognito of jeans, baggy T-shirt and dark glasses, she looked back from the shade of a green awning to see if she'd been followed. An elderly couple in untimely evening dress debouched through the revolving doors of her building and arm in arm made their way toward a waiting cab in a slow fugue-like shuffle. Feeling an opposite compulsion to hurry, Karen swept past them and into the lobby of 1180 Fifth like a woman with a crowded schedule, a full page of pressing engagements.

On her way up to the penthouse, still fretted by an urgency that had no object, she asked Alex the doorman if the elevator was normally this slow? He didn't turn his head, but gave her more answer than she wanted, blaming the car's funereal pace on the extra load the heatwave was placing on the grid, predicting another shutdown like in '77, with looting and riots, worse than LA, smothering her impatience in Lithuanian gloom.

They crawled skyward. She felt the sweat along the ridge of her spine and under her arms turn cool. The tremors of an unspecific fear subsided. The suitcase had been where she'd left it: as an added precaution, she'd changed lockers. There was nothing more she could do now except wait.

Karen stood just inside the front door, her back pressed against it as if to shut out the enemy, her eyes closed.

She never felt comfortable about spending the night at the apartment. It had pretensions to being a home, but in the rich, sterile way that an exclusive hotel suite does, where the fully equipped kitchen isn't really meant to be used; where the sofas and chairs in the over-elegant lounge are always perfectly plumped. Although Ned had a room here, he wasn't encouraged to stay. On the hall table, she noticed there were fresh flowers expertly arranged in a tall oriental vase she had never seen before. Beside it, a stack of unopened mail and a note for Tom from Elvira, who cleaned. After a day or two away, Karen could get the feeling of having walked in on someone else's life.

She kicked off her shoes and went upstairs, one hand trailing the balustrade that rose steeply through the wood-paneled, double-height hall, avoiding the varnished eyes of what Tom called his fake ancestors. The walls were hung like an atelier's with floor-to-ceiling portraits that Tom and his first wife had bought up in lots at auction. Tom claimed to be curious about the people in the paintings. The pleasure, he liked to explain, whenever they had company, was that of discovering some old family photo album that happened to go back centuries rather than years. Karen knew them better as silent witnesses.

On the landing she pulled off her T-shirt and draped it half defiantly over the ornately carved rail of the balcony. She hadn't given a thought yet to what she was going to wear. Tom had only announced last night that she was expected to accompany him to a benefit at the Public Library. It was unlike him to give her such short notice. In other circumstances she might have found the strength to say she wasn't feeling up to it: coming into New York in the heat of the day, leaving Ned at a time like this.

In the master bedroom the exhaust of cool air smelled faintly of lavender. She went over to the windows and drew down thick canvas shades, excluding the wraparound views of Manhattan for which the apartment was generally considered a prize. The heat and noise of the city reduced to a low white hum, she lay down across the bed, unzipped her jeans and closed her eyes. After only a minute or two, Karen reached for the sleep-mask she kept in a drawer of the bedside table, here as at Edgewater.

She must have slept for an hour, maybe more.

She was in the bathroom, watching water cascade into the tub, drowsily wondering why it hardly made a sound. She sat on a gilded wicker laundry basket and drank orange juice from the carton she'd found in the small refrigerator in Tom's dressing room. When the bath was full, she went back into the bedroom and opened the louvered doors of her closet.

She started hunting through the rack of evening clothes, giving consideration only to dresses she thought might please Tom. He liked her to wear simple classically cut gowns: nothing that could be too easily identified, or that would invite comment. She found a short strapless black sheath and held it up to her chest, turning to look at herself in the cheval glass across the room.

She didn't care much for what she saw and let the dress slip indulgently to the floor, ashamed suddenly that she was still trying to seek her husband's approval.

But that wasn't all that was wrong. In the mirror, over her bare shoulder, Karen had noticed that the top drawer of her writing desk was half open. It should have been closed. She swung around, surprised that it hadn't caught her eye when she first came into the room.

The desk, a fine Queen Anne escritoire Karen had turned into a glory hole, was stuffed with paper: odd bits of correspondence, old accounts, unpaid parking tickets, theater programs, invitations—a haphazard record of her New York life, her marriage, her make-over as a society beauty, her less and less frequent visits to the city. The top drawer, which contained the family's medical records, she always kept locked. Although the maid certainly knew where to find the key, the idea of Elvira searching her desk was absurd.

It could only have been Tom.

And why not? After Ned's "breakthrough," he would naturally have wanted to look through Dr. Miskin's reports. She pulled the drawer open now all the way and saw that the folder in question was on top of the pile. But Tom hadn't spent a night at the apartment all week; he would have to have made time to come over from his office during the day. And that, however conscientious a father Tom might be, seemed unlikely.

She picked up Ned's file, which always felt accusingly bulky to her, and leafed through the typed pages of Leah Miskin's analyses. Nothing here had helped Karen to understand why her son, five months past his third birthday, had given up talking as if it was one of life's optional extras. But then Miskin wasn't in full possession of the facts. Karen had told her, in front of Tom, that there had been no warning. Which wasn't true. Soon after she started taking Ned with her when she went to see Joe at Overbeck (always and only on the nanny's day off), she remembered the little boy saying to her, out of the blue: "Mom, I don't ever want to learn to talk."

She would make it up to him, somehow. And, God forgive me, Karen thought, soon.

At the back of Ned's file, buried among prescriptions and growth charts that she should have discarded long ago but for sentimental reasons had kept, she came across a note from the clinic at Lenox Hill, the hospital where Ned had been born. It was an appointment card for June 16, 1990, at 10.30 in the morning.

The appointment she had failed to keep.

Recognizing the name of Dr. Goldstone, Karen quickly

closed the folder, put it back in the drawer and went and sat down on the bed. The anxiety she had felt from the moment she set foot in the apartment returned with a rush.

Was this the information that Tom had been looking for in Ned's file—and presumably found?

She can still see the clock on the wall of the clinic, and herself lying under it on a surgical table, her feet in stirrups, a sheet draped over her knees.

Seven minutes . . .

She has been told to hold this position for seven minutes by the doctor, who has retired to his office, where he sits writing at a leather-top desk. She can see him through the open door if she turns her head and cranes a little. A nurse comes around, peers under the sheet and says something about all being well "down there."

The feeling she has is one of deep dread, of being trapped, of being unable to wake from a nightmare. It isn't the fact that her clothes, which she left neatly folded on a chair beside the couch, have disappeared that prevents her from leaving, but the presence of Dr. Goldstone, who every now and then looks up from his writing and, craning *his* neck, smiles at her in a paternal, encouraging way that makes her feel that she must stay, go through with this ordeal—only another five minutes now, Karen—just to please him.

A tanned, good-looking, older man with thick silver hair and a voice like whiskey and honey, Dr. Goldstone reminds her a little of Walter Cronkite, perfectly cast in the Trinitarian role of father, husband and specialist. She looks from the clock to the desk in the doctor's office and sees him take a tiny atomizer from a drawer and squirt it into his mouth, then, wetting the fingers of both hands with his tongue, vulgarly smooth back the bulging wings of hair (at its thickest and silveriest over his ears) that have strayed from their laquered place. He stands up, straightens his white jacket with the embroidered monogram over his heart and, checking his look in an invisible mirror (apparently unaware of being observed), approves what he sees with a shocking little smile.

He picks up a small black box, toughened plastic, the size of a child's lunch-pail, quickly inspects its contents before snapping the lid shut, and prepares to come through to her.

What if Tom had tried to contact Dr. Goldstone? Had already spoken with him?

But he wouldn't, Tom, would he?

Want to consult a fucking ghost.

There was really nothing to worry about.

Karen lay back in the tepid bath, only half convinced, yet determined not to give way to more unfounded suspicion. Dr. Goldstone didn't exist; by mutual agreement he never had.

She clung to the idea that Monday's revelation about Ned's fantasy friend would have compelled Tom to read up on Miskin. So he'd found the time in his busy schedule to come over here, and ransack her desk; it only went to show how genuinely concerned he was about the boy. Tom might hate the idea of his son seeing a shrink (always referring to her as "gloomy Leah"), but he had a touching confidence in Miskin. There was no reason to think he would have looked any further in the file than her dense and voluminous notes.

"Ned is obviously a high-need child," Karen had read in one of the early reports, "whose universe begins and ends with his paramount sense of being the center of a loyal, supportive and loving family."

The water fell silently from the gold-colored faucet.

She let the heat spread through the bath, controlling the stealthy flow with her toes until some slight adjustments she made suddenly brought back the sound—almost a roar to her ears—of water tumbling over water.

The time for doubts had passed.

She drew a glistening knee back almost to her chin, gingerly clearing a lather of soap bubbles so that she could examine the scratches on the inner and underside of her thighs. The lattice of broken skin, as much of it as she could raise above the waterline, had already begun to fade; the once cruel welts, barely discernible now to the touch, were only tender when she applied direct pressure with her fingertips.

The bitter-sweet sensation, renewing her sense of shame and anger, brought tears to her eyes. But she couldn't separate these emotions from the base conviction that she had gotten no less than she deserved.

Last night, tired after getting back from Chicago, Tom had been uninterested, mercifully, in repeating the lesson. Karen had never doubted that drawing out his marchlands in blood was meant as a warning to her (not even to entertain the idea that she could belong to anyone but her husband). But why had he felt it necessary now to break his own rules of safety— *there must be no mutilation or cutting, no pain inflicted in anger or with any revengeful feelings*—unless he had good reason to suspect that there was someone else?

She remembered the look on Joe's face, Joe saying that he wanted to kill the bastard who did this to her, the wild Celtic light in his eyes when he talked about shooting Tom Welford down like a dog, and a lot of other stuff Joe didn't mean. She wondered now how smart of her it had been to let him know about a side of her life with Tom that he could never understand. It shouldn't have come as a surprise to her that after his temper cooled he seemed to hate Tom for doing this to her a little less than he blamed her for allowing it to happen.

It was when he started talking about evidence of cruel and unusual treatment that Karen realized that her plan had backfired; instead of strengthening Joe's resolve, she had given him another reason to bring up the hopeless question of divorce, another excuse to prevaricate.

There were times when she thought she knew Joe too well.

She closed her eyes.

If there had been any other way, God knows, she would have taken it. But she had let herself be persuaded by him that there was no armor against fate. In this life, Joe had told her his grandfather used to say, what's for you won't go by you.

It was the same sweet stuff he'd laid on her when they first met, were first in love, all that seductive crap about being two of a kind, marked by destiny, meant to be. God! Sometimes she wondered if he had ever even known his grandfather.

And yet she believed him.

It was Joe's vivid and shimmering vision of her that had helped fix in her own mind what she was wearing that night, the way she'd done her hair, the dark Chinese red of her lacquered nails, her different perfume, the small amount of jewelry Tom had allowed her to wear . . .

She couldn't remember now who had brought Joe to the party.

They were standing together in the front hall at Edgewater, she and Tom, receiving their guests (most of whom she was meeting for the first time) when he just walked up out of the June gloaming and was introduced.

They still argued about who had seen who first, and who was the more blown away by that encounter. Joe said he would never forget the look in his hostess's eyes, the sudden dilation of her pupils to an infinity that only he saw, her silent pleading with him not to reveal the coincidence of their having known each other in a former life, and all excruciating evening long the clear signals she gave out that her marriage to Tom, only a few months old, was already unhappy.

Joe always claimed to have had no idea that she was married. The last he'd heard of her in the four years since they'd split up, she was living in a girlfriend's apartment somewhere downtown. Nothing had prepared him, he said, for running into her again in her present circumstances. But Karen had never been convinced by his story of being asked to write a series of articles about Long Island's Gold Coast mansions for a "shelter" magazine—in those days he was supporting his business with occasional journalism—and of taking the opportunity the party gave him to scout Edgewater. At the time she'd played along with the charade of showing him around the house, endured the irony of their going upstairs together to view the master bedroom. She remembered how he had stopped her outside the door, told her that he couldn't take on the assignment, but that he had to see her again. She could only pretend that she hadn't heard.

They had talked on the floodlit lawns like strangers among the other strangers and looked across the dying blue of the Sound to the lights that winked at them along the Connecticut shore. She had treated him with an amicable reserve and, whenever he tried to bring up the past, airily changed the subject. Or made a point of returning to her place at her husband's side. In her heart, she knew it was no coincidence; Joe had tracked her down, had deliberately come looking for her here; and she felt afraid that her excitement would show.

It was really neither fate nor the faithfulness of an old lover that had touched her—Joe had let her down before, she had no reason to think he wouldn't do so again—but the fact that he had come back to her at exactly the right time.

When she needed him most, he was there.

She heard the front door slam.

She waited for Tom to call up to her from the hall as he usually did, but there was nothing more.

Imagined, as she got out of the tub, Tom standing down there at the hall table, going through his mail . . .

She wrapped herself in his white extra-large toweling robe and walked quickly around the bedroom, releasing the shades as she went, letting in the evening light.

Unless, oh Jesus—she stopped dead, staring at the sun crouched like a fiery red beast over Hoboken—he was checking out the contents of her pocketbook, which she'd been dumb enough to leave lying open on one of the hall chairs.

The key to the locker . . . loose among all her other stuff. Shit. Bright orange tag, designed not to be mislaid or missed.

She heard his footsteps on the stairs.

There was nothing she could do now.

"I was getting worried," she said, when Tom finally appeared. He stood for a moment, smiling at her against the gaudy flush of the sunset.

"How was your day?"

He threw his briefcase and a copy of the *New York Post* down on the bed, came over and kissed her. "How was my *day?*" He held the lapels of her robe and used them to draw her face up to his and kiss her again tenderly.

"Aren't we going to be late, honey?"

"Do you have any idea how beautiful you look?" he said. "Tom."

He was nuzzling her ear.

"We've got plenty of time."

"Tom, please." She laughed up into his eyes, and could find there no accusing glint, no trace of a hidden agenda; he was just fooling around. "I'm not even dressed."

"All the time in the world," he sighed good-naturedly as he let go of her, patting her behind. "Long as you haven't decided yet what you're going to wear, I can at least grab a shower."

"Make that a cold one," she heard herself say.

He was loosening his tie; then he was sitting on the edge of the bed pulling off his shoes and socks.

She walked into the closet, conscious of Tom looking at her while she bent forward, her breasts moving freely under the open robe, to slip on her underwear. She turned away.

"You know what I love about you?" he said. "It's your modesty, your irresistible sense of shame."

"For God's sake, Tom." She picked up the black dress she had taken from the closet but discarded and held it up for him. Did a little twirl, which he approved.

Tom in his shirt and shorts going toward the bathroom.

She felt like a traitor then.

"Did you think I wouldn't find it?" The question caught her off guard.

"Find what?" She went over to her dressing table and, removing a couple of bobby-pins, shook her hair free. She could feel Tom's eyes on her back.

"You know what I mean."

Her heart raced. "No, I don't."

"Karen, sweetheart." He was waiting, watching her at this, letting her flounder.

"What?" She looked back at him. Tom was standing in the doorway to the bathroom, legs apart, balancing on the outer edges of his bare feet, like a boy colossus. He held up a small triangle of broken glass.

She laughed, frowning. "What is that?"

He'd found nothing.

"Another exhibit from your private collection." He tossed the glass shard, the size and shape of an arrowhead, on to her desk.

"What on earth are you talking about?" She had to hide her relief that it wasn't the key to the locker. "I've never seen that before in my life."

"It was in the drawer, right there. Honey, I know this isn't something you find easy to share." He was looking at her now with steady, caring eyes. "I can't force you."

"Share *what*, for fuck's sake?"

"It's okay, really." He came up and slipped his arms around her waist. "I just want you to know," he said in a voice so gentle it was like a caress, "that if you ever feel like talking . . . Remember what they said at Silverlake? About it not being such a great idea to deny things? I was real disappointed to see those ugly little cuts on your legs again."

"That's so unfair, Tom."

"I guess I should have known better than to think you'd put all that behind you."

"*You* broke the rules."

"I did? Now you got me all confused."

"Can we please stop with this?" Inside her chest, she could feel a tightness like a hand reaching up and trying to close off her throat. "Please?"

She began to struggle. It was just a game, she told herself. He was gas lighting her. But he held her close a moment longer, his face next to hers.

"You know, you haven't been yourself lately. I've been worried about you, ever since Ned . . ."

Karen twisted around. "Let's keep Ned out of this."

He was silent. His point made that these matters were not unconnected, Tom said at last, "I got some good news."

She broke free from his embrace and, walking over to the bed, picked up her dress.

He followed her. "Don't you want to hear it? I managed to reach Dr. Miskin this afternoon, tracked her down to some gloomy-sounding pension in Bratislavia."

"How enterprising of you," Karen said, tugging the black sheath over her head. Hiding her face. There it was—the innocent explanation. She'd been right after all about Tom searching her desk for Ned's file. He simply wanted to be well prepared when he talked to Miskin.

"Where else would you expect Leah to spend her vacation?" He smiled. "I told her about Ned's imaginary friend."

"How she did react?" Karen pressed her lips together. She felt his hand at the back of her dress, helping fasten her zipper, closing the eyes and hooks.

"She said we won't have long to wait. She wants to see him the moment she gets back to town. In her professional opinion, when Ned does start talking again, it'll be quite 'sudden'"—Tom turned her around and, holding her by the shoulders, forced her to meet his gaze—"and as if he never stopped."

"When does she get back?"

"At the weekend."

"I just hope she's right," Karen said.

"Like a dam bursting—those were her words."

"Oh, Tom." She was close to tears. "It's wonderful news."

"I knew you'd be happy."

They went past the Plaza, jockeying on down Fifth Avenue in a string of ruby tail-lights. The Mercedes pulled over into the left-hand lane and snookered itself behind a delivery van. Eddie Hendricks caught up, went past in the middle lane, then slowed down again, watching in his rearview mirror as the Merc tried to rejoin the stream of traffic.

Way out in front now, Hendricks saw the driver make a turn signal, getting ready to head west on 45th street. He tried to swing the Caprice over into the right lane, with the intention of going through and over to Sixth on the next cross street, but the slot he was aiming for had already been filled. There was a muffled crunch, the hot squeal of rending metal, then frantic honking as he slammed on the brakes.

Stripping his jacket from a hanger over the back seat, he sighed and got out to inspect the damage. There was hardly a mark on the other car, a white Cutlass Sierra, which had hooked its fender behind the Chevy's wheel housing. No point looking for one more dent in the battered flank of his own car.

The driver of the Olds, all white knuckles, was still leaning on the horn. Hendricks didn't feel like getting involved. He shrugged and walked out into the dazzle of Fifth Avenue, making passes with his rayon jacket at the oncoming traffic, until a cab screeched to a halt in front of him.

"What are you, nuts?" the cabbie said. Hendricks waved his private investigator's license and told him he'd have to run a couple of lights if they were going to catch the Mercedes.

"Get outa here, will ya? I should lose my medallion, go to jail. For what?"

"Thrill of the chase," Hendricks said, peeling a bill from the roll he kept in his pants pocket. On the back of the driver's head-rest, a printed sticker read: THANK YOU FOR RIDING YELLOW. THIS CAB IS DRIVEN BY A MORALLY FINE PERSON.

"Wiseguy, you're lucky it's been a slow night."

He stuck the twenty through the Judas-hole in the bullet-proof Perspex grille. The cabbie wasn't quick enough.

"On second thoughts," Hendricks said, pulling it back, "take your time, drop me off at Grand Central."

THURSDAY

1

They ate lunch in the stone-scented shade of the pool-house, its distemper walls a cool Mediterranean blue behind the peeling but still blithe Jazz Age frescos. They ate cold vichyssoise, tuna sandwiches and macadamia brittle ice-cream (each pale course carried down from the house by Darlene) in torpid silence. The two women had given up making small talk for the sake of the boy, lulled by the hot half-wild smells of the garden, the drowsy hum of bees and the popping of a ball-machine from next door's tennis court. Hazel had suggested that Ned wait at least half an hour before going back in swimming. He sat gazing out longingly at the pool and beyond.

August had always made Karen want to be some place else. As a child, growing up in dusty little citrus towns in central Florida, she had dreamed of migrating every summer like the snowbirds to some more civilized northern climate, envying the children whose parents could afford to pack them off to summer camps on Lake Michigan, to Nantucket and Bar Harbor, Maine, and, yes, the Adirondacks.

The irony was that ever since she married Tom Welford and came to share his fairytale life in Locust Valley, they hadn't once gone away in August. Not for a vacation, not for a weekend, not even to the Hamptons, which Tom claimed to despise for reasons that seemed to her obscurely snobbish. It didn't help knowing that Edgewater, built in 1912 by a utilities magnate as a fall and spring retreat, was never intended to be lived in during high summer; that the mansion (relatively modest by Gold Coast standards) had been kept shuttered up during the dead season. Until Tom, that is, bought the place eight years ago for his first wife and turned "the cottage," as he called it, into a year-round family home.

He'd had to wait for the family . . . wait for a child to fill the old house with love and laughter. But he'd always known, he told Karen gratefully, that that was its proper destiny.

It didn't help at all.

The sprinklers hissed and sputtered on again, the lower lawn vanishing under a rainbow mist, then drifting back into focus where the longer grass ran down under tall stately trees to the beach, a perfect half-moon of grayish pebbly sand. At the end of the breakwater that formed an arm of the bay, a sharp-nosed motorboat that belonged to their neighbors gently nudged the dock, riding the sudden backwash of a Coast Guard cutter that had already passed from view.

Karen looked back up at the main house and saw Darlene in her white uniform appear for a moment at the edge of the terrace and, unaware of being observed, lean over and spit into the sea below.

It was only a quarter to two.

In the grounds of Cair, laid out like an English park—to substitute the lake, the majestic trees, the acres of tended lawn, she only has to half close her eyes—it always seemed to be afternoon. There were no fences there either, no obvious boundaries, no areas declared off limits. The place was run along the lines of a country house hotel, where guests are encouraged to make themselves at home, get to know each other, or not, feel free to do just about whatever they please . . . there wasn't a lock on any of the doors.

Why would there be when she was never left on her own, not for a minute, not even to wash or dress herself? Lack of privacy was something you learned to live with at Silverlake, or "Cair Paravel," as she renamed the exclusive retreat (a factual imitation of some Bavarian hunting lodge), where she had spent her lost summer in the Adirondacks.

Each morning she'd listen for Nurse McIver's footsteps descending the corridor that might or might not stop outside her room to deliver the coveted "Cair package." She remembered birds singing their hearts out in the woods, when all she could hear with a wolverine's acuity was the approaching rattle of little plastic cups containing the prescribed medications—silver bullets, for the lucky few.

In her dreams, in her waking thoughts, some of these hot stifling days of August, Karen finds herself back at Cair. She walks endlessly down by the lake, at first with one of the staff or her husband when he comes to visit, and then alone. They are getting her ready for the outside.

Naturally, there is always somebody, who stays just out of sight—just to make sure.

In the muggy afternoon heat, Karen lay by the pool, reading a book that couldn't hold her attention, keeping from behind her sun-glasses a watchful eye on Hazel as she gave Ned his swimming lesson.

The girl was standing at the shallow end, half out of the water, her golden somewhat heavy torso beaded with tiny droplets, her white blonde hair darkened where it hung wet down her back. She held the boy expertly under his scrawny shoulders, encouraging him to scissor-kick his legs as she swirled him around. "Look, Ned!" She pointed out how his efforts were drawing a grinning Flipper, one of Ned's inflatable pool creatures, into their wake. They were laughing, having fun, so completely at ease with each other in their sparkling element that Karen felt a twinge of resentment.

She heard a car in the driveway, heard Bracken bark in a desultory fashion, then suddenly quit, as if he'd been reassured by some familiar scent. She remembered it was his friend the yardman's day for cutting the grass.

It wasn't that she was jealous of the bond Hazel had formed with her son; or, for that matter, with her husband, whose complete confidence she had quickly earned. She'd come to them when Ned was two years old. The clean, reliable, hardworking daughter of New Zealand sheep farmers, trained in England at the prestigious Norland Place School, Hazel Withers, they both agreed, had been a real find, a treasure. There was no question that she was genuinely fond of the boy. For that Karen could have forgiven her almost anything, disregarded all the little things about Hazel which annoyed: the brisk, finical, nanny-knows-best manner that didn't quite jibe with her pretty looks, the suspicion that when there was no-one around she took the easy way with Ned, the cheap perfume she wore on her days off, her irritating habit of saying, "If I were in your shoes, Mrs. Welford . . ."

The page swam before her eyes as Karen tried to find the place where she had given up reading. She thought of joining them in the pool, just to cool off . . . she was wearing a single-piece dark green polka-dot bathing suit with its own matronly skirt that hid the tops of her legs.

She sank back with a sigh on the rattan recliner and watched Darlene come back out on to the terrace, this time headed for the grass steps that led down to the beach and pool area.

It wasn't that Karen would rather have looked after Ned herself. If she sometimes felt nostalgic for the free and easy way she had been raised as a kid, allowed to run wild among the matty groves and crystal lakes of Polk County, she knew better than to share her feelings. Tom would never admit it, but his insisting on their hiring a "dependable" nanny had a lot to do with his doubts about her stability, her competence as a mother. She didn't want him to think that she saw Ned's privileged childhood at Edgewater as anything but idyllic.

Karen's heart beat a little faster as she saw the maid gingerly run the gauntlet of lawn sprinklers, then turn at a more dignified pace along the path toward them.

There were times when she felt reassured knowing that Hazel was there to watch over the boy. It might have hurt her pride a little, but she could even appreciate why Ned had chosen someone outside the family circle as the person to whom he could safely reveal the existence of his talking friend, Mister Man.

It was just that she didn't trust her.

"You have a visitor, Mrs. Welford," Darlene announced as soon as she had caught her breath, her broad placid face dappled by reflections from the dancing blue water.

She looked around for her robe.

How could she trust her, when she knew that Hazel, like all the help at Edgewater, was there to watch over her too?

He was waiting for her in the long sunlit gallery, which ran almost the full length of the first floor, standing under the life-size portrait by Tissot of a woman holding a miniature poodle. A powerfully built man of medium height in his mid or late fifties, the stranger kept his back to her when Karen walked in off the terrace. His hands were thrust into the pockets of a crumpled but expensive white linen suit.

"You know, she looks so serene. Women don't have that serenity any more. Something they've lost. And yet I bet she had her fair share of troubles in her life. Beautiful painting, a real work of art," he said, stepping back from it and hunching his shoulders admiringly.

"I think maybe it was just the way men wanted us to look."

"It must really be something to live in a house like this surrounded by objects of beauty." He turned slowly around and looked at Karen with an appraising smile. "If you'll forgive my saying so, Mrs. Welford."

"You're very kind. We're very lucky. I don't believe we've met, Mister . . ."

"Serafim." A deep voice, a truckload of New Jersey gravel spread over some sort of an accent that came and went. "That's with an *f*, not like the angels."

"Oh . . ." She laughed nervously as he shook her hand.

"You know, the ones that stand up there behind the throne and play better music than Muscle Shoals." He gave a broad grin, and she saw that he had something green stuck between his front teeth. "Victor Serafim."

The unusual name, which Darlene had tried to recall on the way up from the pool but got all twisted around, meant nothing to her. "Are you a friend of Tom . . . of my husband, by any chance? He's not here, he's at the office, in New York."

He shook his head. "Can't say I've had the pleasure."

"Oh, I assumed . . ." She didn't want even to consider the possibility that this person was here to see her.

"But, hey, who knows, now that I got my own place out here? Now we're neighbors."

The smile cut off and on like the beam of a flashlight, leaving his face, in repose, expressionless. It was a strong face, deeply lined and pitted, the prominent nose and high tufted cheekbones suggesting Slav or Native American blood. He had a full head of longish gray hair, brushed straight back, and behind a pair of wire-rimmed glasses dark narrow eyes that didn't hurry over things and made Karen feel uncomfortably underdressed in her robe and sandals.

"You mean, right here on Lattingtown Road?" she said, and at once regretted the note of disbelief in her voice.

"Well, practically neighbors ." The man laughed easily, ignoring or perhaps not noticing the slight. "I just bought a property in Old Westbury, right on the golf course, four bedroom colonial looks out over the first green—you have to see the place, it's a little piece of heaven."

"I'm afraid my husband won't be back until late."

"I appreciate that, he must be a busy man. I just thought it was about time I paid my respects, if you know what I mean."

Karen looked at him, missing something, uncertain how to respond. "I'm not sure that I do, Mr. Serafim . . . entirely."

"My friends call me Victor."

She drew the lapels of her robe tight across her throat.

"Can I get you anything, a cold drink? This awful weather we're having . . ." She went over to the hall table and her hand

shook as she picked up the phone to call the kitchen and ask
Darlene to bring through a tray. "A glass of iced tea?"

She heard him cough behind her; noticed there was a
radio playing somewhere. Looking out the window, she saw
with a sudden jolt of recognition that made her stomach turn
over what had to be Serafim's car sitting in the driveway.

Bracken, happily sniffing around its white-wall tires.

It shouldn't have come as a surprise. Sooner or later they
were going to make contact. A "collector" would be assigned
to her. She knew the score, Sylvia had explained everything.
Only Karen had never imagined they'd get in touch, Christ,
it hadn't even been a week.

"Thank you, no tea." He held up a hand.

Never for a moment thought they'd have the nerve to
show up at the house.

"Yes, Mrs. Welford?"

"It's all right, Darlene." Karen put the phone down.

It was the same gray Lincoln Towncar she'd seen when she
went to pick up the money on Pier 11, Sunday night. Behind
the wheel, the same two bulky young men—she recognized
the overstuffed La Coste shirts in matching gray, like livery—turning now, mouths and hands working, as they spoke
with each other in a delicate flurry of signs.

She had to grip the edge of the table for support.

"If we can dispense with the formalities," Serafim began
in a changed tone of voice, "there's a small business matter
me and you need to discuss."

"Yes, I know. Only not here. You must be out of your mind
coming here. To this house. My husband could come home
unexpectedly. I have a small son, my God!"

"Hey, Karen, take it easy," Serafim said more gently. "I got
two boys myself. I'm a family man. You've got nothing to
worry about. Act like a sensible person and do what's right,
no one gets to know about our transaction, no one gets hurt."

"I'm afraid I'm going to have to ask you to leave—now.
You're not to come here again ever, is that clear?"

"I'll leave when I'm good and ready," Serafim said. "Is *that* clear? Let me explain something to you." He came over to where she was standing and, picking up the visitors' book from the hall table, started leafing through the pages.

"You know famous people," he said, nodding his head as if impressed. "Want me to write *my* name in here? Hey, relax, just kidding. But I get this all the time, clients who think they got the right to come out snotty with me because of what I do for a living. Shylock. Jew. Everyone makes that assumption. It's not fair to Jews, it's even less fair to me. I soon put 'em straight. Tell someone you're from Bosnia these days, which happens to be the truth in my case, only I was raised here in Brooklyn, it shuts them right up."

"I didn't say anything to you except ask you politely to leave. You haven't any right to be here."

"What I do for a living is no different to . . ." Serafim looked up at the ceiling, "it's like going to your bank or a mortgage and loan society, you expect the trust you place in them to be reciprocated. Well, likewise, okay? I come to pay my respects, you pay me yours. You want to act high and mighty, fine, go ahead, but you better know I've been around long enough not to be impressed by any of this." He made a gesture with the flat of his hand that took in house and grounds, and the world of privilege that extended beyond them, then snapped the visitors' book shut and threw it back down on the table.

"You opened your legs and cracked a few walnuts, snared a rich guy, so what? I know too much about you, princess. I know your history. I know your type. You're not in any position to tell me jackshit."

"All I meant was that your coming here like this puts me at risk. I was promised that everything would be handled in the strictest confidence. If my husband finds out . . . well, he'll just kill me, that's all."

"He won't find out. If you're worried about that little something you got going on the side . . . I'd say old Tom was in the total fucking dark."

"You had me followed, didn't you?"

"We have to protect our investment. It's nothing personal. With me all your secrets are safe."

"What do you mean by that?"

"We don't just hand out half a million dollars to anyone and we don't give out free toaster ovens either—even to preferred clients. Borrowing money is a serious business, Karen. There are other people involved here, bankers, businessmen, people like your husband respected in the financial community, they don't play around."

"I think I know what I'm doing."

"It's like you fall down on your mortgage payments, they repossess the house."

"I understand."

"All you got to do is give me the money and I'll be on my way."

"What money?"

"What money, she says. You kill me, Karen, you know that? Didn't Morrow tell you it was six for five? You pay me fifty now, another fifty the end of the week."

"I think there's been some mistake. I have seven days to make the payment. That was the agreement."

"We're talking an unusually large capital sum. If we didn't know your husband was good for the money, we wouldn't have looked at this. My investors want something now, a show of good faith."

"Well, that's too bad. No one said anything to me about 'a show of good faith.' "

"Too bad? Karen, I'm trying to keep this nice, it makes no difference if you take out five bucks or five mil, the principal . . . forget the principal, it's the interest that matters. It's the vigorish, the juice, Karen, the part of you . . . and yours that now belongs to me."

He moved a step closer and she shrank back, thinking he was going to touch her, but he reached behind her instead and lifted the Remington bronze from the hall table. "Heavier than I thought. How much would you say something like this is worth? Fifty, seventy-five, a hundred thousand dollars?

You know I could take it home with me for collateral. My youngest son, Ronald, he's crazy about the Wild West."

The statue was of a cowboy riding a bucking bronco, waving his miniature stetson, one arm thrown back in the classic pose. It was one of Tom's favorite pieces.

"Whatever stone you crawled out from under, Mr. Serafim, I'm afraid you've had a wasted journey. I don't have the money."

"I'm not trying to hear that, Karen. You know I look around your beautiful house that's like a fucking palace and what's on the walls alone must be worth ten, twenty times . . . I didn't come here today to have my intelligence insulted. I came here to collect what you fucking owe me."

"You'll get it Sunday."

"I go to church on Sunday, I spend the day at home with my wife and kids, I don't do business all day."

"The earliest I can manage is Saturday."

He didn't respond. He seemed more interested in the statue, holding it up to the light, weighing it on the flat of his hand and lofting the little cowboy through the air as a kid might play with a model imagining it to be the real thing.

"Would you mind putting that back where you found it?"

"You've got until tomorrow, princess, twenty-four hours. You know the parking lot behind Denny's on Glen Cove Road, meet me there around three. If you don't show, I'll assume you're happy to have me take the matter up with your husband."

"You don't need to worry, I'll be there."

"Then that's settled." He grinned at her and, swiveling his wrist like a waiter, rode the statue back toward the table. "You happen to catch any of *Lonesome Dove* when they reran it last week? How do you like that character whadayacall him . . . Robert Duvall . . ."

Distracted for a moment by the murmur of voices outside on the lawn, Karen heard the dull thunk of the bronze hitting the parquet floor before she saw it fall, as if in slow motion, from Serafim's grasp. Too late for her "No!"

". . . no, it was the other one, Tommy Lee Jones."

She sank to her knees with a little cry, her eyes filling with tears when she realized the statue was still in one piece, thank God. Except that something about it didn't look quite right. She thought she was going to throw up: the cowboy's free stetson-waving arm was bent back now at an impossible angle. "How am I going to explain this to Tom?" she wailed.

"It was an accident." Serafim turned up his palms. "Hey!" He hunkered down beside her. "As God is my witness, it just slid through my fingers. I'm sorry. Accidents happen, Karen. Let me see that." He took the statue from her and made a grimace as he twisted the arm more or less into line. "There, no one will ever know 'the Captain' took a little fall. No harm done."

He set the Remington back on its plinth on the hall table, then held a hand out to Karen, offering to help her up. She meant to reject it, didn't want this lowlife creep touching her, until she saw that his outstretched hand was missing the top half of its middle finger, and felt too embarrassed not to take it. She was conscious of the warm stub pressing into her palm. "Would you leave now, please? Please go."

She looked into his big not unfriendly face, saw only the stillness of the room reflected in his glasses; the blue Persian rug, the windows recessed into white arches that repeated along the length of the gallery . . . then a shadow that moved, and Karen realized that Serafim's eyes had strayed to somewhere over her shoulder.

"I'd be happy to do that for you, Mrs. Welford," he said with a smile that wasn't for her, "but aren't you going to introduce me to the rest of your beautiful family?"

She turned, still adjusting the front of her robe, and saw Hazel standing there in her bikini inside the arched doorway that was open to the terrace, holding Ned by the hand and asking her if it was all right for them to go up to the nursery to watch TV.

"This is Ned and . . ."

"Hello, young man," Serafim said. "What's doing?"

Ned squirmed, canting his head shyly into Hazel's golden thigh.

The collector laughed. "Cat get your tongue, Doc?"

2

While Joe paid for the room, Karen waited in the A & S parking lot on Queens Boulevard across the street from the motel, a dump called the Flying Carpet they had used before in emergencies, when it wasn't safe for her to come to his place.

She kept her eyes on reception, checking her rearview every other moment to make sure she hadn't been followed. She'd called Joe soon after Victor Serafim left, but had told him nothing on the phone. They had a code based on the premise that whoever made the call had reached a wrong number; she was only able to indicate that she needed to see him right away and that time was scarce.

She listened to the pulse of her heart, metering precious seconds. Heard it beat faster when she saw Joe come out of the office and, with barely a glance in her direction, walk along the path that led to the suites reserved for short-stay customers. She hated coming to these places, being part of their remorseless turnover, adding to the permanent reek of stale, furtive little acts of treason. But for once, perhaps because she was afraid, or because she knew it was going to be the last time before they would be together for good, Karen didn't care. She felt a desperate kind of exultation at being there.

She watched him disappear into one of the cabins, waited a few moments, then swung her dark-blue station wagon out on to the street and drove quickly past the Flying Carpet's burlesque frontage of domes and minarets and into the motel court.

She parked in the appropriate space opposite 1002, not bothering to take advantage of the wooden paling an understanding management had erected to screen cars and license plates from the curious. Joe was wearing the black fifties bowling shirt with his name embroidered on the back in tall purple letters that she'd found in a thrift shop and given him their first Christmas in New York. A nice touch, considering he never liked the shirt and could only be wearing it to cheer her up.

The door opens before her hand reaches the bell.

She sees his eyes go out beyond her to check that the coast is clear then loses them again in the rush to find herself in his arms. A little cry escapes her, a still needful whimper, as if the familiar comfort of his embrace is not yet sanctuary enough. Then he's kissing her, covering her mouth with his, and she feels the blissful loosening of what has been like a steel band around her throat, the feeling of release so intense she can't help shaking.

"Are you all right?"

"Scared, that's all. Hold me."

She wants to laugh, it feels so good just to be with him.

"What's happened?"

"Not out here."

"It'll be okay. You mustn't worry."

"There isn't much time. I have to be back by six."

"If you like we can just talk."

She smiles. "That would be nice, Joe, but look at you."

They stand a moment longer swaying on the threshhold, as heedlessly framed as newlyweds against the suite's bilious carmine lobby, the spermicidally cool smell of Pine-fresh seeping out behind them into the roaring afternoon.

"Oh, God, and feel me," she whispers in his ear, the thrilling indelicacy catching in her voice, "I think I'm going to die if we don't."

She leaps up then, the way a child does, and straddles him upright, wrapping her bare arms and legs around him, trying to get a purchase off the narrow walls until Joe, surprised but

not slow to respond, carries her inside with both his hands
under her haunches, under her dress, dragging down her
panties that have been wet half the drive over, as he kicks the
door shut behind them; then has to lean against it, while she
undoes buttons and zippers and her shades slip off her nose
and he has the sense to keep on sucking her already proud
tits until she's achingly ready to collapse with him through the
pinkish gloom on to a bed she feels heave and billow beneath
them: a caged wave that's meant to transport you out of
Queens to the wilder shores of some paradise island in the
Arabian Sea . . . as Joe insists on reminding her when she is
almost there, ready to believe almost anything.

They lay, breathless, laughing up at the hundred tiny reflections of themselves in the mirrored mosaic of the disco-ball
that hung above the still undulating water bed.

It had always been like this with Joe. This comfortable, this
funny, this undemanding. His desire for her had never lost
its urgency. Her desire was only for his. They didn't try to pretend that things were the same as when they were first in love.
But Joe, unlike Tom, whose obsessive need it was to peel back
the layers and search out the core of her being, as if he hoped
to find an answer there . . . God knows to what—Joe had
learned to let her be herself and show her the tenderness she
wanted most of all.

She wasn't good at sleeping with two people.

More often than not—and lately, since Tom had become
more insistent, nearly always—she faked it with Joe. She
didn't feel there was anything dishonest or demeaning about
doing so, because she believed for certain that when all this
was over and they got away together, everything about their
relationship would come right again.

She just didn't think he knew.

It would be sort of nice, he'd surprised her by saying one
afternoon, if you could maybe get off once in a while.

Be patient, Joe, she'd whispered, snuggling close and

sounding, he'd said with a groan, like a coed on a date who's saving herself—but knowing what she meant.

They shared a history going back to the year of her exhumation, the year Joe had taken her out of Winter Haven, the "cemetery with lights," as he'd christened the retirement town in central Florida where she lived with her mother in an RV park on Lake Lucille. The year her life began.

Eighteen years old (which would make it the summer of 1981), Karen had just graduated from St Joseph's Catholic School and was working two jobs, for an artists' supplies shop during the week and at Cypress Gardens as a tour guide at weekends, to pay for her college tuition. With the grudging approval of her mother—a clinging, bitter woman, who, since Karen's father walked out on them ten years before, had found comfort in Christ and the bottle—she was planning on going to Florida Southern in the fall.

One Sunday that August, Joe had turned up out of the blue and found her, dressed in a rinky-dink Southern Belle costume, showing a group of Japanese tourists one of the gardens' main attractions: a swimming pool built in the 1950s for Esther Williams to showcase her aquatic skills after Hollywood let her go. Interrupting the tour, Joe had taken Karen aside and asked her if she remembered—they'd met briefly at a spring break beach party in Daytona—expressing an interest in driving with him to California, taking their time about it, seeing some country on the way. Well, he'd lifted his shoulders slightly, he was heading out that afternoon. How about it?

She'd turned scarlet and in her confusion dropped the azalea bouquet she was obliged to carry as part of her uniform in the Esther Williams pool. Joe retrieved it for her, then explained to the smiling Japanese that he'd come all the way from New York City and wasn't about to leave without the girl he loved. You'll get me fired, she said, are you crazy? The tourists applauded and took photographs of the two of them arguing, which she would like to have now. At the time she

was so mad at Joe she could hardly speak, but it hadn't
stopped her climbing into his Ford pickup, still wearing her
outfit of peach blossom tulle, slamming the door and setting
off across America with this person she hardly knew, but who
had a look in his horizon blue eyes she didn't know how to
resist.

They wandered the best part of two years, drifting from
one small sun-whipped town to another along the dusty back
highways that took them all over the South and West, through
Texas and New Mexico and Southern California. They would
stop every few weeks or so, usually when their money ran out,
choosing places where either one or both of them could find
work. The longest they ever stayed anywhere was three
months. When they started to aquire possessions or get to
know people, Joe would say it was time to move on. He told
her they were free spirits, they didn't need anything to slow
them down. Unique hearts . . . that was another phrase he
used.

She fell in love with Joseph Skye Haynes and laughed at
his country music fantasy of the two of them as small-town
outlaws roaming the American West. They only once, as far
as she knew, resorted to crime, and that wasn't serious. Just
for the hell of it, they stole a car, a 1976 Cadillac Sedan de
Ville, a big gold boat, which, when it broke down 300 hundred miles later, they'd abandoned by the side of the desert
highway with a note of apology for the owner.

In the badlands of Arizona, they made a detour at her suggestion through the Papago Indian reservation to see San
Xavier del Bac, a mission church built by the Franciscans in
the eighteenth century. Arriving after sunset, they found the
church doors locked. It was a warm evening and they stood
listening to the Papago choir inside endlessly practice a Tex-
Mex version of "Faith of Our Fathers," all guitars and tinny
trumpets, as the first stars came out over the rose-colored
Santa Catalina mountains. Karen decided that if Joe should
ever ask, this was where she would like to be married. But she
knew better than to expose her fantasy to ridicule.

The summer of the following year they traveled up through the Rockies to Wyoming, Montana, Oregon, then headed east.

Karen called her mother in Winter Haven and told her that she'd always wanted to see New York. She talked about the dreams and plans she and Joe shared until the silence on the other end grew reproachful. When are you coming home, honey, her mother asked. I am home, Ma, she had to stop herself saying.

It was in New York that their free and easy, often precarious existence began to unravel. They'd been together almost five years when Joe announced one day that he was leaving, he wasn't ready to settle down. Determined not to repeat the mistake her mother had made—Karen would never let herself believe that salvation lay in a doomed commitment—she could only cut him out of her heart, out of her universe.

"You want to tell me now?"

"He knows, Joe. He knows about us," she said, her face turned away, getting the words out with difficulty. "That's what happened."

"Jesus," Joe said. "You sure about this?"

"He's having me followed."

"Has he said anything?"

"No, not exactly, Tom would never . . . I can't explain, he hints at stuff. It's got to the point where I wish he'd just come out with it."

"Then you can't be a hundred per cent."

"There's been this car lately, different cars, parked across the street wherever I happen to be. It's more than a feeling, Joe. I pick them up in my rearview mirror, and just before it gets to be too obvious, the first one disappears and another takes its place."

"That only happens in the movies, not real life." He smiled, leaning over her to kiss her forehead, the movement setting off a tango of ripples under the surface of the water bed. "You know maybe you're just imagining . . ."

"For God's sake, you're starting to sound like him. That's what *he* does, all the time, keeps telling me I'm not well, I'm paranoid, I invent things."

"Okay, now take it easy."

"Take it easy? When I'm living in the middle of a fucking nightmare?"

"Were you followed here?"

She shook her head, no.

"Well, that's a start."

"But don't you see what this means? We're going to have to move everything up. We have to do this thing now, or I don't know . . ." She hadn't rehearsed what she was going to say. It made lying to him easier. If she was to convince Joe that they no longer had a choice, that there wasn't any room for maneuver, for turning back, it had to sound spontaneous, as if it came from the heart. "I mean like the weekend."

"What? Now hold on just a minute."

She started sobbing. "I can't take much more of this, Joe, being torn apart like this."

"Torn apart?" He looked at her. "When he treats you the way he does? That asshole. You're letting him get to you, that's what this is really about. You're letting him mess up your head again."

"No, I only ever wanted to be with you. I only love you," she said, closing her eyes and letting the tears escape into the pillow. She wanted Joe to make the decision for her. She wanted him to be forceful and decisive so that she could know she was doing the right thing. Or not have to think about it. She was so used to Tom being in control, overseeing every aspect of her life, looking after her, she was afraid that Joe would only let her down, like he did before. "I want to get it over with so that we can be together, that's all."

"You think I don't want it too?" he said gently, holding her closer, wiping the tears from her face and neck with a corner of the sheet. "Just because I happen to be able to see things from more than one side, because I say we shouldn't rush making a decision we're going to have to live with the rest of our lives. The fact is nobody can be sure that if you divorce him you won't be awarded custody."

"Joe, don't, DON'T. It's too late to be talking like this, it's too late, don't you get it?"

"It might not even have to go that far. A guy like Tom, you know, a man of wealth, well known and respected in the business community, with his position to think about, don't tell me he isn't going to—I mean he would have to regard his privacy as just about sacred. The prospect of a lot of very dark and intimate stuff coming out in court could be enough to persuade him to cut a deal."

"Who have you been talking to?"

"Okay, so I told Herb. I told Herb. I told him the whole story. Just as a hypothetical case, of course. He thinks . . ."

"I'm not interested in what he thinks. Tom will be extreme. He won't care. He'll do everything he can to make our lives a misery—win or lose. But it's not that, it's not even the question of custody, I just can't stand the thought of Ned being exposed to the emotional trauma, the publicity—I mean, aged four, to be dragged through the worst kind of media horror? On top of everything else. Do you have any idea what that could *do* to him right now?"

"And if we get caught? How's that going to help Ned?"

"They won't catch us, not if we go ahead now. The way we had it planned. By Sunday morning . . ."

"It doesn't give us enough time."

"Enough time for *what?* Tom to find out? He'll kill me, you understand? The moment he knows, he's going to figure everything out. We've got forty-eight hours, not even."

It wasn't far from the truth, or what the truth would be if they left off making a decision much longer. It had occurred to Karen that her anxiety to get this thing over with had as much to do with denying her own guilt and uncertainty—her ambivalence about giving up the security of Edgewater for a late shot at the simple life—as with persuading Joe.

But Serafim's visit had settled any lingering doubts. The threats he'd made, the look he'd given her when he'd spoken to Ned, his *"Cat get your tongue, Doc?,"* had frightened her badly. How could he possibly have known about Ned's reticence or Tom's pet name for their son?

Unless someone had talked.

"Wait a minute," Joe frowned. "The moment he knows? I thought you said Tom already knew. Something's not right here. Are you holding out on me?"

"I withdrew the money from the bank this morning, that's all," she said coolly. "I closed the account at Citibank, I mean closed it into a suitcase right there on the floor of some little manager person's office. Then I took a cab over to Grand Central and put the case in a locker—so we'd be ready."

"You left half a million cash in a locker?"

"What else could I do? Bring it out to you at Overbeck? That would have meant taking it home with me first. Safety deposit box? I tried. Every bank in New York has a waiting list. Besides we need to know we can get the money any time, not just in business hours. Look, I brought you the key to the locker, okay? I'd collect it myself, Joe, only you know if I *am* being watched . . ."

"I'll do it. I just wish to hell you'd never accepted his goddamn money in the first place. A small settlement, Jesus."

"It's my money now. Even Tom would have to agree. Does it really matter where it came from? I *earned* it, Joe."

"Yeah, I guess you did," he said in a voice that was both savage and tender with regret. "When I think what you've had to put up with . . . that sick fuck . . . at least it helps to make things clearer."

"You don't have to say it. I dreamed that it happened once, but I never wished for it to happen. He'll only be getting what he deserves." She bit into her lower lip, aware of having gone further than she needed. "I mean if anybody deserves anything."

"Then why do I feel so bad about this?"

"It's going to be all right," she said, quietly confident,

knowing now that she had him. "What we're doing is right. We have to keep on believing that. We have a moral obligation to be together. I believe God is watching over us, I believe what we're doing has His blessing. We are family, Joe. We had no choice but to go on knowing each other . . . It's just like you always said, unique hearts."

"Meant to be." Joe smiled, a little too bravely, she thought, as his eyes dipped and went past hers, escaped on azure wings to the mock-tented ceiling. She would always wonder if she hadn't chosen Joe Haynes because, like her father, he was one of life's deserters.

But then he kissed her and she didn't worry.

A siren rising above the hum of rush-hour traffic on Queens Boulevard brought Karen back to the world, revived her own diminished sense of urgency. More insistent the closer it came, letting off furious banshee wails as the driver got held up, she imagined, at the lights north of the Flying Carpet. Look at the time, Joe, we have to go. But didn't say it yet, wondering how long it would take her to get home if she used Tom's favorite shortcut through the Valley.

"I really do have to go." She laughed, a wild dry inadvertently harsh sound. "Will you stop . . ." Pushing his hand away, feebly.

She sat on the edge of the bed and looked for her clothes, which were strewn around the floor of the room. Tried to get up. But he was kneeling close behind her, and deftly slipped his arms under hers and crossed them over her chest, trapping one of her full white breasts in each opposing palm. She could feel his prick harden against the ridges of her spine. With a sigh of resignation, only please be quick, she placed her hands over the backs of his, which made her think of a crusader's, then let herself fall backward in place.

If you moved fast enough, Karen believed, you could catch up with the past. Couldn't you?

"We're in this together," he whispered, and she parted the curtain of her hair that covered his face, which she'd read somewhere was unlucky, and so that her swarming tongue could find the smile at the corner of his mouth.

"Saturday night we're invited to the Davenports," she said through the open window of the station wagon. Against her better judgment, she'd let Joe walk her out to the parking lot. "It's only next door. They're throwing a party, a charity ball, for Christ's sake. Everyone will be there."

Joe said, "Is that what you meant by perfect opportunity?"

"Plus the fact that Thurston and his wife are going to the Jersey shore for the weekend. After the maid goes home at six, that leaves only Hazel in the house. I can take care of her."

"What about the dog?"

"He won't bother you, not if Ned's there. He worships Ned."

The image of a pining Bracken sent a guilty pang to her heart. The cheaper the sentiment, in Karen's experience, the more you could rely on it to expose the weakness of your defenses. For the boy, her darling Ned, losing Bracken would be hard, maybe the hardest blow of all, but he'd get over it, surely, in time? She hadn't figured out yet what she was going to tell him about his father.

"What if the sonofabitch wakes up? I mean this could go either way . . ."

"He'll have had a few drinks at the Davenports. I told you, Tom is a heavy sleeper. You've got the key to the terrace door. I'll meet you downstairs. We just have to agree a time."

Karen kept looking around to make sure they weren't being watched. "I'll call you when we're getting ready to leave."

"I don't like it," Joe said, shaking his head, "creeping about the place in the middle of the night, too many damned things can go wrong. Why not wait until morning?"

"We need all the lead time we can get. You said that, you said you wanted to put at least four states between us and New York before breakfast."

"A few hours isn't going to make a difference."

"Don't start, please. You'll have to pack up the apartment on your own. Unless I can get away tomorrow sometime."

She cut on the ignition. The radio came in loud and she didn't turn it down.

Joe leaned his head through the window.

"What about the money?" He screwed up his eyes at her, but the reluctance still showed in his honest, disorganized face; she wondered how much good Joe would be under pressure.

She smoothed his hair. "You can handle it."

"If we're really leaving Saturday," he hesitated, "I'll have to drive to Connecticut tonight and close the business, tidy up a few loose ends. I guess I could always collect the suitcase in the morning. It'll be rush hour."

She nodded. "Rush hour's good."

He started to say something. She kissed her fingers and laid them on his lips.

"We're leaving, Joe."

II
DOUBLE BIND

FRIDAY

It was eight thirty when Tom Welford strode through the lobby of Burlington House, a gaunt slab of brown-tinted glass that rears above the Hilton on the west side of Sixth Avenue. He was wearing a dove-gray Huntsman worsted, Oxford-blue shirt and a Yale tie—torturously unsuited to the dog days of August but giving off the right image of gentlemanly conceit, he believed, for putting the barbarians at their ease.

He was meant to be taking them for lunch at Twenty-One. The entire board of RT Inc.'s directors, necks as red as Georgia clay. Depending, of course, on the outcome of the meeting.

Acknowledging the deferential chorus of "Good morning, Mr. Welford" from doormen and security guards, he gave a brief nod in response to a hardly less respectful "How's it going, Tom" from a scurrying colleague, paused to scan the headlines on the newsstand, then strolled over to the bank of elevators that served the top five floors of the building.

"It's gonna be another hot one," someone predicted as he joined the waiting crowd of drones, mostly secretaries and messengers, toting their coffee and donuts in steaming little brown paper bags. Tom kept his distance.

He never played at being one of the guys, preferring to let his natural reserve and the patrician sense of entitlement he had arrogated from a life devoted to hard work, to the gaining of leverage, suggest a barrier.

"Hotter than a motherfucker out there."

"You believe the subway's up to 120 already?" A thin, nasally voice, close behind him.

Tom didn't turn around, but made a point of studying the bronze panel that showed the position of the express cars as they rose and fell through the building. Impatient with the delay, his shirt sticking uncomfortably to his back, he regretted walking the ten blocks from a breakfast meeting at the Royalton. He'd barely left himself enough time to grab a shower and clear his desk before the day's onslaught.

"It's not the heat that drives 'em crazy," one of the weather experts whined on; it sounded like he was suffering from a bad cold. "When it's a hundred out, the caldron's simmering, they don't have the energy to start anything. Too busy just trying to get enough air. It's the first cool night you worry about."

The elevator doors slid open. Tom hung back while the rest of the crowd got on, hoping the conversationalist at his elbow would follow. The doors closed. He hit the "up" button again and stood back, hands thrust deep in his pants pockets, staring down at his tasseled loafers.

"It's the first cool night you worry about, Mr. Welford."

Tom turned then, and was confronted by a pair of owlish sunglasses perched on the bruised and swollen nose of a small plump man in a seersucker suit.

"A tree tried to hug me, okay?" He made an attempt at a disarming grin. One purple nostril, Tom noted with distaste, was packed with cotton that badly needed changing.

"Do I know you?"

"Eddie Hendricks. I'm an independent investigator, Mr. Welford." He took a folding wallet from his inside pocket and held it up so that it tumbled open, revealing a three-by-five-inch card behind a celluloid window stamped with the seal of the state of New York, and Hendricks's photograph beaming fatly from the upper left-hand corner.

"Do you mind putting that away," Tom said, looking around quickly. "What do you want?"

"I'm here to tell you that my client has the information you requested at your last meet. He appreciates that you're a busy man, but seeing how this is a delicate matter . . ." Hendricks paused, looking at him over the top of his Baccarat shades with watery, slightly protruding eyes. "You said you didn't want any phone calls, right?"

"Tell your client I'll call him."

"This'll only take a few minutes of your time. If you would care to talk to him in person, he's waiting for you right now at a nearby location. I got a cab outside."

"I'm sorry. You'll have to excuse me."

Tom turned away, saved by the arrival, as if on cue, of the next elevator. At the same moment two young women he recognized as typists from Mergers and Acquisitions came skittering up on heels that echoed through the marble hall like unruly castanets. They thanked him, mistakenly, for holding the elevator and went to stand at the back of the car, resuming a low, earnest conversation.

"If you could hear what my client has to say, Mr. Welford," Hendricks insisted, the intolerable whine pursuing Tom as the detective took a step forward to prevent the elevator doors from closing, "I think you'd agree this really can't wait."

There was a hush from the back of the car.

Tom sensed the exchange of glances, the pricked ears of the two women behind him. He weighed the harm of their aroused curiosity—there was no telling what this little creep might say or do next—against the possibility of being a few minutes late for the meeting. He had already calculated that he could see Hendricks's "client" and be back in time to prepare for going head on with the board of Rolling Thunder. It went against his principles to let his private life encroach on business, but sometimes you had to make an exception.

"How far from here?"

Hendricks gave a lopsided grimace as the automatic doors bucked impotently against his small almost dainty foot.

"Three-minute ride."

* * *

"The name Juan Perez doesn't ring a bell?"

"Perez?" Tom shook his head.

"He was this Puerto Rican kid climbed in the bears' cage out at Prospect Park, seven, maybe eight years ago."

"I don't get it. So what?"

"You ever take your kid to the zoo? I used to bring my boys when they were younger," Victor Serafim said, stretching his legs out in front of him, basking in the hot glassy sunlight. "It was all different then."

"I was told you had something for me that couldn't wait. I didn't come here to chat, Mr. Serafim."

"Relax, friend. This won't take long."

The two men were sitting on a park bench across the plaza from the polar bear habitat, a hollow mountain in miniature with a Perspex wall that let you see into the bear's invitingly green tarn. Watching the huge animal swim backwards and forwards underwater reminded Tom that though he helped fund the zoo's refurbishment, he'd never in fact taken Ned. Always had the intention, just never found the time.

"The cops got there too late to save him," Serafim went on, "but iced the bears anyway through the bars of the cage with .38s and 12-gauge shotguns. Teddy and Lucy. They never gave out the names of the officers. They got so many hate calls they had to shut down the precinct switchboard.

"The kid's mother complained that no one seemed to care about the death of her son. But little Juan had been taunting the bears, pelting them with bricks and bottles. There was a sign in Spanish and English said, LOS OSOS SON PELIGROSOS NO ENTRE A LA JAULA. BEARS ARE DANGEROUS, DO NOT ENTER THE CAGE. Maybe the Perez kid couldn't read, maybe he wasn't too bright. One thing is sure, the animals didn't invite him in . . ."

"Do you mind telling me how this is relevant?"

"The way I figure kids growing up these days are too much protected from the notion that bad or foolish actions can have dire consequences." Serafim smiled. "It's a cautionary tale, Tom."

"Who is it you're saying should be careful?"

"When the wife of a seriously rich man takes out a loan of half a million bucks from a guy like me, you have to wonder."

"Are you trying to threaten me?"

"What for?" The older man's pitted face took on a mock pained expression. "You know why I let you in on this in the first place. Purely business, friend. All I'm interested in here is looking after my investment. If I can help you into the bargain, at the level of two human beings, so much the better."

"I still only have your word for it."

"Well, there's more now," he smiled. "A lot more."

Tom took a deep breath and straightened his back against the park bench. The more organic air of the zoo had a strong feral smell of dusty sun-warmed animals. But it was the proximity of the man that made him uneasy. Even talking to this kind of person, he thought, you risked infection.

It was exactly a week since Serafim had made his first approach, flagged him down as he was jogging around the reservoir, and told him, a total stranger, he had reason to believe his wife was in trouble. He should have kept going. He shouldn't have listened. But the way Karen had been behaving lately, it hadn't altogether come as a surprise. He couldn't afford to ignore the possibility that she was slipping back into her old ways.

He'd made discreet inquiries. There were people Tom knew on Wall Street, who knew people—low, low down the food chain—who occasionally resorted to borrowing money from loan sharks. They'd heard of Victor Serafimovic, the "Angel of Kings," a tough guy of Balkan extraction with backing from a Brooklyn-based crime syndicate. But they didn't do business with him.

"What have you got?" Tom asked, almost reluctantly.

"You wanted me to check things out." Again the twist of a smile. "We checked them out. This was no Dun & Bradstreet job, Tom. Your wife doesn't even have a fucking bank account."

"She gets a sizeable allowance . . ."

"With strings attached. She feels the urge to spend, it's credit or charge only. Right?"

"Karen had some problems in the past. I'm afraid that's not exactly a sealed book. I just keep an eye on her."

"I didn't get this in the gossip columns. I know about your wife from an old friend of hers, Sylvia Morrow, used to be a dealer on the downtown club circuit—'Starlite' they called her on the street—before she went over to steering for the people I work for. Sylvia set up the loan." He paused. "They don't play around."

"Neither do I."

Serafim gave him a searching look. "I'm trying to make this easy for you. You're out of your world."

Tom shrugged.

"Half a mil buys an awful lot of harmful substances, Tom. You ever find the key to that locker?"

He shook his head. "I didn't look for it."

He could feel the curious unrelenting eyes trying to lock on to his. In fact, he had searched Karen's pocketbook at the first opportunity and come across the orange-tagged key, number 129, almost too easily. He saw no advantage in sharing this with Serafim. The key could have been a plant.

"You didn't ask her what she was doing last Sunday around six thirty? Or where she spent Tuesday afternoon?"

"No, I didn't," Tom snapped. "I'm not in the habit of interrogating my wife. The time you say she was having a rendezvous with this guy—whatever he's called—I talked to her from Chicago, Ned too. They were home."

"Call forwarding. He's got a second line on his phone just so that she can hook up to it before she leaves the house."

Tom cleared his throat. "There's something you maybe should know . . ." He hesitated, wary of telling Serafim too much; his first concern was still to protect Karen. "Before we got married, I put my wife through a rehab program at Silverlake. When she came back, her doctors advised me . . . The fact is she isn't completely well yet, her behavior can sometimes be erratic."

"It's been going on a long time, Tom. Ever since he's been renting that garage apartment in the Wheatley Hills, your wife is a regular visitor."

"How can you be so goddamned sure?"

Serafim turned and waved to the detective, who was waiting in the shade by the zoo turnstyle. "Hey, Eddie, want to step this way a moment?"

"You said you'd get back to me with proof."

Tom watched the butterball with the ridiculous injury make his way toward them through a throng of school-children. "Some sleazy little private eye you happen to have in your pocket isn't exactly what I had in mind."

"He does a good job. You'll see. Eddie's a pro."

"I guess it's really what *you* do for a living, Mr. Serafim, that I have a problem with . . . I mean, I'd have to be a fool to think this was anything but a set-up."

"You wouldn't be here," Serafim smiled, "if that was what you thought. You'll get your proof."

Tom glanced at his watch. Ten more minutes and then he'd need to go. If this did turn out to be an elaborate attempt to extort money, he might regret not having talked to his lawyers, even to the police. Instinct told him the less fuss, the fewer people involved, the better. Karen's timing as always was lousy. But one thing was certain—he stood to lose a lot more than half a million dollars if he screwed up the Atlanta deal.

The detective approached the bench, mopping his brow with a handkerchief. He wore his hair, or what was left of it, in an elaborate comb-over that only drew attention to his baldness. It reminded Tom of the old gag about living in New Jersey and parting your hair in the Bronx. Sweat stains showed under the arms of his mustard stripe suit.

"Eddie, why don't you tell Mr. Welford what you got on Joseph Skye Haynes?"

"Sure, what do you want?" Hendricks stood in front of them thumbing through a notebook. "He's thirty-five, single, male Caucasian, drives a Chevy Suburban with a bumper sticker that says I BRAKE FOR WILD HORSES, which doesn't place him too high in my estimation."

"No, skip that stuff, tell us what you found."

"Okay, about noon yesterday, I made an illegal entry at 1154 Wheatley and had a quick snoop around. I didn't know any different I'd have said the subject—your wife that is, Mr. W.—actually lives in the apartment. There's a whole closet full of female clothes, her size, most of it never been worn, personal belongings, suitcases, letters going back to her high-school days . . . like she has this whole other life."

"A life on hold, Tom, waiting to be lived."

"They even got toys for the kid for when it's the nanny's day off and she has to bring him along . . ."

"Why should I believe you?" Tom interrupted.

The detective looked at him over the top of his sun-glasses.

"Before he moved to Long Island, Haynes had a place out on the Connecticut shore near Old Lyme. He still runs his business from a couple of barns in an orchard he rents up there. Calls himself an architectural salvage consultant. He buys up old colonial houses that were going to be torn down anyway, takes 'em apart and sells the bits to somebody who wants them put up someplace like Ohio, for a lot more than he paid. At least, that's the idea."

Tom lifted his shoulders slightly. He'd a vague memory of a conversation he'd once had with Karen about something of the kind. A salvage contractor. "Where'd she find this guy?"

The name Haynes meant nothing. It could be someone she'd known from before. They had a pact not to discuss what she called "ancient history": Tom never brought up his first marriage, and she never spoke of former lovers. But they weren't the threat. It was the chance encounter.

"The business was failing even before the recession," the detective said. "Haynes has no money, no assets. I ran the usual credit check. The guy's obviously a flake. I don't know how they met. Jesus, I wasn't in there long enough to . . ."

"Eddie, tell him what else you got," Serafim said.

Hendricks sniffed modestly. "Five in the afternoon, yes-

terday, I tail the subject to this motel in Queens, a hotbed
joint they call the Flying Carpet. The rooms there got walls
that are nothing but sheetrock, no insulation. The décor
sucks, but I got a definition on the tape that's truly outstand-
ing. You hear a lot more than the bedsprings."

"You're disgusting, you know that?"

"Take it easy, friend," Serafim said. "He's just saying there's
more to this than . . . it's not what they get up to in the sack
you gotta listen for."

"What are you talking about?"

"As an impartial observer, Eddie, tell him what it is they
seem to have uppermost on their minds."

"Well, I can't say a hundred per cent, but . . ."

"Go ahead, take a shot at it."

The detective shrugged. "I'm sorry, Mr. Welford, the way
it looks your wife is paying Haynes the money she borrowed
from the firm to kill you, or have you killed."

"Kill?" Tom felt the air suddenly go out of him so that when
he started to laugh it was on an intake of breath and sounded
like a rattle. "Are you serious? Karen kill me? For what?"

"Subway tokens. What do you think?" Serafim said.

"But that's crazy. If this was about money, all she'd have
to do is get a divorce. I signed a prenuptial agreement my
lawyers said was generous beyond . . . No, no, Karen knows.
We split up, then she stands to benefit. If I predecease her,
it all goes to Ned."

"Then why doesn't she divorce you?"

Tom didn't answer.

"She's afraid she might not get custody of the kid," Hendricks offered. "With her history of drug abuse, rehab clinics,
mental . . . 'scuse me one second." A beeping sound was coming from Hendricks's person. He opened his jacket and fished
about under the overhang of an ample gut for the Motorola
pager attached to his belt. "What did I tell you? Loverboy's on
the move." Giving them a professional look, he clipped the
pager back on and hitched up his pants. "Sorry but I gotta run."

"Thanks, Eddie, I can take it from here," Serafim said.

"We're tailing Haynes as well as your wife, Mr. Welford," the detective explained. "That's him now just coming up to the Midtown Tunnel. Mrs. W. handed over her key to the locker at the motel yesterday, told him to pick up the suitcase. I'd say someone's about to collect his paycheck."

"You might as well tell me," Serafim said when they were alone again. "There's a lot involved."

Tom sat for a moment staring ahead of him at the glass wall in the side of the little mountain where the polar bear had just executed another clumsy underwater turn, its long white pelt flattening like the brushes of a car-wash against a windshield, before it faded into the green murk.

"It wasn't anything. No big deal. Ned had a fall when he was about a year old. Broke his arm. Karen was meant to be looking after him at the time. Only she happened to be drunk, so damned cockeyed she remembered nothing."

"Any witnesses?"

"The nanny—not the one we've got now—came back and found them both."

"Let me get this straight," Serafim said. "If your wife initiated divorce proceedings, you'd fight for custody of your son, right? You'd instruct your lawyers to dig this up and use it to show Karen as an unfit mother?"

"There've been other incidents . . . Look, I have to get back to the office."

"Wait." Serafim put a hand on his arm. "Would you fight for your kid?"

Tom hesitated. "Of course."

"Then she has to see you being taken out of the picture as a possible solution."

"Solution?"

Serafim nodded gravely.

In spite of his distaste for having to deal with this kind of lowlife, Tom recognized what was impressive about the man. He gave off an aura of unexercised power that he knew it would be a mistake to ignore.

"Why I'm talking to you, at all," he said pompously, "about these very private matters is because I don't believe that Karen wants a divorce. And I happen to know she doesn't have in her whatever it takes to commit murder. She needs me too much. She needs me for just about everything."

"She has the motive."

"Somehow I don't think so."

"What are you saying? That she's not seeing this guy? That she didn't borrow the money? That it's just a fantasy? We've got them ice-cold, for Christ's sake . . ."

Serafim took a manila envelope from his jacket pocket and laid it on the bench between them. "It's all here, Tom."

"Let me explain something to you," Tom said, "my wife has a tendency to blame herself for things that aren't really her fault—just bad luck, bad timing—or, that never even happened. Maybe because she was raised a Catholic, she feels she should do penance for her 'sins.' I'm talking about a medical condition that goes way back with her."

"Now what? You're pleading insanity for her?"

"She first started hurting herself when she was a kid, secretly lacerating her arms and legs with twigs, knives, compass points and so on. Became what's known as a cutter. She's always denied it, of course. There was a doctor she talked to once. He told me it's not uncommon in young girls from her kind of family background—dysfunctional is the word he used. Her father sold insurance, peddled installment deals, anything that kept him on the road. The times he did come home, he was drunk and abusive. He finally walked out on the family for good when Karen was eight. The mother took it out on her, my wife . . . on herself."

"Tom," Serafim said softly, "in my line of work, I hear a lot of hard-luck stories. What beats the crap out of me is why someone like you decides to marry one."

"You wouldn't be the first," Tom laughed, finding it easier to talk now. "When I started going out with her—we met at some party downtown—people couldn't wait to warn me that she was bad news. Beautiful, smart as a whip, but not a girl to get involved with." In fact, it was only after the party that he'd noticed Karen shivering on the sidewalk in her black marabou jacket and sunglasses. It was a bitter February night and he'd offered her a ride. "Where you headed?" Tom had asked. There wasn't, as he recalled, a cab in sight. "Crazy," she'd murmured as she slid gracefully into the back of his limousine, "and don't spare the horses."

But there would always be those who insisted it was no accident that brought them together.

"She was dangerous to know. Maybe that was the attraction. Karen got a kick out of putting herself in harm's way. It wasn't only the booze and drugs. She liked to go out 'walking,' wandering the streets of New York, in the worst neighborhoods at all hours of the night, alone. I'm not a sucker for every damsel in distress, believe me. But I used to have her followed—just to make sure she'd be all right."

"And you're still watching over her, still paying to have her tailed. Is that how you see this?"

"I didn't find out she was a cutter until after she came back from the clinic. I began noticing these marks on her body, tidy clusters of nicks and slashes, usually in places where it didn't show. She always had some quite plausible explanation. Then one time, soon after we were married, I came across a child's plastic lunch-pail hidden at the back of her closet in our bedroom. The initials KS scratched on the lid. Hers from when she was at school, she was Karen Straw then. The pail was full of Stanley blades, razors, nails, rosary beads, bits of broken glass."

"Jesus." Serafim shifted uncomfortably.

"A little shrine to suffering. It may sound strange to you, but I realized then how much I loved her. I got her to agree to more treatment and for a couple of years, while Ned was a baby, everything seemed fine. They explained to us at the clinic that Karen uses self-injury as a way of controling emotional pain, a way of releasing unbearable tension. Well, she was happy. I'd given her everything anybody could possibly want, and in return she'd given me a son.

"It flared up again briefly about six months back, right

around the time Ned lost his voice. A couple of nights ago, I happened to notice the marks were back."

"Something you're not telling me, Tom."

"She's been under a lot of pressure lately."

"What is it? If it ain't the way it looks. What does she want the money for?"

"I haven't the slightest idea."

"And why come to me? Borrowing from loan sharks, you know what they call it? A self-inflicted wound."

"Isn't that what I've just been saying? It fits the profile. Karen can be quite creative when it comes to self-injury— this whole thing could simply be another way of exposing herself to danger."

Serafim turned his head and looked at him.

"You're the one who's exposed, Mr. Welford. Listen to the tape, you may want to change your mind about your wife's 'profile.' This guy she's screwing. She puts her heart and soul into it, you'll hear."

Tom looked down at his hands. He had a sudden urge to wrap them around Serafim's throat. But he willed himself to remain calm, and changed the subject, asking almost casually, "Did your man find out about Haynes's medical history?"

"He's still trying. Medical records are never easy. What you worried about, AIDS? They're planning to croak you, for Christ's sake."

"What I propose doing is talking to Karen's doctors, once I've considered whatever's on here." Tom picked up the manila envelope and slipped it into his jacket pocket. "Then maybe you and I can discuss coming to some arrangement."

"It would have to be the same terms agreed with your wife."

"If I can be satisfied that the transaction actually took place, you'll get your money back." Tom rose to his feet. "I hope after that never to see you again."

He nodded curtly to the loan shark and, with a glance at his watch, strode off toward the zoo exit. Serafim caught up with him at the turnstyles opposite the Arsenal.

"We're talking about principle plus interest for the week

my money's been lying dead and what would have accrued if the loan had gone to the agreed period, which in your wife's case was one month. At six for five, on a weekly basis, that's another four hundred thousand dollars. On top of the five plus one—I'll waive the fee for the surveillance—what do you say we call it a million even?"

Tom kept walking. "You've got a hell of a nerve."

"We're both businessmen. We understand each other."

He wheeled on him. "Let's just get one thing straight. You and I have absolutely nothing in common."

Serafim grinned and lifted his eyes heavenward.

They came out of the park together and stood in silence under the shade trees on the west side of Fifth Avenue. Tom was sweating, feeling the heat now; during the short time they were at the zoo, the temperature had crept up into the low nineties. He looked around impatiently for a cab.

"Give you a lift anywhere?" Serafim asked.

He gestured toward a gray Lincoln Towncar parked across the street. A young heavy-built man with a shaved head was leaning against the hood, his long swollen arms folded over his chest. Behind was all tinted glass. Tom didn't answer.

Serafim shrugged and stepped off the sidewalk, then hesitated, as if he'd forgotten something. Holding his hands out to the side, he weighed the air in his palms.

"You know what I'm also taking under consideration?" he said. "The fact that someone in your position can't afford to be mixed up in anything like this. It wouldn't look good."

"You think you can blackmail me?"

"Do me a favor, Welford, I'm offering you protection."

2

His office, which looked north over the park, was like a captain's bridge suspended in the sky, narrow and spare with floor-to-ceiling windows on two sides that made it seem as big as all New York. Staring out across the isometric sprawl of the city, Tom steepled his fingers under his chin, resisting an impulse to call Karen and confront her with the evidence; before he did anything else; before even examining the evidence himself. The thick manila envelope Serafim had handed over at the zoo lay unopened in a locked drawer of his desk. Pending.

Rocking forward in his chair, he gathered up the silver-framed photographs of his wife and son and laid them face down on the desk. He had twenty minutes, less than that now, to prepare his speech for the board of Rolling Thunder: he couldn't afford any distractions.

He'd already asked his secretary to hold his calls.

Tom didn't expect trouble over the deal with RT Inc. But like all the battles he'd ever fought, he saw it as the one he had to win. Otherwise, he believed, anybody who wanted to pick a fight with him in the future—even if they hadn't a dog's chance of winning—would feel they had the right, no, the obligation, to challenge him.

A year ago he'd accumulated 20 per cent of preferred stock in the Atlanta-based container and chassis leasing company with the aim of gaining overall control. As chairman, he'd soon started agitating for change; not exactly out for blood, but you didn't turn around a troubled business without kicking a few shins, bruising a feeling or two. When it began to look as if he might get his way, a majority of the board had resisted and, at a hastily called meeting, ousted him as chair. He could still picture the faces of those good ol' boys down in Atlanta, hardly able to suppress their glee at the success of their ambush, like cavemen dancing around a predator they've been lucky enough to trap in a spiked pit.

Tom didn't bear grudges. They were little people, fighting for their survival in a changed world. But after the débâcle in Atlanta he'd started buying up any Rolling Thunder shares he could get his hands on. Last week his stake in the company had climbed to 36 per cent. The board had asked for a special meeting. Scheduled for ten today.

He had no doubt that they were coming to surrender.

He swung around to the windows again and leaned back, hands clasped behind his head, one foot resting on the base of a seventeenth-century celestial globe his first wife had given him to "correspond" with the brass telescope mounted on a tripod that stood in the opposite corner. Wouldn't it be better to get this thing over with? Listen to the tape now, or at least part of it, enough to know whether or not it was genuine? Reflected in the glass, he could see the green glow of the Quotron machine spitting out stock prices behind his back; above it, on the paneled wall across from his desk, hung the small painting by Manet of a black packet-steamer plying the English Channel that was the single most valuable thing he owned. There was no other art or furniture.

The night he got back from Chicago . . .

He'd known by then, of course, about the money. It was one of the reasons he took the trip, but even if he hadn't been looking, it was obvious that something wasn't right.

He had a clear memory of the amused, couldn't-give-much-of-a-damn look in Karen's eyes, her low self-deprecating laughter, as she'd described her eventless day—utterly convincing, if only because she always was able to convince herself. That was how it began the last time, with a little lie.

But murder?

The room was almost silent.

It wasn't a question of vengeance, but of persuading a bunch of antebellum rednecks . . . Tom stood up and, as if it might help concentrate his mind, began to pace . . . that even these days when the pursuit of wealth has fallen into moral disfavor—another way of saying, gentlemen, that America has its head so far up its ass it can't see shit any more—the world has to change, time goes on, and a business like yours that's losing money . . . well, he took pride in the fact that nobody had ever been able to say of Tom Welford that he left a trail of destruction in his wake.

He came back to the desk, sat down, found the key and

swiftly unlocked the drawer. Then he leaned across and hit the intercom button and told Mrs. Strayhorn that he didn't want to be disturbed for any reason at all.

His hands shook a little as he fitted the cassette into the tape-recorder.

At first he hardly recognized the woman's voice, and it gave him hope. Voices could be cloned, surgically altered in a studio, made to sound like someone else. He wanted to believe that Serafim had access to that kind of technology and had doctored the recording, concocted the whole thing.

He took soundings from the tape, stopping at random, only allowing himself to listen in when he heard conversation, fast-forwarding over the long explicit silences.

It helped that he knew what he was looking for.

He could ignore Hendricks's hi-fidelity effects, the cries and whimpers that didn't sound at all like the Karen he knew; the rhythmic slapping of flesh on flesh accelerating toward predictable abandon. It wasn't her style. Karen was passive by nature. The girl on tape came across as enthusiastic to the point of being wanton, her voice slipping now and then into a low husky Southern drawl, for God's sake, or breaking into dirty laughter like a two-bit whore.

It was quite a performance.

But the more he listened, the harder it became to pretend that he was eavesdropping on someone he didn't know, couldn't even picture, an absolute stranger drowsily murmuring in the ear of some loser in a motel room that she loved only him.

By the time he came on the relevant passage, he no longer had any doubts. She sounded different, but in a subtle way Tom didn't care to analyze; the Karen he knew was talking another language, a foreign tongue she'd picked up for the sole purpose of excluding and humiliating and betraying him.

He pressed rewind and played the section back.

Karen: *"I dreamed that it happened once, but I never wished for it to happen.*

"He'll only be getting what he deserves . . ."

What *I* deserve? Tom smiled. An unkind cut. After all that he'd done for her . . . but then Karen always had a tendency to be melodramatic. He let the tape roll on.

Haynes: *"Why do I have such a bad feeling about this?"*

You have to ask, you little prick? He could see how Serafim and "Eddie" with his ear to the wall might have gotten the idea that they were planning his murder.

Karen: *"What we're doing is right. We have to keep on believing that. We have a moral obligation to be together. I believe God is watching over us, I believe what we're doing has His blessing. We are family, Joe. We have no choice but to go on knowing each other . . . just like you always said."*

She sounds crazy, though, awfully crazy, he thought.

Haynes: *"Meant to be."*

Listen to him. Jesus, where'd she find this guy? Tom hit the stop button, and slipped the headphones off his ears; it was the "we are family" bit, the sickening whiff of righteousness that really turned his stomach.

He had an image of Karen's face, her upper-lip beaded with sweat, her dark honey hair threshed on the pillow.

The pain caught him unawares—a knifing pain vicious enough to make him double over.

He stayed that way until it eased, hugging his knees, stunned, trying to decide what to do. Then slowly Tom sat up. It was almost time to meet the people from Rolling Thunder. But this had to take priority. Picking up a telephone, he dialed the general number for Lenox Hill Hospital and asked to be put through to Dr. Goldstone's clinic.

While he waited, tapping out a rhythm with the George III shell skewer he used as a letter-opener, he examined the rest of the envelope's contents. Apart from Hendricks's report, they consisted of five photographs, all taken with a long lens. He spread the color prints on the desk: Karen at the wheel of the Volvo, turning into a driveway; Ned playing in the yard of a white frame-house; Karen's silhouette at window of same; a fuzzy profile of Joseph Skye Haynes; and then a shot of them together, Joe and Karen embracing each other, while at their feet Ned trailed his green security blanket in the dirt.

He thought he knew the face. It swam a little further out of focus. The pain in his stomach sharpened. For a moment he felt as if he were going to black out, but the icy spasm passed.

He couldn't really be sure.

"This is Dr. Goldstone's office. How may I help?"

Reaching for the face-down framed photographs of his family, Tom restored them to their upright position as if they were icons with protective powers.

"I have an appointment for tomorrow at eleven thirty. I'd like to change it. The name's Welford."

"Certainly, Mr. Welford. When would be more convenient? We have two or three openings next week. Let's see now."

"I'll be there in ten minutes."

"Excuse me? I'm sorry, Mr. Welford, but Dr. Goldstone has a very tight . . ."

Tom put the phone down, hesitated a second, then buzzed his secretary and told her that something unexpected had come up. He had to go out on an emergency. Would she be kind enough to let Jerry know, ask him to present his sincerest apologies to the Atlantans and hold the fort?

"But they're all waiting for you in the boardroom. Mr. Turbidy's in there with them."

"Stall them, Mrs. Strayhorn. You can handle it."

He sat with his head in his hands.

They weren't planning to kill him. They had no need. It was worse than that—they were going to take his son from him. Which was what he had been obscurely dreading all along. Against odds that he'd been assured were impossible, she had found him.

Her Mister Man.

But Tom had to be sure.

He rose from his desk and walked over to the windows,

holding the slim black tape-recorder against his chest like a
preacher clutching a prayer-book. The need to hear them together now too strong to resist, he wound the tape back to
the beginning and, looking out across the green rectangle of
park to where Harlem Meer glinted like a spill of quicksilver
through the haze, turned up the volume.

A train rumbled out of one of the upper track bays followed
by the sound of running footsteps. Hendricks imagined as
they clattered to a halt over his head the frustration of some
outward commuter who'd cut it too fine. Down here in the
bowels of the station there were fewer travelers, fewer viable
people about.

He searched his pockets for change as he watched a party
of three leave the restaurant, the glass door held open for

Hendricks waited until he could speak without having to
raise his voice. "He coulda been trying to shake us," he said.
"You know, he walks in the joint, straight through and out the
other side. The old routine."

He was talking from a pay phone under the tiled arches
outside the Oyster Bar on Grand Central Station's lower level.
The detective had seen Haynes take the stairway that led
down into the Oyster Bar's wood-paneled saloon (a back room
with check tablecloths, stuffed marlin arched over a neon
scribble, a little more privacy), leaving him no choice but to
come around the long way by 42nd Street, cutting across the
main concourse and down through the tunnels to the lower
level. He'd been staked out nearly an hour, and still no sign
of movement. From where he stood, Hendricks could see
into the cavernous main eating hall, but not the saloon. His
back-up, Frank Cicerone, was parked on Vanderbilt Avenue,
watching the restaurant's street-level entrance.

There was the usual burst of static as the phone company
robot cranked itself up to interrupt the call.

"Please deposit another ten cents."

"Shit."

"Ten cents please . . ."

He searched his pockets for change as he watched a party
of three leave the restaurant, the glass door held open for

them by the Oyster Bar's unofficial doorman, a grimy old veteran in a child's size clear-plastic raincoat. The way they looked through him, he might as well have been invisible.

". . . or your call will be terminated."

Hendricks gave Frank the number of the pay phone, made him repeat it and told him to call him back.

"You mind telling me what's going on?"

"Hang up, Frank."

"Eddie, you sure about this being a routine matrimonial?"

"Hang up the phone."

He cut him off, holding the button pressed down, but going on talking as another customer—this one, on his own, pausing to check his reflection in the glass door—strolled into view. On the plump side with a little Latino mustache no thicker than a girl's eyelash, he wore a cream silk suit, a cream shirt and tie, and pointed shoes with lattice-weave tops, also cream. Looking down distastefully at the shrink-wrapped bundle of human misery at his feet, he patted over the pockets of his double-breasted jacket.

Hendricks felt a light tap on his shoulder.

"Are you going to be much longer?"

A chunky young woman, his height, in a navy linen business outfit and sneakers, stood there swinging her briefcase.

" 'Fraid so." Hendricks turned away.

He saw the spic bend down to drop a ten-dollar bill in the doorman's Styrofoam cup, and reveal the shadow of a gun snugly holstered under his left arm. He straightened up; the piece didn't spoil the line of his suit. He was looking now right at Hendricks. Something about him seemed familiar.

A pro with charitable instincts.

"Excuse me, but I have to make an urgent call. It's really important," the girl persisted, none too politely.

Hendricks ignored her. He wondered if his partner had taken the number down wrong. Frank all over.

The phone rang at the same moment that Hendricks saw Karen Welford leave the restaurant, ushered out by the captain, a squat little grinning guinea in a tux and a hairpiece.

The unofficial doorman had melted back into the shadows.
He released the button.

"I just spotted him," Frank said. "He's out on the street,
looking up and down, this way now. Shit, I think he made me,
Ed, he's heading back to his vehicle."

She was alone, and uneasy about it, casting around her the
way stylish women do, taking in the palatial subterranean
concourse and its scumbag indigents, like she was getting her
bearings at some fancy social gathering. A frigging gazelle hiding behind those Jackie O shades would have attracted less
attention. The detective flattened himself against the pillar,
edging around to its blind side until the cord of the pay phone
would stretch no further.

"They done a switch, Frank. Stay with Haynes."

The girl with the briefcase, pursuing him, said loudly,
"Anyone can see you're not really using that phone."

"Take a hike, sis."

"What did you say?"

He held his free hand over the mouthpiece, as if there was
still someone on the line, "Listen, sweetcups . . ."

"I'm not your sweet anything, asshole," the girl barked at
him, then turned on her heel and stalked off, flexing powerful calves that piano-legged into a pair of pink Reeboks.

"Yo, bitch!" a young black kid who'd witnessed their exchange called after her. "Beauty's only skin deep, but ugly's
to the BONE."

Hendricks shook his head, things going from bad to worse
as he caught the eye of the registered charity in the cream
suit, who gave him an easy little smile before sauntering on
up the ramp to the station's upper level.

He still couldn't place him. Unless he was one of Victor's
people.

A hint of expensive perfume hung on the air, cutting the
thick smell of roasted pretzels, hot dogs and human stale that
wafted through the tunnels. With the tail of his eye he saw
Karen walking in the other direction.

He watched her—almost to the end of the concourse

now—circle around and make her way past a ragged cluster of tunnel-people, ignoring the catcalls and come-ons, deflecting potential nuisance from a young girl with too-bright eyes and what looked like a rat clamped to her breast. Then, with a glance over her shoulder, the subject quickly approached the bank of lockers tucked in behind an archway at the back of the hall.

He saw her fish something out of her pocketbook, most likely a key, only her back was turned and from that distance he couldn't be sure. Hendricks was in no doubt that she'd come to pick up the suitcase. Haynes had simply been used as a decoy.

He couldn't stay longer, but made a note of the time for the report of investigation: it was ten after ten.

Somebody had just walked into the locker area, walked up right behind her. The purposeful stride and heavy squelch of rubber-soled shoes, surely a man's, made Karen's heart beat faster. She had to force herself not to look around. Tucking her hair behind her ears, she pretended to rummage in her pocketbook for the key with the orange tag that she already held in her hand. She heard something soft being placed in a locker, the metal door bang shut, the plunk of quarters. She waited.

Why in God's name didn't he leave?

Her eyes lifted to the imperial cornice that wouldn't have seemed out of place in the anteroom of a basilica, then tracked slowly down again to the lockers. One hundred twenty-nine was right in front of her. She could have found it blindfold. Top row, third bank, seventh from the left. The man was just standing there, breathing through his mouth.

She heard him give a polite cough, and closed her eyes. What was he going to do, start a conversation, try to pick her up?

The footsteps retreated.

She let her breath out gradually. It wasn't over yet. They could be waiting for her to come out with the money. They

could be anywhere in the station, watching . . . she didn't even
know what they looked like.

Karen turned her head, but there was no sign of anyone.

On the way in from the country, there'd been a white
Dodge van, desert panorama painted on its mirrored rear
window, hanging a couple of cars back from Joe's Suburban.

She slid the key into the lock.

The same white van that was parked now outside the station on Vanderbilt. It was Joe they were watching, not her.
At the last minute, she'd decided to drive her own car into
the city. Just to make sure everything went to plan.

Nothing happened.

She tried twisting it the other way, but the key refused to
budge. Karen felt her skin flush hot, then cold. Her fingers
shook a little as she withdrew it and checked the tag number.
Two two nine. The slot in the door was marked *one* hundred
twenty-nine . . . Easy, easy mistake. Wednesday, when she'd
moved the suitcase, she'd just shoved it in the next locker
down.

This time the key turned, setting off a flutter of satisfying
clicks as the tumblers fell. Five hundred thousand in small
bills. She remembered exactly how heavy that felt.

"Spare some change, lady?"

Karen wheeled around, keeping her back pressed up
against the unbolted locker.

The young girl she'd seen nursing a baby in the hall, and
had taken care to avoid, was staring at her from the doorway
with accusing eyes. "I need money to buy the formula."

"I'm sorry, what did you say?"

"Just a coupla dollars." She came forward and stood by the
first bank of lockers. "He's on Similac."

"Oh," Karen forced a smile. "How . . . how old is he?" she
asked politely, looking down at the girl's too-big galoshes,
wondering if it could have been her she'd heard earlier.

"Eight weeks. Won't suck." Her thin shoulders went up inside the half-buttoned blouse. "He just cries all the time, day

and night. I don't keep him quiet, sooner or later somebody down here'll save me the trouble."

She was stroking the baby's matted head, holding it tightly to her so that the hidden curve of its cheek pushed up her dingy insufficient breast. Karen listened with sympathy to her fluent pitch about being homeless, always afraid, destitute.

Yet she obviously had *some*thing . . .

"This is really no place for you, or your baby."

"Sssh!" the girl whispered. "He's sleeping now."

She raised a finger to her lips, and Karen saw a tiny foot escape from the rag bundle she held cradled in her arms. It had the rigid unseparated toes of a china doll.

. . . something that she felt was worth putting in a locker for safe-keeping.

"Look, I'd really like to help you out," Karen said gently, trying to suppress the note of alarmed pity in her voice. "How much do you need?"

"Well, fuck you," the girl suddenly shouted and, turning away, sobbing, banged her fist on the lockers. *"Murderer!"*

"No wait, please wait!" Karen called after her, but she was off striding through the marble hall, galoshes squelching as she headed back in the direction of the tunnels.

I've got money . . . plenty of money.

Karen tugged open the locker door and reached inside.

Her heart slammed up against her ribs.

Three minutes later, when she came back up on to the upper level, Hendricks was waiting. He stood under the Merrill Lynch clock, studying a train schedule behind a trio of Barney's suits who were too engrossed in the financial news tickertape to notice they were being used as a shield. Something was wrong. He knew the second he saw her face, turned briefly his way, pale, wild-eyed (the shades gone), blind to everything. He felt it now, the invisible bond between them.

The subject, he noted for his report, was acting in a distraught manner: walking fast across the concourse, now and then breaking into a little trot, constantly looking behind her, pausing just long enough to glance up at the overhead clock, as if she had only moments to spare . . .

Which is how most people would act if they were carrying half a million dollars through Grand Central Station. But Karen was empty-handed: there was no sign of any suitcase.

Anticipating her running for a train, Hendricks broke cover and started toward the track gates, only to observe her at the edge of his vision suddenly double back the way she'd come. Out in the open—it was a trap he'd walked right into— all he could do was hover by the escalators to the PanAm building, gazing up at the winter zodiac on the stations' blue vaulted ceiling like a dumb tourist.

When he looked again, the subject was gone.

One moment she was standing there, silhouetted against the empty north wall where the Kodak colorama, the largest god-damned lantern slide in the world, used to hang and brighten the days of commuters until some half-assed committee deemed it esthetically incorrect: it had changed once, magically, in front of the detective's eyes from fall in Vermont to a glorious view of Mount Rushmore.

The next, she was history.

3

They were unmistakably Americans, a group of medical symposiasts mugging for the camera on the infamous "Sea" green of the Old Course at St Andrews, some kind of golfing trophy at their feet, the Royal and Ancient looming mistily in the background. Tom got up and walked over to take a closer look at the photograph. He didn't at first recognize Goldstone's among the larky hats and clip-stretched grins. He'd met the man once for twenty minutes five years ago, sat in this same room with Karen and discussed the most intimate details of their marriage, then put the sonofabitch out of his mind forever, or what he'd hoped would be forever.

He was curious now to know how it happened, how two total strangers in a city of eight million people . . . it couldn't have been chance. He should have paid closer attention at the time, but the whole business had been so utterly distasteful, he had preferred not to get involved.

He never even asked her about it, not once.

They had to go on knowing each other, Karen had said on the tape. They'd had no choice. What could she possibly have meant by that? One thing Tom was sure about, whatever it was that happened here—God, it must have seemed like a miracle to her when she found him—he had no intention of leaving this room until he knew the answer.

It wasn't hard to figure Goldstone for the one in the middle with the bluest eyes, the deepest tan, the whitest teeth. The walls of his office, lit by halogen spots recessed into the ceiling to create a soft chiaroscuro, were covered in framed diplomas and more photographs showing the director of the Repro-Gen Center in various sporting poses—skiing with his family, at the wheel of a 1937 Packard rumble-seat convertible, strapped into the chair of a tarpon fishing boat—smiling the same costly, reassuring smile.

Enjoying all the good things.

A door in the oak paneling behind the desk opened and an erect, well-preserved man of about sixty with a full head of meticulously coiffed silver hair entered the room. He had on gray pinstripe pants and a white double-breasted jacket with the letters HG stitched over the heart in red.

"Mr. Welford? Thank you for being so patient." It was the rich, melodious voice Tom remembered. That and the hair. "Harvey Goldstone." He advanced a lean brown hand across the top of the desk. "I apologize for my secretary giving you the run-around . . . she can be a little overzealous when it comes to protecting my schedule."

The doctor's handshake was firm and dry and left behind it a faint odor of rubbing alcohol.

"I understand," Tom said. "I'm sure you know I wouldn't be here unless it was important."

He'd had to threaten breaking down the specialist's door for this five-minute audience.

"Have a seat, Mr. Welford. Now how can I help?"

Tom continued to stand, hands in pockets, legs apart, balancing.

"I'll try to be brief," he said, noticing the little grimace Goldstone made as he lowered himself into the swivel chair behind his desk.

"When my wife and I first came to see you . . ."

"Word of warning. Never play tennis with your grandkids"—Goldstone smiled ruefully—"and expect mercy. I'm sorry, I interrupted you. You were saying?"

"When we first came to see you," Tom began again, "before she started treatment here . . ."

"I know the name, of course, but I've a lousy memory for dates. Roughly when was this?"

"Five years ago."

"Five? Okay, good."

"You assured us that everything that happened in this office would be handled in the strictest confidence."

"Your wife became pregnant from the treatment?"

Tom took his time before answering.

"We have a son. His name is Ned." He sat down, then almost at once stood up again and, approaching the front of the desk, leaned on it with both hands. "Do you stick by what you said?"

"One of the rewards of working in my field is that it's never too late for congratulations." Goldstone beamed. "I'm delighted, really, I couldn't be happier for you." His uplifted eyes snapped at Tom's like stars. "Was it by donor insemination, or your own?"

"Would you mind answering the question."

"Sit down, and I'll be glad to." He waited for Tom to return to the chair. "Everything we do here is subject to a rule of anonymity. The very tenet of AID is that the donor will not know about his children and the children will not know about the donor. Without that bond of secrecy, I always say, our work at Repro-Gen could never . . ."

"There's been a leak."

Goldstone frowned. "You mean somebody other than you and your wife knows how she became pregnant?"

"I used to worry about that," Tom said. "Now . . ." He shrugged.

"You can be absolutely certain that no client information of any kind has ever left these premises."

"Look, I had a hard time coming to terms with the idea of calling another man's child my own. It took some doing, but I made it—made that 'emotional leap' you said I'd have to take before I could accept it completely."

"To be perfectly honest with you, Mr. Welford, I have no recollection of your case. I rather make it my business to forget."

"Then I suggest you consult your records."

"Ah," Goldstone held up his hands, bringing the fingertips slowly and precisely together. "There, if you will, lies the proof and guarantee of our discretion. We don't keep any records."

"Is that right?"

"Saves on the paperwork." He laughed, leaning back a little in his seat. "No, but seriously, most people think of fertility medicine as some kind of brave new frontier. That's baloney. It's been with us a long, long time. Second oldest profession, I always say. The ancient Sumerians used the services of anonymous donors whenever a dynasty looked like becoming an endangered species; they ensured their anonymity by having them put to death. We have to make do with the best safeguards available to us."

"Safeguards," Tom said, nodding. "If you want to avoid a malpractice suit, Dr. Goldstone, I recommend you either find some account of what happened here or unscramble that lousy memory of yours pretty damn fast."

"I'm sorry, I seem to have missed something." Goldstone

looked bemused. "What is the exact nature of your complaint?"

"You told me that the chances of my wife and the biological father of the child ever meeting were beyond the realms of possibility."

"I may well have done, or used words to that effect." He smiled uneasily. "I find most husbands need reassuring. The odds are incalculable, of course. But I'd bet the farm on it, sure. Wouldn't think twice."

"Well, I'm here to tell you that the impossible is precisely what has happened."

Goldstone shook his head. "Some mistake."

"They not only know each other. They have become lovers."

"There's really no way."

"Then prove it to me," Tom said. "You prove it didn't happen, or I'll sue your goddamned ass."

His professional smile still holding, Goldstone rose slowly to his feet. "I'm sure there has to be a perfectly rational explanation. As I said before, the absolute confidentiality we guarantee our patients depends on the keeping of incomplete records, but in certain special cases . . ."

"Well, gee whiz. Is that how it works? The least threat of a lawsuit or maybe having your license to practice medicine withdrawn, and suddenly there are 'special cases.' "

"It's unlikely I'll be able to help, Mr. Welford. There's just an outside chance. Excuse me one moment."

He slipped out by the door in the oak paneling.

Tom caught a glimpse of him in the next room, padding around the business end of a gleaming steel table fitted with stirrups. He imagined Karen lying there, naked, defenseless, under restraint . . . Then Goldstone moved away. He saw her legs miraculously break their bonds and fly up around the back of someone whose looks, height and build matched his own; her blind heel feeling for the cleft in the man's absurdly pumping buttocks, spurring him on. Tom closed his eyes. He hadn't learned yet how to shut out the instant replays, the uninvited highlights from his wife's bravura performance at the motel; after listening to the tape, he knew you could only cauterize such deep, tender wounds with equivalent loathing.

He could still hear the tiny sound of her ankle bracelet, cutting through everything; it was like a constant singing in his ears.

Goldstone returned after only a minute or two, carrying a slim gray folder. "You're in luck," he said, looking at him over a pair of half-moon reading glasses. "This was indeed an unusual case. I remember now. Only too well."

"You're full of shit," Tom said. "So who was the donor?"

"All I can do," the doctor said, consulting the contents of the folder, "is give you a broad-brush pen portrait. We only record the chief characteristics—build, color of eyes, hair etc.—so that we can fit them to the would-be father's. Never the donor's name. Here, if you don't believe me."

He slid a single sheet of paper across the desk.

"We had difficulty coming up with a match. But then you're not exactly standard issue, Mr. Welford. And we're not into designer babies here. By the way, when was your son born?"

"June 21, 1991," Tom said, picking up the sheet. He saw at once what Goldstone had meant. The description of the donor hardly tallied with his, but what was more significant— Tom felt his heart make a sudden lurch—Joseph Skye Haynes didn't have brown eyes and blond hair either.

"If this is right," he said quietly, "then I owe you an apology. It's not the same guy."

"According to my notes," Goldstone was saying, "your wife was inseminated three times on consecutive days during her first cycle after treatment was agreed. The reason she was unable to conceive by natural means was due to her husband's sperm being infertile."

Tom smiled. "Tell me something I don't know."

"I have a feeling I'm about to do just that. I don't know if you're familiar with the term 'traducianism.' It's the theory that the soul is transmitted to the child in the act of generation. Takes the old 'one flesh' argument about sexual union being a spiritual event a step further. It's what your wife said she believed in when she came back to see me at the end of her first month—not yet pregnant."

"She's a Catholic. So what?"

"She was very upset. She said she'd been thinking things over and had decided that it was wrong to 'go against nature.' I got the impression, Mr. Welford, that she was under a certain amount of pressure to conceive. She talked about how you'd 'saved her life' and how she felt that the least she could do was to provide you with a son and heir."

"What nonsense. If I had any ulterior reason for wanting Karen to get pregnant, it was because her doctors thought it might help stabilize her. She has a history."

"At the end of our discussion, she told me that she wanted to discontinue treatment. That it had all been a terrible mistake. I didn't try to persuade her." Goldstone paused and looked at Tom over the rims of his half-glasses. "I have a note here to the effect that she had already discussed the matter with her husband.'"

"She tells lies. She can't help it." Tom looked down at his hands. "What exactly are you trying to say?"

"The last time I treated your wife was May 30th, 1990— a full year, it seems, before the baby was born. In other words, conception did not take place as a result of her visits to this office."

There was a moment of silence.

"I see." Tom coughed. He looked up at the ceiling and loosened his tie, then put a hand to his forehead. "Excuse me, I find this . . . more than a little embarrassing."

Goldstone waited before he said, "I'm sorry. I can imagine what you must be feeling. This must be very hard for you." He paused again, shifting his weight in his chair. "Maybe I *should* have tried,"—he bit his lower lip—"I mean, tried to convince your wife that we don't just fool with nature at Repro-Gen. What we do here has its moral dimension too. We can't claim the higher ground, but in a secular age . . ."

He shrugged, then ran a finger along the desk-top, absently checking for dust.

"We needn't discuss this any further. I had no right to say the things I said, and I apologize. I've wasted your time." Tom pushed his chair back.

"Wait just a moment," Goldstone said. "We could be jumping to conclusions here. You don't by any chance happen to know your son's blood group?"

"Yes, it's the same as mine. I always assumed that was part of your 'matching' service. We're both type 'O,' along with a few billion others. So what?"

"How about DNA testing?"

"What are you getting at?"

"When did you last have a full sperm count? You know, Tom, stranger things have happened."

"No," Tom shook his head, "now you're wasting *my* time." He slid the sheet of paper back across the desk, then, changing his mind, held on to it as he rose to his feet. "I presume your rule of strict confidentiality still applies."

"It goes without saying."

"Then you won't miss this," he said, picking up the gray folder with his wife's name windowed in the top left-hand corner, and restoring to it the page of her case notes, "since it never really existed."

There was only the slightest hesitation. "As you wish."

The director of Repro-Gen, wearing a grave smile, came around his desk and walked with him to the door.

He held out his hand.

"It may be none of my goddamn business, Tom," he murmured, his buttery voice now gruff with concern, "but don't be too hard on her. The yearning to have a child can sometimes breed . . . well, acts of desperation."

"You're right," Tom said, "it is none of your business."

What he needed was a drink—before he could even think of facing the Atlantans.

Halfway back to his office, he told the cabdriver to turn

around and drop him instead at the Madison Avenue entrance to the Carlyle. Force of habit, as much as anything, drawing him to an old-world haunt, where he had always enjoyed taking Karen for dinner when it was just the two of them. But the moment he set foot inside the hotel, expecting to find in its dependable sameness—the muted Art Deco wall-paintings, the scent of expensive flowers, the quiet smiling voice of the hat-check girl who greeted him by name, and asked politely after Mrs. Welford—a temporary shelter from the storm,

. . . and little Ned, he must be *how* old by now?

Tom realized his mistake. Spotting a hunched figure at the bar who looked vaguely familiar, he kept going around the revolving doors and left.

He walked ten blocks.

On the corner of 66th and Madison the pain in his gut became acute. Bad enough this time for him to have to stop and, showing an abrupt interest in the window of a jewelry store, lean against its shuttered glass and take several deep breaths. His forehead felt clammy. He wondered if he were going to suffer the humiliation of throwing up on the sidewalk. A young Asian woman in nurse's whites being pulled along by a fan of yapping dogs asked him if he felt all right. Tom thanked her with unfailing courtesy and said it was just the heat.

Sweat broke out on his back as the spasm passed, leaving him staring at his own hazy reflection in the glass and behind it the center-piece of Fred Leighton's window display: a high collar of pigeon-blood rubies with a zigzag of small diamonds running through them like a row of jagged teeth. The card on the green velvet stand said: FOR THE WOMAN WHOSE PRICE IS FAR ABOVE VIRTUE.

Tom gave a mirthless snort. He closed his eyes and felt his insides shrivel as he tried to think back. Five years was a long time to be married to someone, and not know. It meant that she'd been cheating on him, his wife of five years, almost from the very start. He had a vision of Karen resting by the pool at Edgewater when she was pregnant with Ned, her silken skin without blemish, the glow of lazy contentment in her shaded eyes that he hadn't put there. It's going to be fine, Tom, she'd squeezed his hand, everything's going to work out just fine. And all the time . . . a time of closeness and sharing and growing trust . . . making mockery of every moment of pleasure they'd ever given each other, of all the happiness Ned had brought them . . . she was being unfaithful. When he considered what he'd done for her, the risks he'd taken, the sacrifices he'd made—frankly, it was beyond comprehension.

He took a deep breath and set off again down Madison Avenue, hands thrust in the pants pockets of his Huntsman suit, managing to cut his usual impressive figure. His height and big loose-limbed Midwestern stride gave Tom the invincible air of a man used to viewing the world from a pinnacle. Other users of the sidewalk moved aside instinctively to let him pass, never suspecting that such a parade of confidence, such obvious natural superiority, could conceal the smallness he felt inside, the little seizures of rage and panic that threatened to overwhelm him.

There are days that change everything, he thought, days that tell you after this nothing will ever be the same again.

Naturally, he'd been jealous before. He'd had his doubts, entertained those suspicions about Karen that every beautiful woman invites. Like the time he'd found a sachet of birth control pills in the bathroom—birth control, honeybunch, for what?—and she'd told him the doctor had prescribed them to regulate her periods. He'd believed her, if only because she was always testing him, pushing compulsively against the limits of his trust. On that occasion, it hadn't prevented him from checking out her story. But he'd learned to interpret the subterfuges, the paranoia, the little harmless lies she told as part of her condition. At the clinic they'd advised him to give her "plenty of space." It made her deceiving him, when he was trying his best to help her, all the harder to swallow.

And that wasn't the worst of it. If she'd simply screwed

some guy and gotten pregnant, then come and told him about it, he might have been able to forgive her, the marriage could have survived. After all, half the people one knew weren't who they thought they were. But the trick that she'd played on him had a cold, scheming deliberateness about it that was straight from hell. In making the effort to accept Ned completely as his own, he'd invested every penny of his capital in their joint project of human manufacture. He'd made Dr. Goldstone's emotional fucking leap all right. And she knew.

He really loved the boy. Ned *was* his son, goddamn.

He called the office on his mobile as he walked and heard that the meeting with the Atlantans had gotten under way at ten thirty. He told Mrs. Strayhorn he was coming home, which wasn't what he'd meant to say. It was now ten forty-eight. He still had time for that drink. He walked three more blocks, found a bar that was down some steps, a dark empty tavern, and ordered a double Scotch straight up.

There were legal aspects to consider, and then there was what might be called the social picture. Clearly, he needed to talk to his lawyers—Boz Geary about the possibility of changing his will and Phil Zimmerman on the divorce angle— and before the end of the day. He wanted to be able to consider his options over the weekend with all the facts at his disposal. Tom knew that under New York State law he was Ned's legal father, but the fact that the boy wasn't after all the result of donor insemination was bound to complicate matters. He could only imagine that should it come to a custody fight, it would improve Karen's and her lover's chances. But if that was the case, then surely she would have been more tempted to start divorce proceedings against him?

He'll only be getting what he deserves . . .

Tom picked up his mobile and tapped in the number of his family law firm. The switchboard operator answered just as the bartender came over and asked if he wanted a refill. Tom shook his head, then, changing his mind on both fronts, flipped the phone shut. And let the man pour him another shot of whiskey.

He needed more time to think.

Haynes had been right about one thing. The prospect of all this coming out in court horrified him. He could imagine the field day the media would have at his expense, feeding a salivating public the intimate details of his marriage, the furtive visits to a sperm bank (disclosing his infertility, which doubtless would be confused with impotence), making a martyr of the beautiful troubled wife who finds solace and fulfillment in . . . Jesus Christ . . . and at the heart of it all, the innocent boy who knows nothing, says nothing—it didn't even bear thinking about.

Tom had been raised in the old-fashioned way to shun all publicity. His father, who'd barely spoken to him since he'd married Karen, had taught him that a gentleman never exposes himself or his family to ridicule. Holman Welford, a blunt square-jawed Missourian cattle rancher and former senator in the Ford administration, could neither understand nor forgive his oldest son for leaving his Brierley-educated first wife, with her thoroughbred looks and impeccable Eastern pedigree, and a year later marrying a gold-digging tramp—"that hillbilly with lipstick," as the old thug had once referred to Karen—who couldn't help but drag the Welford name into the mud. Ironically, the birth of a grandchild had brought about a slight rapprochement, but the thought of giving his father, whose brand of paternal discipline had been castigating, absolute, vengeful . . . the satisfaction of being proved right was another reason he couldn't afford to let this happen.

No, Haynes had hit the nail on the head. He did regard his privacy as sacred. And if any of this came out, it would, they were both smart enough to know, quite simply destroy him.

He called the barman over and asked for one more drink and the check. He felt in the inside pocket of his jacket for his bill-fold and then searched his other pockets for the scrap of paper with the number on it that Victor Serafim had handed him at the zoo. When he found the note, he spread it on the bar beside his portable phone. He drank the whiskey.

If he had to redraw the map of his life, Tom decided, because past and future were no longer the continents of certainty and hope he once thought they were, then he would do so—whatever the cost.

He dialed the number and, when Victor answered, said, "Yes, we were talking earlier . . ."

"Now do you believe me?"

Tom cleared his throat. "I think there's a chance we might have something to discuss."

"I knew you'd come around. Business is business, right? Look, I got someone with me right now. Let me call you back."

"No, I'll call you."

He heard Serafim give a low chuckle.

4

They'd assumed physical shape before his eyes, and Hendricks hadn't even noticed. One minute, nothing; the next, there they were, standing on the sidewalk opposite, their molecules reassembled like what's the guy in *Terminator II*, staring at him through the beach traffic with those dead-end eyes.

Nobody could call Victor's crew inconspicuous. The tall, skinny one, Donut, had on scarlet warm-up pants, a white singlet and sneakers so new they still squeaked . . . not that he would know. Roy Roy, shorter but with the body of a weight-lifter, wore a baggy T-shirt that said DEF PREZ NOW across the broad shelf of his chest. A pair of reflector shades hung from a gold loop around his neck.

Hendricks wondered if he wasn't losing his edge. You get distracted, a careless second is all it takes. It worried him more that the tension he felt was written all over his face.

He had no idea how long they'd had him in their sights before he spotted them. The D was the only train to arrive at the Coney Island terminal in the fifteen minutes he'd been waiting. He'd watched its graffiti-stained, mostly empty cars snake slowly around the elevated track behind the condos on Stillwell Avenue. But he never saw them get off and, if they used the stairs, missed them again exiting the station at street level.

There was no sign of Victor.

Earlier he'd seen his gray Lincoln parked outside the Italian restaurant across the street. He had the time to drive around the block and run a make on a couple of limo plates in the restaurant lot with Datafind. The kind of people Victor was sitting down to lunch with wouldn't appreciate a show of muscle from an unmade shylock. Out of respect, he would have instructed his crews to find their own way here.

Cautiously, they started to cross the street, sniffing the air first, then looking rapidly to left and right, swiveling their heads each time through ninety degrees as they negotiated the traffic on Surf Avenue. You could have mistaken them for out-of-town kids on a spree, eager to check out the girls and rides, sworn to find some action. Hendricks realized he'd never seen them alone before. On the loose, like this. For a moment he wondered uneasily if Victor was planning to show.

They came up to him with easy grins—Roy Roy bobbing and weaving like a boxer—wanting to shake hands, only the detective had a Nathan's chili-dog with extra relish in one paw and a plastic cup of Miller's Lite in the other. Helpless, he gave a fat little shrug; holding up his lunch like an offering: "You boys hungry?"

Donut didn't answer, just reached out and took the chili-dog from him and crammed the whole thing in his mouth.

"What the . . ." Hendricks began, too surprised to hide his dismay as he watched Donut wolf it down, leaning forward to stop the chili sauce messing his clothes, his bony Adam's apple working like a turkey's.

Roy Roy, finding this funny, relieved the detective of his beer also and handed that to his partner.

"You dumb sons-of-bitches, I didn't mean for you . . ."

Mistake.

Donut drew his mouth across the back of his hand, then put a finger up to his thin greasy lips. Smiled. Still chewing.

"Yeah, right. Excuse me for speaking with my mouth full." Hendricks gave a ratty laugh. "I forgot."

Thing One and Thing Two, he called them.

He had no idea how much they understood, whether they could really lip-read. He just talked to them like anybody else.

"Well? Is he coming?" He wiped sweat from his brow with the paper napkin he'd been left holding.

They watched faces. Fear they could smell.

Roy Roy produced a hawking sound from the back of his throat and pointed to the Nathan's sign above their heads. FOLLOW THE CROWDS SINCE 1916. He inclined his head. The way to the amusement park, sprawled between them and the ocean, lay down a deserted lane flanked by empty lots, chain-link fences and a few boarded-up side-shows. Even in broad daylight, it looked a route to avoid.

"It's okay with you two girls, I'll just wait here."

They made a brief exchange in Sign. He saw their eyes agree something before coming back to rest on his. A pause that had the weight of silence. Then skate quickly past him.

"Ever try the soft-shell crabs, Eddie?"

He turned to see Victor Serafim, standing behind him. Like the others, from out of nowhere.

He shook his head. "I could really murder another hot-dog, though." Suspecting this was somehow all arranged.

"They're the best in town."

"Are you kidding me?" Hendricks, not a little relieved, made as if to protect his stomach. "I'm allergic to seafood, anything that swims, or crawls."

"You don't know what you're missing."

A fanfare of hunting horns cut through the steady thump of rap music from the arcades, heralding the start of the same race-track game Hendricks remembered playing out here twenty years ago. Making his first bets on mechanical horses.

"I know what I've missed."

Victor smiled. "The boys been taking good care of you?"

He looked harmless, hanging there in his crumpled suit, wire-rimmed glasses and white bucks; a straw hat pushed jauntily back on his sunburned forehead. Like somebody's favorite uncle.

"Sure, we were just running out of conversation".

"Fried in batter with hot sauce on a soft roll? Hard to beat, Eddie."

"Give me a break, will you?"

Victor threw an arm around the detective's short neck, scragged him a little, as if to show there was no call for hard feelings. "Let's go."

He'd been working for Victor over three months now, ever since he'd started falling seriously behind on the payments. A run of bad luck in Atlantic City and the future had looked bleak until Victor had offered him what seemed an easy way out. The chance to work off his debt by going on to his payroll. Doing credit checks mostly, the odd surveillance job, maybe an illegal entry here, a phone tap there. Nothing too heavy. He had friends in the Department who understood that sometimes a private had to do these things to get results. Out on his own for twenty years, he'd paid his dues as a fraud investigator with an insurance company in Gary, Indiana. It wasn't the first time he'd worked the wrong side of his badge, but he could see the day coming when it wouldn't be so easy to go back. There was a line you crossed.

At least, that was how he was planning to put it to Victor when he got through telling him the news about Karen Welford.

Eddie Hendricks wanted his independence back.

He knew exactly what he had to say. The hours he'd put in on the Welford case, the information he'd gathered, the growing evidence of criminal intent that would normally leave him no choice but to go to the cops: he was getting too involved. The trick was how to say it without appearing to threaten anyone's interests, without arousing suspicion. With Victor you could never be too careful. He had an unpredictable nature. But he didn't like change and he let nothing slip.

Accepting money from a loan shark, Hendricks had never had any illusions, was like cutting your throat later rather than cutting your losses now. Made no difference whether it was in cash or kind: you didn't pay, you knew what would happen.

There were other strollers besides them on the Regelman boardwalk, but nowhere near the usual August crowds. People sought the shade, finding the day too hot to enjoy without anywhere to cool off. Since the hospital-waste scare had come back to haunt the city beaches, few were risking the water.

The sun, still high over Brooklyn, was like the bright blade of an axe stuck in the sky. He might have known Victor would insist on walking, knowing he hated the beach.

He kept up a merciless pace, his pair of trained dingos loping along not far behind. More or less to heel. Hendricks struggled to stay ahead of them.

After five minutes the detective was breathing hard, his nose starting to throb again, the sweat stinging his eyes.

"Can we talk?"

"Sure." Victor stopped to wait for him under the rusted tower of the Parachute Jump, an old fairground attraction that had been out of commission long enough to be declared a landmark. "You hear that sound?"

Its spidery rigging gave off intermittent, doleful clangs like a buoy out to sea.

"The metal expands in the heat," Victor said, setting off again as soon as Hendricks caught up. "Reminds me of Brother Soldo, our parish priest when I was a kid, ringing the Angelus."

He braced for one of Victor's reminiscences about growing up in Brooklyn after World War Two. An orphaned refugee from communist Yugoslavia, Victor Serafimovic had been raised by his father's sister in Bensonhurst, or one of those greaseball neighborhoods. Hendricks had heard it all before. How he'd dug graves for a living, spun dough in a pizza-parlor, run errands for local gangsters—the old-style "dem, dese, dose" guys who'd given him his start when loan sharking was the best business organized crime had going for it.

"We really need to talk," Hendricks puffed. He didn't like the fact they seemed to be heading away from where there were people. They could have talked anywhere.

"It reminds me of being hungry," Victor said, "hungry and scared and five fucking years old."

"I think Karen and Haynes are planning a move."

"It was hot like today," he went on, ignoring him. "I'd gone up into the woods behind our village, Gudovac, to look for food. This was the summer of '41, everyone was hungry and scared then. Serbs and Croats were doing shit to each other that makes the latest go-around look like a fucking picnic.

"Imagine. Five years old, existing on a diet of shoe-leather and squirrel, and I come across this big crop of mushrooms under a tree in the forest. They give off a smell so sweet . . . I can still smell 'em."

Victor had to stop again to let Hendricks catch up, and get his own breath. Donut and Roy Roy kept their distance.

"I heard a creaking sound, looked up and saw that the branches of the tree were all bent, weighed down with the swaying bodies of hanged men. I counted nineteen, mostly from Gudovac. Among them, my two elder brothers, Anton and Mladin, and my grandfather. Their tongues were black as berries and sticking out further than I ever thought tongues could go. The mushrooms, I figured, must have popped up during the night after the assassins left. Or they'd have been trampled on.

"You know what's funny, Eddie? I picked every last one before I ran home to break the news to my mother."

Hendricks asked weakly, "What had they done?"

"They were suspected of being traitors."

When what he'd wanted to say was, Why are you telling me this? Victor never told you anything without a reason.

"Tugomir Soldo had ratted on them to the Ustaše, the Catholic Croatian militia, whose uniform he wore openly after that. Still kept his priest's cross around his neck, right alongside a second necklace made up of the eyes and tongues of Orthodox Serbs."

"Jesus Christ." The detective looked away.

"I couldn't talk. But she already knew. My mother was a Serb, my father Croatian—mixed marriages were not healthy then." Victor had started walking ahead. "Or now. You know what it is to have divided loyalties, Ed?"

He laughed. Hendricks was silent.

"What about your mother? The rest of your family?"

"The Ustaše came back and took us to the camp at Jasenovac. As a Catholic and respected local businessman, my father had some influence. He used it to save his own skin, denied we had anything to do with him. At the camp, they gave him an important job converting the old brickworks into a crematorium."

"Holy shit. What happened?"

"You really don't want to know."

"Then why the fuck bring it up? Does this have something to do with the Welford case?"

Victor shrugged.

"Maybe not. But I'll tell you something, I haven't been able to look at mushrooms since."

They were halfway to Sea Gate, a wealthy retirement colony huddled behind security barriers on Coney Island's western tip, before Victor finally got around to asking.

"Frank brought in a fresh tape," Hendricks said.

"Yeah?"

Victor joined him at the wooden rail that was for leaning on and enjoying the view.

"Karen went over to Haynes's place this morning after

taking the kid to kindergarten. She stays fifteen minutes, they argue, they fuck, then she and Haynes drive into town. In separate cars. It isn't the way we had it figured. They're not out to clip anybody."

"You came all the way down here to tell me this?"

"No, there's more."

"I hope so, buddy." Victor yawned. "Because I never thought for one minute that they meant to kill him."

"You heard the tapes, same as I did. You said . . ."

"What I fucking said, Eddie, was that it wouldn't hurt to let Welford think his life may be in danger."

"Hey, look, I just supply the information. What you do with it is your business. You want the truth, I prefer not to know."

"You were there. You told him yourself."

"I told him what I believed at the time."

A patrol car crawled past, making the slatted planks of the boardwalk sing and shudder as it headed back the way they'd just come. Victor leaned over the rail to study something on the beach below.

"What I'm getting now," Hendricks said, "is that all along they were planning to leave, take the kid and just disappear. Start a new life somewhere. Only Haynes was dragging his feet until Karen starts pressuring him. If you think about it, the clothes, the suitcases, the personal stuff she keeps at the cottage, the money—it was staring us in the face."

"You're the detective," Victor said, looking around for Donut and Roy Roy, who'd given up trying to extort change from a seaside telescope and were sitting up on a bench, bored, sharing a cigarette.

"Did Haynes pick up the money yet?"

"I'm getting to that part. But I'll tell you now there's no way they're gonna pay it back."

The patrol car pulled up beside the mutes. Hendricks heard the crackle of its radio as the window rolled down. Then without warning it took off again at speed, blue dome light flashing.

"Who asked you?" Victor said, staring at him.

"What?"

"Who the *fuck* asked your opinion?" In a tone so suddenly vehement it froze him to the marrow.

"What's the matter with you? I don't get it."

"Don't fuck with me, Eddie. You ever fuck with me, you fat jerk-off, I'll give it to you in three seconds flat."

He sheered away. Stalked a few paces, then stopped.

"Take it easy, Vic, all I'm giving you is . . . facts." Thrown off balance by this outburst, frightened by it, Hendricks blustered. "I work for you, remember?"

"*You* remember," Victor said.

Then, slowly wheeling around, came back to him with that big Uncle Jack grin spread all over his face. "Hey!"

He tapped him on the cheek. "Just blowin' a little steam, that's all. You do a good job, Eddie."

"I wanted to talk to you about that," Hendricks said, deciding to grab the best opening he was likely to get. "The thing is, Vic, I'm turning down a lot of offers lately. Above the board PI work. I'm having to turn them down. And it's good money. Real good."

"Aren't you forgetting something?"

"I'd like the chance to get out there and work for myself again."

"You owe me, you owe the firm . . . what do we got, thirteen, twelve and a half? And you want to quit."

"I'm getting too involved in this thing. If Welford decides to go to the cops, shit, I could lose my license. You don't need me any more, Vic. How about we go back to when I was on my own making regular payments? The way it used to be."

"What are you, a comedian? Regular payments? The last three months you tried to duck me every time I came to collect. This arrangement was for your own good. I did you a very big favor. If I'd wanted to talk to you like a scumbag, Eddie, I'd have said, 'Eddie, let me tell you, this is what you fucking owe me and that's it.' I've been trying to make things easy for you."

"No, I appreciate that. I really do."

"You want it to get out of hand again? All it takes is a word and you're in big trouble with these guys, Eddie. At lunch today, they asked after your health. You are in big trouble. One word, and that's it, they're out of patience. They stop the clock."

"I appreciate that too." Hendricks gave a nervous laugh, not that he believed that Victor's friends were even aware of his existence. "It's just that . . . well, shit, you know me, last of the independents."

"You have any idea how stupid that sounds?"

"Depends on what you want out of life."

Victor bowed his head for a moment, rubbing a hand around the back of his neck as if deep in thought. When he spoke again, it was in a gentler, more confidential tone of voice.

"The way I see things, Eddie, this mess Welford has gotten himself into—okay, so his wife got him into it, but marry a head case like that you've only yourself to blame—it could be the opportunity we've been waiting for. I took a big gamble putting out all that paper on Karen, but I always knew I would end up dealing with the husband. Now it's just a question of being patient, waiting to see how things develop before I make my move."

"I don't want to hear about it."

"But you have to hear about it. You're part of this, Eddie, you were in on it from the beginning. And don't fucking tell me you didn't see the potential."

"Oh, I saw the potential all right—for getting screwed. Marion, my old lady, warned me to stay off this case . . . she said it didn't look right on my chart. She's a reader."

"Yeah? Listen to me." Victor put a hand on the detective's shoulder. "This thing could go huge. It could be my last chance to make a big enough score to get out of the rackets for good. I don't intend to let it go by. I'm 59 years old. I'm tired of this fucking business. It isn't what it used to be. New York City belongs to a preteen nigger with an Uzi. I don't want to end up as garbage on Fountain Avenue dump. I got my family to think about too. In fact, you and me, we're a lot alike, Eddie. Which isn't the only reason I've decided to offer you a deal. But it's one of them."

"What kind of deal?" He'd been about to tell Victor that he and his wife were planning to move down to Fort Lauderdale, but thought better of it.

"Maybe there's a shot of you coming out of this after all, you see it through."

"You mean I can come out of this clean?"

"Smelling rosebuds, owing nothing."

"Let me get this straight. If I continue to work for you on the Welford case, you're willing to wipe the slate?"

"Interest and principal." Victor smiled.

"After that, I'm on my own?"

"Whatever you want."

Hendricks didn't have to do any arithmetic. In interest alone, one way or another, he was paying Victor more than fifty thousand a year. With no reduction on the original sum borrowed. He couldn't turn the offer down. Victor knew that his whole life was a quest to get out of debt, to just for once be able to stop worrying about money. But the detective didn't want to appear too eager to accept either.

"I can live with those terms, I guess."

They shook hands.

"As long as we understand each other. Anything slips, Eddie, you're the one that takes the beating. If anything happens, they'll leave you for dead."

"What was the other reason?" Hendricks was thinking about the story Victor had told him. The tree of hanged men.

"I need a couple more days to get this thing set up. I need you there on the inside."

"You don't have that long. She's running scared."

"I'm meeting with her later to collect the vig. I can talk to her, make her see sense."

"I wouldn't count on it."

"You mean Haynes didn't pick up the money?"

"She went herself. I followed her down to the lockers. I

even got there first, but I couldn't get near enough to see what happened. All I can tell you is Karen didn't walk away with any suitcase."

"What are you saying?"

"She came to collect the money."

"Maybe she just took what she needed to make the payment. Left the rest in the case for Haynes to pick up later."

"You didn't see the look on her face. I thought she was going to have a friggin' heart attack."

Victor went over and leaned against the rail. He looked back at Hendricks. "Well, I'll be damned."

He tipped the brim of his hat to shield his eyes from the sun. "They are screwed. You know that?"

"If you didn't take it . . ." Hendricks said, tentatively, as if he meant it half as a joke. "You think maybe Welford?"

Victor smiled back at him, giving away nothing.

Hendricks had begun, he might as well go on. "Wouldn't he want to find out if what you told him about his wife was true? He could have sneaked the key to the locker without her knowing. Had it copied. It would have been easy for him.

"When he opens the locker door, discovers the loot, he thinks what the hell, it's his money anyway. If he takes it, it'll make things awkward to say the least for Karen and her boyfriend, who he thinks are planning to kill him."

"He denies absolutely finding any key."

"He would."

"They are *all* fucking screwed."

Out to sea, a long spar of haze had appeared on the horizon and was drifting slowly onshore, bringing the visible edge of the world closer.

Victor said, "I used to love to come down here when I lived in Brooklyn. Take a walk beside the ocean."

"I remember you telling me."

"In the days when this was a fit place for human beings to live. Each time, I'd say like a prayer, thanking the lucky stars that brought me to the USA. I never took what this country gave me for granted."

"You ever been back? Over there, Bosnia, I mean."

"You can still ask that question?" Victor looked at him and blinked. "After what I just told you?"

Hendricks said, "Victor, I gotta go. I got things to do."

"No, I want you to hear this. You asked me what happened at Jasenovac. The day after we arrived, they brought a load of Serb women and children in from the villages. The Ustaše ordered them to sit on the ground. Then they went to work."

"Knock it off, will ya?" Hendricks gave a shrill laugh.

"They attacked the crowd with hatchets, clubs and iron bars; slashed or beat them to death where they sat. Some of the killers were female, good-looking broads in uniform; they had arm sheaths with knives attached that made it easier for them to cut their victims' throats. There were so many it was late afternoon before they got around to my mother. She held my three-year-old sister, Nadja, tightly in her arms. They died like that. My father was tied to a post by the brickworks and made to watch. So they could see if he was telling the truth."

"Look, Vic, I can't even begin to . . . I mean, Jesus, this ain't something you talk about, is it?"

"Through it all I never took my eyes off my father. He was a tower of strength. They brought me over to him and told him to bite off one of my fingers. Pop didn't hesitate. He looked right through me as if I was nothing to him, not his, not even human. He said I couldn't be his son because I was half Serb. I can never forget that look, nor forgive it, but it saved his life. And, you know something? Mine too."

"Why didn't they kill you?"

Victor looked out at the flat sea.

"You're right, Eddie," he said, his eyes unblinking, "it was a long time ago. Ancient history. Back home, the fires burn too fucking deep, nothing stays buried for long. But this is America."

"What you been through, Jeez, I'm sorry, Vic, I had no idea." He saw that Victor wasn't going to answer the question. "You made it over here, that's the main thing."

"My father's Ustaše friends got us out through the Croatian Red Cross. After the war they put him on a boat to Paraguay, where there was a demand for skilled immigrants and no questions asked. I was sent to his sister's in New York. He promised her he'd come for me, but we never heard any more."

Hendricks watched a young Hispanic woman in a bikini walk up off the beach, yacking away in Spanish at two small plump kids lugging umbrellas, mattresses and a beer cooler the size of a bathtub.

"Why tell me?" he at last had the courage to ask.

"In the camps," Victor smiled, "I played dumb to survive, and lost the habit of speech. By the time I started to talk again—my aunt put me through a couple of years at the Brooklyn Institute for the Deaf—I was dreaming in American."

The woman, waiting for her kids to catch up, hung her head to one side and shook the water from her hair. Her breasts did a teasing jig with gravity. He saw Donut and Roy Roy exchange a grin and a few signs he took to be lewd.

"You think maybe the Welford kid . . ." Hendricks hesitated. Victor had invited the comparison, and yet it seemed somehow inappropriate, even disrespectful. "You think maybe he had some kind of bad experience?"

Victor laughed and pushed his hat back on his head.

"Nah, rich kids screw up easier, that's all. By the way, I got a call from Tom Welford, wc had an interesting little chat."

"Yeah? What about?"

"He's with you in thinking his wife and Haynes're ready to run. He wants them stopped, Eddie."

"Why do I feel depressed all of a sudden?"

"Give me a child before he's seven, as Brother Soldo used to say." Victor turned, holding out his hands, palms up, like a supplicant. "And he's mine for life."

Hendricks frowned. "I still don't get it."

They'd reached the edge of the amusement park. Victor put an arm around his shoulder. "Tell me something."

The detective took off his sun-glasses. He'd felt a breath of wind, warm, salt-laden, just enough to turn sweat cool on the skin.

"You were in their shoes, Eddie, what would you do now?"

5

Even with the rear seats stripped out the Suburban wasn't big enough to hold all their stuff. Joe prided himself on being someone who traveled light, who had sworn never to let possessions weigh him down; he had his music collection, some paintings he had an idea were worth a buck or two, his books and papers. The rest, he said, he could either take or leave. He would have liked to have taken the best of his architectural models, his tools which filled an old sea-chest and the stereo equipment—playing Van Morrison at full volume while they packed—but only if there was room.

He was prepared to make sacrifices.

Karen was hardly listening as they worked side by side among the piles of junk heaped on the living room floor. Dust floated in the slanting shafts of sunlight.

Anything loose went in the cardboard boxes she'd collected earlier from the local market, though they'd already filled more of them than could possibly fit in the wagon. Joe was still for hiring a U-Haul trailer, which he reminded her had been part of the original plan. She said there was no time.

"What difference can a couple of hours make?"

Her own suitcases were packed and ready to be taken down to the garage. Only Joe insisted on measuring them first, driving her nearly insane with his agonizingly methodical calculations. She'd have been more than happy to jettison anything that might delay their departure. What about

Ned's toys? They all had things they didn't want to leave behind, Joe said peevishly, this was his whole life they were talking about. And hers? Or didn't what she was giving up count?
The sacrifices she'd made? The strain telling, she suddenly
began to shout at him. The risks she'd taken? She hadn't
even had time to say goodbye to her horses. He just looked
at her.

Still in the dark. It wasn't Joe's fault.

She glanced up at the clock.

Her rendezvous with Victor Serafim was less than ten
minutes away. She felt her scalp tighten. Had there been the
slightest hope of stalling him, of buying more time, she would
have kept the appointment, driven by Denny's in Glen Cove
on her way to pick up Ned . . .

A fresh surge of panic.

Oh, God. Even another hour.

She reached for the handle of a suitcase, but was unable
to complete the action. She had no luggage, hands empty as
she ran through Grand Central Station, some mistake . . .
Karen stood transfixed, slowly waving her head, eyes brim-
ming as the images flooded back. Now, on the lower concourse, she was opening the locker door . . . going through
the sequence of shock, disbelief, then frantic denial as she
reached again into that unforgiving void. Probed and palpated
every inch of its metal walls like a person newly blind—but
there *hadn't* been any mistake.

They wouldn't have long when Serafim realized she wasn't
coming. The only question was would he go to Edgewater
first or would he know to come here?

Looking for her. She twisted her head, as if an unfamiliar
hand had fallen on her shoulder.

"Hey, take it easy."

Joe had come up behind her.

"It's going to be all right." He slipped his arms around her
waist and held her tight, his hands clasped over hers. "We'll
survive without it. We've got each other is all that matters."

"You don't understand," Karen said.

"It's not the end of the world. Money isn't everything."

"For God's sake, Joe."

She had been reluctant to discuss what had happened. What was the point? The money was gone, there was nothing to be done now, except pack and get out. She couldn't very well tell him who she thought had taken it. We should have picked the case up sooner, was all she'd said, not that it would have made a difference. They were watching us, Joe, from the start.

He hadn't pressed her; he hadn't seemed upset or even that surprised. She wondered if Joe had ever really believed that the money existed.

"You want to know the truth," he said. "I'm glad we're not going to be building our future with Tom's money. It would have come between us, oh, yes, sooner or later."

"We really have to leave now."

"I see this as a kind of deliverance."

She couldn't make him understand the need for urgency. It was imperative now that he do so. Her intention had been to explain everything later, when they were safe.

"It was my money," she said quietly. "It didn't come from Tom. I couldn't ask Tom for a lousy twenty bucks without having to account for it down to the last cent."

"What are you talking about? How could it be your money?"

"I lied to you." She turned around to face him, keeping her eyes level with the top button of his shirt. "I lied to you, Joe. I'm sorry, but there was no other way. I couldn't handle the idea of suddenly having nothing again. I did it for us, for Ned, for our family."

"Did what, Karen?"

"If you don't have money," she said, looking up and bleakly searching his amiable face, "you die in this country."

"What did you do, rob a bank?"

Joe, with his little smile on. The eyes that were like a piece of the sky.

He was her bottom line now, for better or worse, the reason, though she would never say it, that she had felt obliged to take out insurance, a cushion for the journey back.

"Remember Starlite?" she asked.

Joe walked over and turned down the stereo.

She told him how she'd run into Sylvia Morrow a few weeks ago in New York outside Bergdorf Goodman, and let herself be talked into going back with her to a loft downtown, where they did some catching up over a bottle of Absolut and a couple of lines just for old times' sake and she'd ended up telling her that crazy as it might seem she needed a loan.

Sylvia knew someone.

She told him how easy it had been to get the money, how Sylvia had taken care of everything and how she planned to pay the interest on the loan out of principal until they were ready to leave. These were business people, she heard herself say, echoing Serafim. After she'd gone, they would know to get in touch with Tom to recoup their investment.

"You were going to let him pick up the tab?"

"Why not? He can afford it. A divorce settlement would have cost him twenty times more. He's getting off light."

"No, you're right. I'm just . . . surprised at you. Blown away by this whole thing, I guess."

"You think Tom didn't get his money's worth?"

"Nobody's judging you."

"If we ever get out of here, I plan to write Tom and explain everything. About Ned, about you, and the money. He has a right to know why we're taking Ned away from him. He loves him too, Joe. Look, don't think this has been easy for me. I pray to God every night, asking Him to help Tom try to understand and forgive us."

Joe was silent.

She told him then about the collector, Victor Serafim, and the threats he'd made, the payment that was due that afternoon: leaving Joe in no doubt about the seriousness of their predicament or the lateness of the hour.

He started pacing the room.

"You could've told me, for Christ's sake. You love somebody, you're meant to share things with them."

"You would only have tried to talk me out of it. There was
no need for you to know."

"He's *our* son."

"I'm sorry," she said, tears running down her cheeks. "I'm
sorry I screwed up."

"How do you suppose that makes me feel?" He took her
by the shoulders. "When we both know I'm the one that really got us into this mess. If we'd stayed together, if I'd been
able to make a commitment when you wanted, you wouldn't
have had to . . . none of this would have happened."

"We're wasting time, Joe."

"Maybe we should talk to the police. It's not too late to
change our plans . . . We can call Herb, ask his advice."

"Joe, listen to me."

She left him loading the Suburban behind closed garage
doors; bringing the stuff down from the apartment by the inside stairs, in case anybody was watching the house.

She set off in the Volvo to pick up Ned from Edgewater.

They had enough money for the trip: or they would have
after closing Joe's modest savings account at the Chemical in
Westbury. Enough to get them as far south as Raleigh, where
they had planned anyway to sell the wagon.

Then they'd be rich, Joe had said. She wasn't altogether
sure he was joking.

By evening, he reckoned, half the police departments in
the country would be looking for her and Ned. The more
miles they could put between them and New York before
dark the better. But she needn't worry. He'd worked up a
game plan—this part of it, the disappearing act, had always
interested Joe—for how best to cover their tracks.

On the phone to Edgewater, she'd told Hazel that she
would be home in ten minutes, and instructed her casually,
but firmly, to have Ned ready to go out. She'd decided to take

him over to swim and get an ice-cream at the club. No, there was no need for her to come too. Thanks just the same.

Wondering now if she should risk running up to the nursery and throwing Ned's security blanket and a few other things into a tote; if she could do it somehow without setting off that bitch's alarm bells.

She slowed at the end of the driveway.

Then had to slam on her brakes, slewing to a halt in front of the gray Lincoln that had just pulled in off Wheatley Road, blocking her exit.

Without hesitating, Karen shifted into reverse and started to back up, before she remembered there was no other way out. She central-locked the doors, turned up the air and the radio and jammed her hand down on the horn. She saw Victor Serafim get out the far side of the Towncar, walk slowly around it, then come over to knock on her window. She kept looking straight ahead. Heart in her mouth.

"You're going to be late, Karen," he said, and for a moment it puzzled her that she could hear him so clearly, "if we don't get you out of this jam you're in."

Serafim was leaning through the Volvo's open window, his mouth almost to her ear.

"Is the picture dark enough for you?" they used to say at Cair, where guests tended to watch a lot of daytime TV.

The Lincoln's cool gray interior smelled of cigars and stale sweat and the hint of a sweeter something (masked by a cheap floral air-freshener) that Karen couldn't get, beyond that it was faintly medicinal, the kind of smell you feel loath to analyze too closely.

She sat stiffly the other side of a plump leather arm-rest from Serafim, holding the crystal glass of Chivas he'd handed her wrapped in a quilted napkin. She'd been too scared to refuse the whiskey. Joe, who was up front, wedged between Donut and the driver, hadn't been offered a drink from the mini-bar. From time to time she'd catch his eye in the parabolic rearview mirror that extended the breadth of the windshield, but they had no information to exchange. She feared for Joe's safety more than for her own.

Victor had refused to reveal their destination, promising only that the ride was to be "an education." After they left the Interborough at Highland Park, Karen gave up looking out for landmarks. One rundown residential section of Queens or Brooklyn (she had no idea which borough they were in) looked very much like another.

They had been driving half an hour. Nobody spoke.

Donut, slumped in his seat, one foot up on the dash, watched her and Victor in the long mirror; hard little oh yeah eyes squinting out at them from under a spinnaker of greasy hair.

"Turn that thing down, will you?" Serafim said into the mirror. The mute leaned forward to kill Mel Tormé's greatest hits booming from the speakers.

"They're going to give you a piece?"

Serafim was talking on the phone.

"A piece to get after who?"

"You want my advice, Harold. Just lay there quietly in Brooklyn before you get a slap."

"I like to keep the chart always straight, straight, buddy. You missed me over three weeks already. Harold, I got it written down here, Harold, I'm watching."

He kept his eyes on Karen while he spoke, in case she missed the point that he was doing this partly for her benefit.

"What's the shot? What's the chance of your coming up with some money, Harold?"

"I'm sorry to hear that."

Victor put his hand over the receiver.

"He's H-O-M-E." Spelling it out for the eyes in the mirror.

Then held the phone away from him, as if to show her that nothing Harold could say would make the slightest difference.

"How do you like this creep? This is what I have to deal with. This is how I spend my life, talking to scumbags."

Karen shook her head, getting that medicinal smell again, stronger than before.

"He's giving me all excuses, Karen, he's giving me he's working . . . listen." He put the phone to Karen's ear for a second, long enough to let her make out the pleading litany at the other end, then took it back.

"What's that, gas money? Who are you kidding, Harold? I know you got buying power."

It had a putrid reek to it, like a soiled bandage.

The car slowed to a crawl.

"Harold, you sonofabitch, you got until noon tomorrow, or you'll get a beating every week till I get my money back, every single week, I'll take a piece out of your body, you fag. You fat fucking fag."

He switched the phone off and crashed it down in its cradle, then lay back in his seat with a satisfied expression. One hand gently slapped the arm-rest.

"This the house, Roy?"

The Lincoln had pulled into the curb opposite a large dilapidated Victorian shaded by plane trees, its jungly front yard littered with abandoned toys, rusted machinery, the skeletons of household appliances. An old climbing frame overtaken by weeds made Karen think of Ned. He'd have been ready now these past thirty minutes, listening out for her car on the front steps at Edgewater.

The name on the mailbox said UNTHANK.

The driver looked up at the rearview and nodded.

"Well? What are you waiting for?"

Roy Roy made small incoherent noises as his thick fingers rippled fluently in the mirror.

"He's not going anywhere," Victor reassured him. "Are you, Mr. Haynes?"

Joe could only shake his head.

"Let's hear some music. M-U-S-I-C."

Donut turned up the volume on the stereo. His partner had produced from somewhere a foot-long lead sash-weight and was rolling it up inside a copy of *The New York Times*.

They got out of the car and walked swiftly up to the front door of the house and rang the bell.

The door was opened by a middle-aged man in swimming trunks holding a can of beer. Karen saw the look of surprise in his red puffy face turn to fear as he recognized his visitors, and tried to slam the door shut, nothing like quick enough.

Dragging him out into the yard, they threw him to the ground. Roy Roy sat on his back, pushing his face into the grass, while Donut went to work on his arms. Raining down short dull blows of the weighted newspaper on the same spot just above one of the victim's dimpled elbows.

He could have been chopping wood.

In the back of the Lincoln, Karen, numb with revulsion, hardly flinched when she felt Victor's hand come to rest on her knee. The lush sounds of Mel Tormé on the stereo almost drowned the screams. She saw Donut bend the man's arm back the wrong way, let it fall, then move on to the other.

"They have an edge when it comes to hurting people. If you don't know what pain sounds like, it's a lot easier to dish it out. Me, I can't stand even to hear a baby cry."

Karen looked away, shrinking back into her seat as she felt the stub of Victor's middle finger softly investigate the crease behind her knee. She prayed that Joe wouldn't see what he was doing, and try to start something.

"A family guy, four kids and a mortgage"—Victor leaned close to her ear—"defaults once too often on a payment . . . how else do you make a creep like that face up to his responsibilities?"

"I'll get the money, I swear," Karen said, as she watched Donut and Roy Roy walking back toward the car. "I just need a couple more hours."

"Harold shouldn't have went to the track."

"Harold? The one you were just talking to on the phone? But you told him he had until tomorrow."

Victor shrugged.

"Sometimes you gotta, you gotta, you can't be nice to

nobody. Sometimes you gotta do the right thing and they come across."

He leaned forward suddenly and gripped the head-rest of the seat in front. "Isn't that right, Mr. Haynes?"

As the doors either side of Joe slammed shut and the Lincoln peeled away from the curb, tires singing.

"Hey, Joseph. I'm talking to you."

"I wouldn't know," Joe said.

"You wouldn't know?" Victor, looking back at Karen, gave her a wink of shocking complicity.

"I don't seem to be making myself clear here. Donut, show this asshole your collection of forfeits."

Karen thought she was going to throw up. But Donut's "forfeits," smelling to high heaven, turned out to be in the trunk of the car. Their exhibition would have to wait.

"This isn't how you get to my place," Joe said.

They were on Northern Boulevard, coming up to the junction with Glen Cove Road. She saw that Roy Roy had his left-hand turn signal on, which would bring them on to Cedar Swamp or Duck Pond and then into Locust Valley.

"Where are you taking us?"

"Home, princess."

"For God's sake, you can't." She gulped her whiskey and put the empty glass back on the tray.

"I want my money, Karen."

"The money isn't there."

"It could be." Victor smiled and patted her knee. "We swing by the house and wait for your husband to get back from the office. Then we can all have a little chat. Straighten things out."

"Don't do this, it won't work," Karen pleaded. "Please, I'll get you the money."

"You tried to duck me once already. Why should I listen? I know you're in trouble."

Karen hadn't much doubt that it was Victor who'd taken the suitcase from the locker, stolen back what he'd lent her, but she didn't dare accuse him—just in case she was wrong, and he didn't know yet that the money was missing. Then they would have no chance.

"I can get it by tonight, I swear to God."

Victor laughed, crab-walking his hand along the inside of her thigh. "What you gonna do? Peddle this?"

Was he admitting it now?

Joe tried to turn around, but the mutes, wedging him in with their elbows, forced him to face the front. "If you so much as touch her . . ."

"What's that, a threat?"

They both laughed. At least, Donut got a lopsided grin on his face with air rushing in and out of it; Roy Roy made a little noise that sounded like tiss, tiss.

"I'll pay double what I owe you," Karen pleaded.

"I'm rapidly losing patience here. You don't seem to realize this is a serious situation you people're in."

"Won't you please give us a break?"

Victor settled back in his seat. He took off his glasses, breathed on the lenses and polished them on the sleeve of his jacket. Unprotected, his eyes were more noticeably oblique, and revealed a softer, almost vulnerable side to his face that made Karen look away.

"Maybe we can work something out. Maybe we can work this out to everybody's satisfaction."

"All right," she said quickly, imagining he meant to up the percentages, squeeze a little more juice from the loan. "Just let's get it over with."

"There'll be some extra cost involved. But if it gets you out of this mess, I wouldn't nickel and dime over it." He held his glasses up to the light, checking for smears. "Handled discreetly, you'll have no worries on that score. Nothing to connect you. You won't even know how or when."

"What are you talking about?" Karen frowned.

She saw Donut slot another tape into the stereo and wondered how a deaf person would know when it was time to change the music.

"A contract."

Serafim had waited for the band to strike up again, for Sarah Vaughan to start singing "What a Difference a Day Makes," before he answered.

"What did you just say?"

"Tom."

"You've got to be crazy," Joe said.

"Twenty-four little hours . . ." Serafim sang along with the incomparable Sarah. Was this a joke?

"It had to cross your minds." He put his glasses back on, smiling at her. "I know it did. Where else do you think I got the idea?"

Karen shrank back, shaking her head no.

"Conversation recorded yesterday afternoon in a motel off Queens Boulevard . . ."

"Oh, Jesus, no, this isn't true."

" 'He'll only be getting what he deserves . . .' Sound at all familiar, Karen?"

"You got your wires crossed, man," Joe blustered.

"Do I? There's a lot involved."

She felt her head spinning. "All I meant was that if I left Tom . . . and he had to take care of any debts . . ."

Joe nodded. "That's right. He'd have to pick up the tab. You could do a deal with him."

Victor ignored the suggestion; he didn't let up on them.

"Imagine," he said softly. "All your troubles over. No need for the vanishing act. I get my money back and you . . . hell, you would have it all. The kid, the house, each other. And how much? Seventy-five, a hundred million dollars? Sound good to you, Joseph?"

Joe said nothing.

"You don't have to say yes or no. In fact you wouldn't have known anything about it, if you hadn't been planning to do a Houdini."

"You have no idea . . ." Karen shook her head.

She found her lover's eyes in the mirror. "Tell him, Joe. Tell him what happens. The money's all locked up in trusts until

Ned reaches his majority. I stand to inherit next to nothing."
She turned to Victor. "If you don't believe us, I can get a copy
of the agreement Tom made me sign when his son and heir
was born. You're wasting your time."

Victor wasn't listening.

"The two of you planned this thing, you're in it together."

"We're not murderers, for Christ's sake."

"We just wanted to go away together."

"This way is better." He paused. "This way you can be sure
no harm comes to the kid."

"Look, you've got us all wrong, we're not even prepared
to discuss . . . What do you mean?"

It was as if she'd been standing in a strong wind that had
dropped without warning. She held out her arms to save herself, thinking she could fall.

"Accidents happen."

"You're sick," Joe was shouting. "We'll go to the cops first,
we'll talk to . . . we'll do anything."

"Pipe down, Joseph. I know your type, don't give me that
shit, it would break your heart. You cocksucker."

"I would go to the police," Karen said quietly, "I would.
I'd tell them everything."

"Everything," Victor repeated, then shook his head. "What
have you got, a threat? If I say to you, I know where Doc goes
to school, Karen, it's a busy street for a kindergarten to be on,
is that a threat, is it a crime? Or am I just advising you as a
concerned neighbor to take care?"

Looking out the window, Karen saw that they were already
halfway along Lattingtown Road. Less than half a mile from
the gates of Edgewater.

"Okay, okay," she sobbed.

"I told you, princess, borrowing money is a serious
business."

Avoiding Joe's eyes in the rearview, Karen said, "Maybe we
can talk about this."

"Roy Roy, pull over."

* * *

They drove back to the Wheatley Hills in silence.

Karen watched the round metallic blue tank of the water tower hovering above the trees get closer through the shimmering heat haze. She thought how foolish to imagine you could hide something that ugly against the sky.

When the Lincoln came to a halt at the bottom of Joe's driveway, Victor leaned across her and opened the door.

"Just don't try to leave town or anything," he smiled. "Not for a few days. It wouldn't look good."

6

The ritual of summer weekends at Edgewater began on a Friday evening when Tom got back from the city. It didn't matter how late or how stretched he was, they always had a glass of champagne together, rain or shine, in the old pavilion out on the headland.

The Temple, as it was known, stood in a grove of sycamore trees almost to the end of the wooded cape which acted as a buffer between Edgewater's secluded bay and the municipal beach at Dosoris Park. An old pier ran out into the Sound there and on the cliff above it hung the upper deck of a ruined 1920s bath-house, where guests once picnicked and swam, descending from its tiled changing rooms by wooden steps to the sea, and where dances were held on moonlit summer nights. Now unsafe, most of the structure had collapsed on to the shore below, the heap of tumbled stones usefully blocking public access to the estate—keeping out what Tom called, only half joking, "the mud people" or "the vandal hordes."

The summons had come at seven thirty with a discreet knock at their bedroom door, the odd, mildly reproachful note in Thurston's voice (Mr. Welford was wondering if you could spare the time to join him in the Temple for a drink before dinner) suggesting something more, Karen sensed, than the chauffeur's old disapproval of her.

She shouldn't have needed reminding.

Their weekend rendezvous was a sentimental tradition. Tom had proposed to her on the Temple steps and four months later married her under the sycamores in a quiet ceremony attended by people who worked on the place, and a small group of his friends—nobody Karen knew (by mutual consent, they hadn't invited family). Unless you counted the doctor from Cair, who'd drunkenly advised her to think of "this wedding" as the first day of the rest of her life.

"Thank you, Thurston, tell him I'll be right down."

It was the tone of regret, his choice of the words "spare the time," that had pricked her conscience and brought home to Karen the inescapable reality of what had been agreed to in the back of the Lincoln. She suddenly felt sick with dread, afraid her guilt was already written in her face, plain for all the world to see. It would show now in everything she did . . . or failed to do.

Tidal repetition, Tom's phrase.

She flashed on an ice bucket, carelessly overturned, rolling away from his feet and bumping down the marble steps behind a flood of wine, water, ice cubes, splinters of glass.

The importance of not drawing attention to herself, of doing things as usual . . . all those precautions she'd taken had acquired a new, loathsome significance. She wondered how much longer she could hold the seams together.

How much longer before blood began to flow.

She walked out of the night-nursery, where she had been reading Ned a bedtime story, to find Hazel waiting for her on the landing. Oh, it's you, Mrs. Welford. The girl wore her hostility like a badge of merit. Unable to ask for an apology or at least some explanation of why Karen hadn't come home when she'd said she would, she made do with a tart: "Ned's been a little angel, considering how much he was looking forward to his outing to Piping Rock . . ."

"Would you mind just finishing the chapter?" Her hand shook as she handed Hazel the book of fairy stories; then couldn't resist going back in on the blonde's sullen heels to steal from her son another last goodnight kiss.

"Mummy's so sorry," she whispered.

Was it her imagination, or did the bubble that formed and burst against her ear contain a word? Did he cling to her as if more than his life depended on it?

"I'll make it up to you, sweetheart Ned, I promise . . . Tomorrow."

The pitying look he gave her—before calmly laying his head back down on his Spiderman pillow and its protective ring of stuffed animals—was to let her know that tomorrow his father was taking them all to the beach. *He* hadn't forgotten.

She had told Ned once, when he was going through a difficult phase, about the Recording Angel who keeps a chart of the good and bad things every person does.

She could see Tom sitting there, niched like a statue in one of the pavilion's classical arches, his head and shoulders outlined against the dove-colored sky. She felt his eyes on her as she walked up the path that led from the house.

She waved . . . the simple gesture appalled her.

When she got close, Tom rose to his feet; his impressive bulk, diminished in silhouette, slowly detached itself from the hoop of light.

"I was getting ready to give up on you," he said with a smile, coming down the steps to meet her, a glass in each hand. "How is he?"

"Looking forward to tomorrow. You remembered?"

He kissed her on the forehead. "I'll try, honey. The damned Atlanta thing isn't over yet. I told him I'd do my best."

"We all know what that means."

She moved inside ahead of him and sat down on one of the chintz-covered rattan chairs. The interior of the rotunda was white with an aquamarine dome, four arches open to the sea breezes and a Renaissance stone altar ("rescued" from a ruined church in Vicenza) set in the middle of the tiled floor. After their wedding Tom had had the altar deconsecrated (for her sake) and converted into a bar with a small refrigerator fitted in the space once occupied by the tabernacle. In the old days, when garden temples were the fashion on the North Shore, the original owner used to meditate here or, some said, hold seances where she would try to get in touch with a son lost in a boating accident.

"Have you had a tough day?" Karen asked, the slight echo showing up the forced casualness in her voice.

"You don't really want to hear." Tom stretched out in the chair next to hers. "New York's getting to the point . . . I must need a vacation. How's Ned been otherwise? Any more cracks appeared in Leah's famous dam?"

"For God's sake, Tom."

"You think I don't know what's going on?" His eyes half closed, hands clasped behind his head. "I know."

"Oh?" She felt her heart knock against her rib-cage. "What's that supposed to mean?"

"The reason why Ned stopped talking in the first place. We never discuss it now, do we? But I finally figured it out."

She sipped her champagne, then had to put the glass down, her hand was shaking.

"This morning on Madison Avenue, I was walking past the Carlyle when it suddenly hit me. You know how you used to say we didn't spend enough time together as a family? That I was too caught up in my work? That I neglected Ned because of the difficulty I had accepting him as my own son?"

"Let's not get into *that,* shall we?"

Tom moved forward and put a hand on her arm, so lightly that she couldn't avoid looking at him.

"No, but you're absolutely right."

His face was grave, the restive eyes steadied by a glaze of sincerity she didn't trust herself to doubt.

"He stopped talking in protest," Tom said, lowering his

voice significantly. "The boy doesn't get enough attention from his father, so he clams up. He discovers the power it gives him over us, and what's more he likes it. Which encourages him to turn up the heat. Enter 'Mister Man.' Only this isn't just any imaginary friend. He's a real person."

"I don't understand. Who is?" Her mouth dried suddenly.

"Flesh and blood." Tom waited, watching her. "Isn't it pretty obvious?"

Something in the room stirred and she realized that Bracken was lying there under the sofa. For an absurd moment she thought he meant the dog.

"You're looking right at him, babe."

"Oh, Tom." She managed a weak smile. "I don't think so."

"He invents the father he would have me be. I'm his Mister Man. At least, I'm going to have to try to become him."

She should have felt relieved, but she wasn't even sure that it really mattered any more how much Tom knew. Only that she musn't start to feel sorry for him.

"I'm afraid it's more complicated than that."

Tom reached for the bottle of champagne and generously filled both their glasses. One glass of wine was her usual limit.

"Well, anyway, I've been doing some thinking. What we all need—you, me and Ned—is a change of scenery. I've decided to take a couple of months off work. As from the week after Labor Day, I become a man of leisure. I thought it might be fun to travel, maybe go to Europe."

It came out of left field; it was so unlike the Tom she knew that Karen was at a loss how to react.

"But what about your office? You always said the whole thing would fall apart if you left them alone for a day."

"They'll survive. It'll do 'em good." He gave a laugh, a short rallying shout of mirth that alarmed her. "We'll do the grand tour, stay in the Crillon, the Cipriani, the Connaught, hit all the best spots . . . maybe even rent a house somewhere. Just the three of us, babe. You can make a list. We'll catch up on all those things we've talked about doing but never had the time for. What do you say?"

She got up and came around behind his chair, one slender hand alighting on his shoulder for a moment as she bent
down to kiss her husband's cheek.

"What can I possibly say," Karen murmured close to his
ear, "except that I . . . I think it's a wonderful, wonderful idea.
Just give me some time to think it over."

He reached up for her hand, but it had already gone.

She moved almost languorously to the westerly outlook
and stood there, an arm resting against the ivy-entwined pillar that divided the arch, staring off through the twilight at
the fading line of the American continent. Breathless, she
drained her glass, the champagne making her feel a little
dizzy but not enough to make the difference. In a world this
fucking perfect, there was no need to think anything over. She
could have laughed, it was such dumb irony. Afraid to examine either the implications of what Tom had just said or her
conscience, Karen couldn't allow herself to see beyond the
fact that his offer had come too late. It was the view, she
thought, the always beautiful view from the stern of a liner
slipping out to sea on a doomed voyage.

"When did you say we could leave?"

The evening was loud suddenly with cicadas, frogs, the
rustle of dry wings: an invisible orchestra that had struck up
again after a forgotten interval.

She turned when Tom didn't answer and saw that he was
busy helping Bracken to extricate himself from the sofa's
wicker undercarriage. The old brown dog, his dignity hardly
ruffled, padded off down the steps into the stifling dusk, anticipating by a few seconds the telephone, which rang twice
before his master got to it.

"Tom Welford."

By the way he spoke, by the way he was looking at her, she
knew that she'd said the right thing; and that that, God help
her, carried its own penalty.

Tom raised an eyebrow. "Tomorrow?"

He was speaking to her, she realized, as if she were the
person at the other end of the phone. "Wouldn't that be

great? Listen, if it were at all possible . . ." he said—talking
right through Thurston's windy announcement that dinner
was served—"Why don't we plan for, say, the end of next
week?" He put a hand over the mouthpiece. "I love you.

"Yes, Thurston, I *am* still here."

"You're crying," Tom said.

"I don't deserve this, you're being too nice to me."

"You absolutely deserve it," he said earnestly and put an
arm around her as they walked. They crossed the croquet
lawn and, overtaking Bracken, started up toward the house
as the last of the light, catching its pink and black brick façade,
turned all seaward windows the same coppery blue as the bay.

"Who was the last to leave?" Tom, looking back the way
they'd just come, drew her attention to a lamp one of them
must have left burning in the Temple. The glow migrated and
Karen pointed out that it was just the deck lights of a boat off
the headland; through the trees, it had seemed closer than it
really was. Tom laughed at his mistake.

"I want this to be a happy occasion," he said.

They sat opposite each other at either end of the candlelit
table in the dining room. Thurston, sporting a white cotton
jacket, served them a rich and indifferent dinner cooked by
his wife. Karen hardly touched her food.

"I'm glad we didn't invite anyone," Tom said quietly, when
Thurston was out of the room. "Besides, I wanted us to be
alone tonight. Are you feeling all right?"

"Just not terribly hungry," she said.

Whether or not they had company, Tom insisted on eating in the dining room when he was at home. What's the point
of living in a beautiful house, he would argue (whenever
Karen suggested having something on a tray in the library),
if you can't enjoy the place as it was meant to be enjoyed?
Only the right setting, he'd once paid her the stuffy compliment (his broad hand including in its sweep the eighteenth-
century Chinese wallpaper, the carved Adam fireplace, the

soft luster of Georgian silver) could do justice to her beauty
at night.

He expected her to dress for dinner. When he instructed
her as to what she should wear or how she should fix her hair,
Karen knew that it was a prelude to another protracted ritual that would only begin after they went upstairs.

But there had been no instructions.

He was, on this night, at his most charming and solicitous
toward her; affectionate and touchingly proud when he talked
about Ned. He weaved seductive itineraries for their forth-
coming trip ("just the three of us," a constant refrain) and outlined new schemes and projects for Edgewater, assuring her
that when they returned from abroad he planned to spend
more time, a lot more time, at home.

She'd heard it all before. How much they, his family,
meant to him, how much he loved this place, how he wanted
to leave Ned something more than just money. He liked to
think that Edgewater (perhaps his only lasting achievement)
could still be a sanctuary, an island in a sea of encroaching
suburbia, an outpost of continuity with a more civilized past,
fifty, a hundred years from now. She didn't think it unusual
that he should be talking this way.

She did her best to share his enthusiasm. Tom kept filling
her glass, as if on this occasion normal rules didn't apply. She
remained subdued, rigidly tense; he only grew mellower as
the evening wore on.

Then, without much warning, his mood changed.

They were having coffee in the library. Thurston had come
in to ask if there was anything else they needed, before wishing them goodnight. He and his wife, who had a small apartment in the stable block (only Hazel slept in the main house
with the family), were spending the weekend at the Jersey
shore and hoped to make an early start.

"Why is it," Tom murmured after he'd left the room, "that
that man always has to choose the most awkward time to take
the weekend off?"

"I didn't think . . . Mrs. Thurston asked me ages ago if it

was convenient. We don't have guests, Tom. We're not even going to be here all day tomorrow. Remember?"

"It's a question of security. This place is wide open. Jesus, anybody could walk in and . . . poor old Bracken would probably run right up to them wagging his tail."

"Tom, please!"

He sat and drank his brandy in silence.

At a little after ten, Karen said that she felt sleepy and was going up to bed. There was a movie on 13 she wanted to watch. Tom frowned as he made an impatient show of stubbing out his half-smoked cigar.

"Have you thought about what you're going to wear? I want you to look . . . I want to be able to say, you look radiant."

"I'm sorry?" Karen stared dully back at him. Going to wear? He hadn't given her any instructions, or had he? She looked down and tried to recall choosing the cream silk halter she had on, the gold belt and sandals, the dark burgundy crêpe-de-Chine skirt that reached almost to her ankles.

He gave a little smile. "I've a reason."

Her head swam. "Isn't this all right?"

"I'm talking about tomorrow night—the Davenports, the party, for Pete's sake!"

"Oh, God!" She closed her eyes. "It's not . . . you've got to be kidding, it *can't* be tomorrow. Are you sure?" Knowing perfectly well.

"They've only got a marquee as big as Grand Central Station going up across the bay. Or hadn't you noticed?"

It was tomorrow night that Joe was to have slipped into the house and taken Ned, then waited nearby in his Suburban until she could join them. Now that there'd been a change of plan, the idea of going with Tom to a charity ball seemed grotesque.

"I just assumed it was . . . *next* Saturday."

She bowed her head. A week from now . . . The heels of her palms pressed against her temples, suppressing the reflex thought that a week from now Tom would most likely be dead.

"The invitation is sitting up there on the mantelpiece. How long since we got it, a month?"

"I'm sorry, honey. I'll try to find something. What would you like me to wear?"

"I'm having a little difficulty with this," he said, putting down his brandy glass. He came and stood over her, legs apart, his back to the empty fireplace. "It's just too damned casual. They're our neighbors."

"I said I'm sorry."

"Didn't hear you, babe."

"Sorry." She was no louder.

"I thought we agreed to banish that weasel word from our vocabulary."

"What do you *want* me to say? I made a mistake, I get things muddled sometimes."

"I think you're lying."

"No, Tom."

"You know the consequences."

"It won't happen again, I promise." She looked up into his eyes and saw the trap he'd laid for her.

She took a deep breath. "Okay, I lied. I knew the party was tomorrow. The truth is I'd much rather stay home and just be with you. It's not too late to send our regrets, is it?"

"Some things," Tom shook his head, "I guess you'll never learn." Then, opening his dinner jacket and hooking his thumbs in his waistband, he said, "I know you've had a lot on your mind lately, Karen, but this . . . this was so avoidable."

"I just don't feel like going." She dropped her voice to a whisper. "Please. I'll make it up to you."

"You're jumping the gun, babe. Let's not spoil this. I've got something, a surprise for you."

He helped Karen up and, gently supporting her under one arm, led her out into the hall. They stopped in front of the first of the long Venetian mirrors which hung at intervals the length of the gallery. It was lit by a pair of sconces with dimwatted bulbs shaped like flames, a simulated dribble of wax running down the side of each candle. The mirror's dark silvering was faded and blistered so that in places it gave back no reflection at all.

Tom was standing up close behind Karen, but his face was a distant blur.

"Now put your hands over your eyes and don't take them away until I tell you to."

As if she was a child . . .

On a rare Christmas morning when her father was home, he'd played the same game. He'd made her hide her eyes, made her wait an eternity, it seemed, until she'd finally let her curiosity and excitement get the better of her and opened them. A brand new candy-apple red bicycle with white seat, pump and handle-grips was waiting for her in the hall, but her father had gone, had slipped away under the cover of darkness.

She felt his fingers untie the halter at the back of her neck. She resisted an urge to catch at the thin cloth as it slid over her breasts and fell from her waist to hang like an apron. She heard a tiny clinking sound, then shivered as her skin reacted to something cold at her throat that suddenly grew tight, tighter . . . she recognized the sensation, and didn't worry. It wouldn't have been the first time.

"Go ahead, you can look now."

She felt herself sway and might have fallen if he hadn't been there to steady her, holding her by the shoulders.

"Oh, dear God"—she put her hand up to her throat—"it's too beautiful. Tom . . . I don't deserve this."

The choker of pigeon-blood rubies had a chevron of diamonds running through it. The stones were tiny but gave off a deep lustrous gleam that (even to her inexpert eye) said they were the genuine article. Her heart beat faster. It had to be worth a hundred thousand, Karen thought, maybe more, maybe even enough to pay off Victor Serafim.

"Now you have something to wear tomorrow night."

"You know you shouldn't have done this. I feel so ashamed. You don't even like jewelry on me." She began to cry.

Tom had told her once, soon after they were married, that he'd never bought his first wife important jewelry, furs or valuable pictures. Why give an adversary negotiable assets, he'd kidded in lawyer-speak? But the way things had turned out (divorce after a couple of years, and who would have guessed sweet, gentle-born Helen would turn termagant and try to take him for all she could), his lawyers had advised him well. The line he took with Karen was that she was too beautiful to adorn.

She wondered what had made him change his mind.

In the early days of their affair, she'd asked him about his marriage, where it had all gone wrong.

I just woke up one morning, Tom had replied with a sincerity she'd never doubted, and realized that I still hadn't met you.

His reflection had vanished from the mirror. Then, through a prism of tears, she saw that he had only stooped down behind her to unfasten the hooks and eyes of her skirt, before gently lowering the zipper. She felt his hands on her bare hips as her clothes pooled around her ankles, felt his mouth's fastidious caress between her shoulder blades and, at the same time—she almost cried out in terror—the sensation of someone wetly licking the nape of her neck between the clasp of the choker and her hairline.

She whirled around, but there was only Tom.

The music he'd left playing on the CD was loud enough to cover his returning footsteps, the telltale creak of the screen-door. She would only know that he'd come back into the room by the fall of his shadow on the wall, or the first cut of the whip. She would hear nothing.

The mask he'd chosen for her was stifling. Karen was forced to breathe with her mouth pressed to a small feathery opening under the creature's beak. The sweat ran down her cheek-bones and, because her head was tilted back, glutted her ears. The eye-holes, set too far apart, gave her a partial view of her bent knees and the rope between them furcating the dark arrow of her pubis. He had tied her legs at the ankles, and again just below the knees, run a rope above and below her breasts, and another around her waist which passed between her legs and attached to her wrists; then he'd hog-tied her in a balled-up position, the "crapaudine," Tom called it, which drew everything tight, before sending her up to heaven. She could see the iron ring in the ceiling that had once supported a chandelier and from which she now hung, indecently cradled above the bed, with her head lower than her rear end, which he'd left exposed to the fullest extent.

Then he'd gone out on to the balcony, abandoning her.

Terms of ordinary entreaty being open to misinterpretation, they had a safe word, "Home," which she could use if things got out of hand, or she wanted him to stop for any reason.

Tom didn't always play by the rules.

She'd never had occasion to use it, but there was comfort in knowing the word was there. Home.

In the beginning, when he was breaking her in, when there was still the risk of revolt, he'd been careful. Not that the discovery of her husband's prescriptive tastes had shocked Karen. They seemed harmless enough, and the contrast between the sober, clean-cut image Tom presented to the world and this other side to his nature intrigued her. There was no real pain involved. He once told her that he couldn't find pleasure in giving free rein to his impulses, that love had to be a disciplined art, that he believed in restraint in all things. But gradually his need to discipline and control her—always for her own good—had turned into something over which she felt he had less and less control. Noticeably, after she became pregnant with Ned.

They had warned her at the clinic that her husband might display signs of insecurity. Dr. Goldstone had given her fatherly advice: try and see it from his point of view. You get pregnant by another man's seed, even if it's out of a vial, there's likely to be some subconscious reaction, a risk of irrational jealousy on your spouse's part. It'll pass . . . as the child grows. Naturally, she put the change in Tom, the mistrust, the possessiveness, his growing appetite for punishing her, down to that same unspecific resentment.

He was frightened of losing her.

But it didn't pass as Ned grew. And, because she knew that if Tom had "irrational" fears they were only too well founded, Karen had no choice but to continue putting up with his demands—seeing Joe all the while and planning their future together—however odious those demands had become to her.

He left her alone for an hour, it could have been longer, she had lost all sense of time. The few strands of rope that bound her might just as well have been ties of steel, the bondage was so irrevocable. She wondered if the knots felt tighter than usual, the bindings harsher, but she had confidence in Tom's judgment. She still trusted him. She felt a kind of freedom at being helpless, at being relieved of any responsibility.

A breeze got up, fluttering the awning over the balcony. The night air, charged with the scent of lilac from the garden, cooled her skin. She began to imagine that it was the house, not Tom's ropes, restraining her, preventing her escape. For one disordered moment, she allowed herself to think what it might be like to live at Edgewater with Ned and his real father. They would never be able to stay here, of course, after it happened, even for the boy's sake, but then, as Serafim had pointed out, they wouldn't be able to leave either.

After it happened? As if she had already accepted this ghastly thing as done. After it happened . . . the day unmarked as yet on the calendar, but a firm date in hell.

Tom had never made her wait this long before.

He beat her with a riding crop of green braided leather that tapered prettily to a looped thong. The cuts stung most that fell on old wounds. Each time her flesh recoiled from the blows, the rope between her legs chaffed cruelly. She couldn't tell if there was bleeding. She moaned but didn't cry out. The pain she would describe as rosy.

Afterwards, he took her down and lay her across the bed. He untied the ropes and removed the mask and rubbed her aching joints and limbs with ointment to bring back the circulation. Sometimes she thought Tom needed to punish her so that he could comfortably express his undoubted love for her. He asked her, almost tenderly, if she were ready now to do anything that he required of her.

When she didn't answer, he caught her by the wrists with one hand and drew back the other and slapped her across the face. She fell sideways and rolled from the bed on to the floor. He stood over her, his arm raised to strike her again and she cowered away from him, pulling her knees up to her chin. "You know I am," she sobbed.

He helped her to her feet, but only so that he could hit her again, harder than before, his hand glancing off the back of her head where the bruise wouldn't show. She swayed but didn't fall.

This wasn't a game, was it?

She had a sweet taste in her mouth. She thought about using the safe word, but was frightened to squander it; or worse, discover that in these circumstances it would have lost its power to prevent savagery.

It would be no less than she deserved.

He told her to get down on her knees. Obeisant, abject in her desire to be humiliated by him, she kneeled before Tom and with sweaty trembling fingers undid the sash of his robe.

At last he pushed her away, and from the look he gave her she understood that this was his revenge, he knew everything and now he was going to kill her.

He suddenly reached down behind her back and she felt his hands close around her ankles, on which her haunches rested, and then he stood up, lifting her whole body into the air with him. Her head fell back, her exposed throat gashed

by the ruby choker rested for an instant on the edge of the
mattress, before he threw her down on the bed. Keeping hold
of her ankles, he twisted her over on to her belly, slowly drew
her toward him, and kissed up the backs of her legs to the
fiery welts at the top of her thighs.

"I want you to be happy, that's all," Tom said, leaving off
what he was doing to speak; she felt like begging him not to
stop. "I want you to promise me you won't do these dreadful
things to yourself any more."

"Please, Tom . . ."

He walked away, ignoring her.

He turned up the stereo and she recognized the heavy
swell of Verdi's *Nabucco* chorale, which she remembered
him once saying was a piece of music that never failed to lift
his spirits when he felt low.

Watching his shadow while he put on a blindfold.

"Oh, God, no, please." But she didn't try to move.

Her face buried in a pillow, she held her arms crossed over
the small of her neck in an irresistibly submissive gesture of
warding off and at the same time inviting the final, inevitable
blow. She felt the diamond clasp of the choker hard under
her fingers. Her whole body stiffened as he turned her over
and opened her thighs. Then something gave, the tightness
around her throat suddenly eased and the rubies spilled on
to the sheet in a dark glistening pool.

She gave a little cry and, in the next moment, he entered
her. Karen closed her eyes the pain was such sweet agony,
realizing even before he began to thrust that she was going
to come and that there was nothing she could do to stop
herself.

By the time she came back from the bathroom, the sky in the
east had started to pale. Tom was already asleep. She stood
a moment gazing down at him as he lay on his side, his gray
head resting on the crook of an arm. The boyish things in his
thick spoiled face had risen to the surface. He looked a child
again, untroubled, trusting. She turned away, wondering at

the power she had to settle his restive demons . . . and he hers. She thought of waking him, and telling him everything, laying bare her soul. She got as far as putting a hand on his shoulder, but when he didn't stir she took it as another sign.

Tom had already made the decision for her. He'd helped pick up the strands of the ruby choker and its broken clasp from the bed, then taken the gift back into his safe-keeping. Told her he knew a place on 47th where they'd have no trouble fixing it in time for her to wear to the party tomorrow night. It had been her last chance.

She got into bed and sat propped against the pillows, waiting for the Seconal to work. She felt the accusing warmth of Tom's body next to hers and closed her eyes. The old footage of Ned falling from his crib when she was too damned drunk to lift a finger came back to haunt her. Then the image of Victor Serafim's thugs bending back Mr. Unthank's arms . . . the smell in the trunk of the Lincoln.

She couldn't find any way out.

III
DEADLIGHT

SATURDAY

1

A warm gust off the bay stirred the shade of the locust tree, tugging at a corner of the newspaper Tom held in his lap. He sat in an old Adirondack chair, one foot braced against the stone parapet that edged the cliff, looking out at the golden expanse of the Sound. He felt the sun for a moment full on his face as he leaned forward and drank the last of his coffee, then glanced back at the house. The shades of the bedroom windows were still drawn.

Tom got up and walked over to the corner of the terrace where he could see enough of the beach to tell that the fish were back. He'd had a talk earlier with the groundsman about how they could limit the damage of the "brown tide." Along the slack, ailing tideway of the Sound, starved of oxygen, choked with reddish blooms of algae, the news all summer had been of polluted clam-beds, of dolphins being washed up on town beaches, of swimmers getting sick from water-borne viruses. Just below the house, Tom had seen lost armadas of horseshoe crabs, those shy primeval throwbacks whose blood runs the color of blue sky, sluggishly patroling the tepid shallows. By night, you could sometimes hear a soft susurration as the algal blooms breathed and multiplied.

He'd tried to explain these things to old Dominic, who came from generations of Baymen, in simple scientific terms: how the Sound wasn't holding enough oxygen to sustain life; how the algal blooms, which created oxygen like any other plant during the day, consumed it all and more at night because they needed to breed—which led him on to his favorite theme, that the pressure of population on resources would soon destroy Long Island's capacity to support any life except that of the urban commuter, which was no life at all.

He looked at his watch. If Karen wasn't down before he left for New York, he'd have to call her from the car or his office. It wouldn't be the kindest way to break their date, but then nor would waking her after the skinful she'd had last night. Lately, he'd been careless about keeping the booze under lock and key.

Even if he were partly to blame for her lapse, when all this was over she was still going to need professional help. She would deny it, of course, just the way she always denied everything. He'd made her take a look this time at what she'd done to herself, forced her to feel the cuts with her own hands, even as she stood there in the mirror, saying what cuts, what are you talking about, I don't see anything . . .

Absolutely convinced. Which was why she was so good at keeping things to herself—Karen had no curiosity, none: it was how she preserved her mystery—all that time she was cheating on him. And screwing her Mister Man.

The wash of a boat he hadn't noticed go by slapped against the rocks below; the throb of its engines, the departing sounds of music and laughter, drifting back across the water. Whether he should get in touch with her doctors at Silverlake now—just to be on the safe side—was something he would have to consider carefully.

What had happened between them last night didn't change anything. He understood now that her need to punish herself had been more than a maladjusted fantasy. It was justified. But in time the wounds, all wounds, he liked to think, would heal. If you loved someone, then you could forgive them anything.

Wasn't that how it worked?

He watched a long seine of weed heavy with debris ride

the oily swell and move a little closer to the beach. One thing about Karen, she healed well.

Dominic had shrugged off his disaster scenario, making it clear that he regarded his employer's concern for the natural world as a rich man's indulgence—he blamed everything on the weather. He'd cleared the beach three times already that week, he grumbled, but however many loads of fish he took away, more seemed to come. "It's kinda like your parable of the Sermon on the Mount, Mr. Welford," he'd added slyly.

Tom had felt like putting it to him that if it had been his beach, he wouldn't think it so goddamned funny that it was permanently decorated with a silver trim of stinking belly-up fish. But then Dominic had said first that what he smelled was rain, rain before the weekend.

This was Saturday and there wasn't a cloud in the sky.

The cavalcade came to a halt outside the front door under the natural porch formed by two overgrown wisteria bushes that were as old as the house: Ned clinging on to the gnarled branches; Tom laughing because Ned really didn't want to come down from his shoulders. When the game had to end, Tom seemed almost reluctant to hand the boy over to her. Say goodbye to Daddy, Karen said, we'll see him tonight. He hugged them both in an awkward display of affection; then ran down the steps to where the car was waiting to take him into the city.

The chauffeur—an unfamiliar stand-in from an agency—looking sweaty and sullen in pearl-gray livery and dark glasses, held the door open for him.

Involuntarily, Karen put a hand up to her mouth, then let it fall, as if she'd thought better of what she wanted to say. How could she warn him that it wasn't safe? As long as they were planning to spend the day together, he wouldn't have been at risk. In the city, on his own, he was anyone's target.

On the point of ducking into the back of the limousine, Tom hesitated. He looked up and waved at them, calling out to Ned, as if the idea had just occurred to him: "I owe you one, Doc.'"

The little boy waved back, then turned his head the other way, disconsolate, as the Mercedes drove off.

"Never mind, pumpkin. We'll go to the beach," Karen said with a visible effort, "we'll do something."

After last night, she'd been disappointed but hardly surprised by Tom's decision not to come with them. Watching him earlier from the bedroom window, sitting out on the terrace, briefcase at his feet, the strong neck and back to his head as sleek and vulnerable as a seal's, she'd realized there was no hope. She'd done her best to persuade him not to go. He was letting Ned down, she'd argued, he'd given the boy his word. But Tom wouldn't listen.

It was white flag day for Rolling Thunder. The Atlantans were starting to squeal. He had those Crackers by the balls.

Don't forget to water the horses—his parting shot.

"Oh, Hazel." She turned abruptly to the girl, who was standing behind them in the shade. "Why don't you take the rest of the morning off? My hair appointment isn't until four, so why not . . ." She smiled and threw up her hands. "Why not?"

"Thank you, Mrs. Welford, but if it's all the same to you, I'd just as soon come along. You know how I love the ocean."

"No, I insist. You have a little break. You deserve it."

She crouched down beside Ned, who had already gone back to playing with his video game, his fluent thumbs hammering the controls, as Sonic the Hedgehog chittered out its maddening electronic reprise. The expression of fierce concentration didn't change as she bent over to kiss him.

"We'll be fine, just the two of us. We'll have a great time, won't we, Ned?"

He looked up for a moment and cut his eyes in his nanny's direction. She had on a white cotton shirtwaist, white jeans and white sun-glasses. Ready for the beach.

"I think Ned would feel happier—and Mr. Welford too— if I were there to give him support. In the water, I mean."

Karen stood and looked at the girl, taking in the defiant tilt of her chin, the hard set of her pink glistening mouth.

She suppressed a rush of anger.

"Well, I sure do appreciate your concern. I'll be extra careful. Shall we go get our things, Ned?"

Hazel took a half-step forward. Undecided what to do with her hands, she stuffed them in her pockets and frowned at the ground. Dug at something with the toe of her sneaker.

"You're really, like, er, putting me on the spot, Mrs. Welford." Her voice grated like sandpaper on glass. "I'm sorry to have to tell you this, but your husband said—he gave me strict instructions last night that for the next couple of days I wasn't to let Ned out of my sight."

"Did he now?" Karen smiled, forcing herself to remain calm. "In that case, Hazel, we better call him right up and explain that due to your not feeling well, we both agreed you should take it easy this morning."

"That isn't true," she protested, flipping back a wing of bone-white hair. "I feel great, tip-top."

"But you do have your period," Karen said, not unkindly, as she went into the house with Ned, leaving the blonde to follow. "I'm sure my husband will understand," she called over her shoulder. "He feels bad enough about this, I doubt if he'd want to deprive Ned of his day at the beach altogether. Any more than you or I would."

A thin bald man wearing a Hawaiian shirt left the altar rail and with the help of two sticks came shuffling down the aisle toward them. It wasn't until he drew level with their pew that Karen realized that he wasn't much older than she was and that he smelled like a hospital. By which time she'd already put out a hand to stop him and ask if the priest was still hearing confessions. He nodded but didn't speak and with a smile for Ned, who sat beside her playing his video game with the sound turned off, continued on his painfully slow way.

She heard change fall into an alms box, the scrape of the man's departing sticks, then the doors swing back on their hinges, leaving the church silent and empty, its cool dark interior reeking of candle grease and ether.

Sanctuary.

She made a sign of the cross and, leaning over to whisper to Ned that she wouldn't be long, started down the aisle. At the foot of the altar she genuflected, crossing herself again, then walked to the far end of the transept, where the confessional stall stood like a sentry box at the entrance to a side chapel. She looked back to see that Ned was all right before turning on the little signal light and parting the velvet curtains.

She sat on the edge of the hard wooden seat waiting for the priest, not sure whether she wanted it to be someone she didn't know, or Father Michael. The last time she'd gone to him and poured out her troubles—seeking guidance as much as forgiveness—she suspected that the old parish priest had simply been overwhelmed by her story. But at least Father Michael wouldn't need to be put in the picture.

It was two years now since she'd disclosed to him that her husband—she remembered lowering her voice out of an irrational fear that somehow Tom would hear—hadn't even told her until after they were married. "Told you what, my child?" She'd leaned closer to the grille. The reason, she'd murmured in her confessor's ear, she went along with Tom's wishes was because he seemed to want a family so badly. She'd thought she could handle it. But then, God must have taken pity on her, something inside her had rebelled. He'd sent her off to a clinic, she was just lying there—Karen mortified to be talking about this kind of stuff to a priest—her feet in these stirrup things, feeling trapped, irrevocably bound, when she first heard the sound of beating wings.

The old man had shifted uncomfortably. She could almost hear him thinking, maybe this person isn't altogether . . . maybe she needs more than spiritual help.

The hardest part had been convincing him that she felt too frightened of her husband to disobey him: "I couldn't tell Tom that I'd quit Repro-Gen, father, I just couldn't. I'm not trying to make excuses, but you have to understand"—looking around her in the dimness of the confessional—"that my husband is a man who's capable of almost anything."

A door closed somewhere, probably the vestry, Karen thought; then, from another part of the church, came the measured sqeaking of rubber soles on stone, heading her way. She joined her hands in an attitude of prayer.

I understand, the priest had said, it must have been very difficult for you. Then, ponderously, he'd reminded her of the church's teaching on artificial fertilization. As if she'd needed to be told at that point that it was wrong. As if she didn't know from gut instinct, as well as her own shaming experience, that a popsicle of frozen sperm tends to deprive "conjugal fruitfulness" of its unity and integrity.

She'd tried to do the right thing, hadn't she?

He couldn't seem to grasp the idea that she'd deliberately set out to commit adultery with an old lover in order to get pregnant. That she'd only done it to fulfill her husband's wish for a child and so to preserve their marriage. That she'd had no intention of telling anyone. Not at first, anyway. It was always meant to be her secret, and only hers.

She'd thought she could handle it.

Her heart fluttered as she reached up to draw the velvet curtain, craning her neck first to check on Ned. He looked like a little angel, she thought, hunched over in his seat, as good as gold, not moving.

The footsteps stopped and retreated. Came on again.

She kneeled forward and bowed her head to make an act of contrition. It had been how long since her last confession? How long to get from there to here? From what had once seemed a harmless deception, a desolate sacrifice for the husband she had never loved but owed a debt of gratitude . . . to complicity in his murder? She closed her eyes, squeezing her thighs together until the pain brought tears of equivalence.

Her hand shook as she opened the small missal that had been a gift from her mother. Its diaphanous pages speckled with mildew stains had an unwelcome power to evoke the past: the dank, hard-scrabble years, after her father left them, when they'd lived in trailer parks at the edges of cypress swamps and the eerie little Florida towns whose names she was still trying to forget. Her mother, who'd gone off her twist in the last of them, had raised her a Catholic; taught her that the only way to really meet God was through suffering and sacrifice; taught her to live by a code that along the way might have gotten a little blurred at the margins, but still allowed Karen to think of herself as basically a good person.

Even now, more than ready to acknowledge her guilt, she couldn't help wondering what it was she'd actually done wrong. Borrowing money, after all, wasn't a crime. Nor was loving someone.

It was out of weakness, Karen had confessed, that she went on seeing Joe. One time, soon after Ned was born, she gave into not curiosity but an irresistible urge to visit him with the baby; then, as their son grew, found herself arranging things so that whenever possible the three of them would be together. Although she'd resolutely kept Joe in the dark, it gave her a sense of completeness she'd never known before. What they had going, she'd appealed to Father Michael, felt natural and right and surely had to be more pleasing to Our Lord than a marriage based on fear, on cruelty and on lies . . . *they* were the real family, in the eyes of God, surely?

But the verdict had been uncompromising. Father Michael told her that she must give up her adulterous liaison, and warned her that it would do more harm than good to let this other man know that he was the boy's father. At the time, convinced that the old priest's views were out of the ark, muddled, simply wrong, she had defied him. Now, she wondered if she shouldn't after all have heeded his advice.

Karen was startled by a discreet cough from the other side of the stall. She saw the silhouette of a small, sharp-faced man behind the cloth-covered grille, then heard an unexpectedly deep voice intone, "Lord Jesus Christ, lover of our souls . . ."

It wasn't Father Michael. She should have felt relieved. At least she would keep the comfort of anonymity. Instead she was stricken by panic; a shapeless uprising of fear and remorse that suddenly turned so acute it felt like a ravenous ferret gnawing at her insides.

"I grieve from the bottom of my heart that I have offended thee, my most loving Master and Redeemer, to whom all sin is infinitely displeasing; who hast so loved me that thou didst shed thy blood for me, enduring the torments of a cruel death. In nomine Patris . . ."

His narrow hand floated up to deliver the blessing and she saw the glint of a watch at the priest's wrist and in that same instant Karen realized there was something wrong. She opened her mouth to begin the response but suddenly couldn't remember the words: even the prayer of contrition she'd prepared refused to come. Confess. It was as if the ferret had forced its downy head up into the back of her throat and, red little eyes gleaming, had guzzled her tongue.

She was suffocating, she had to get clear of the box, she needed air. She drew back the stall curtains and stumbled into the aisle before she took in with a chilling lurch of awareness that Ned was no longer sitting where she had left him.

She ran out into the middle of the church. The empty rows of pews scanned instantly. He wasn't among them. Forcing herself to slow down and search more carefully, she called his name—finding her voice now. Frantic, saying to herself over and over, please God, don't let this happen, she ran on again; calling Ned, louder, turning around as she went, knocking into things, getting back only the echo.

The birdlike priest looked out cautiously from his side of the confessional; he had on a black T-shirt and a leather lace around his neck that dangled a wooden cross and yellow smile button. "Be of any help here?" he boomed.

There were plenty of dark corners, a hundred places to hide, but ignoring him she pushed open the swing doors and ran out through the lobby into sunlight, where the danger was more immediate. Making a visor with both hands, she blinked at the peaceful suburban street that fell steeply toward the harbor of Glen Cove. There were cars parked under trees. A young couple on bicycles pedaled by with a dog. Everything looked normal. Then she saw the battered Dodge Tradesman, a picture on its mirrored rear window, slowly pull away from the curb. Desert scene, cactus with arms up like traffic cops, the skull of a longhorn whitening in the sun.

The faint stirring of recognition was lost in the split second she realized that Ned couldn't be inside the van. She'd felt something soft underfoot. The boy's green security blanket was spread like a tattered flag on the church steps. She swung around and saw him sitting across the yard, hugging his knees in the shade of a fieldstone buttress, calmly watching her. When he waved, she couldn't be so sure.

But she'd heard him say *something* . . .

Karen let out a little cry as she went over and squatted down beside him, laughing through the tears she couldn't hold back, letting the relief flood over her.

"Thank God." She closed her eyes, saying nothing more, so grateful to be back on firm ground. There could be no clearer sign, no other course for her now.

"Hey," drawing him close, "I got an idea. Why don't we stop by Mister Man's place before we hit the beach?"

Ned didn't answer.

"Bitch."

The answering service had put her on hold again. Karen slammed the phone down. Not that it mattered, she had the information she needed: Miss Morrow was out of town for the weekend . . . no, she hadn't left a number where she could be reached. As a rule she called in for her messages Sunday afternoon.

This is an emergency, Karen had pleaded.

That's what they all say, honey.

"It won't work, Joe." She started pacing the floor of the bare living room. "It won't work. We're too late."

She'd tried earlier to reach Victor Serafim on the phone,

but the listing was either under another name, or he'd been lying about having a place on the Island. She remembered him saying he'd be in touch. Almost certainly that meant *after* the job was done. There was nothing more she could do now to stop him: getting word to Victor through her friend Starlite had been their last hope.

"Aren't you forgetting something?"

She looked at Joe lying on the couch, bleary and unshaven, smoking a cigarette over a glass ashtray balanced on his stomach. It was barely a month since he'd told her he quit, for the boy's sake.

She wiped her forehead with the back of her wrist.

"Forgetting what?"

"The threat he made to hurt Ned if we pull out."

"It's only good as long as Serafim's got something over us."

"You owe the guy half a million dollars."

"We can't go through with this, Joe. I know it, you know it. We don't have a choice here. I'm calling the cops."

"The cops?" Joe snickered. "You're crazy. What you gonna tell them? Some story about borrowing money from a Brooklyn loan shark? Mrs. Tom Welford, married to one of the richest men in Nassau County . . . Forget it, they'll probably refer you to the nut farm at Stillwell Woods."

"I know how to make them listen."

"Yeah?" He took a deep drag of the cigarette and blew smoke at the ceiling. "Okay, let's just say you tell them you're afraid someone's going to kill your husband, and then the 'accident' does take place. How do you think that's gonna look? Hell, we don't even know it hasn't happened already."

"I never wanted you involved. It was all my idea. I'll tell anyone that."

"We're in this together, remember?" Joe stubbed out his cigarette and sat up. "Did it ever occur to you that Serafim could be bluffing? The guy's just a small-time crook. He knows about scaring the shit out of little people who don't pay their debts on time, but he's not a hitter. Why would he complicate his life with this?"

"He said other people were involved."

"They already got their money out. No, no, something's not right here, I can feel it. I think we should forget the whole deal and leave as planned."

She shook her head. "It's too late for that."

"We take off now, *right* now, what can he do? Listen, when I saw that you'd brought Ned, I thought, man, this is it. We just get in the car and drive. Karen, look at me. No one's going to find us. Remember New Mexico, that little place near the border, way down in Apache horse country?"

"I don't think so . . . vaguely. It was a long time ago."

Wrenching herself away, she walked over to the screen-door and looked out at Ned playing in the yard. The sky over the wood was hazy white and she wondered if there'd still be sun at the beach. They'd have to be back by two if she wanted to get into the city in time to get her hair done. She felt like a stranger in the room, surrounded by boxes and suitcases, Joe's forlorn belongings piled where he'd left them after their aborted getaway.

"You know I love you," she began, and had to moisten her lips. She'd made her decision, now she wanted to get it over with. "All I ever dreamed was for us to be together. Just the three of us. Be a family. But things don't always work out."

"What is this?" Joe jumped up and came over to where she was standing. "What are you talking about?"

"You only get one chance in life," Karen went on, avoiding his eyes. "You only make one decision. This is mine. And, it's already been made for me, wouldn't you know." She smiled slightly. "The right thing, the only thing for me to do now is go back to Tom, and . . . I can't just warn him, Joe, I'll have to tell him everything."

"Do you know what you're saying?"

She took a deep breath. "About you, and Ned."

"It comes down to choosing between us," Joe said bitterly, "and you don't even hesitate. It comes right down to it."

"We don't have any *choice.*"

"Jesus!" Joe hung his head and ran a hand through his hair. He walked away from her and came back.

"Money, right? That's what this is about. Money. You don't give a damn about anything else, about me or the boy, your 'real' family . . . shit, he's even got you thinking like he does. All you care about is living in that big house with the lawns and horses and tennis at the club and dinner-parties and an army of people waiting on you hand and foot, making you feel safe. Money."

"You know that isn't true."

"I don't blame you. No one would. So why not admit it?"

"You are my family, Joe, always were, always will be. It breaks my heart to think . . . Joe, I was ready to go with you anywhere in this entire fucking world. All I ever wanted was you, and Ned. You wanted it too, Joe, we shared the same dream, a house full of children and laughter . . . not money. Not money."

"He's got you, kiddo. You'll never get away from him now. Never break the habit."

Karen tucked her hair behind her ears, thinking of last night. She hadn't meant to let it happen, she'd been betrayed by her own conscience. She started to shake. "We have to do what's right," she said. "Do what's best for Ned. We're talking about having the man he thinks of as his father *murdered*. How could we live together as a family after that?"

"He isn't his father. And if he was here right now, I'd gladly waste the bastard myself."

"Don't talk like that. You didn't screw up, Joe, I did."

"No, it's my fault for listening to you, for going along with what I always knew was a mistake. I should have insisted that you take him to court. He may have a right to Ned in the eyes of the law—and, sure, because he's loaded, chances are he would win a custody fight—but I have the right to him by blood, and because I love him. Ned is my son."

"I know you do. I know he is." She looked up into his eyes

and started to cry. "But you *didn't* insist. You'd have been perfectly happy to let things drift on as they were for ever."

"I was just trying to straighten out my life. Put a little cash by so we could get off to a fair start. But that wasn't good enough for you." He paused, shaking his head. "You go right ahead, tell Tom the truth, I'll be interested to know how he takes it. I only hope for your sake that he can."

"What's the alternative?" she asked. "If we went to the other end of the world, sooner or later he'd find us."

"I'm going to keep trying, Karen. I'll take it the distance, all the way to the Supreme Court, if I have to."

"It's over, Joe." She turned away, hardly able to get the words out, tears running into her open mouth. "I'm sorry, but I've got to go now, I promised I'd take Ned to the beach."

He gave a short laugh. "The beach. The beach. Perfect day for it. Hey, I'll come with you."

"No, don't." She felt his hand on her arm, the bond of first love between them still uncut. "Don't touch me . . . please, Joe. It'll be easier for everybody if we make this a clean break. Remember last time?" She managed a bleak smile. "We can't go through all that again."

The hand fell away. "Then let me say goodbye to Ned."

She hesitated. "All right, I mean, of course, you must. It's just . . . I don't know how to say this, my poor Joe, but you won't do anything to upset him, will you?"

"Like tell him who I really am and ruin his life?"

Standing by the white picket fence, the boy playing in the grass at their feet, they appear a handsome couple, young, healthy, optimistic . . . a little wistful perhaps, but then Hendricks knew their history.

The photographs were taken from the usual place at around ten that morning. In one of them, the most telling, Ned is busy retrieving what looks like a small stuffed animal from the back of the Suburban. Another shows "the family" saying goodbye; the camera catches Karen's forced gaiety (making an effort for the kid's sake) while Haynes looks past her, his empty gaze fixed on the horizon. The last frame, they are in each other's arms, Joe and Karen, leaning against the tailgate in the middle of the driveway.

The I BRAKE FOR WILD HORSES bumper sticker was partly obscured by their long entwined legs. They were vain together, Hendricks decided, looked like they were posing for a fucking Ralph Lauren ad, nostalgic for a cloudless American future. He could see why the gods might want to have their revenge.

And something else.

What was troubling him most about the pictures. The three lives packed in the back of the wagon. They showed how near they'd come to getting away.

Hendricks knew that he was responsible for stopping them, for spoiling their chances—he wasn't proud of it, but he had a job to do, his own life to think about. *His* escape. Look at this one . . . Behind their heads, the pale sky and a clump of skeletal shade trees, leaves ravaged by June's plague of gypsy moths, give an untimely impression of winter.

But it captured the moment.

The boy and Haynes solemnly shaking hands . . .

It was Marion who'd first put the idea in his head. She'd picked up an earlier photograph of them and without knowing who they were remarked on a family likeness. Unable to see it himself—probably it was one of those female intuition things—he'd always recognized the possibility that Haynes was Ned Welford's natural father. There was nothing on the tapes. No compelling reason, therefore, to share his suspicions with anyone. But why else would a woman trail her four-year-old kid along when she went to visit her lover?

A half hour after she drove away, Haynes was seen by Hendricks's operative setting off alone on a walk through the woods behind Overbeck. At ten thirty-five the phone rang. The caller left a message on the answering machine, which

Hendricks's recording equipment also picked up, though the tape was no longer being monitored.

"I hear you were looking for me."

Victor Serafim's voice.

2

She was like a tigress on heat, Eddie Hendricks said, as the gray Lincoln Towncar turned off Piping Rock Road and nosed its way down the oak-lined avenue that would bring them into Locust Valley. The detective was telling the others about the night he got lucky sitting up with an angry wife outside a house in Queens watching her husband cheat from the back of the family car. I'm not kidding, he gave them a knowing look, I didn't think I'd see daylight again.

Live to tell the tale, he'd meant to say.

Nobody even cracked a smile, the mutes up front taking their cue from Victor's habitual deadpan, or maybe it was because they really couldn't follow him, the way he kept running on at the mouth. One of the advantages of using hearing impaired muscle, Victor had explained to him, was being able to talk freely in its presence. But only if they weren't watching. A white Prelude . . . I'll never forget it, Hendricks said, wiping the sweat from his face.

Settled deep into the upholstery, Victor was watching a Knicks game on TV with the sound turned low. He wore a white cashmere sweater over an open blue shirt, dark blue pants and white patent leather loafers. Donut was staring out the window, chewing on a toothpick, checking on them from time to time in the extra-wide rearview mirror. Roy Roy drove.

"Eddie, you worry too much," Victor said without taking his eyes off the little screen.

"Why do you say that?" Hendricks laughed uneasily.

"We're on a sightseeing tour."

Leaving the Tudor Village shopping center on their left, they drove on at a crawl up the hill into Locust Valley. The past two weeks, the detective had gotten to know this affluent little burg with its packaged country charm and magicwand boutiques—convenience stores for the rich that could make the shiniest wish come true, long as you had the cash or plastic to wave back at them. He hadn't found it the easiest place to work a surveillance from; no question here of trying to blend in or get chummy with the locals, he'd've stuck out like the balls on a tomcat. It being a Saturday afternoon, the main street was jammed with tourists and summer people. The crowds would help, but whatever kind of "sightseeing" Victor had in mind Hendricks's concern was that someone would recognize him, if anything went down.

He was getting a bad feeling about this already.

They turned on Oyster Bay Road, turned again off the continuation of Route 107 on to Feeks Road, then down a side street bordered by a privet hedge that cast strong geometric shadows across the roadway. They carried on thirty yards or so before slowing to a halt opposite the Holy Child kindergarten.

"Why we stopping?" Hendricks asked, trying to sound casual, his voice coming out treacherously hoarse. He cleared his throat. "There's nothing here worth seeing."

The school was closed, the short street deserted, still as a canal in the blue early dusk.

"You ever been inside one of these places? I used to have to take our two boys," Victor said evenly, hitching a leg over his knee to reveal a yellow sock patterned with crossed golf clubs. "Fucking bedlam. My wife never stopped breaking my balls about how she needed some time to herself. I think children ought to be home at that age, out . . . out of harm's way." Victor put back his head and laughed. "Isn't this where the Welford kid goes to school?"

Hendricks nodded.

"What's the routine?"

"It's in my report."

"Refresh my memory, Eddie."

"The chauffeur drops him off, right there, in front of that little gate. Weekdays, around nine thirty. Then picks him up again back of noon."

"Does what's-his-face, Thurston, get outa the car?"

"Doesn't have to," Hendricks said.

"How's that?"

With obvious reluctance, Hendricks went on. "Hazel, the nanny, goes with them. She always takes the boy inside the building and brings him back out to the limousine—'cept on her day off when Karen Welford usually does both runs herself in the Volvo. They're very careful."

He laughed. "They should be careful."

"Look, if this is what I think it's about, I don't want any part of it. Okay?"

"Eddie, Eddie," Victor said softly. "The facts is all I'm asking. Isn't that what I pay you for?"

"I know my limits."

"We're talking about a seam job, a simple snatch. And don't fucking give me you never done this kind of thing before."

"Only one time and it was a custody case, above table, perfectly legal. We even had law enforcement on our side."

"Yeah? Well, this is a custody case too."

"I dunno." Hendricks shook his head. He didn't *want* to know. He felt like blocking his ears. "I mean, snatch the Welford kid, I don't get it, Vic. What's the angle? Suicide?"

"Let me worry about angles. What I need from you, Ed, is where's the seam? Any point where Ned Welford is left unattended, where he goes from one minder to another that isn't air-tight."

"I told you, they don't take chances. A neighborhood like this, people with money that have kids learn to be security conscious the moment they toddle out into the real world. They still talk about Lindbergh, for Christ's sake, like it happened yesterday. The girl sticks to Ned like white on rice."

"There's always a seam."

The detective glanced up and saw that Donut and Roy Roy, identically dressed in white button-down shirts and narrow club ties, were tightening the harnesses of their seatbelts. Staring back at him in the mirror. He felt like saying it's been nice knowing you, gentlemen, getting out of the car and walking away. While there was still time.

Instead of which, he said, "Your only hope is a Monday."

He wouldn't have made it to the end of the street.

Victor smiled. "Now you're talking."

"Mondays," Hendricks continued, "the nanny stays at the kindergarten all morning. When they come out, she and the kid wait by the side of the road here for the limo, which is usually late 'cause Thurston likes to stop off in the village for a cappuccino. There's this joint he frequents, the Stables Café. He's got something going on the side with one of the waitresses."

"How late?"

"Last week, they had to wait five minutes."

"Here's the thing, Ed." Victor leaned toward him. "This is what you do and it can't fail. You'll be up front with Roy Roy. It won't be this car, but Roy'll be driving. He pulls up alongside them and you start chatting to the girl."

"Now wait, wait just a goddamned minute, no one said anything to me about going in any car . . ."

He swallowed, his mouth dry.

"All you do is engage her in conversation. You know, like ask for directions or something. Donut, who happens to be strolling past, comes up from behind, snatches the kid and bundles him into the car." The palms of Victor's hands opened up like a book. "Simple."

But he should have known. He should have seen it coming, figured that this was what the man had been planning all along. How could he have been so fucking dumb? He'd been set up to play a part in it from the very start.

"No, no, this is crazy. I never agreed to get mixed up in nothing like this. Jesus fucking Christ, Vic, it's a federal rap. You'd be looking at twenty-five to life."

Victor settled back in his seat. "We always knew it was a situation that had potential."

"In front of all those witnesses?" the detective carried on, but less shrilly. "The sidewalks swarming with mothers, kids, teachers . . . it'd stir up a hornet's nest. And why me, for Christ's sake? You don't need me. I'd just be a liability."

"I'm doing you a very big favor, Eddie, I'm offering you a piece, a two-way split. What do you say to we go eighty-twenty? We're talking retirement money here."

"It'll never work." Hendricks loosened his tie. He thought of telling Victor about the possibility that Ned wasn't Tom Welford's son. If he hadn't already figured it out, it would lend a certain weight to his argument. But with Victor you could never be sure, and Hendricks didn't want it to look as if he was backing away from anything.

"It'll work," Victor said patiently. "I had another meeting yesterday with Welford. I got my money out already, or as good as. He agreed to take care of his wife's debts. Plus some extra. A legitimate guy like that gives you his word, Ed, you can depend on it. We have an understanding."

"What does that mean?" Hendricks saw his only chance was to play along, but he wanted it to look as if he was coming around slowly to Victor's offer. "You trust him because he went to Hotchkiss and Yale, because he's a big swinging dick in the finance markets?"

The more convincing he made it, he believed, the better his chances of easing himself out of the situation later on.

"It means Tom Welford won't be in any hurry to call the cops when he gets the ransom note Monday. If it came out that his wife was all mixed up with the wrong people on this . . . no, it'd finish him, he won't want any fuss."

"Maybe not," Hendricks said thoughtfully, "but these things never run as smooth as they should. There's always a hitch."

"It's the break we've been waiting for, Eddie."

"What about the wife? What's to stop her going to the cops?"

Victor took off his glasses, breathed on the lenses, rubbed them on a corner of his sweater, then held them up to the light. "You know, Eddie, she and Haynes were real upset about the money being gone from the locker. They couldn't pay the vig. They were shitting themselves." He looked at Hendricks and smiled before slipping the glasses back on. "I offered to help them find a way out, I offered Karen—it's not as if this was something she hadn't already considered—a contract taken out on her husband. It's all down on tape. I even got witnesses. Isn't that right, fellas?"

Donut and Roy Roy, attentive in the rearview, nodded.

"You mean they agreed to do him after all?"

"You got it. They needed a little persuading but not that much, Eddie, not that much."

"But you weren't serious."

"It was one way of stopping the lovebirds flying the coop. They were all set on taking the boy with them, which would have interfered with our plans. But, as far as Welford's concerned, what's the difference? If the kid's mother is involved, okay, you get bleeding hearts in the picture, but it's still abducting a minor, it's a kidnapping, soon as they cross that state line. We take him, at least Welford knows, if he pays, he'll get to see his son again."

"I guess so. I guess, I never looked at it that way."

"What you reckon we should ask? Ten, twenty?"

"What makes you think he'll pay?"

"Oh, he'll pay. She'll see to it that he does. You know what this guy's worth; you did the income evaluation, you ran the checks on his credit . . . Eddie, twenty million's a drop in the ocean to him. A couple of phone calls, it's done."

"Twenty million dollars," Hendricks said, shaking his head.

"Listen, when they get the kid back, they won't care what it cost, it'll be like Christmas in August—everyone's happy. You know, I think it might even help their marriage. Bring the family closer together. I'd kinda like that."

"You really are some piece of work."

Victor grinned. "You gotta play all the angles, Ed. You

have to learn to be flexible, to adapt, if you wanna stay ahead of the game."

He made a sign in the mirror to Roy Roy, two fingers performing the easy pantomime of departure, and the Lincoln pulled away from the curb.

"You make it sound like you'll be doing them a favor."

"I always try to think positive. Do you know how rich we're gonna be? Do you have any idea?" He hesitated. "Eddie?"

"Yeah." Hendricks had already calculated his share, which had delayed his getting around to wondering why Victor was being so nice to him.

"I got one more thing I want you to do."

They kept the stereo on full volume—Hot 97 FM playing a safe mix of latest hits and oldies—as they drove back to the train station at Mineola where an hour before Hendricks had left his Caprice in the parking lot.

Slouched in his seat, the detective watched Victor and his crew carry on a desultory conversation in Sign from which he was naturally excluded. For all he knew, they were talking about turning his balls into shish kebab. He looked for give-away gestures and facial expressions among the quick wild flights of hand and finger telling—babble, to his eyes—but found none, which only deepened his suspicion that he was deliberately being kept in the dark about something.

They were gliding up the ramp into the parking fields when he realized that Victor was talking to him now, giving him his instructions. The music was so loud Hendricks could hardly hear himself think. He stared straight ahead, looking at cars, trying to remember where he'd parked.

Victor put his mouth close to his ear. "I said, my people want their money back, Ed."

"What? What money? I don't get it," he shouted back, laughing, not to give out he was rattled. "I thought you said that Welford had agreed to pay his wife's debt."

"Yeah, but she don't know that."

"The fuck she don't."

"I want you to go over to Haynes's place and talk to him."

Hendricks chuckled nervously. "Yeah? What about?"

"You all right, Eddie? You look all squeezed out."

"Never better." Hendricks swallowed. "You want me to swing by the cottage? Okay. What am I supposed to do if Haynes ain't home? Last report I got he went out. We don't have a tail on him any more."

"You wait is what you do."

"What if he comes back and he's with somebody?"

"You tell him you'd like a word in private."

"This isn't my line of work," the detective said. "I don't think I should be the one that has to do this. It's getting late, I told Marion I'd be home in good time . . ." He couldn't come up with any more excuses.

"Aren't you forgetting something?"

"No, this is it for me," he flared suddenly. "I want out."

He felt around for the door-handle, keeping his eyes on Victor. He tugged at the lever, the door was locked. Victor leaned over and put a hand on his shoulder.

"Get a hold of yourself, Eddie, you're in way big. You can't come out. Remember, you still owe me, I can stop the clock for you too, at any time."

He squirmed under the soft heavy grip. "You're getting your money's worth."

"Don't get snotty with me," Victor advised. "Hey, morons, turn that fucking thing down."

Donut, popping his bony fingers to the Eurythmics' "Would I Lie to You," just missing the beat, shrugged and reached forward to snap off the radio.

Hendricks looked down: he had on a pair of Docksiders, badly scuffed, old friends . . . imagined them caught in the coils of a chain chasing an anchor overboard. On the phone, Victor had told him he wanted to show him his boat, a 35-foot half-cabin cruiser he kept at Glenwood Landing. Maybe take it out for a spin, if there was time.

But the offer of a cruise hadn't been repeated.

"We had to teach this guy a lesson once," Victor was saying, "I forget his name. I said, 'You can do yourself a favor, friend, pay what you owe or we'll spread you all over the lot.' He starts whining about this and that, so I said, 'You mother, open your yap again and Donut here'll crash you.' He didn't say another word, only Donut you know doesn't hear too good. Boom, he hit him right in the fucking eye, then he started to kick him, he was ripping."

"All right, all right, you don't have to pull your tough guy act with me, I hear what you're saying."

A minute reduction of light behind Victor's glasses let Hendricks know he'd overstepped the mark.

"He got banged up for nothing, Eddie. You shoulda seen his mouth, like this, all banged up. He thinks he's what was that guy, Rock Hudson. He thinks he's beautiful. You know these guys, knock a few of their fucking teeth out and they can't sleep nights. Ever hit these faggots, the first thing they do is go like this." Victor held his hands up in front of his face to demonstrate. "Protect your stomach, over here's important, your liver, your kidneys, your most important part of your body. In here . . ." He leaned across the arm-rest and gently speared a couple of fingers into the detective's well-covered ribs. "Fuck the face, what's important about your face?"

"Never get into a fight with an ugly person," Hendricks wheezed. "They got nothing to lose. You told me that."

"You little cocksucker," Victor said, and hit him with the back of his hand across the nose, hard enough to open the old wound and make the blood run.

Ah, Christ! Hendricks spluttered. What'd you have to go and do that for?" He fished for his handkerchief.

"Get any on the seats, I'll give it to you again."

"The fuck is the matter with you? Do I look like a Rock Hudson?" His eyes watering.

"Not any more, you don't."

Donut and Roy Roy cracked up at that.

Never guess looking at them, would you? They were related, brothers even, nobody knew for sure. They were certainly close. Shared everything, money, clothes, girls . . . and a talent, Victor was telling him, that was wasted in their present profession. Astronomy, I'm not kidding. A night sky full of stars was music to their eyes. Roy could draw you a current map of the heavens; he could sign the names of distant constellations; he knew more about the mountains and mares of the moon than a fucking astronaut.

There it is, Hendricks interrupted to point out his Caprice, the worst-looking piece of junk on the lot, ha-ha. But still there, right?

As for Donut, Victor went on, he'd made a hobby of memorizing the alignment of the planets on significant dates in American history. What Donut didn't know about the transits of Jupiter or the oppositions of Mars in August . . . wasn't worth knowing.

Yeah? You and Marion should get together, Hendricks thought of saying; he was never gladder to see a Chevrolet.

Their teachers at the deaf orphanage in Brooklyn (where Victor had spent his first years in the States and returned more than once to recruit personnel) had been impressed by their ability and predicted a bright future for these two. That was before Donut learned to whistle (in a manner of speaking) the spacious skies of June 7, 1986, when under the chilly blaze of a meteoroid shower he and his partner had wasted their first earthling. Just some drunk lying in the street . . .

Up until that moment in the story of the universe, Victor laughed, they could really have been somebody.

Hendricks, bleeding into his handkerchief, said no shit, trying to avoid Donut's alien gaze in the rearview.

They were to accompany him to Overbeck.

You might as well drive, Ed, you know the way, the boys'll ride shotgun, Victor said, meaning it as a joke. It was a known fact that neither of them ever carried. Donut and Roy Roy provided a personal service. Guns were impersonal. They specialized in hurting people with whatever came to hand, they were masters of improvisation. Mostly, though, they didn't need to do more than be there, their presence was enough.

They drew into the parking space next to the Chevy. The four men got out of the Lincoln Towncar. Victor climbed back into the driver's seat. Hendricks opened the doors of his car wide and left it for a minute with the engine on and AC running. At six thirty, it was still a miserable ninety degrees out, the air thick enough to bite on.

"I'm trusting you to handle it, Ed," Victor said from behind the wheel of the Lincoln, where he looked oddly out of place.

"Then why do I need them?" He flicked his head.

"You might be grateful for the company."

"That long, huh?" Hendricks wiped his nose, which left a rust-colored smear on the back of his hand. "You mind if I call my wife, tell her I'll be late?"

"Why don't I take care of that for you?"

"Spare me the flak." Hendricks nodded. "Sure. Go ahead. Don't forget to tell her . . . ah, fuck it, she knows the score."

"I'll tell her you love her, Ed."

"Can't hurt." The detective blinked. "And what do I tell Joe Haynes?"

"It never hurts," Victor said.

"Does he expect this . . . visit?" He remembered the message Victor had left on Haynes's answering machine and wondered if he'd ever gotten back to him, and if so what had been said. What he really wanted to ask Victor was, did this have anything to do with Monday's plan to snatch the Welford kid.

He was in over his head.

"Sooner or later, Haynes has to come back to the cottage and, when he does, you say there's been a change of plan and ask him for the money, which he doesn't have."

"Why go after him, then?"

"It's part of the deal."

"Jesus Christ."

Hendricks turned to get into his car. He stood for a moment waiting to let the Babylon local trundle out of the station. East, the sky was overcast, a long high shutter of cloud moving in off the ocean with the night behind it so that you couldn't tell if it was a storm coming or just plain getting dark.

"He starts crying," Victor called across, "you just tell him sorry—the boys'll be there to back you up—but Mr. Serafim is out of patience."

Donut and Roy Roy were already in their seats, belting up.

3

She held her face between thin strong hands. Tears had softened the lines that Karen looked for in the silver-framed mirror, leaving only the gray havoc of her eyes, which Tom always said were her best feature, in need of repair.

She wanted to make herself beautiful for him.

She bathed her eyes in an indigo glass eyecup filled with a herbal solution until the whites came clear. It was like swimming underwater without a mask.

She drank the Absolut from a tooth glass.

An hour earlier somebody she didn't know from Tom's office had called to say that he'd been delayed. She was to go ahead without him; he'd meet her there, at the party.

Undressing in their bathroom, so grateful for the news that she'd had to go around touching anything that belonged to him, robe, toothbrush, cologne, razor, she'd remembered a prayer for the reprieved that began, "O kindest Jesus, hide me within thy wounds." Her heart could have soared.

She'd stood a long time under the shower that was like a birdcage, detained behind its nozzled struts and bars at her conscience's pleasure. She'd let the cold salt-water needles revive last night's angry graffiti, angling the tenderest parts of her body to meet the strongest jets, the sweetest fire, until, burning all over, she'd at last felt clean.

Relief that he was still unharmed had blurred into feelings of gratitude toward her husband.

Who could do this to her.

Whatever happened now, when she told Tom, he would know how to handle the situation. Know what was best for her.

Just to please him, she'd used hardly any make-up, leaving her complexion its natural pallor. But her nails and lips she'd had done in town at the Red Door, where the girl had matched them to her description of the ruby choker. The green silk dress she was wearing, which made her look in a hipshot stance with her dark honey hair, slightly sunken cheeks and long elegant legs like a forties vamp, had also been chosen to set off Tom's absent gift. She didn't even know if the clasp would be fixed in time. There'd been no message, no special delivery. But no word either to counter the instructions he'd given her to dress plain and leave her throat bare.

When she was more or less satisfied with her look, Karen went out on to the balcony to get some air. She drank what was left of the vodka from the bottle. Then, screwing its silver cap back on, she tossed the empty out into the darkness, hearing it thud on the croquet lawn below, where it would certainly be found by Dominic in the morning and produced as evidence of marauding hooligans from next door. Guests had already started to arrive at Nonsuch; she could hear the cars coming up the driveway, tailed back, it sounded like, to Lattingtown Road.

Before going inside, Karen stood for a moment gazing up at the light over the balcony. Its white bowl-shaped shade was darkened on the underside by the summer's harvest of dead insects; it made her think of the moon when it was half in shadow. She stepped through the window and drew the curtains behind her.

It was tonight that Joe was to have come for them.

She cracked the door to the night-nursery.

Ned was sitting in bed propped against the pillows, hair

neatly brushed, clean shining face, eyes a dark scurry like mice running for cover. She thought she'd heard voices.

When she came in, he didn't look up.

She sat on the edge of his narrow bed, feeling like an intruder. Waiting for the room to stop spinning. She took care not to muss her gown of stiff crackling silk.

"Sweetheart?" She reached a hand out to one of his, which lay inert on top of the sheet.

Ned looked at her in all her finery. Unimpressed. He made her think of Joe again.

"We won't be far away, just next door." Her voice, at least, sounded like her own. "Listen, can you hear the band?" The music coming in billows from across the bay.

The boy sucked his thumb.

"It's not that you're going out," she heard Hazel say behind her. She was over standing by the window. No sign of a book in the girl's thick hands: they couldn't have been reading.

Yet she was sure she'd heard something.

"He's upset because we can't find his security blanket. He won't go to sleep without it. We thought maybe somewhere on your wanderings . . ."

"It wouldn't be the first time," Karen said, "I'm pretty sure . . . Honey, didn't blanky stay in the car when we went down to the beach?"

She turned her head. "Did you check the Volvo?"

"We searched everywhere," Hazel said. "Ned thinks he may've left it at his friend's place."

"His friend's place?" She laughed, staring at a Babar poster on the wall. "What friend's place?"

" 'They' were talking earlier," Hazel said archly, "Ned and his imaginary friend. Just before you came in, Mrs. Welford."

The whisper of voices, the boy's troubled look . . . he'd had to hide him from her, vanish Mister Man in a hurry. She wondered if Hazel hadn't secretly broken through into "their" private world. Now privileged not just to listen in on their conversations but to ask questions, and get answers.

The girl knew. She was building a case against her.

"Imaginary friends don't have 'places,' " she said coldly. "He must mean the church. We stopped by St Mary's on our way and he . . ." She saw herself gathering up the tattered green blanket spread on the church steps. "Ned, honey, in the morning we'll go back and take a look. If somebody handed blanky in, you can bet your bottom dollar Father Michael will have kept him safe."

She squeezed his hand. The look he gave her was full of reproach. She would forgive Ned anything.

"I'll read to you, sweetheart. Mommy'll stay with you until you fall asleep. It's all right, Hazel, you can go now."

The nanny shrugged, turned her back to straighten the curtains, then came around the other side of the bed and squatted down to kiss Ned goodnight. He clung to her. "I'm not going anywhere," she whispered.

"If it's any help," Hazel offered, innocently, as if on the boy's behalf, "Mister Man told him that he left it under the tree in the yard where he usually plays."

"Really?" Karen forced a smile. How long has she known, she thought, who else has she told?

"It's a real place. He didn't just dream it."

Not that it would matter soon.

"I'd like a word," Karen said, you bitch, still smiling.

When the girl got up to leave, gently disengaging Ned, who was still holding on to her T-shirt, Karen followed her out through the door and closed it behind them. She leaned against it and took a deep breath.

"In the morning," she said quietly, "I want you to pack up your things and go. You're fired."

Hazel gazed at her uncomprehendingly. She closed her eyes and opened them again. "Have I done something wrong?"

"I think you know the reason."

"I'm not sure I do, Mrs. Welford." A hand going up from her hip to twist at a lock of pale blonde hair; she raised her eyebrows at the nursery door. "Shouldn't we, em, be discussing this somewhere else? His hearing's sharp."

Karen walked down the hall with her until they were by an open window, out of earshot of Ned's bedroom. She'd already lost the advantage.

"I'll write you a reference," she condescended, turning on Hazel with a rustle of silk. "As long as you're out of this house by tomorrow. I'm not having you here spying on me."

The girl shook her head. "I honestly haven't a clue what you're talking about."

"What is it you *want*? Money?"

"Oh, that's rich," Hazel laughed derisively. In the dim light of the hall her face looked ashen.

There was a silence.

Less sure of her ground, Karen lifted a wrist up to her forehead, her fingers trembling. She couldn't remember if she'd taken the pills Tom had left her, only that she'd found the half of Absolut vodka in her rainy-day stash to wash them down with. She regretted now having said anything at all to the girl. She should've just kissed Ned goodnight and gone straight to the party.

"Your husband did warn me this might happen," Hazel said quietly. "He told me when he engaged me about your off days. He told me how Ned broke his arm when he was a baby. Are you sure you'd be able to manage without me, Mrs. Welford? We'd have to discuss it with him first." Her tongue came out and touched her upper lip. "In the morning, perhaps. You don't seem yourself tonight, if you'll forgive my saying so."

"So he put you up to it. You admit that much."

"Put me up to what?" she frowned. "All it is, all I'm doing is my job. Can you honestly hold it against me, after two years, that I care what happens to Ned?"

Hazel looked up at the ceiling, tears welling behind her white eyelashes. "I may only be his nanny, but that doesn't mean I can't love him too. He's such a special little boy, if you just . . . he's so vulnerable." She hunched her swimmer's shoulders. "I know he's yours. It's just I sometimes wonder if

you quite realize . . . He needs all the support he can get, he
needs friends, he needs protecting."

"Who from?" Karen almost jeered. "Who does he need
protecting from? You can tell me, Hazel, I won't hold it
against you. You're just doing your job." But asking herself
now whether she could possibly have misjudged the girl.

"What I'm trying to say, Mrs. Welford, is that if I were in
your shoes I wouldn't want to make things any harder for Ned
than they already are. He needs me here right now." She
wiped her eyes. "You both do."

It was the hand falling damply on her bare shoulder.

"I'm sorry," Karen murmurs, not sure how to take this, moving past her to the open window.

She could badly use a drink.

Leaning out into the wide starless night.

She focuses through the trees on their neighbor's driveway lined with flickering torches like an airstrip in the jungle. She can hear the surf of animated voices, splashes of
laughter and music carried on the warm air. The party in full
swing. Karen, who has always thrilled to the lighted candle,
feeling impatient suddenly, afraid of missing something.

"Would you mind reading to Ned?" She takes Hazel's arm
for support and steps back. "I'm already late."

At the top of the stairs, Karen stopped to listen, one hand
clutching the swaying banister. The house was silent, the
whispering now all inside her head.

These things took time, she thought, everything would
come right, given time. They were going to Europe in a day
or two. Ned would get over this. Kids have short memories,
she'd read in one of her books on how to be a parent: it was
how they survived their childhood. He'd forget all about his
Mister Man, and when they got back . . . She saw how the
hands stood on the clock in the hall below.

She descended the staircase slowly. She had a vague feeling there was something she'd forgotten, something she was

meant to have done. But it didn't come to her. When she listened again, she heard only the rapid uneven pulse of her heart.

On her way out, she decided the night was too warm for the wrap she'd chosen and left it draped over the hat stand just inside the front door.

4

"Darling!" Tamara Davenport cried as she took both Karen's hands in hers and carefully missed one cheek, then the other. "But how divine you look." Her strong weathered face, when it came back, showing polite dismay. "And how brave of you to come alone. Where's Tom?"

"Isn't he here yet?" Karen said gaily, doing her best to look unconcerned. "You know what he's like. Always the last to arrive. Tom wouldn't miss this for the world."

She was passed quickly on to Tamara's husband, Chip, a wiry bronzed little man in his seventies, whom Karen sometimes met jogging along the beach before breakfast. Gallantly, he escorted his neighbor into the garden and found her a drink. There were only a few faces in the crowd she recognized.

Not the usual bunch, Chip Davenport observed amiably. She couldn't tell whether or not he was enjoying the fact that people from "all walks of life," as he put it, had invaded his burnished lawns in support of a good cause.

Behind them, the white colonnaded façade of Nonsuch—confidently named after Henry VIII's demolished palace in Surrey and one of the few really grand shore places still standing—was ablaze with light.

Karen's host kept her by his side, talking about the splendid coalition his wife had formed to fight the building of an incinerator in Hempstead Harbor. A thirty-story smokestack that would cast a blight from Sands Point to Oyster Bay could only be described as a potential atrocity. Karen agreed. It was something, she said, she knew Tom felt strongly about.

She escaped at last into the marquee, where guests were beginning to discover their dinner tables, admiring the lavish floral arrangements and, amid loud laughter and the popping of champagne corks, writing tax-deductible checks for Tamara's war-chest.

Sitting down to dinner with an unpromising group, Karen turned her chair so that she could keep an eye on the main entrance to the tent.

She felt the reassuring pressure of his palm on the middle of her back as he steered her on to the crowded dance floor, making for an apron of space close to the orchestra.

"Let me get a good look at you," Tom roared against the music and spun her away from him, holding her at arm's length.

"It's the only thing I have that goes," Karen said, meaning her dark almost black green silk dress.

He gazed at her approvingly. "Belle of the ball. Everybody's saying it. A total stranger pointed you out to me as the most glamorous woman here."

"Tom, for God's sake," she shook her head, "he must have meant someone else."

The word stranger.

Tom smiled. "*She* was dead right."

"More likely dead drunk."

She saw him make a face as the front line of saxophones, cadaverous old men in white tuxes, rose solemnly to deliver the grandstand riff from Stevie Wonder's "Master Blaster." The halting sound big enough to raise the hairs along the back of her arms. Tom mouthed something.

"What did you say?" she laughed.

He reeled her in again. "No contest."

"You really mean it?"

"Radiant doesn't even come close."

"Now you're making me embarrassed." She put a hand up and touched at the delicate hollow of her throat. "Is it still there?" Unsure for a moment whether the tightness around her neck was real or imagined.

"Maybe," Tom spoke close to her ear, "you're the one who should go easy on the sauce."

"I'll be all right," she said, gripping his hand, "now that you're here. Oh, Tom, I'm so happy for you."

"It's only money," Tom said distractedly, his eyes skimming the crowd.

Her cheek came back to rest on his broad shoulder. She was still getting up her nerve to tell him.

She'd had to wait until halfway through dinner before she knew that he was safe. Unable to touch her food, drinking steadily, she'd looked up and seen him making his way toward her from the far end of the marquee, stopping to apologize to his hostess, working the tables, lavishing his sincerest attention on people who didn't matter. Tom could be so charming. She'd watched him with the growing certainty that she'd made the right decision.

Stooping behind her chair to kiss her cheek, he'd murmured his good news—Atlanta's all sewn up, babe, you were right to start celebrating—then, without another word, slipped the ruby and diamond choker he'd had fixed by the little man on 47th around her neck. A repetition of last night's ceremony in front of the mirror, only this time the way he did it was like putting a collar on a dog, like saying in public that he owned her.

Once again she'd started at the coldness of it, making her eyes wide, her mouth prettily like an O, getting the stock response of delight and confusion just right, then reached her hands back to help him, still fellating the air—the trophy wife who couldn't be humiliated.

Karen didn't care. It was just another reminder, like the tenderness of her thighs on the gilded cane chair, that she deserved whatever punishment was coming to her.

She'd had to sit through the embarrassed applause of her dinner partners, then lead them in laughter at Tom's little joke (as if she'd never heard it before) about the danger of giving one's wife negotiable assets. An owl-eyed man asked the rubies' provenance, and she'd learned along with everyone else that they came from the Mogok mines, just north of Mandalay in Burma. Never been cooked or heated up to reduce the "silk," the secondary mineral lines that cloud lesser stones. Tom had revealed an assayer's expertise that to the other women around the table—Karen had seen it in their molten eyes—would have sounded romantic, the next best thing to being told how much the rubies had cost.

Was this why he'd bought her the necklace? A mocking allusion to the price of her virtue? Karen couldn't help wondering, when he heard from her own lips what she suspected he already knew, how much her life would be worth?

How much should she tell him?

After dinner he'd smoked a cigar, rocking back in his chair, basking in the ignescent rumor of his success. A man she recognized as something on Wall Street came over to shake his hand; and was joined by a stout, pink-faced lawyer, who'd been to their house for tennis but she knew only as Boz. He paid her an elaborate compliment and laughed at whatever Tom said, his voice unnaturally loud.

Others followed, more casual, slapping his arm or murmuring a grave "Tom" as they passed. Each time it happened he'd shoot her an amused look. Toadeaters, he called them.

There was no way she could tell him about Ned.

Tom had a slight cast in one eye that became pronounced when he was tired. She could see the lash fibrillating. He trapped it with his fingers like an insect.

Karen said across the table she felt like dancing.

She had to drag her husband on to the dance floor, he was enjoying playing down all the attention.

"I have something to tell you."

She closed her eyes as if surrendering to the music.

"Are you all right?"

They were the couple everyone was talking about, among

couples they knew, gliding now to a tune called "Nashville
Nightingales." The orchestra paying homage to Gershwin.

"No, I need to talk. About us."

"Well, gee whiz, honey, can it wait? I mean this isn't exactly . . ." He blustered, doing his Jimmy Stewart thing.

"*Tom.*"

The look of wry bemusement gave way quickly to a concerned frown. "What's wrong? Is it Doc?"

She shook her head. "I've a confession to make."

"In nomine Patris . . ." His solemn face broke back into a
boyish smile. "Go ahead, I'm listening."

"Tom, please."

"What did you do this time?"

"Not here." Letting go his hand.

She gathered up a glass from a floating tray of champagne,
and left him to follow her out through the open side of the
tent on to the floodlit lawn.

A crowd of familiar faces threatened to halt their progress
but melted away at the last moment. Karen moved ahead, descending some stone steps into the garden, where there was
a second bar under a tree hung with Japanese lanterns and
more tables for sitting out. She waited for him to catch up
with her, and then they went on arm in arm, avoiding the
whorls of revelers, taking the path that led down to the beach.

She felt intensely drunk suddenly. "Tom, you won't . . . you
won't be too angry with me, will you?" Hating herself for the
flirtatious way that sounded as she leaned against him and
slipped off her shoes to walk barefoot in the sand.

Tom said nothing.

It was the route they often came with Bracken last thing
at night. The water that glimmered at their feet gave off a
strong marine odor that seemed almost contagiously foul,
but Tom didn't comment. Neither of them spoke again until
they had left the boat dock, which marked the boundary between Edgewater and the Davenport estate, well behind.

On the cusp of their own half-moon bay, on home ground,
she told him. Her face scarcely visible in the darkness.

Tom bent down to pick up a pebble and, turning with an athlete's grace, danced it back across the water. He repeated the action. The third time, his silence began to frighten her.

"I've sometimes wondered," he said at last. "I guess it had to come. How long?"

"A year, not even," she answered, not ashamed to lie if it made this any easier for him. "It's all over, Tom, I swear. It's all been a terrible mistake. Somebody I knew from before I met you. An old friend. He's . . ."

He put a hand on her shoulder.

"If I let you go on, you'll tell me a name. I'd rather not know too many details." He cleared his throat. "Is this the first time it's happened?"

"Yes."

"Why?" he asked gently.

"It wasn't anything . . ." She knew she had to keep it simple. "I was bored, I guess. Mostly just lonely. You were never there. I felt like a prisoner."

She could see the lights of Edgewater, the outline of the house gaunt on the cliff above them.

"Perhaps I expected too much from you."

She began to cry. "You had the right . . . God, to a little loyalty at least. I feel so ashamed."

"No apologies either."

"I'm not asking you to forgive me. It's just . . . it took my doing this to open my eyes, and now that I know what's really important in my life, it's too late."

"You didn't have to tell me."

"There's a reason, Tom."

"You felt guilty," he said. "Isn't that why you go to church, so you can unload on a priest?" Then he added, his voice low and flat, "You're not pregnant, are you?"

She shook her head. "I didn't plan to hurt you, I just can't keep it inside any longer. I tried, God knows."

"I'm glad you told me. Really, I want to help."

She cried quietly. She'd expected him to be angry, even violent with her. She didn't deserve his sympathy.

"Hey, now, take it easy."

He stopped and turned to face her, taking both her hands in his. "Did it ever occur to you that if you couldn't feel guilty, you wouldn't do these things to yourself?"

"This isn't about . . ." Karen hesitated, unwilling to go down that road. "I may have had some problems in the past, but I'm clean now, I'm not crazy. You know I'm not."

He pulled her close, one arm going around her bare back. He slipped a hand under the fat silk bow attached to her waist, eased it down inside her skirt between the silk and her skin.

"What are you doing?"

She made a feeble attempt to push him away.

"Why?" Wrapping her closer. "Don't you like it?"

"Stop, I can't. This isn't right."

"It's not what you think. Let me show you something."

"I've been having an affair, Tom, screwing another man, don't you get it?"

"I can live with that as long as you can."

His other hand on her breast.

"You don't believe me, do you?" She was trembling, suddenly afraid. "My God, you think I made this whole thing up."

"Of course, I believe you," Tom murmured, kissing her shoulder, her neck, her ear. "It's just that I know you, I know how you blame yourself for things you can't really help."

"I let you down."

"You're not the only one. I've a lot to answer for the way I've neglected you and Ned. I won't let it happen again, I promise."

He kissed her mouth.

"Tom, don't," she moaned, confused by her feelings, ashamed of her body's independent response, as a nipple rose under the crudely insistent flicks of his fingernail.

"Somewhere safe. Just until we go to Europe."

"What are you talking about?" She twisted her face away from his.

"I was thinking," Tom went on, "you could maybe run up

to Silverlake, not to stay—well, maybe just for a couple of days, just so you can talk to somebody about all this."

"Please, please don't."

"You know the doctors up there, they know you, there's that one you like, David something. He's okay."

"Don't do this to me," she wailed.

"I'm only thinking of what's best for you," Tom said.

Her legs were like water, she had no defenses against the kindness that gave him authority over her. But wasn't that why she'd come back to him? To lay down her burden. She remembered how restful it had been at Cair, where every hour of every day was like the moment just before sleep. She remembered the way she'd felt soon after she and Tom first met, when he declared that he wanted to look after her always.

A shudder ran through her. The only way she knew how to shed her skin was through blind obedience.

"See how it is?" he said, pulling her closer with the hand that was inside her dress.

"I can't help it," she sobbed. "I love you."

"I spoke with him on the phone today David Beckworth. I told him I've been real worried about you."

She felt him dig deeper. His fingers feeling for the cuts, reading them like Braille. She drew in her breath sharply.

"I'm not hurting you, am I?"

She bit down on the inside of her lip.

"You sure about that, sugar? Quite sure?" He tightened his grip on her harrowed flesh, then swung her around so that the blaze of light from the Davenport house fell on her face.

"If you'd just admit it, Karen"—his mouth was a line— "we'd both find it easier to know when you're telling the truth."

Her eyes fluttered shut. "Home."

But he'd already withdrawn his hand.

Abandoned her, it felt like. When she looked again, he'd moved a short distance away. He was standing down by the water, hands in his pockets, staring out to sea.

"You can say we had this conversation," Tom said over his shoulder. "Tell them you admitted to an indiscretion and I forgave you. But, as far as *I*'m concerned, it never happened. If the subject should ever come up again, I won't know what you're talking about."

She felt something warm and wet splash on her arm. It was the first drop of rain.

"There's another reason," she said faintly, "something else I haven't told you."

The air was absolutely still.

Eddie Hendricks pushed in the little metal stud at the side of his watch. The numerals glowed a tawny red, the color and size of money spiders. He held up his wrist in the dark.

Tapping the glass. "You see what time it is?"

He let a few seconds blink by before he released the button.

"We're coming down to the wire, team," he said, keeping up his habit of talking to the mutes like anybody else. Even under blackout conditions.

The room, empty except for basic furniture and a few packing cases, had a slight echo. Each time after he'd spoken, as if to himself, it seemed to lapse into deeper silence.

Donut and Roy Roy, whose silhouettes he could just make out against the wall opposite, were crouched like stone temple dogs on chairs they'd placed either side of the door. A distance of maybe twelve feet separated them from where Hendricks sat more comfortably in an armchair by the fireplace, listening out for the Suburban turning off Wheatley Road into the driveway of 1154. His own car they'd been smart enough to bring inside the garage below and close the doors behind it so that when Haynes drove up he wouldn't guess he had visitors.

Whether or not they knew it, the detective had a bet on with Victor's crew—ten grand that said Joe Haynes wouldn't be home before midnight.

They'd found the door to the apartment unlocked. Nothing in the refrigerator but some moldy cheese and a six-pack of Coors he'd shared with his partners, which got things off to a flying start, except that when Hendricks had to go to the bathroom, Donut came too, making it clear how far they trusted him. Apart from a suitcase of Haynes's clothes and some personal effects (shaving things, alarm clock, framed family photographs) thrown together on the bed, everything pointed to his having cleared out.

"He walks through that door in the next twenty minutes," the detective said, "you win, you take the ten. If he doesn't, what the fuck, he probably isn't coming back anyway, and we call it a night. We all get to go home. Deal?"

He waited, not for an answer but, peering through the gloom, for some sign that they were at least aware that he'd been talking. He remembered Victor on the subject of how the hearing impaired developed a more acute visual sense, that it was nature's way of compensating . . . What he wanted to know was how well his gonzo astronomers could see in the dark.

"All right," he went on at last, "why don't we up the ante, make that a hundred thousand dollars?"

They didn't stir, not for a hundred thousand; they didn't even look as if they were breathing. He wiped sweat from his face with the back of his hand. They had all the windows open, and the heat inside the living room was stifling.

"Dumb assholes," he said disgustedly, knowing he would never have had the nerve in better light. "You think I'm kidding? You think I'm not good for that kind of money? Well, read my fucking lips."

He heard one of their chairs creak and wondered if he'd found the right frequency.

5

They walked back in silence along the beach.

Karen hitched up her skirts, shaking them now and then

to keep the sandflies off her ankles. With every step she took, her thighs chaffed and burned, but she gave no sign that she was hurt, still waiting for the soothing endorphins that kick in with the release of confession.

Bobby Shafto, everybody, bonny Bobby Shafto . . .

A tidal wave of applause for the cabaret star swept down through the gardens. Tom held up a hand and they stood and listened to the singer's bewitchingly hoarse valediction—I love you all, have a wonderful evening, and God bless . . . God bless America—accompanied by a jubilant sign-off on stride piano that left his audience baying for more.

The guy's a legend, Tom broke out, shaking his head, as if—incredibly, she thought—he resented missing an act he must have heard a thousand times.

Ahead, through dark elms, the glowing marquee seemed to hover above the Davenports' lawn. It reminded Karen of the space station in a drawing Ned had brought back from Holy Child, blades of light radiating from the open sides of the mother ship as antennaed stick people spilled out on to the colorless grass.

I happen to *like* New York, the legend croaked for an encore.

This was the part she dreaded most. The prospect of plunging back into all that fucking hilarity, when all that she wanted now was for her husband to take her home.

"One thing I'm having trouble with," Tom said, rubbing the back of his neck. "Your friend, the golfer in the Lincoln, expects me to hand over the money *after* I've had the accident?"

"I know, I know it sounds crazy." Karen laughed uneasily. "Tom, he's not a friend."

He waited while she put her shoes back on.

"There are people here," Tom resumed, "people I call *my* friends, who'd love to be able to say I told you so if they knew about this. They warned me what to expect when I married you. Sooner or later, they said, she'll show her true colors. Breeding counts, Tom. Well, I didn't buy that crap then and

I don't buy it now. But I'll be damned if I'll give them, or my family, any chance of satisfaction. If you owe this Victor fellow some money, I'll take care of it first thing Monday."

Tom drew a deep breath, looking around importantly as if he felt his speech, however private, merited an audience.

"Thank you," she said quietly. "I don't deserve this. After what I've done to you, I'm not worthy to . . ."

"Hey, lighten up, will you?" He put an arm around her shoulders. "Let's go look for a drink."

They turned up the steps into the garden. Karen, glancing behind her, noticed a couple on the dock leaning over the wooden rail that carried a string of lanterns far out into the Sound. The man's face was turned to the girl, who had on a white low-cut gown and gold sandals, and might have been half his age. Karen heard her give a low throaty laugh at something he'd said. He put a finger in her mouth.

The rain was holding off.

Unable to sleep, she had gone to the window and, looking down, seen him slide like a shadow behind the wheel of his Buick convertible. He'd driven away without lights, taking the less-used track that ran through the citrus groves and along the still dark edge of the lake. She remembered the water, glassy calm, the same starved blue as the sky, reflecting a thin gray line of palm trees at the horizon so flawlessly if you looked long enough it became hard to tell up from down. She had a memory of him waving back at her, but now couldn't really be sure.

It was the last she saw of her father.

"She doesn't have friends, she has place cards," murmured Tamara Davenport, louder perhaps than intended, as she took Karen's arm to negotiate the obstacle course of sprawled couples holding conversations on the stairs.

The party had moved into a new looser phase, a far cry now from those fashionable North Shore affairs that ended the moment they began, once everybody had been seen or not seen.

The woman Tamara had disparaged, a rival queen of the charity circuit, had just passed them on her way down, cutting a determined froufrou in a cloud of Joy-scented rainbow tulle as she returned to the fray.

"I heard that, Tam," she sang without looking around.

Karen could only pretend not to have heard. "Thanks for saving me from Mr. Abogado," she said to her hostess.

"Is that who that was?" She paused to catch her breath as they reached the landing. "My dear, you look a little peaked, are you sure you're feeling all right?" Tamara showed Karen to the door of a guest bathroom, then made her promise to wait for her so that they could go back down together.

"I'll be fine," Karen said almost impatiently. "Really."

Whatever was keeping Tom—it was twenty minutes since he'd wandered off to fill their glasses—she wanted to be there when he got back. He had left her at the mercy of a Brazilian realtor called Abogado, a pony-tailed, open-shirted oilcan, who had tried to interest her in the beach house of her dreams on Shelter Island. Tamara had discovered Karen backed under the sweep of the double staircase, wasting away, as she put it, and immediately whisked her upstairs "to have someone to gossip with in the little girls' room."

The threat of intimate small talk had faded as soon as the two women were alone. "It's too ridiculous our living cheek by jowl and just never seeing each other," Tamara said lightly. "When things quiet down, after Labor Day, let's you and I put our heads together and hatch a plot."

"Let's," Karen said, smiling as she closed the door.

Locking it.

She sat on the floor by the bathtub, her skirts drawn up over her waist, her thighs spread before the full-length mirror attached to the wall. She used cotton dipped in a solution of water and cocaine to bathe the reopened wounds. Grateful for Abogado's generosity with the vial and spoon that he'd unclipped from a gold chain around his neck, she snorted what remained of the precious powder and licked the spoon. Then she swallowed the dregs of the pinkish anodyne she'd mixed in a tooth glass. In the old days she'd have sucked the bloody wipes, not to waste a drop.

After she'd finished, she kneeled before the same mirror and, crossing herself, said a prayer. She'd done what she could to convince Tom that the danger he faced was real, though she doubted that he'd take the threat seriously. It worried her that there had been so few questions: he'd listened to her agitated, not always coherent account of borrowing money from Victor Serafim with hardly an interruption. He hadn't even asked what she needed the half million dollars for. Just told her again, he didn't want to know too many details.

"And you say he took the money *back?*" He'd looked at her with that sincere, slightly mocking air of incredulity.

"I can't prove it."

"Maybe this fellow's not all stupid."

"He's an operator, Tom, don't underestimate him. I walked right into it. A damned fool could have seen the only reason he agreed to the loan was to get at you . . . your fortune."

"That isn't a word I use."

She'd looked away. "I think what he wants now is to deal with you direct."

"How much is involved again?"

"Half a million dollars, I told you."

"So well north of that if you add interest at what four, five hundred per cent?" He shook his head. "You'd come to me for a loan, babe, I'd have offered you better terms." Tom smiled. "We all make mistakes."

She'd wanted to believe he wasn't merely humoring her.

"He said he'd kill you."

"They always threaten. It's the way these guys do business. I'm not too worried about your Mr. Serafimovic."

"He'll do it, Tom, if he doesn't get his money. I've seen what happens. He lets his thugs loose on people, he can't call 'em off. They don't hear, they don't talk, they have that shut-down look in their eyes . . ."

"How do I reach him?"

"He told me he'd be in touch."

"There's no one in the city I can't get to by making a few calls. If we strike out, what the hell, we'll turn it over to the police. They can be discreet."

"I landed us in this mess, Tom. It isn't what you deserve. Maybe your friends were right."

"You've really been through it, haven't you?" Tom said kindly. "Hey, chin up." Arm around her shoulders, he'd given her the silk handkerchief from his breast pocket so that she could dry her tears before they rejoined the party.

"Just don't send me back up to Silverlake," she pleaded, wiping her eyes, "I need to stay here with you. I have to be here to look after Ned."

The scent of his cologne had reminded her how the twisted cloth felt against the back of her tongue, how bitter it tasted. Like the cocaine, only sweeter.

"It'll be okay, you musn't worry," he said, hushing her. "We can put all this behind us. I still love you, Mrs. Welford. Nothing is ever going to change that. We need you too."

"You do believe me, then? Tom, look at me." His eyes, when she briefly held them, were twin black lakes each re-flecting her own supplicant face in miniature. "I haven't made any of this up, I swear to God."

"I know that now," he said calmly.

In the mirror, asking God to make good by his infinite mercy the defects in her confession, Karen begged Him to give her grace to be now and always a true penitent.

The only lies she'd told her husband were lies of omission; she'd done what Father Michael had told her to do.

She came back, her face newly fixed, her spirits revived, the numbness between her thighs feeling like the breath of snow rising from a wintry sidewalk. She stood a little shy of the edge of the balcony. A huge unlit chandelier with reducing tiers like an inverted wedding cake overhung the crowded hallway. She could look down through its dim lusters, shimmering to the thump of the bass drum in the marquee, without being seen.

There was no one she wanted to talk to other than Tom.

The cocaine made her heart race at nothing. She listened to the band, on a predictable trawl through the sixties, play "Me and Bobby McGee," which she remembered Joe saying had been the theme song at his parents' wedding; he was their best man. In the tent, well-oiled, well-heeled fifty-somethings were roaring out the chorus, lamenting missed chances and broken dreams with the raucous authority of Janis herself. Karen didn't know whether to laugh or cry. They knew all the words to "Hang on Snoopy" and "Mustang Sally." She didn't envy them their nostalgia for the youth they'd lost to more innocent times.

She spotted Tom at last in the crush by the front door, holding two glasses of champagne above his head, looking round for her. She waved but he didn't even glance up, and she started dutifully toward the top of the stairs.

"There you are, dear!" Tamara fell in behind her. "Help me with this, will you? I've been galavanting around half naked all evening and no one seems to have noticed."

Karen obliged with a smile, stooping to fix a couple of eyelets that had parted over the older woman's ample back.

"Hey, Tom!" someone hollered below. "Over here!"

She looked down through the chandelier and saw a hand reaching up from the throng: another toadeater trying to get her husband's attention, making a path toward him. She had only a partial view from behind of a heavy-set man with straight collar-length hair—she thought for a moment it was Boz—before the image became fragmented by the web of wire and crystal.

"Over here, Tom!" He'd pushed his way through.

Laughing at something the person next to him had just said, Tom turned the wrong way as the fraternal hand came down on his left shoulder. She almost cried out.

It couldn't be him . . . not *here*.

Her heart hammered in her chest. For a brief moment, indecently exposed against Tom's black velvet smoking jacket, she'd seen the pink stub of a docked middle finger.

Tom swung around, slopping their drinks. His face registered surprise, then a darker flush of what might have been anger or alarm—she couldn't tell which, seeing him caught in the high beam of Victor Serafim's party grin.

"Now where's that divine husband of yours?" Tamara bubbled as she swept past her to the banister. "I haven't been able to get within a mile of him all evening."

He was going to kill him right there.

Karen froze, helpless. "It's too late."

Victor in a tuxedo and white silk polo neck, one hand thrust deep in his jacket pocket.

Tom saying something as he backed away.

"What on earth do you mean? There he is, poor man, stuck over by the door. Oh, my stars . . ."

He had to be holding a gun on him. He had to be crazy, in front of all these people.

". . . just look at who's buttonholed him now."

Karen moved closer to the rail, open-mouthed, her heart missing a beat as Victor slowly drew his hand out of his pocket and, turning it palm up, harmlessly weighed the air. The warning died in her throat.

Whatever Tom had said to him, Victor appeared to be considering with some amusement. She saw her husband put a hand on Victor's arm, trying to move him along, herd this interloper back out into the night; and Victor affably but firmly stand his ground. I've as much right to be here as you, pal, he seemed to be saying. Victor, clearly enjoying the encounter, was doing most of the talking, while Tom kept looking around with a stiff flickering smile, as if he was anxious to get away, as if he was afraid of being seen in undesirable company. He was making it too obvious, she thought. Acting like they were total strangers.

There was room for doubt but not for coincidence. Karen

felt weak suddenly. If the two men did know each other, it could only mean one thing.

She managed to say, "Who is that Tom's talking to?"

Her head throbbing, she stepped back from the edge of the balcony, as though it had been a precipice.

"Oh, that's our fallen angel, Mr. Serafim," Tamara gushed. "Everyone tells me he's mixed up in the Cosa Nostra, you know, but he made such a generous donation to *our* little cause, I couldn't very well not invite him. He just bought a house out here on some golf course. Shall we go down and rescue Tom?"

The idea seemed laughable now.

It could only mean that she had gotten everything back to front.

The sympathy Tom had shown her, his ready acceptance of her story, the way he'd referred to her sins absolvingly as another symptom of her "condition"—concerned about her, but with just enough anger under the surface to let her know he *was* jealous. I don't want to know too many details, he'd said. Christ, she'd felt real pity then, she'd trusted him. But he'd said it once too often. She might have expected him to play down a threat to his life. But for Tom not to want to know every last detail about a financial transaction that involved his money . . . *that* took on a new alerting significance. Her heart started hammering again.

Joe had warned her. What if his suspicions were right?

"How stupid of me," Karen made a tiny drama of searching her pocket book, then snapping it shut. "I think I must have left my compact in the bathroom. You go ahead. I'll join you in a minute."

She had to find a telephone. As far as she knew Tom wasn't aware that she'd seen them together; she couldn't be so sure about Victor. There wasn't much time. Tamara, when she got among them, was sure to say something.

She retreated in order across the landing, then turned down the bedroom hall, which she remembered exited through a green baize door on to the back staircase. The moment she was out of sight, Karen started to run.

The first door she tried was locked. The second opened into an unoccupied guest room decorated in a pale yellow rose chintz. She closed the door behind her and turned the key. She didn't need a light to make out the telephone beside the bed.

Her hand was trembling so much she had to redial.

Come on, Joe, pick up.

She heard the number ring four, five times . . . drumming the night table with her lacquered nails . . . six. She could just picture him, sitting there in the living room at Overbeck, staring into space.

Pick *up*, damn you.

6

"Joe? Joe, it's me."

The low urgent whisper came from the answering machine on the floor at Hendricks's feet. Leaning forward in his chair, he dropped a hand down behind the arm-rest.

"Something's wrong . . ." A slight hesitation in her voice, as if at any moment she expected Haynes to pick up. "Victor showed up at the party, I saw him just now, talking to Tom. I thought at first . . . Joe, you there?"

The detective had his hand on the receiver. He could have snatched up the phone and gotten off a warning, told her to call the cops, any damned thing.

"Only they act like they know each other."

Could have. While it was still ringing. Now that the machine had answered, he knew he'd left it too late.

"Joe, please pick up the phone."

Alerted by the green message light, first call they'd had all evening, one of the mutes, Donut he guessed, had flitted across the room and taken up position behind his chair.

"I know I should've listened. But whatever this means, you're not safe there. Get out of the house. *Now* Joe, you must leave right away."

He felt a tap on his left shoulder. Just in case he got any bright ideas. The hand slipping inside his shirt collar.

"I have to go . . . somebody's coming."

There was a click, the tape made a noise like a zipper being yanked as Hendricks hit the play-back button, then the whirr of the rewind mechanism. He let go the breath he'd been holding as he eased himself back in his chair. It was a chance missed, but look on the bright side, something—call it good instinct or a failure of nerve—had saved him from making the wrong move. He'd tried to be a hero, it would only have ended in tears, at the very least earned him a beating, and for what? He couldn't have told Karen much more than she already knew. Her husband kept the same lousy company she did.

Victor's message from this morning was still there on the answering machine.

I hear you were looking for me.

His instructions were to wipe the tape. He hadn't liked the way that sounded. Get rid of the evidence. Liked it even less now. What was Victor doing at a frigging charity ball, Hendricks thought, unless fixing himself an alibi?

He twisted his head around. "Hey, knock it off, will ya?"

Donut's thin bony fingers were expertly kneading the back of his neck. For Christ's sake . . . Unaware of his objection, the mute kept going, he made a hissing sound while he worked like a groom currying a horse. In spite of himself, Hendricks could feel the tension ebbing.

"You know something?" He flexed his shoulders. "That feels pretty good. Donut, you ever quit your present job, you'll still have a future hurting people."

Left of the door, Hendricks saw a circle of light briefly halo Roy Roy's shaved head. He was holding a pencil flashlight, holding it between his teeth: a red-cheeked gargoyle as he bent over a pad to scribble something.

He came up to him with the note. The masseur was still working, his thumbs deployed to the pressure points behind the detective's ears. It wasn't a comfortable feeling.

Roy Roy held the light for him and they both peered over his shoulder while Hendricks supplied an answer to the childishly printed query, WHAT DID SHE WANT?

These guys were beautiful. How the *fuck* did they know?

"That was Victor," he wrote without hesitating. "Said to tell you Haynes won't be coming back tonight. We can go HOME."

It had to have something to do with vibrations . . .

Donut, finishing up, gave him a not so friendly slap upside his head.

Tiss, tiss.

He heard Roy Roy do his impression of a laugh as he took the scrap of paper from him. Then the light went out. The detective rubbed his ear, still ringing, as he watched their shadows melt back on to the chairs against the wall. Presently he recognized the sound of paper being scrunched and tossed in a corner.

It was worth a try.

"I've thought about it," the girl in the lavender dress was saying. A stocky blonde with an alert, confident manner, not more than eighteen, somebody's daughter . . . Tom Welford had an uncomfortable sense of genetic *déjà vu*. "A lot of people have said that I could be an inspiration to others. There's a big life out there."

"New York's a dying town," drawled her young escort, who looked so much like her he might have been her twin; he was sloppy with drink. "Big life, my ass."

"I don't suppose that either of you kids . . ." Tom tried to interrupt.

"The way things are right now," the girl went on earnestly, "I don't care too much about *not* being out there. People don't have any respect for life or anything any more. But you have to believe in the world getting better . . ." She looked up at

Tom with eyes that matched her dress. "Hi, I'm Cassandra. What do you think? Is it? Getting better, I mean?"

"Yes, I expect so," Tom said distractedly.

They were standing by the marble steps of the swimming pool, around which an alternative party had developed, kids mostly, sitting on the grass smoking reefer, hanging out. It was where someone had told him they thought they'd seen Karen headed only minutes ago.

"I'm looking for my wife. You won't know her, but she's kind of tall and has dark . . ."

"It's easy to get lost at these things," Cassandra said, "they invite too many people. I don't even know what I'm doing here." She shook her head. "We wouldn't have seen her."

"There're only one or two people I see in New York," her twin mistakenly corroborated. "There's almost nobody left really."

"Oh, Beaumont," she glanced at him impatiently, "why do you always have to be so negative?"

She slipped an arm in Tom's and asked him if he wanted to dance. The best way to find someone, she laughed, dragging him forward in her enthusiasm, was to let them find you.

Awkwardly, Tom disengaged himself and moved away across the lawn, heading back up to the house. The rain was still holding off but there was talk of moving the fireworks display forward half an hour, just to be on the safe side.

He wandered through the crowded marquee where a second supper was being served to the strains of a jazz quartet, looking for Karen, saying dryly to friends as he passed, "I seem to have mislaid my wife." Not wanting to appear too concerned.

When a stranger came up to him and asked if he'd had any luck, Tom knew it was time to leave. He walked on under the garlanded porch into the house proper with the intention of doing one last sweep of its almost deserted reception rooms.

There was no sign of her.

Probably she'd just felt "tired"—the word Karen used in the old days when she'd had too much to drink—and had gone home to Edgewater. It was getting on for twelve o'clock.

The worst that could have happened, Tom rationalized as he climbed the stairs, was that she had seen him talking to Victor Serafim. The man had to be insane coming here. All got up in that ridiculous monkey suit, letting him know he'd received an invitation. The way he'd hailed him like an old college friend . . . Jesus! But at least Serafim hadn't stayed long, just said what he had to say and left. Apart from Tamara, who wanted to be complimented on her sense of chic in welcoming lowlife to the charmed world of "Nonsuch," no one had mentioned him. If Karen *had* witnessed their encounter, he needed to find her and explain things before she got the wrong idea, got it all twisted around inside her head.

A question of damage control, he tried to convince himself, but not the end of the world.

It was Tamara who'd told him that she and Karen, her "new best friend," had gone upstairs earlier to powder their noses; that they were talking on the landing, and then somehow had missed each other. Not exactly insinuating, Tom thought, and yet . . . he'd seen something, a flash of pity in the older woman's eye that had filled him with rage.

He'd waited for his hostess to move breathlessly on before taking a turn up to the bedroom floor.

In one of the guest rooms, imagining he caught a hint of Karen's perfume lingering on the air, Tom stood stock-still, as if he sensed that she was close, that the trail must end here; then, wiping his mouth with the back of his hand, discovered absurdly that the source of her musky scent was his own fingers, still redolent, after their walk on the beach, of the lies she'd told.

She was saving her skin, he could hardly fault her.

After listening to her "confession," Tom had wondered if the sensible, the decent thing wouldn't have been to let Karen go, let 'em both go. But, of course, it wasn't that easy. He had certain responsibilities. There was no one who could give them what he could, no one who would cherish them as he did. They were dependent on him. And he on them. What else could it mean to be part of a loyal, supportive and loving family?

The more he thought about it, her Mister Man—like all benefactors—really should have remained anonymous.

He heard running water coming from the bathroom. There was somebody in there. A woman gave a rapturous giggle . . . more than one person. Tom didn't hesitate, but going around the bed approached the connecting door which he could see now had been left ajar. He pushed it back another inch, letting out groans of delight over the hiss of the shower, a whispered curse, the comic slap-slapping of wet bodies . . . then they were fully at it, grunting like pigs.

He could have laughed, but was convulsed instead by the jealous certainty that it was his wife in there. Screwing her brains out.

The urgent little cries on the motel tape, the wanton jingling of her ankle bracelet, still fresh in his memory, Tom stepped across the tiled threshold and was about to tear back the shower curtain when he noticed a gas-blue frock and white panties lying at his feet, discarded in hot haste, but not Karen's. Not hers.

"I'm most terribly sorry," he mumbled in retreat.

He stood outside in the corridor, shaking with emotion, knowing he really had to get a hold of himself.

Another five minutes crawled by.

Hendricks got up to stretch his legs; no one made any attempt to prevent him. He walked over to the window and stood looking down on to the empty gravel circle with the big oak-tree in the middle and the outhouses beyond, just enough glow in the sky to put a line around the shapes of things. The traffic on Wheatley Road had dwindled to almost nothing. He tried to guess how much lead-time he'd have once he heard the Suburban turn in the driveway. Ten, fifteen, twenty seconds at most, before his partners would see the lights.

He was still gambling on Haynes not coming back.

The other message on the answering machine was a call-back from Haynes's lawyer friend, Herb Meltsner, letting him know he'd be stuck at the office a couple more hours. Reference to an earlier conversation. Moderately pissed-off sounding, Herb had said that he might be able to find a hungry lawyer willing to take on the case for the publicity—in response no doubt to an inquiry from Haynes regarding his chances of pursuing a paternity and custody claim through the courts—but without even the support of the mother? "Not a hope in hell, buddy. You really don't have a prayer."

He remembered the conversation in the motel room, Karen refusing to let Joe even talk about legal alternatives to their plan of running off together. Now here he was, the born-again loser, going it alone. You had to give him credit, though, for still wanting his kid.

Herb Meltsner had suggested meeting for a drink around seven at the Hyatt on 42nd Street. Joe was sure to have gone along, listened to the bad news, but then what? Call up an old girlfriend, try to drown his sorrows, or decide to cut his losses—more Haynes's style—and hit the road?

Why drag his sorry ass back here? It was just that Karen had sounded so damned sure he'd be home.

He turned away from the window and went back to his chair by the fireplace. It was starting to feel too comfortable, warning him that he was getting tired. Tired of sitting there trying to think how he could use the slight advantage his hearing gave him over the others, when the time came.

He was an expert at fighting sleep.

Hendricks waited.

Something, a dry scraping sound out there in the night, made him jump. Probably rats or a raccoon maybe sniffing around the garbage cans in the stick-shed. He never liked scavengers.

Earlier, he'd watched the mutes prepare for Joe Haynes's reception, using the little flashlight to assemble wire, kitchen knife, duct-tape, plastic garbage bags and a decorator's caulking gun they'd found in the garage. They'd put the stuff in a

J.C. Penney's shopping bag and left it handy on top of the kitchen counter.

He was getting too old for this shit.

Victor wouldn't have sent him along if the idea was to take care of Joe permanently. Would he? Just put the blocks to him, that's what he said. Tell the cocksucker I want my money back. They needed him to do the talking. Not for any other purpose.

He felt himself dozing off, his eyelids becoming heavy. He wondered if Victor had kept his promise to let Marion know that he'd be home late. He tried rubbing his temples, pinching his lip, old tricks he'd learned for staying alert on long surveillances. He pictured her sitting up in bed watching the late movie, still waiting for the phone to ring.

Tom was calling her name even before he'd gotten the front door open, fumbling with the keys under the dark tunnel of wisteria, his hand a little unsteady.

The lights were on in the hall. He saw her wrap hanging on the hat stand, looked for the set of keys she usually threw down on the brass trestle tray just inside the door. Not this time. He came up the short flight of steps into the long gallery; at the far end, the glow of a lamp left burning in the library gave him hope.

"Babe, you down there?" He didn't need to raise his voice the house was so still.

Nothing.

She must have gone straight up to bed.

Tom undid his bow-tie and the top button of his shirt. He unlocked the mini-bar under the stairs and poured himself a nightcap. Only now noticing that Bracken hadn't wandered out from his lair to greet him. A deep grumbling whine came from behind the dining room door. He smiled as he went over to open it, wondering how long the dog had been in there; and whether Karen—a half-empty bottle of Diet Coke on the mahogany sideboard caught his eye—could have shut him in by mistake: it wouldn't have been the first time.

He bent down to give the Lab's broad head a pat as he brushed past, putting on a stiff-legged display of injured pride. It wasn't long, though, before Bracken relented and came back to his outstretched hand, wagging his tail furiously.

Tom let him out on to the terrace through the french windows in the breezeway. He saw the dog lift his leg against an urn, kick up some pebbles, then go zigzagging off into the night, nose to the ground. He followed him outside and stood sipping his brandy and soda, looking up at the house: a light was showing on the balcony outside their bedroom. He didn't doubt now that Karen was home safe. He almost felt sorry for her. Picturing her half asleep, propped against the pillows, waiting for him, he felt his goddamned dick get hard.

He made himself concentrate on what he was going to tell her if she asked about Victor Serafim. How this guy he'd never laid eyes on before had come up to him and demanded half a million bucks. He'd realized who he was, of course, but remembering what she'd said about the threats he'd made hadn't exactly encouraged the conversation.

It wouldn't hurt, Tom thought, to reproach his wife a little for all the trouble she'd caused.

What Victor had in fact brought him—he took a long swallow of brandy—was the news that everything was set for tonight. Tom would have preferred not to know. But he could see the advantage now in letting Karen think that he'd told Serafim to get lost—which wasn't a hundred miles from the truth—told the creep that he never mixed business with pleasure . . . no, better than that, told him he had no intention of paying him a red cent.

He had already turned to go in, forgotten all about Bracken, when he heard growling from the direction of the knot garden. He called him back with a low whistle. The dog barked once, then almost immediately came padding up out of the dark. It wasn't until they were both inside the house that he noticed that Bracken had something in his mouth. A young rabbit, Tom thought, until he saw that what had been dutifully laid at his feet was a child's slipper.

He recognized it as one of Ned's.

Hendricks woke with a start as the light came swinging in the windows, falling first on the empty seats by the door so that for a moment he thought the other two had gone. Then the room brightened again, and he saw Roy Roy standing motionless by the counter of the open-plan kitchen.

He doubted he'd have gained much time had he been fully alert. He could only just hear the engine now over the sound of tires crunching gravel, the wagon rolling to a halt under the windows. He waited for the driver to cut the lights before getting up from his chair. Knowing Donut was somewhere behind him but not expecting the arm he threw around his neck, or the little-toothed blade of the Kitchen Devil he held like a finger to his lips.

Roy Roy had already slipped out into the hall.

The detective heard a car door slam, then somebody walking up to the front of the house. He must have parked outside the last set of garage doors. Haynes didn't usually bother putting the Suburban away. Hendricks listened for a break in his step—hoping that he would at least take a look inside the garage and see the alien Caprice sitting there—but the footsteps on the gravel came right on. The screen-door screeched open, and banged shut.

They stopped at the foot of the stairs leading up to the apartment. Something wasn't right. Maybe he could sense danger. There was a significant pause before a light came on in the hall. Hendricks kept his eyes fixed on the white strip under the living room door.

He heard the cautious tread and thought for Christ's sake, no, you can't let this happen. If he kicked sideways with his foot he could probably reach the answering machine, the smallest noise would be enough to warn, but as he edged his left leg forward he felt Donut's knife rein him back until its serrated blade was scraping his teeth.

* * *

At the head of the stairs, Tom found the other slipper. He picked it up, far from reassured, then made his way quietly along the hall to the night-nursery.

He stopped outside Ned's room and listened. Tom always made a point of looking in on the boy last thing at night. During the week, more often than not, it was the only time he got to see his son. There was no sound of breathing.

Sometimes he'd open the door and Doc would just be lying there, wide awake. He didn't find it difficult talking to him then. When it was just the two of them, he felt comfortable with the boy's silence: it encouraged him to believe they had a special understanding.

The rabbits were his favorite slippers.

He turned the handle, eased the door open. In the dim glow of the nightlight he saw that the bed was empty.

He felt his insides tauten. Still telling himself there had to be a simple explanation.

The bedclothes had been pulled back, the red and black Spiderman pillow and some of Ned's stuffed animals had slipped to the floor. He turned on the light at the door and quickly checked the corners, the closet, the bathroom, even looked under the bed, making sure that the boy wasn't hiding anywhere. Then he strode on down the hall to his nanny's room, calling out her name.

He didn't worry about waking the household now.

There was no answer to his knock. He opened the door, getting a faint smell of suntan lotion and Johnson's powder as he advanced hesitantly into the darkened room. Hazel?

Tom looked down at the bed, caught a glimpse of her nakedness, the flurry of eau-de-Nil limbs and paler bikini areas, as the girl drew a sheet over her. The only source of light, a fluorescent strip in the aquarium on top of the dresser, cast a sickly green flush over everything. He remembered Hazel kept sea-horses; she'd asked his permission before buying her first pod or string, whatever you called the damned things, from a mailorder firm in San Diego.

She had on a pair of headphones, which she slipped down around her neck, then reached over to turn off the CD player on the bedside table.

"Mr. Welford?" Her eyes wide with alarm. "Is something the matter?"

"Ned's not in his room."

"Oh, my God! What?" She sat up against the pillows, holding the sheet to her throat. "But he was there . . . I checked him just before I turned in."

"How long ago was that?"

"About eleven. He was sleeping soundly. Are you sure? I mean if he'd woken, and something was wrong, he knew to come through to me . . . there has to be a mistake."

She looked bewildered.

"I don't think there's any real cause for alarm," Tom said calmly, wanting to believe it. There'd been nothing to suggest an intruder, he'd found no signs of a struggle. If the boy hadn't gone through to his nanny, then Karen must have taken him . . .

She wasn't here in the house, he knew that now.

. . . come back from the party, taken Ned, left again.

It was so fucking obvious. The only question was, did she do it because of what had happened tonight, a spur-of-the-moment decision, or had she been planning this all along?

"Did you hear my wife come in?"

"Your wife." She ran a hand through her hair. "Umm . . . I can't think. There was a car. I assumed it was her or both of you coming home from the party . . ." She hesitated, clearly embarrassed. "Mr. Welford, would you mind giving me a minute and I'll put something on?"

It didn't take Tom much longer than that to confirm that Karen was not waiting for him in their bedroom. He came back to the nursery wing and found Hazel standing in the hall wearing a blue Japanese happi coat. Nothing on her feet. She wanted to search every room in the house, but he stopped her.

"When did you hear the car?"

"Maybe half an hour ago. I actually only saw the lights.

I . . . I'm sorry, I was listening to music. I wasn't paying a whole lot of attention. There's been so much activity out there."

"So you didn't hear anything? It's all right, Hazel, no one's blaming you. I just want you to tell me what you know. Did you see the car leave again?"

"I'm not sure," she said.

"What do you mean?"

"I was lying there, half asleep. You know how reflections sort of slide across the ceiling, you can't always tell where they come from? I think I saw lights about five minutes later. It just never occurred to me that it could be the same car. They seemed more remote somehow."

"Because you believed Mrs. Welford was home."

"I guess so." She looked down at her bare feet, curling her toes into the pile of the carpet. "It's possible that I did hear someone, inside the house, a door banging or something."

"Home for the night." Tom frowned. He thought about Bracken shut in the dining room. "Did you hear the dog barking?"

She shook her head. "Mr. Welford, what's going on? I feel so terrible. If anything has happened to Ned . . ."

"I'm sure it's nothing to worry about," he said. "I think my wife must have come back here, then maybe she decided to drive into the city, taking Ned with her. They're probably spending the night at the apartment."

"Why would she do that without telling you?" she said quite sharply. "I'm sorry, but I feel I have the right to ask."

"I understand." Tom caught himself looking at Hazel's breasts and shifted his gaze. "As you know, Karen . . . my wife . . . is not entirely a well person. She's been under a lot of pressure lately, her behavior can be erratic."

Hazel nodded. "We had an argument earlier, before she went out—she accused me of spying on her." The girl drew the lapels of her happi coat tighter, leaving a hand folded across her heart. "She told me to pack my bags, I was fired. It didn't make sense. Maybe she's jealous of my relationship with Ned, I dunno. I just hope I'm not somehow responsible for what happened here tonight."

"You mustn't blame yourself for anything. You do a good job, Hazel, I'm grateful. There's no question of your leaving."

"She was acting pretty strange."

"She's not going to hurt Ned, we both know that. She loves him . . . as only a mother can. I appreciate your concern, but really there's no need."

"You don't think we should call the police?"

"No, I don't." Tom smiled, reaching out and patting her shoulder. "I'm sorry if I alarmed you. Now why don't you go back to bed and try to get some sleep?"

"I couldn't sleep before. Would you let me know if there's any news?" She started to turn away, then hesitated as if she'd forgotten something. "Mr. Welford?"

"It'll be all right. Don't worry."

"I'm not sure whether I should be telling you this," she said quietly, lowering her eyes. "Ned spoke to me for the first time tonight. He was upset because he'd left his security blanket at what he called Mister Man's place. The way he was talking . . . it's a real person, Mr. Welford, not make-believe."

A tear rolled down the girl's cheek.

"The important thing," Tom said, "is that he spoke."

7

The white frame house was in darkness.

Karen stood in the doorway and felt around the walls of the narrow entrance hall for the light-switch. As often as she'd visited Joe's place, she'd never come at night. Her fingers crept along the rail, past the corner of a picture frame, a familiar tear in the wallpaper, the disconnected bell push— getting her bearings as she edged forward into the deeper black of the stairs.

She felt something hard under her feet, a pile of magazines she remembered Joe refusing to jettison.

She was almost certain that he'd been here when she'd called—too stubborn to pick up the phone. Behind her, the screen-door creaked mournfully as it settled on its hinges. His Suburban wasn't in the driveway. If he'd gotten her message, they must've only missed each other by minutes.

One hand on the rail, the other holding up the skirts of her ball-gown, she climbed the steep wooden stairs to the apartment. In the dark, it was easy to get the feeling she was trespassing. The house where she'd acted out her fantasy of escape already felt alien to her. The old garage smell of motor oil and dust was spiked with a scent she couldn't identify . . . and something else that hovered just beyond the threshold of recognition.

She put it down to the strangeness of returning to a place she never thought she'd see again.

The tune came into her head as she climbed, one step at a time, getting used to the blackness now. She remembered, in the back of the Lincoln . . . Victor Serafim singing along.

Twenty-four little hours . . . She heard it in the whisper of silk against her legs—accusingly loud, suddenly. You get one chance, make one decision.

It was only that morning that she had driven off with Joe's image growing smaller in her wing mirror. He was leaning against the old rail-and-post fence, an unlit cigarette in the corner of his mouth. Beside her, in his car seat, Ned had gone on waving goodbye long after he'd faded from view.

It felt like an eternity.

He'd told her they'd be back.

Smiling into her eyes when he'd said it, trying too hard after his earlier outburst to be cool. It was so typical of Joe. Don't become strangers now, you hear?

She'd come straight from the party to warn him.

There was a small sound, a scraping from above that stopped as suddenly as it began. A squirrel on the roof . . .

She stumbled over a step that wasn't there, her heart racing as she found a switch at the head of the stairs and cut on the lights.

She had to shield her eyes from the sudden brightness. At the end of the hall, the door to the living room was closed. She had a memory of Joe saying he always left it open at night so that the air could circulate. One thing he and Tom had in common, they didn't believe in air-conditioning. She advanced cautiously, pushing open doors and looking into each of the rooms as she went.

In Joe's room she took in at a glance the empty unmade bed, a half-packed suitcase, and her son's green security blanket draped over a chair—almost as if it had been left out for her. Was that what he'd meant? The reason he'd been able to predict with such certainty that she'd come back? But Joe would never have done anything so petty as to let Ned go, knowing he'd left his most treasured possession behind.

Would he? She felt a quick rush of fear.

Behind her the lights in the hall had snapped off.

She swung around: "Joe?"

Somebody was in the room with her.

A darker mass moving through the doorway. She recognized the smell now—the cheap air-freshener from the Lincoln masking the stench of stale sweat. Of decaying flesh. She started to scream but Roy Roy's hand had already closed over her mouth. His other arm circled her waist.

She saw no sense in struggling.

Bundled into the living room, she felt herself pushed down on to a wooden chair just inside the door. It was the skinny one, Donut, who gave her the once-over with the flashlight; big grin on his face that said, well, look what we got here.

She felt Roy Roy's hand slip around to the nape of her neck and finger the clasp of the choker. Then, as if he'd had a better idea, he pulled her head back and kissed her on the lips, his mouth open. He walked away from her, snickering. The flashlight went out. She heard the slap of a handshake as he

joined Donut at the kitchen counter. Congratulating themselves no doubt on their luck. There was a clatter of uten-
sils . . . it sounded like someone rummaging around in a
drawer, or maybe a shopping bag being emptied.

She shuddered as she wiped her mouth, doing it quickly,
not wanting to show her revulsion. Then sat hugging her
arms to her rib-cage. Her breath came in ragged gusts.

She was being watched.

There was enough light from the windows to let Karen
make out a third man standing by the fireplace; for a moment
she'd thought it might be Victor, but he was the wrong build,
too short by at least a head.

"Don't mind Roy Roy, the kid doesn't mean any harm, just
not house-trained."

The short man came over and squatted down in front of
her chair with his back to the two mutes. She could see his
scalp under thin carefully deployed hair, small light eyes in a
fleshy face, rosebud mouth. A light-colored sports coat. He
was no one she'd ever seen before.

"Where's Joe?" she asked.

"We were hoping you'd be able to tell us," he said amiably
and held out a small hand. "I'm Eddie Hendricks, a private
investigator, Mrs. Welford. I work for Victor Serafim. It's a
pleasure to meet you at last."

"And I've heard so much about you, asshole." It was the
insinuating tone of voice she resented. She remembered Joe
in the motel room telling her she was paranoid because she
thought she was being followed. "What are you doing here?"

"The door was open . . . I figured nobody would mind if
we made ourselves at home." He let the hand fall to his knee.
"We really need to talk to him, Mrs. Welford." The detective
cleared his throat. "We can wait—all night if necessary."

"You'd be wasting your time. Joe isn't coming back tonight,
or any other night. He doesn't live here any more."

"Then why did you come?"

"We had an argument earlier," she answered smoothly, trying to remember what she'd said on the machine. "Joe doesn't

always pick up the phone, I thought . . . He was driving to his sister's place, upstate. I thought maybe I'd catch him before he left. Obviously I'm too late."

"You're lying, Mrs. Welford. I can't help you if you lie," Hendricks said softly. "Mind if I sit?"

He got up and brought the chair over from the other side of the door, turned it around and sat astride it with his arms resting on the back. "They sent me to tell your friend, Haynes, that there's been a change of plan. Mr. Serafim's calling in the loan, stopping the clock."

"Well, why didn't you say so?" Karen sat back in her chair.

"He wants his money back."

"I don't have any problem with that. As a matter of fact, I've been trying to reach them all day. My plans have changed too. Tom knows now, about . . . well, he knows everything. But it's all right. He promised to take care of my debt."

"I'm afraid Mr. Scrafim is out of patience."

"But I just saw Victor and my husband at a party—twenty minutes ago—the two of them were putting their heads together. They probably got it all worked out by now. If I were you, I'd call your boss before taking this any further."

"We still need to talk to Joe, Mrs. Welford. Where is he?"

"Joe's got nothing to do with it."

"Mr. Serafim thinks he does."

"Look, I'm the customer. You can talk to me."

"Mr. Serafim is out of patience," Hendricks quietly insisted. "You hear what I'm saying? I'm truly sorry."

"What the fuck do you mean, you're sorry?"

"You tried to tip him off, didn't you?" She saw his eyes shift in the direction of Donut, who had moved away from the kitchen and was standing in the middle of the room. Roy Roy remained hunched over the counter, using the flashlight to write something. "I want you to know, Mrs. Welford, if I'd had the chance, I'd have done the same."

She could hear the tension in his voice. The detective's moon face was shiny with sweat.

"Why should I believe you?"

"The money isn't important," Hendricks went on in the same flat tone. "They're gonna take Joe out, whatever happens. Try not to overreact. Our dumb friends here got some kinda sixth sense. It's all part of a set-up. Victor's going big casino . . . Will you for Christ's sake look at me, Mrs. Welford? He plans to kidnap your son."

"Oh, God," Karen closed her eyes. "I knew . . . I *knew* this was coming." Wishing now she'd heeded an impulse to stop by Edgewater and check on Ned before rushing over here. "When?"

"After he gets out of kindergarten, Monday. They'll be there to collect him before the chauffeur . . . we have to make this quick, somebody's feeling left out of the conversation."

Roy Roy came slouching over.

"Hard to say what they'll do now—your showing up here tonight complicates things. Don't worry, I'm gonna get you out of this. Just don't let anybody stop you calling the cops."

"My husband's involved, isn't he?"

"He doesn't know about the boy."

"But he ordered Joe killed."

"It's a possibility," Hendricks said.

She saw him smile and shake his head, but not for her. He was looking at Roy Roy as he went on: "The door to the backyard isn't locked. I make my move, about thirty seconds from now, you go through it and run like hell. Don't try to get to your car, head for the woods. Use the only advantage you've got."

"Why are you doing this?"

Hendricks laughed as he reached out to take a piece of paper from Roy Roy. The mute put the flashlight on the note for him.

"What's this, Roy? Another poem?"

They know that he's strayed from the script.

It isn't just the note. Hendricks can tell by the way Donut has moved in close behind him that they're getting ready to start something. He keeps talking as he slowly pushes himself up—we're going to have to let Mrs. Welford go home, Roy—slips the chair out from between his legs; then, dropping the balled-up note, changes his grip on the chairback, still grinning at Roy Roy as he says to the cat-slant eyes behind the flashlight, the whole thing's blown now because of her. You understand, you dumb fuck?

The flashlight cuts out. Hendricks lifts the chair up over his head and, wheeling around, crashes it into Donut's face.

The kid gives a surprised grunt and stumbles backward.

Yelling at Karen to go, the detective gets the door to the hall open. He sees her hike her skirts over her knees and launch herself from her chair—Roy Roy doesn't try to stop them, just stands there shaking his head—and then Hendricks's through the door and running blind, going for the stairs with the idea that if he can get down to the garage and the Caprice before they catch up to him . . . far as he knows his gun's still in the glove compartment.

He hears the girl scream, the sounds of a brief struggle, the back door slam shut—in that order, bad news—then coming up fast behind him the scamper and squeak of rubber soles on bare boards.

He puts on a spurt, but there's no juice, no fucking pickup, the message isn't reaching his sawed-off legs. It's a race he's run before, time and again over a lifetime of bad dreams. He hears a sound like a whinnying horse. His unprotected back prickles with anticipation, almost as if the dread of letting this hell gain on him has turned to longing. He nearly trips over a packing case, saves himself by careening off the wall, and keeps going. There's only a couple more yards now to the top of the stairs. You can do it, Eddie. Back to thinking maybe he's got a shot at this after all, when a high scragging tackle from behind brings him down.

The momentum carries him forward, he gets a hand over the lip of the first step and pulls himself along on his stomach. For a second Hendricks imagines he can still make it as he tries to swim headfirst down the murky stairwell. He doesn't feel the undertow, the weight on his legs holding him back, before the breaker smashes down and rolls him under.

Roy Roy keeps the foot on his neck while he tears off a length of duct tape, then squats down and binds his wrists behind his back. Any attempt to move on Hendricks's part sets off small explosions of pain and light at the base of his skull.

Not worth the effort.

The throbbing in his head meshes sickeningly with the engine noise down below. He realizes Donut must have brought the Volvo inside, which makes perfect sense. He hears the engine cut out, the garage doors scrape shut. His head's still pounding. Roy helps him up and, in case he should misinterpret the gesture, mashes his face into the wall.

Then leads him by his necktie back into the living room.

"You know something?" Hendricks, wheezing, finds a piece of broken tooth with his tongue and spits it out. "Victor isn't going to be any too happy when he hears about this."

Roy Roy pushes him down on to the couch, throws the tie in his face, and walks away.

"He hears how you screwed up his plans," Hendricks shouts after him, twisting his neck to try to loosen the knot. "He'll take a dim fucking view . . ."

He can hardly breathe, his head's on fire, he's got a mouth full of blood and debris, a lump coming up over his right eye the size of a child's knee—things could be worse.

He watches Roy Roy's outline as he moves back and forth between the windows, hands in his pockets, shoulders hunched.

"We have to haul ass, Roy. You know Haynes isn't coming. The girl says she talked to the cops." He winces as air reaches his shattered tooth. "Give her a piece of paper, you don't believe me, let her write it down."

"Oh, sure, and ask them if I can use the phone, while you're at it." Karen's voice comes over low and sardonic. "Don't you see you're wasting your time?"

"Are you hurt, Mrs. Welford?"

She's sitting on the other end of the couch. The way she's leaning forward he can tell her hands are also taped behind her back. "You've got to be kidding."

He turns at the familiar pop of igniting gas, sees Donut in a blue glow bent over the kitchen range.

Donut heating water in a saucepan.

"Maybe it didn't work out like I'd hoped," he wheezes. "But we gave 'em something to think about. These two are smart enough to know they're out of their depths. The way things are now they gonna have to talk to Victor."

"Then what are you worried about?"

He doesn't answer. Just sits there watching Roy Roy pace, and listening to the small domestic sounds from the kitchen.

"They're not planning to talk to anyone," Karen says at last, "and you know it."

"I can still get us out."

"Jesus." She laughs.

"Trust me on this, it'll work."

"Why should I?"

"Because I'm trying to help you, Mrs. Welford, and I'm all you've got." He can't believe the balls on her. A woman in her predicament, she doesn't even seem ruffled. "Worst case only, okay? We offer them a deal."

"You think you can buy them off," Karen says doubtfully, "buy off their loyalty to Victor? He's like a father to them."

"It comes down to money," Hendricks says, "we all speak the same language."

He hears the sound of water coming to a boil, the scrape of the saucepan being removed from the hob.

She clears her throat. "I'm wearing a necklace that's supposed to be worth something."

Water being poured.

"What happened to you?" he says to Donut, who comes over with a cup of coffee and sits between them on the couch. "You look all squashed up."

In the dark, he can't be sure how much damage, if any, he inflicted with the chair.

Ignoring him, Donut switches on the TV, an ancient 19-inch Zenith, using the remote to kill the sound. He surfs the channels, flipping backward and forward between David Letterman and a nude chat show, before he settles for an old black and white movie.

"Damn," Hendricks sniffs, "that coffee smells good. You think we should offer some to our guest? Hey, fellas, I won the bet, didn't I? Fair and square. He's not coming. What do you say we all go home?"

There's a note-shaped scratch on Donut's chin, his hair's a little mussed, but that's all. Wearing glasses (same accountant-style wire-rims as Victor's) to watch the tube, he looks like a harmless geek, sitting there sipping his coffee, staring at Audrey Hepburn and Cary Grant in . . . whatever. Hendricks forgets the name of the picture, but he can guarantee that if his old lady's still awake this is what she'll be tuned to. It gives him the feeling of being in touch.

"She doesn't know it yet," he announces proudly, "but I plan to take my wife on a cruise this Christmas. Sunline, first class all the way to Santiago, Chile. She's got relatives down there." He pauses. "Okay, how much? We can do the transaction right here. Keep it simple."

There's no take-up on the offer.

His tooth is starting to throb. His left eye has almost closed. To get his mind off the pain, Hendricks flirts with the notion, which he knows to be dangerous, that she's watching him through the TV. Marion, who likes to think she's clairvoyant, can see them sitting on this cheap couch by the gray flickering light of the TV screen. She knows how the movie ends, which is why she's got that vacant look on her face. Didn't she warn him to stay off the case?

Eddie said to say he loves you . . .

He gets a flash of Victor Serafim standing in the hall of their apartment. He's come to deliver the message in person.

But what's he doing now? Squinting down the dark corridor to the light around the door of the bedroom beyond.

It's called *Charade*. Get a fucking grip, Eddie.

"Mrs. Welford?" He looks across at Karen and, seeing how beautiful she is, how close they are to the beginning of terror, he wonders, only for a second, if his first hunch about her wasn't the right one. But he trusts her, he has his speech all prepared: "I just want you to know, Mrs. Welford, whatever happens, that I never meant by anything I did to put you or your family at risk."

Karen murmurs something he doesn't hear.

The door opens. Marion's sitting up in bed, wearing the silk robe he bought her yesterday from Lord & Taylor, a taste of the good life he's promised her for so long it's not funny any more, but that's Audrey Hepburn on the screen, her eyes wide with alarm, not Marion . . .

Jesus Christ, not Marion—he looks away only to find the image reflected in Donut's stupid glasses—she doesn't know anything. He starts shouting.

"She's got nothing to do with this." He leans into Donut, barges his shoulder to get his attention, making him spill his coffee.

"How much do you *want*, for fuck's sake?" he yells and sees Roy Roy turn away from the windows. "Look in my jacket pocket, I wrote her a note. We can cut a deal, we can talk."

Donut puts his cup down on the floor, calmly wipes the knees of his pants, then picks up a heavy green glass ashtray and without warning crashes it into Hendricks's face.

His head flies back, blood sputters from his nose.

"Talk." He hears the echo.

Tiss, tiss.

Roy Roy, coming over to help, gets behind the couch and throws an arm around his neck. Stuffing his necktie in his mouth, the mute draws out a length of silver duct tape from the roll he wears like a bangle on his wrist and quickly secures the gag. Then wraps the adhesive strip round and round the detective's head until the spool is empty.

All done in the twinkling of an eye.

His eyes and nose are streaming. A bloody clam of snot hangs from one nostril, the other's almost completely blocked. He has to breathe slow, keeping the passage open against the flow of blood and mucus, suppressing panic as he coaxes from this sucking and bubbling valve minute increments of air.

It's breathing out that takes discipline.

He's aware of Karen trying to scramble up off the couch, and being casually knocked back into place by Donut. The kid does it without taking his eyes off the TV screen. He's still glued to Hepburn and Grant when he bends forward and, reaching under his seat, comes back up with the caulking gun.

Hendricks hears her say, Oh, God, no.

A metal skeleton frame that holds a cartridge of sealant on a spring, and a nozzle: all you need to pack a seam. He knows Dow Corning, the maker's name. They're up in Michigan some place, not far, so happens, from where he was born.

A humiliating warmth between his thighs signals he's lost control of his bladder. Bad timing, you could say, but the truth is he held out overlong.

Left it too late to tell Karen he's sorry for getting her in the mess she's in. It was me that took the money from the locker, I'm the one . . . But the note offering to split the loot with Victor's crew is right here in his right-hand jacket pocket. If she leaned across, behind Donut's back, she'd be able to fish it out for him. It's their only hope.

He catches her eye, tries to make her understand by tilting his head to one side and straining with his bound hands.

She just stares at him. Probably thinks he's fighting for breath, or cracking up.

He should have seen this coming. It didn't take genius to figure out that sooner or later he'd be less useful to Victor alive than dead. Once, not long after they first met, Marion offered to do a reading for him. All he remembers is that she made him shuffle the cards again. Over and over again.

He wonders if Victor and his astronomers know about the

syzygy, a rare alignment of planets the weathermen claimed was playing havoc with the tides along the Eastern seaboard, and Marion had warned would visit mayhem, a season of violence and insanity, on the city.

As if it made a difference.

He thinks of Marion and how he'll be leaving her with no one to share her memories, but can't say either that he's not afraid for her future.

Roy Boy vises his head while his partner inserts the nozzle of the caulking gun in his left nostril, the choked one, as luck would have it, and squeezes. It takes for ever to travel up the tube, maybe the filler's dried solid. He sees the tendons standing out on Donut's bony hand. Then something gives, he feels the plug hit home and suddenly there's so much of the stuff, it's oozing back out, running down over the silver bandaging and globbing into his sodden lap.

He takes a deep last breath before Donut transfers the nozzle and seals his good side.

Tom put his glass down on the hall table next to the little Remington cowboy. He poured himself another brandy. She must have gone around the back of the house—that would explain Ned's slipper being on the terrace—just in case she ran into him coming home from the Davenports.

Karen planned this, she had to have done. Left the party at the appointed time, like fucking Cinderella. Haynes would have been waiting for her, helped her carry the kid out to the station wagon, which she must have parked down on the shore road, and then driven off with them—a thief in the night.

Unless Serafim had gotten to the sonofabitch first.

Tom sipped his drink, noticing out of the tail of his eye something different about the Remington: the bronco rider's arm was all bent out of shape. He touched the twisted bronze limb and, to his dismay, the miniature stetson along with the cowboy's right hand came away in his fingers. He laid the hat at the base of the statue, then in a sudden gesture of fury swept the whole broken thing on to the carpet.

He walked out on to the terrace, taking his glass and the brandy bottle with him. He found a chair and set up his little bar on the parapet before removing a portable telephone from his jacket pocket. He punched out a number on the luminous dial, wondering if the detective still had a tap on the phone at Overbeck. If he didn't speak, the call couldn't be traced.

Could it?

He had to know. It didn't change anything, but he had to be sure that he was too late to prevent this.

He sat in the dark and watched the first rockets go up from Nonsuch, drizzling the low clouds with gold far out over Long Island Sound.

The number was ringing.

The mutes didn't try to stop Eddie Hendricks as he rolled from the couch on to his knees, then got up again and, almost knocking the TV off its stand, made a frantic stumbling charge for the kitchenette.

Karen watched the little fat man behind the counter turn his back to the kitchen range so that he could reach the controls with his hands. She heard the gas ignite. Saw the flames leap up. There was a wet hiss as they changed from blue to orange. The seconds payed out. His body blocking her view now, she knew from the nauseating smell of burned flesh that he was holding his bound wrists over the jets. Then suddenly, wheeling around—even though he must have realized by now that the tape was fire-resistant—Hendricks lowered his mouth into the ring of blue flames.

She didn't hear the telephone.

Only the small sound bottled in the detective's throat, a stifled squealing that absorbed everything and sent shivers through her as he came lurching back into the middle of the room, hair on fire, eyes bugging out of his head. She saw Roy

Roy step aside to let him past, laughing at his antics. Then, colliding with a chair, he pitched forward on to the rug.

The phone rang again.

She looked at Donut, still sitting quietly beside her, watching television. It could only be for Joe, or her.

Struggling up from the couch, Karen ran over to where Hendricks lay and sank down on her knees beside him as if to comfort the dying man. There was little she could do. She used her skirt to smother the flames in his hair. What was left of the elaborate comb-over smouldered fitfully along his true hairline.

At the third ring, knowing she must reach the phone before the answering machine cut on, she crawled around his still shuddering body to the fireplace and nudged the receiver off its cradle.

"Help me, for God's sake," she sobbed into the mouthpiece. The detective's heels were drumming on the floor, beating an involuntary tattoo a yard from her ear. "There's been a murder."

Silence the other end.

"They killed him. Do you hear me? There's been a murder."

The killed man sat bolt upright, like somebody waking from a bad dream, then toppled sideways with a shockingly loud and long release of gas.

She babbled her address, pleading with the other party to call the police, aware now of Roy Roy standing over her.

As Hendricks's last spasm subsided into stillness, she felt a hand on her shoulder gently pulling her away, then Roy Roy bent down to pick up the receiver.

She heard the line go dead.

Karen sat on the floor, her head bowed, watching them sign back and forth in the livid glow of the TV, their fingers making stuttering shadows on the wall.

They were still arguing—she could guess about what—

when Donut, pointing his remote at the screen, brought the discussion to an end. No more talk.

They seemed to have reached a decision about her.

She shrank back as Donut came over and kicked the detective's body before hunkering down beside it. She saw the gleam of a small blade and, remembering the collection of forfeits in the trunk of the Lincoln, turned her head away. She couldn't escape the sound.

He went away whistling tunelessly.

When they came to take her down to the garage, it was Donut who held her arm on the stairs. At the first touch of his hand, sticky with Eddie Hendricks's blood, she felt her legs give way beneath her.

But they wouldn't let her fall.

Roy Roy removed the choker from her throat. She couldn't tell which of them then pushed her back on to the hood of the Volvo, or whose hands suddenly lifted her skirts above her waist. The laughter that accompanied their discovery that she was wearing no underwear seemed to come from another room.

From the pit of her stomach the numbness spread slowly outward. She began to shiver uncontrollably.

There was a gray circle in the darkness, a single deadlight on to the backyard where Ned used to play. She concentrated on the spot as if it was a mandala with the power to keep them safe. Whatever happened, she had to get through this for her baby's sake.

The two pairs of hands moved over her body in harmony as though they were used to working together, sharing.

She heard above the little animal noises they made Joe's wagon coming up the driveway. She knew it was the Suburban from the note of the engine. It was showing no lights.

They kept on doing what they were doing.

The car stopped outside, its engine running, music on the stereo—a Disney tape she remembered Joe had bought for

Ned's last birthday. She heard the three little pigs chirp in confident unison: "I'll build my house with bricks."

She tried to call out but one of them had covered her mouth with his. Then the car door opened, letting light escape briefly from the Suburban's interior and fall in a yellow thread across the floor of the garage.

I'LL BUILD MY HOUSE WITH BRICKS . . .

Slammed shut.

They froze. Donut stayed with her, keeping his tongue in her mouth but with a knife pressed against her belly, while Roy Roy, zipping his pants, shuffled over to the garage doors.

She could make out Joe's voice now, talking to someone in the wagon, saying he'd only be a minute. With a visceral jolt, she heard a child answer.

He closed everything into the suitcase on the bed, except for the green security blanket, which he stuffed inside his sweatshirt. Then he returned to the window to check on the boy: still there, safely strapped in the front seat of the station wagon, his white face pressed against the glass. Joe waved down at him, but there was no wave back.

He looked at his watch. Thirty minutes. For a ride that should have taken ten. You couldn't blame the kid for acting up. At his age, how was he supposed to know this was okay? Naturally he felt scared. They were well clear of the house and into the trees before Ned had woken in his arms, crying and struggling. He'd managed to calm him by telling him they were going to collect "blanky." Then set off together on a great adventure.

When the two of them got better acquainted, they'd learn to trust each other: the blood thing would make the difference. The fact that Ned had spoken to him just now in the wagon—the first time he'd ever heard his son talk—only bore out his theory. Joe believed that his coming for him had done the trick. His intervention, call it karma if you like, had helped the boy find his voice.

He took a last look around the room before he cut off the

light, then stood a moment longer, listening to the low idle of the Suburban's engine and, after a short pause on the tape he'd left playing for Ned, the sweeping overture to "Once upon a Dream" from *Snow White*. Suitcase in hand.

He walked through the hall toward the living room.

The door was ajar and the sweet acrid smell of burning he'd noticed as he came upstairs grew stronger.

Then he stopped suddenly.

The sound of footsteps that had been shadowing his own carried on. There was somebody moving around down below. He heard the garage doors go, a heavy tread on the gravel outside, the click of a car door opening. He ran back into the bedroom and, looking out the window, glimpsed a squat powerful figure on the Suburban's blind side swing up in the driver's seat.

He saw the boy's head twist around.

At that moment the skinny one, Donut, came out of the garage with what looked like a tire iron slung over his shoulder.

They'd been there all along, waiting for him.

IV
EDGEWATER

SUNDAY

1

Tom Welford hadn't moved from his outpost at the border of the terrace and the upper lawn. A balloon of brandy in one hand, cigar in the other, he sat slumped in his chair watching the navigation lights of an ocean-bound merchantman out on the Sound. He followed the ship's obscure profile through the fixed lights of Rye, and then the string of small towns it briefly eclipsed along the receding Connecticut shore, until, with a last extended groan of its fog horn and the red wink of a starboard beacon, it faded into the night.

He let another minute go by, holding out against his own impatience for the telephone to ring, listening with marginal hope for the homecoming slam of a car door under the loggia—then reached for his mobile, which lay beside him on the broad wooden arm-rest, and touched the redial button to call Overbeck. If Karen picked up again, he wouldn't be able to speak, but he'd know at least that they were safe. It was the fifth time he'd tried in the past half hour.

He waited until the last moment, and cut the line before Haynes came on. Not wanting to hear the sound of his voice preserved by the answering machine.

He took a swallow of brandy, absorbing its comfortless fire, then refilled his glass. He noticed he was sweating, his armpits drenched, as if he'd been running.

There was nothing he could do, but wait.

Brooding over a picture he'd taken from his pocket—his

mistake had been to let her out of his sight at the party, even for a minute—Tom tried to convince himself that sooner or later Karen would have to come home. She had nowhere else. Things might have taken an unpredictable turn, the reins slipped from his grasp, but whatever happened she had to realize now that this was where she and Ned belonged.

Now that it was just the three of them again.

Leaning forward, Tom picked up a heavy Tiffany lighter from the garden table and held the flame to a corner of the photograph. One of the detective's more revealing efforts, it was the only physical proof in his possession that he had ever been aware of Haynes's existence, had ever suspected his wife of cheating on him: ever imagined that their son might be anything more than the satisfactory outcome of her juice-less surrender to a turkey baster and a reheated dribble of jism from a nitrogen tank.

As Dr. Goldstone had pointed out this was not a business where it paid to keep records. Everything else, the whole sordid contents of the manila package Serafim had handed over in the park (photos, tapes, documents, reports of investigation)—all proving beyond a doubt that Joseph Haynes was guilty of trying to *embezzle* his family—Tom had destroyed that afternoon at his office.

This last piece of evidence—a skyline shot of Haynes and Karen basking in post-coital glow while Ned plays innocently at their feet—was slow to combust. In the wavering flame, he could make out those points of likeness between Haynes and Ned that he'd ringed and arrowed earlier in black Magic Marker on the glossy print. If anything, the resemblance seemed stronger—a trick of the light, perhaps—but now that the donor had been returned to anonymity, Tom could imagine a time when he would look at his son and see only Welford lineaments.

It was what he'd already blinded himself to do, ever since he'd first laid eyes on Ned, newborn, a miniature Winston Churchill asleep in his mother's arms.

He regretted now dialing Overbeck. He hadn't heard

enough, and he'd heard too much. Karen's cry for help was still ringing in his ears. The frantic drumming of her lover's heels, so close to the receiver he must have died in her arms, would haunt him. He wasn't sure whether knowing what she had gone through would make it easier to show her compassion.

She wasn't meant to be there.

No witnesses. Wasn't that the deal?

When it finally caught, he dropped the burning photograph into an ashtray and watched as the flames licked at the man's features, darkening, distorting and peeling away the map of his face until it scrolled upward and was consumed. What if Ned had been forced to witness it too? He stumped his cigar out in the ashes, then got up and walked along the parapet to where the cliff fell sheer to the water and tipped the still smoldering contents of the ashtray over the edge.

Surely Karen would have tried to protect him? She'd given her address: call the police, she'd pleaded. "Tell them I'm at 1154 Wheatley." Not we. No mention of Ned. Where was he when it happened? Asleep in the car?

Or somewhere else?

The long trail of smoke from the fireworks had drifted out to sea, leaving a faint smell of cordite on the humid air. Tom stood for a moment looking back across the bay to the blaze of light from Nonsuch, his patrician eye drawn by a shoal of silver reflections a few yards off the beach that appeared to dip and shimmer to the raucous pulse of the dance.

He heard the muffled sound of a footfall.

"What the Christ . . ."

Tom swung around.

He saw a figure step over the low stone balustrade at the far end of the terrace.

"How's it going, ace?" Victor Serafim said, as he strolled up out of the deep shadows.

"The hell are you doing here?" Tom turned his back, walked over to the table and, replacing the ashtray, picked up his brandy. "You think you can just turn up at my house any time you feel like it? You must be out of your mind."

He sat down heavily.

Victor smiled and shoved both hands in the side pockets of his jacket. "Do I hear an invitation?"

Without waiting for an answer, he came around in front of Tom's chair and squatted on the edge of the parapet, his back to the water. "I dunno, Tom, sometimes . . . I swear. That's the second time this evening you told me I had no right to be somewhere."

"You know what I'm talking about."

Victor shrugged. "You look as if you could use the company. Waiting for news of your loved ones can be a lonely business."

"Where are they?"

"You don't need to worry."

"I was expecting a call."

"It's not the kind of news you'd want to hear over the telephone. We got the security angle to consider."

"You didn't seem too worried about the goddamned security angle when you showed up next door. My wife isn't stupid. If she saw us together, or anybody happens to mention to her that I was talking to some guy who looked like he got lost on his way to a Mott Street social club . . ."

Victor chuckled, viewing Tom over the top of his glasses with glittering eyes. "Some party, though, wasn't it?"

"Where are Karen and Ned?"

"I paid a lot of money for that glass of warm champagne, the one you brought me, Tom." He cleared his throat. "But, hey, look at the class of people I got to rub shoulders with, the celebrities that were there. I'm a little disappointed you never introduced me to none of your friends, Tom. Where I come from, a new face moves into the neighborhood . . ."

"Some other time," Tom snapped. "I'm still waiting to hear what happened."

"You know who I was chatting with? Mandy Patinkin. The movie star. When it comes to playing bad guys, forget about it, no one can touch him. They ever make a movie of my life . . . I told him what I do for a living, Tom. He thought I was bullshitting. Said he couldn't quite picture me as a loan shark. I looked too mild, too respectable, more like a lawyer or your accountant type individual. We all swim in the same water, I said. He laughed, but he still wasn't getting it . . . I told him about us, Tom."

"You did *what*?"

"No names. I just said: Mr. Patinkin, take a look around, would you believe there's a person in this room, a wealthy, well-respected member of society, who hired me to fill in his wife's boyfriend? The hit's scheduled for later tonight. You spot him? Well, that's my exact point. Now look in my eyes and tell me what you see."

Victor took off his glasses, trapping one of the metal stems in his mouth. He smiled at Tom.

"Are you asking me?"

"You shoulda seen his face. I wanted an autograph for one of my boys. Patinkin was real nice about it, but you could tell, the prince of villains couldn't wait to get away."

"You really are crazy."

"I'll be honest with you, Tom, things didn't go strictly to plan. Your wife was with Haynes. Seems like they decided to pull a scoot after all. We had to improvise, but I'm here to tell you the problem has been taken care of . . . permanently."

"What about my wife and son?" Tom demanded. "Where were they when this was happening?"

"Never in any danger. She knows what went down, but she wasn't in the house, she saw nothing, the boy neither. She should be on her way home by now."

Tom thought for a moment. Victor was lying. There could be more than one reason why. "She'll go to the cops."

Victor smiled again. "Now you know better than that."

"Why didn't you wait until he was alone?"

"And let them get away?" Victor's eyebrows went up. "Is that what you'd've wanted?"

"All you had to do was keep a tail on them. What happened to that detective fellow? What happened to making this look like a fucking accident? Jesus Christ."

"With your son along, way too risky. Look, we'd known Haynes was going to grab the kid, it coulda been handled differently. What matters is we stopped him, we nailed the little fuck. Your wife believes his getting done was an 'enforcement' issue, to do with the loan. Naturally she's upset, but she'll get over it, and you come out of this smelling of roses."

"It's all screwed up, Jesus, but isn't it? You let those dumb animals of yours loose and they screwed up."

Victor shook his head. "And here I thought you'd appreciate what we achieved tonight. A job well done. As one businessman to another, I have to say, partner, I was hoping . . ."

From the base of the cliff came a sudden boom of surf as the wash of the long-departed freighter broke on the shore and was sucked back through the tumbled-down masonry blocks of the old sea wall. Victor paused, waiting for the roaring to abate as if it were the applause of a crowd.

"I was hoping you'd show a little more gratitude for getting your boy back safe and sound." Breathing on his glasses, rubbing them on the sleeve of his jacket. "What a terrific kid you got there, Tom. You must be real proud of him."

He held the lenses up to the lighted windows of the house, then put them back on. "Your son and heir."

Tom sat staring ahead, one eyelid tremoring at the dulled periphery of his vision. He'd seen it coming, seen this monster dimly taking shape around him. But had been reduced in his impotence to thinking that if he only denied it light, it could never happen. Even as the implications of Victor's wheedling rebuke slowly sank in, he still believed the world could be put back the way it was, the equilibrium of their lives at Edgewater magically restored.

"What the hell do you want?" he burst out.

"What do I want?" Victor leaned forward and, lifting himself from a crouch, went around behind Tom's chair. "What do I want?" He put a hand on his shoulder and bent down. "How about everything you've got?" he said, close to his ear.

Tom gave a scornful laugh.

The collector laughed with him. Then he stood back and, holding out his hands, palms to heaven, turned slowly on the spot. "Everything. House, gardens, stables, the beach, this croquet lawn, this view, this . . . beautiful life of yours."

The smile fell through a trap-door.

"Only kidding."

Tom scrambled to his feet. "Where is he?"

He came at Victor. "Where's Doc, you sonofabitch?" He stood over him, swaying too much to be a threat, his big fists clenched at his sides. "Where?"

Victor said, "You open to a piece of advice, Tom?"

She rises toward the surface.

Drawn by a far moonlike glow that comes slowly into focus as the deadlight over Joe's workbench. She remembers the voice from the Suburban, the miraculous small clear voice.

"Can we go home now?"

The car door slamming shut.

She sinks back, unable to move for the ropes, the stirrups, the ties that bind her.

They didn't have to hit her so damned hard.

"Can we go home now?" The boy's first words float past again on a swirl of ether. "My dad will be worried about me."

Her tear for his safety gives her strength; she breaks her bonds, the shroud flies from her knees . . .

His dad.

Opening her eyes, Karen lifted her head from the concrete floor and listened. They must have gone. The silence in the garage was deep enough to convince her that she was alone. Only a faint hissing sound came, or seemed to come, from the apartment above. When she sat up, her head swam and she realized the ringing was in her ears.

She felt the side of her face, her temples, the back of her neck, finding tender places but no evidence of real damage. Now she wasn't sure that one of the mutes had knocked her down; she could have fainted, hit her head in the fall. She

crept forward on all fours, groping in the dark, hampered by
her ball-gown and her bare feet, which kept getting caught
in its torn trailing hem. Her shoes were still upstairs.

They'd taken them from her just before the killing.

The details of what happened flooded back—the last she
remembered was being muzzled by the slimy gag of Donut's
tongue. She shuddered. Was it only her mouth he'd violated?
The thought made her skin crawl. Sick with apprehension,
she slipped a hand between her legs.

Thank God, she heard herself moan in the darkness.

Joe had gotten there just in time, hadn't he? The present
came rushing up like a wall. They'd taken Ned.

That was all that mattered.

Another sound, the slow steady drip of water on metal.

Karen stopped dead, holding her breath. A leaking pipe,
she decided, nothing more.

Pulling herself up on the tailgate of the Volvo, she leaned
against the rear window's coldly comforting glass. There was
no telling how long a start they had on her. She only knew
that she had to get after them and that every second counted.
Still not steady on her feet, she felt her way along the body
of the station wagon as carefully as if she'd been standing on
a high ledge, until she reached the driver's door.

It was locked.

She tried the car parked next to hers that must have belonged to the detective. Also locked.

There was a light on in the hall.

Joe had gone upstairs to get something. She thought
she remembered hearing him coming back down again, but she
couldn't be a hundred per cent. Every place she turned, she
did so with dread, convinced she was going to find him lying.

Outside in the driveway she'd come across what might
have been signs of a struggle. It was beginning to look as if
they'd taken him with them.

Which meant Joe could possibly still be alive.

In the living room she kneeled down beside Hendricks's

body. Keeping her head turned so that she wouldn't have to see his mutilated face, she went through the dead man's pockets. She found a key-chain attached to his belt that snaked under him into the left back pants pocket. It took all her strength to push him over on to his side.

His head, when it rolled, gave a sticky squelch like a candy apple being lifted from a plate.

She worked the keys off the ring, then hesitated.

Look in my jacket pocket, Hendricks'd said.

Karen had an idea it might have been important. But she couldn't bring herself to touch him again. Just couldn't do it. She hoped the note was something he'd scribbled to his wife, and that when they found the body someone would deliver his last message. Collecting her shoes and pocket book, she ran back down to the garage.

The drip was hitting the Caprice's sun-roof, falling more frequently now; inside the car, its insistent tap-tapping seemed to echo her heartbeat. Karen hardly noticed. She turned the key in the ignition. The engine coughed, spluttered ominously, then roared into life, and she slammed the shift into reverse. She'd already started backing out of the garage when she remembered to switch on the lights.

The windshield was streaked like a delta with rivulets of what appeared to be motor oil. Oh Jesus Christ, she breathed, don't let there be something wrong with this fucking car. Then, glancing up at the beam and board ceiling that also formed the floor of the living room, Karen saw the source of the drip. A dark, weeping stain that suggested the detective's head lay immediately above the spot where they'd parked his Chevy.

The wipers spread the blood into a thin even red film. She found the washer button and kept hitting it, in a frenzy of revulsion, trying to see through the clouded surface as the de-icing foam turned everything a sugary pink, before the windshield finally cleared.

By which time, doing fifty, she was almost to the junction

with Wheatley Road, trying to figure out which direction the
mutes would have taken in Joe's Suburban.

On the terrace at Edgewater, they were talking numbers. It's
only money, Tom remembered saying to Karen when he'd
danced with her at the party. Victor wanted twenty million
dollars.

At that price he couldn't afford to let himself dwell on what
the boy must now be suffering. In the end, there would have
to be a negotiated settlement. Or no deal. He knew better
than most the importance of keeping a level head.

"Twenty million?" Tom took a deep breath and exhaled
slowly.

He frowned, rubbing his chin and nodding as if he were
giving the amount serious consideration. "You want me to
hand over twenty million dollars. When you receive the
money, you return Ned. This is what you propose."

"You got it," Victor grinned. "A nice round figure, the way
it sounds is even good. Twenty million. But, hey, what is that?
What's twenty million to a guy like you?"

"I don't keep that kind of money lying around the house."

"You crack me up, Tom, you know? We're not talking you
have to deliver a sack of cash anywhere. We're talking about
a legitimate business transaction, all straight and above board.
The funds can be transferred to an investment company we
set up together, you and me, first thing Monday. We become
partners, Tom. Hell, we already *are* partners. You shouldn't
have any difficulty making a few assets liquid, and by Monday evening, if you and Karen cooperate, I guarantee you you
will have your son back, safe and sound."

"As if nothing had happened."

"You took the words out of my mouth."

"And you expect me to believe this wasn't planned?"

"It was planned," Victor said modestly, "we just had to
move the timetable up a day or two."

"That could be quite a problem," Tom said. "You're saying this'll take forty-eight hours. Ned can't be away from

home that long. He has a condition that requires constant supervision, he needs all kinds of medication."

"I know about his 'condition,'" Victor laughed. "Kid's a little fucked up, Tom, that's all. He'll be well cared for, you don't have to worry."

Tom poured himself a brandy, then held up the nearly empty bottle to Victor, who declined with a wave of the hand. "I drink that stuff this time of night, I don't sleep good . . . it gives me nightmares."

"Another difficulty I can't see a way around," Tom said slowly, crossing his legs. "What you're suggesting is not actually feasible. Not in the real world. I don't have twenty million dollars and, even if I did, in these days of tight regulations . . . it just wouldn't work."

"Don't insult my intelligence," said Victor. "An hour ago we were at a party where all anyone could talk about was the killing Tom Welford made in Atlanta. Now I happen to have friends down there who're in the trucking business. They told me you came out of the Rolling Thunder deal with at least double what I'm asking."

"Well," Tom laughed, "I don't know where they got their information, but I can tell you it's way, way off target."

"Let's cut the crap, all right?" Victor turned slightly and fixed him with a hard stare. "It comes down to one thing. You wanna see the boy alive again, or not?"

Tom looked down at his brandy glass, examining the way the dark liquor clung to its sides as he swirled it around. "I'm sure we can work something out," he said, showing more confidence than he felt. "You have to give me a little more time here. I need to talk this over with my wife."

Tom glanced back at the house. He only had to think about Karen and his large hands would start to shake with the effort of controling his anger. But he couldn't blame her for everything that had happened. He wanted her to come home.

"Until she gets back—Jesus, I only have your word for it that Karen *is* coming back—there's not a lot of point in your standing there making threats."

Victor was silent. He stood with one foot on the parapet, hunched over, the thickest part of the night like a hump rising from his back.

"Mind if I use your phone?" he asked at last.

He picked up the mobile from the arm-rest of Tom's chair and punched in a number, then after a couple of seconds cut the connection. "You know what they got now? Bleepers for the hard of hearing. Ain't that something?"

Tom wasn't listening.

Half a minute later the phone rang. Victor leaned over and pushed the instrument toward him: "It's for you."

In random pursuit of the Suburban, Karen drove west on the Long Island Expressway, trying to ignore the voices in her head that kept telling her that she'd made the wrong choice, she should turn back.

Even if New York was where the mutes were headed, the odds against catching up with them, she knew, were lengthening with every mile that brought her closer to the city.

She caught a glimpse of herself in the rearview mirror, her pale tense face straining forward in the intermittent glare of oncoming headlights.

It was the thought of Ned, and Joe maybe too, in the hands of those animals . . . she had to try, she had to do something.

Coming up to Douglaston—less than fifteen minutes after she'd set out from the Wheatley Hills—Karen made up her mind that if she hadn't sighted the Suburban by the next exit, then she wasn't going to: better to turn the car around and head home to Locust Valley. She knew she couldn't handle this alone.

She didn't blame Joe for what he'd done. How could she, when it had been her idea? She'd told him, God help her, that they'd be out all evening. He must've gotten into the house through the french doors that opened on to the terrace. Just as they'd planned. It was her fault. She'd meant to ask him to return the key, but somehow hadn't had the heart.

She kept driving, afraid that if she turned back now, she'd miss that one chance. The traffic bound for New York was light, and with every car she passed Karen found it easy to convince herself that the next set of tail-lights, just up ahead, glowing red in the steadily narrowing distance, belonged to the Suburban.

The exit sign for the Cross Island Parkway North flashed by. She held her foot down, pushing the decrepit Chevy to its juddering limit, the needle hovering between 95 and 100. If she got pulled over by the cops or a state trooper, her decision would be made for her; she would know what to say. She gave herself another five miles.

But why had Joe gone back to the cottage? To pick up his things, Ned's security blanket . . . or was there something else? If he never got her message, he'd no reason to think that he was in any danger. He couldn't possibly have known, could he, that Victor's thugs would be waiting for him?

She went over again what had happened. The Disney tape on the stereo . . . louder when the car door opened, *I'll huff and I'll puff* . . . Joe promising he wouldn't be long, Ned's voice, Ned saying he wanted to go home, then the door slamming shut. They didn't try to stop Joe going upstairs. She'd listened to his footsteps in the hall overhead, hoping that he'd enter the living room and discover Hendricks's body. But he only got as far as the bedroom. That was when she heard the door of the Suburban open and quietly close again, and knew that Roy Roy was in the station wagon, alone with Ned.

Waiting, presumably, for Joe to come back down.

She'd struggled her hardest to get free then, and either Donut had hit her, or she'd fallen, but there was nothing more that she remembered.

No words were spoken.

The childish whimpering at the other end was instantly and chillingly familiar.

Tom waited, his jaw muscles bunched, breathing through his teeth. It had started to rain. He hardly noticed.

Nothing could have prepared him for the sudden howl of pain and terror that burst against his ear.

Victor's eyes were on him.

His hand shook a little as he released the talk button. It seemed as if the scream went on, an echo that carried faintly across the Sound. He hit the button again.

"Wrong number," Tom said with a careless shrug, then sat back in the chair so that his face was in shadow.

Victor removed his glasses and pinched the bridge of his nose. His deep voice fell softly.

"Let's take this step at a time, Tom, shall we?"

2

"I gotta tell you something," Victor said, shaking the water from his clothes. He put his head on one side, stuck the stump of his middle finger in his ear and wiggled it vigorously. "Earlier in the week, Wednesday maybe, your wife was down the Village food shopping at Balducci's—"

"Tell me where they've got Ned," Tom broke out, leaning against a pillar for support while he caught his breath. "Tell me. Or I swear I'm gonna beat it out of you."

They were standing just inside the breezeway, out of the rain; in the few seconds it had taken to run in from the terrace, the two men had become drenched.

Victor laughed. "She's waiting in line at the meat counter, right, when these two bulls in uniform come strolling through the store. The way they're sniffing around the radicchio and the cumquats and what-have-you you can't tell they're getting ready to bust the joint on a violation, or buy something for dinner like everyone else."

"What the hell you talking about?"

"No, wait, Tom, this is pretty fucking funny," Victor went on, his glasses beaded with moisture. "So now the manager, all nervous and oily, comes over and says, 'And how may I help you gentlemen?' The cops exchange a look and one of them getting his courage up goes: 'I was wondering, ah, you happen to carry any like exotic meats? Such as buffalo, or lion.' "

"You crazy sonofabitch, where is he?"

"I'm serious. Lion! King of the fucking jungle! Lion-meat for New York's finest! We're talking about fucking Balducci's here. The manager doesn't miss a beat, he just says, 'No buffalo today, gentlemen. 'Fraid we're fresh out of lion too. But if you'd care to step over to the fish counter, shark can be very tasty.' " Victor was laughing so hard he could hardly get the words out. "Shark!"

"Karen found this amusing? Frankly, I'd be surprised."

"She'd already gone. Given our man the slip. The moment the cops walk in, she's out of there. Eddie let himself get distracted again. Between ourselves, I was doing the guy a favor using him for this kind of work. But like you said, your wife has a guilty conscience."

"I don't get it," Tom frowned, looking fixedly at Serafim, wanting to give the impression of being drunker than he really was. "What does this have to do with the boy?"

"Nothing. Everything."

"He's somewhere close, isn't he?"

"Shark," Victor said, no longer laughing, "also happens to be the name of my yacht. Funny coincidence, right?"

"Your what? You trying to tell me he's on a boat?"

"A 35-foot half-cabin cruiser, one previous owner, signed her over to pay off a debt. You think I'd pick a name that fucking cute? You're not much for sailing, Tom, are you? Me, I love to be on the water."

Tom, silent, stood staring out at the rain. The downpour had come at last without any warning. The sky had opened up, no monitory rumble of thunder, not even a glimmer of lightning—just the rain suddenly roaring down out of the blackness. He watched it batter the dust-dry earth and withered clumps of Mediterranean shrubs in the knot garden.

A smell like sulfur thickened the air.

"See that mooring light out there?" Victor was pointing in

the direction of the Temple. The cloudburst had reduced visibility to a few yards; Tom could hardly distinguish the outline of the headland, but he nodded anyway.

"She's tied up to the end of your dock. They're watching us, Tom. They got keen eyesight. Strange, isn't it, how nature makes up for some of its defects, and not others?"

Tom stared at him. "I suppose so," he said without any expression.

"Anything happens to me, understand, you let anything, anything at all slip . . ." Victor drew the stumpy finger across his throat.

"You already made your point."

"I hope so, Tom. Because that's a real nice kid you got there, and in the human kindness department, my boys are one hundred per cent deficient. You know what I'm saying? Morally challenged, otherwise fucking abled?" He laughed again. "But then you could say they never had a fair crack of the whip.

"You do the right thing, pal, and Doc's got nothing to worry about. Just don't go getting any bright ideas."

They were relaxed now. Different people.

Sat across the table from each other in the saloon, hunched over a game of magnetic checkers, smoking, enjoying a couple of beers, as if nothing had happened.

They even threw Joe a cold one.

It was the mood swings he had to watch. There had been no further attempt at communication. Donut would glance at the brass clock on the wall behind the ladderway, looking right through him like he wasn't there any more.

They were waiting: every few minutes, taking it in turns to go up on deck with the binoculars and scan the house and grounds from the topside pilot seat.

Joe wondered what more he could have done.

The boy lay beside him on the gold plastic-covered couch, his head buried in a pillow; the sobs that had racked his small body had eased at last to a fitful trembling.

He told him not to be afraid, he was safe now, everything was going to be okay. He promised, knowing how empty it sounded, that he wouldn't let the bad guys hurt him again.

A child's cry often sounds worse . . . He imagined Tom trying to comfort Karen. She'd be sick with worry, but she was bound to realize that he'd taken him. They were still in this together.

Joe asked Ned where it hurt. If he gave an answer it was drowned by the noise of the rain drumming on the overhead decks.

Ned wouldn't talk now. His dark eyes had withdrawn into that glassy far-off stare he used to punish them with on his mother's afternoon visits to Overbeck. Awkwardly Joe stroked his hair, feeling their son shrink away at his touch—as scared of him, he realized, as he was of the others.

He never saw what they did. There were no cuts or bruises, no marks on his skin. After the phone rang—two rings, and he'd picked up—Donut had grinned and taken the instrument from him. Then, putting on a creepily saccharine mime of a small, frightened boy calling home, had beguiled Ned past the galley into one of the staterooms. Caught off guard, Joe had been about to follow when he heard the scream. He'd sprung up, hurled himself after them, but Roy Roy, who'd stayed in the lounge, had calmly hooked him back into his seat using the claw-end of the tire iron.

He understood then how it was going to be.

"Who else is there in the house?" Victor asked casually as he led the way down the hall, making for the library, showing that he knew his way around; he didn't need to be told that Thurston and his wife had the weekend off.

He even seemed to know where they'd gone in Jersey. The thought occurred to Tom that he'd sent them away himself.

"What about Mary Poppins? The nanny with the nice tits. She still up in her room? Why don't you ask her to come down and join us for a nightcap?"

"You really think that's wise?" said Tom. In the half hour

since he'd talked to her, he'd hardly given Hazel another thought. Now he saw in the girl's undisputed loyalty to Ned a chance of gaining some time, even a little leverage.

"All right," Tom shrugged, "if you insist. She's probably asleep, but I'll run up and . . . What do I tell her?"

He turned and started back toward the stairs.

Victor, laughing, reached out and caught his arm. "What I meant, Tom, was for you to call her up on the phone. She's got a phone by her bed, doesn't she?"

"I believe so." Wondering why Victor would want to bring the girl into this—unless she were somehow part of the plan.

"Thomas, you old dog, you know she does." He threw him a friendly punch as they stopped in front of the mahogany double doors that led into the library.

"You give her a tinkle now." He ushered him into the room with an absurd flourish. "Oh, and mind you tell her not to touch any of the lights on her way down. Nothing on, nothing off. You got that?"

Tom sat on an arm of the white sofa.

The insolent way Victor stood in front of him with his back to the fireplace, clearly aware of usurping his position, suggested another possibility. What if he saw her as a loose end and simply meant to kill her? Tom picked up the telephone and pressed the button on the intercom panel for the night-nursery and nanny's room.

On the third ring Hazel answered.

He sank down into the sofa's deep pillows, burying the receiver in his shoulder so that Victor couldn't see he had it clamped not to his ear but flat against his cheek. The ivory phone was the old-fashioned kind made of heavy-duty plastic that doesn't broadcast the other party's voice.

He talked right through the nanny's dazed and frightened-sounding "Is that you, Mr. Welford?", looking Victor in the eye and saying with the right ring of hesitant finality, "Nope, no one's there. She must have left already."

"Whaddya mean, she's not there?" Victor was instantly

suspicious. "How could she do that, just leave? Does she know the kid's missing?"

"My wife fired her earlier this evening," Tom deftly segued his reply. Through the bones of his face he could hear Hazel feebly protesting her presence.

"Karen told her she wanted her out of the house first thing in the morning. The girl probably thought why wait, why not just slip away and avoid any awkwardness. She knows there's trouble between us."

"Well, I'll be damned, I was right! You've been banging the help. Naughty boy, Tom." Victor gave him a finger-wagging look. "You been taking your spoonful of sugar from Mary Poppins. Is that it? That how you been getting even? So now we have your side of the story."

"You know, you're beginning to really piss me off," Tom said as he hung up the phone. "I'm not into 'banging the help,' as you put it. I had to stop Hazel calling the police."

"Yeah? What did you tell her?"

"That there was nothing to worry about. I told her my wife had probably taken Ned up to town."

Victor nodded. He was quiet for a moment, then came over to the side-table and picked up the phone.

"Mind if I try? It's not that I don't trust you, partner, but you never know, she might have stepped out for a minute."

Tom waited, wondering if Hazel had gotten the message, if he'd been explicit enough in his attempt to warn her.

"Even nannies sometimes have to answer the call of nature."

But there was no answer.

Out the window of the Caprice a forest of white crosses flickered through the highway divider. Karen sped on past the dark rolling fields of Calvary Cemetery, knowing that she had no hope now of catching them.

A mile from the last exit before the Midtown Tunnel, she slowed down for the overpass. The glittering towers of Manhattan rose on the horizon, startlingly close. She saw no build-

ings, no city ahead, only dense thickets of light drawn up before her to form an impenetrable barricade.

There was a phone in the detective's car. She reached for
it and dialed 911. She told the Emergency Services operator
that she wanted to report a kidnapping. Then opened the window, letting in the drumbeat of the night. Ned is out there,
she cried into the phone, he's four years old.

It was while she was waiting for the police to come on the
line that Karen changed her mind.

There *had* been something else.

When Joe had driven up in the Suburban, she remembered now, Donut had looked at his watch; she'd noticed the
luminous dial out of the corner of her eye. Maybe she was
being paranoid, but it was almost as if he'd been checking to
see whether Joe was on time. As if they'd been expecting him.

She hung up the phone.

She put on her turn signal and with a long, drawn-out
squeal of rubber pulled over into the feeder lane for the
Greenpoint Avenue Exit. The voices in her head telling her
she should have trusted her instincts, she'd have to drive like
the wind now if she wanted to get home before it was too late.

"Where the hell is she?"

"Relax, partner."

"You know what time it is?"

"It won't be long."

Tom got up and, going around behind the sofa to the
drinks table, poured himself a couple of fingers of malt
whiskey. From force of habit, he held the decanter up to his
guest.

"Well, maybe just a small one. You got any Chivas?"

He carried a tumbler of blended Scotch over to the armchair Victor had settled in by the fireplace. He saw no point
in wasting the good stuff.

"It's a ten-minute drive. She should be here by now."

"Relax, will ya?" Victor growled. "Your wife could be a little distressed after what happened, that's all. You know what I'm saying? She won't be long."

Tom walked across to the library windows and stared out through the rain, then turned away. He had to stop himself thinking about Ned, how desperately afraid and alone the boy must be feeling. There was no sign of Serafim's cabin cruiser, no light off the end of the dock that he could see.

"You're not telling me everything," he said quietly.

"What's that supposed to mean?"

"Your story about Karen not witnessing . . . not being a witness to the killing. I happen to know she was there."

"Sure she was there, nobody's denying it." Victor took a sip of his whiskey. "Depends though what you mean by witness."

"It was done in front of her eyes, you sonofabitch."

Tom came back and stood over Victor's chair and looked down at him. "You know how I know this?"

Victor shrugged, as if he couldn't have cared less.

"When I got home and discovered that they'd taken Ned, I called Overbeck. Who d'you think picked up the phone? I got my wife screaming there's been a murder, pleading with anyone listening to call the cops. She sounded a little distressed, Serafim, you're right about that.

"But you know something?"

Tom paused, searching Victor's stony face.

"Not distressed enough. Not really. Not for a woman who's being forced to watch the life go out of someone she loves."

"The fuck you talking about? I told you already, we took care of the problem. You want proof that Haynes is dead?" Victor jumped up. "Here you go, pal, here's proof!"

He slipped a hand inside his sodden dinner jacket and for a second Tom thought he was reaching for a gun. Instead, he pulled out a small package, which he tossed on to the low glass table in front of the sofa.

The zip-lock sandwich bag landed with a soft plump on a pile of illustrated art books; the one uppermost, a Picasso monograph, showing a detail from the *Three Dancers* on its cover. Tom had an impression of anemic tissue stewing in its own bloody marinade; the frayed caul of white skin and flattened hairs molded into the shape of the bag's clear plastic corners. He looked away before he would be forced to recognize what part of the human anatomy it contained.

"Something else you can't get at Balducci's," Victor laughed. "Not squeamish are you, Tom? I think a man should be able to face up to the consequences of his actions, don't you?"

"His wallet would have been enough," Tom said, convinced now that things must have gone badly wrong at Overbeck, and that Victor was trying to cover up a botched job.

"They took it off him while he was still alive," the collector went on, bending down to retrieve his forfeit, which had leaked a small mattery pool on to the book's cover. "He probably died of shock. You getting the picture now, Tom? Or you want me to spell out what'll happen"—his voice suddenly rose to a ranting shout—"I don't get a little more co-operation around here."

"But I am co-operating," Tom said evenly.

He had resumed what he considered his rightful place in front of the marble fireplace. Over the mantel, the softly lit painting of a hunter in a landscape by George Stubbs gave off its deep sheltering glow. He stood with his legs apart, balancing on the outside edges of his evening pumps.

"Ah, shit!" Victor had noticed the bag was dripping down the front of his tux, on to the antique Persian rug; he did a little jig as he held it away from him. "Where do I put this fucking thing?"

Tom didn't answer. It didn't matter that he couldn't tell whether the gruesome trophy had been cut from Haynes or someone else. He knew now for certain that it *wasn't* his wife's lover he'd heard being killed.

"Excuse me." The loan shark went around his back and threw the plastic bag into the empty grate.

"You ever light a fire here in summer? This kind of heat?" he said, straightening up, wiping his hands on his pants. "See, that's the kind of question the cops're liable to ask." Giving

Tom a sidelong glance as he returned to his chair and sat down. "I were you, Tom, I'd shampoo the rug too."

Victor reached for his glass. "Now why don't we talk about something pleasant—like how I'm gonna collect my bounty?"

Tom didn't answer, taking his time lighting a cigar. They still had Ned, of course. But now that Serafim and his thugs no longer enjoyed immunity, whether they knew it or not, they'd lost their only advantage.

"Before we go any further, there's one thing you ought to know," Tom said at last, exhaling a rich cloud of smoke. "Ned is not my son." He let the words hang for a moment, watching the loan shark's face, then took another puff. "You should really be having this conversation"—Tom turned and tapped his cigar ash into the fireplace—"with the boy's father. Understand what I'm saying, you piece of shit, or do I have to spell it out for you?"

Victor sat there, smiling, shaking his head.

"You think I didn't know that? I didn't do my homework? What do you take me for, an amateur?"

"You're out of your league, that's all," Tom replied calmly. "You ought to stick to what you know, Serafim: fucking over your defenseless nobodies out there. Raise the stakes too high, a door opens up in the green hill and you can go slithering straight down to hell."

"I'll take that chance."

"You didn't hear what I said. He isn't my son."

"I heard you," Victor sat forward, his hands clasped between his open knees, contemplating the stain on the rug, "but lemme tell you something. You're his father, the one that counts. Ask the boy, ask Doc, he'll tell you. You're the one that raised him from birth. You love him like a son, don't you? A man who tried to deny that would be guilty of the worst— and I know what I'm talking about—the very worst kind of betrayal."

Victor looked up, his dark Slav eyes behind their water-smudged lenses blazing with intensity. "I got two sons. God is my witness. If what I'm telling you now ain't the truth, may my sons drop dead with the worst things God can give to human beings."

"You're full of surprises." Tom gave a scornful little laugh and turned away. "It must be hard for you. One minute, to think you're this close to the haul of a lifetime. The next, boom, blown clean out of the water."

Victor said, "I have a wide experience of human failings, Tom, of human degradation. You have no idea how some people live, you can call it living. But you really disgust me, you know that? To stand there and say you're prepared to let the boy die, let him down like this, your only child, and for money you wouldn't even miss?"

"It's not an insignificant figure," Tom said, blowing another cloud of cigar smoke. "You prepared to discuss that?"

Victor was silent.

"I didn't think so."

Tom went over to the drinks table, and refilled his glass with whiskey and water. As he was putting the crystal stopper back in the decanter, he noticed a slight movement behind him; a change in the distribution of shadows at the far end of the hall. Reflected in the silver curve of the ice bucket, he caught a glimpse of Hazel tiptoeing down the steps into the porch.

Why in God's name hadn't she taken the back stairs, used the servants' entrance? Seeing her reach for the front door handle, he grabbed an ice-pick and started hacking away noisily at the almost melted block of ice.

"I did warn you," Tom kept talking while he worked, "when you first came to me with that story about loaning my wife half a million dollars, I warned you about Karen."

He threw down the pick, then added an unwanted chunk of ice to his whiskey. "It may be difficult for you to grasp this, but I no longer give a damn what happens to Ned, or his whore of a mother. Go ahead, break their legs, cut pieces out of them, do whatever it is you do. You have my permission. They're nothing to me any more."

He heard a small sound from the hall.

"What the fuck?" Victor came out of his chair fast and strode over to the double doors.

"Any luck it'll be my dearly beloved wife," Tom said drily, then turned, slopping his drink, so that he could look down the long dim hall. There was no sign of Hazel. "The dog, for Pete's sake. Hey, Bracken, here, boy!"

The old Labrador, emerging sleepily from its lair under the stairs, yawned and stretched, then let out a low growl as he sensed a stranger and came shuffling toward them, hackles raised. She was certain now to go to the police.

"What did I tell you?"

"Yeah, well it didn't sound like . . ."

"Bracken," Tom spoke sternly, "no way to behave."

The loan shark let the Lab sniff around his legs. Then bent down and patted its head while the dog sheepishly looked back at his master for reassurance. "We know each other. Don't we, buddy?" Victor said.

Tom had already moved away. "It seemed like a simple enough job," he said. Going back around the end of the sofa, he placed his glass on a silver coaster beside the telephone and sat down. "But you want a thing done right, these days, you really have to see to it yourself." He put his feet up on the table. "Not rely on some smalltime crook, some grubby little moneylender from Bay Ridge Bosnia, or wherever the hell it is you're from. Jesus Christ, what *can* I have been thinking?"

Behind his back, the flat, patient voice of the loan shark warned, "You're way out of line, Tom."

"Did I say I was unhappy about how things have turned out? A little messy, perhaps, but suddenly my conscience is clear . . ."

"Don't fucking push me, asshole."

"It wasn't Haynes I heard at Overbeck, was it?" Tom went on in the same railing tone. "Joe Haynes is still alive. You screwed up, fell down on your side of the bargain. The deal's off, partner." He reached for the telephone. "I'm calling the station house in Locust Valley to report Ned missing."

"I wouldn't touch that I were you."

A hand came down on the receiver. Tom looked around and started to struggle up from the sofa, but was arrested halfway by the coiled, nothing-to-lose look in Victor's eyes.

The chrome-plated .38 pointed at his head.

"You had your chance to do the decent thing," Victor said quietly. "It makes no difference how, but one way or another I always collect. You won't pay, we have to turn this back around. The way your wife wanted it from the start."

"Good God," Tom laughed. "You must know you can't take anything Karen says seriously."

"She knows what she wants. It ain't you." Sticking the barrel of the gun behind Tom's ear, Victor prodded him forward. "Get up off the couch, you fucking hump, on your feet."

Tom rose slowly.

"Start walking. We're going down the hall. You make a wrong move, I'll let you have it."

"I already told you," Tom said, when they reached the foot of the stairs, "if anything happens to me, the house and everything I own goes to the boy. She won't be able to touch a penny. She gets a small settlement. Nothing."

"Now you're calling ten million nothing?"

"This isn't going to do you any good. By the time Ned reaches his maturity, even if you live that long . . ."

"I'd worry about your future, not mine, pal." He motioned toward the stairs with his gun, but Bracken had come between them and was standing in Victor's way, growling.

"Tell the fucking dog to back off, Tom." He leveled the .38 at the old Lab's head, then put it up. "I got a better idea. Stick him down in the hole. He can be a witness."

Tom, taking Bracken by the collar, led him over to the basement door that was tucked away between the staircase and the dining room. He opened it and shoved the dog inside. Told him to stay.

"If you think that my wife . . ." He straightened up taking his time, conscious of Victor's gun pointed at his back. "No wait, wait just a goddamn minute here, you're not going to get me to believe that . . ."

He suddenly saw how it was meant to work, the way in which he'd been set up, how it must have been from the very beginning. It was as if the steps that disappeared into the darkness behind his dog's sullen, still trusting bulk no longer led down to the basement, but to the bottomless pit that had opened up under their feet.

He closed the door on Bracken's whine.

"Whatever else," Tom said grimly, "Karen is incapable of harming the child."

"You're the one that's to do him harm, friend."

Donut came in from his watch on deck soaked to the skin. This time he didn't rejoin his partner at the games table, but sauntered over to the couch. He picked up a towel, wiped his face and hands, then offered Joe a cigarette.

"Don't use them."

The mute gestured again, holding out the damp pack of Camel Lites, insisting.

Joe realized that to refuse again would cause offense, but he raised his hand like a Boy Scout. "I'm trying to quit."

He saw the listening look in Donut's eye turn dull. This was a prelude to something else.

Roy Roy, who had circled behind the couch, leaned a heavy elbow on Joe's shoulder. He laughed in his ear, then licked it. Joe squirmed away from him. Tiss, tiss. Roy's breath smelled like a fresh turd.

Donut beckoned to Ned.

"TInE to dO, 'oc," it sounded like he said.

Before he could object, the tire iron hit Joe solidly behind the ear Roy Roy had just anointed.

"We're gonna need a shotgun," Victor said, as he stepped back from the balcony windows overlooking the Sound. "Where do I find the key to the gun-rack, the one in the basement?"

"I'm surprised you have to ask."

"Don't fuck with me, Tom. This is your decision."

White gauzy curtains billowed up, briefly enveloping Tom's sweating face. He brushed them away. "It should be in the top drawer of the bureau . . ."

"Hands where I can see them."

". . . in my dressing room."

"Where the fuck is that?"

Tom inclined his head. "Through there."

He was made to lead the way, hands behind his neck, fingers laced. Ahead of them, the door to the bathroom was half open. He could see the gleaming chrome skeleton of the showerstall and beyond it the closed door to his dressing room.

He was looking for something in their path, any kind of object he could use as a weapon. He remembered a pair of scissors in the bureau where he kept the keys to the gun rack. But which drawer? The sweat stung his eyes.

They advanced slowly across the tiled floor of the bathroom. Karen's things were lying everywhere.

"I happen to like my life," Tom said, as they reached the dressing room door. "Why would I want to pull a crazy stunt like this? I'm not the type to kill myself." He was playing for time. "Besides, no one will believe her."

Victor had stopped a couple of paces behind him. "It's not too late to change your mind. Now bring your hands down slowly and ease open the door."

Tom shook his head. "You're making a mistake."

"You think so?" Victor gave a short laugh.

"Karen'll never hold up her end of the deal. She'll give you the same kind of screwing she gave me, she gives everyone."

"Open the fucking door, Tom."

In the confined space, between the showerstall and the wall, there wasn't room for Serafim easily to get by him.

"Or you'll do what?" Tom asked over his shoulder, keeping his hands behind his head but loosening the weave of his fingers. "Shoot me in the back? With *your* gun?"

Tom began to whistle. An old Andrews Sisters number,

"Rum and Coca-Cola," he remembered from childhood and had heard the band playing earlier at the dance.

"Open it, or you're dead. You are fucking DEAD."

Victor's anger, barely under control, was like a third presence in the room.

Tom went on whistling, deliberately taunting him.

"Shut the *fuck* up!"

He felt the gun jammed against his ribs.

His mouth dried. The air that came out hadn't enough shrill to carry the tune. Where it should have dipped down on the last mocking line, about working for the Yankee dollar, Tom murmured, "You got any other requests?"

He turned his head. Victor's face was a mask: the canted eyeslits black and empty behind his shining glasses.

"We're two of a kind, Tom," said Victor, as he skewed the muzzle of the .38 into his spine. "When I have your money, we'll be the same person. Nobody will be able to tell us apart. It'll be like instant reincarnation. The door."

Tom, his back rigid and alert, didn't move.

"The *door,* Tom."

Victor tried to push past him on his right side, not noticing that the tiles around the base of the stall were still wet from Karen's shower, treacherously so.

He threw out a hand to catch his balance.

Tom swung around, getting the whole weight of his body behind his elbow as he smashed it into Serafim's face. He gave a surprised grunt and stumbled sideways. Catching his gun-hand at the wrist, Tom knocked it against one of the cage's chrome struts and kept knocking it until the hammerless .38 clattered to the tiles. He kicked it away, giving the loan shark time to get a leg behind him and, capturing Tom's throat with his free hand, topple him backward. They hit the floor together. Tom was heavier and rolled on top, but the older man didn't lessen his grip. All the power in him surged up through his fingers, his teeth cracking from the effort.

Blackness rolled in behind Tom's eyes. The choking pain in his windpipe galvanized him. He clubbed down blindly with his fist, and connected with Serafim's warm fleshy neck. The loan shark made a grating sound and the pressure from his fingers eased long enough for Tom to fill his lungs. Picking up Serafim's head by an ear and a handful of his thick lacquered gray hair, he banged it back down as hard as he could on the tiles. The fingers at his throat went slack and he wrenched himself free. Diving after the .38, he snatched it up and scrambled to his feet.

"I have the right," Tom gasped, backing away. "Don't think I won't . . ." He was panting like a dog just to breathe. "You took a wrong turn at my gate, *pal*. Now do yourself a favor, get the hell out of this house."

Slowly, painfully, Victor pulled himself up by the frame of the shower. He was an old man suddenly, his mouth cut and sagged but still smiling—the nervous smile that comes and goes—as he limped toward him.

Tom pointed the .38 at his chest.

"You haven't got the balls," Victor sneered. The glasses gone, his eyes like some primitive cave-dweller's were weak and bluish, burning now with the low flame of ancient hatred as he kept on coming. "Do you?"

He held out his damaged hand for the gun.

3

She came in out of the rain and kicked the front door shut with a satin heel, leaning for a moment against the heavy paneled oak while she waited for the world to stop spinning.

She'd heard a muffled echo that might have been a door closing in another part of the house. After her breakneck ride, her heart still pumping adrenaline, Karen found the silence disconcerting. The house seemed suddenly enormous.

She wasn't sure what she had expected: that somebody would be there to meet her? Who could tell her don't worry, Mrs. Welford, everything's going to be fine?

Now that she'd come home.

Ned is here. He was here all along.

Looking down the long empty hall, she noticed that the french doors leading on to the terrace had been left open, admitting occasional spits of rain and the faint but still defiant pulse of music from the party across the bay.

She wondered if that was the way Joe had let himself out, carrying their son still half asleep in his arms.

She moved toward the stairs.

A child's voice in the dark was all she'd heard. How could she know for certain that it had been Ned's? After so long and profound a silence? She wanted desperately to believe that somehow she'd been mistaken; that if she ran up to the nursery now she would find the boy tucked up in bed.

A dull gleam by her shoe halted her. She stooped down and picked something up off the floor: it was the broken-off arm and miniature stetson from the Remington bronze. She saw the horse and rider lying under the round table.

Karen remained crouched, listening now.

There was someone moving about upstairs; she heard the soft heavy tread pass immediately overhead, then, from what seemed a greater distance than was possible inside the house, a man's voice, calling her.

"Karen?"

She lifted her eyes to the landing, and caught a glimpse of Tom's smooth bare legs through the balusters that she once used to worry about the child slipping between. "That you, babe?"

She raised herself slowly, one hand resting on the table, the metal limb and hat concealed in her other palm.

Watching her husband come down the stairs. He had exchanged his dinner jacket for a dark blue toweling robe and tapestry slippers; his hair was wet and slicked back as if he'd just taken a shower, something he always did last thing, before going to bed. It occurred to her for a moment that perhaps he didn't know yet anything was wrong.

She came up to meet him at the turn of the staircase,

where he stood waiting. The look of strain in his large stolid face disillusioned her.

"Oh, Tom," she said miserably. "I'm so sorry."

"You look as if you've been through the wars." He frowned slightly at her stained and torn ball-gown.

She hesitated, then with a little cry folded herself into his arms. "I know what you must think, but I had nothing to do with this, with taking Ned. You have to believe me."

"What happened to the choker?"

She put a hand up to her throat. "They stole it."

He was silent.

"Tom?"

"Sure, I believe you. Why not? It's just that you looked a little surprised to see me." His eyes had a hard feverish glaze.

"I didn't think you'd be back from the party. Hold me."

He let her head fall on to his shoulder, but she could feel him resisting her, not letting her get any closer, refusing to be drawn into the intimacy of a pain she could share with no one else.

"Have you heard anything?"

"I've had a talk with your friend."

"What does he want?" She looked up at him, blinking back tears. "They're not really going to hurt Ned, are they?"

"You're asking a lot, babe."

"*I'm* asking? What do you mean?"

Tom cleared his throat. "I'm afraid it's rather more than I'm prepared to pay in the circumstances."

"You're just saying that, Tom."

"He tried his darndest to persuade me. Didn't seem any too bright, your Mr. Serafim. I had to remind him that it's customary in a kidnapping to negotiate with the parents."

She expelled a little air and, no longer able to meet his gaze, hung her head.

"I didn't know Joe would do this," she said at last. "I told him it was over between us, I swear to God. I would never have . . . I mean, right from the start, if I could have seen how much misery this would bring. It's my fault, not his."

"Spare me your dreary little mea culpas."

"You wanted a child, Tom, as much as I did."

"Almost . . . almost, but not quite."

"I only went to that dreadful place for your sake. I always believed it was wrong."

He smiled thinly. "You know what Dr. Goldstone was kind enough to say in your defense? He said that in some women the yearning to have a kid can breed desperation."

"I didn't know how to tell you I'd quit, not without hurting your feelings. I was afraid you'd be angry."

"You just decided to say nothing and seek alternative treatment. What do they call it—screwing around?"

"What happened was an accident. I never had any intention of letting Joe know that the baby was his. My getting pregnant seemed like a miracle. Like *our* prayers had been answered. It was what we both wanted, don't you see?"

Tom pushed her away from him.

"I thought I'd be able to handle it," she sobbed.

"But you couldn't, could you? No, you had to tell him. You had to go on seeing each other. Why deny yourself something that felt so right, so natural? You fucking *bitch*, you're lying. You're not half as crazy as you make out. You knew exactly what you were doing from the day we met."

She tucked her hair behind her ears. "I don't know what you're talking about."

"A divorce must have seemed too risky," Tom went on. "You wanted to be sure of having it all. Your lover, his child, my money. Of course, you had to wait until I'd learned to accept Ned as part of the family. Until I was ready. You showed me how, you were very patient, you taught me how to love him as if he were my own flesh and blood. There's something there that I find a little hard to stomach."

"Please, Tom." Karen sank down on to her knees, her dress puffing out, breaking over his bare ankles. "Please, this is not about us. This is Doc's life we're talking about. You've got to help him. He's just an innocent little boy."

"Why should I? Give me one good reason."

Lowering her eyes. "He's your son too."

"How dare you say that?" Tom roared suddenly. "How dare you?" He drew his hand back as if to strike her.

"Because you do love him," she whispered. Bowed and trembling, she waited for the blow. "Tom, please."

He unclenched his fist.

"Oh, that's pitiful." With a little scornful laugh, letting the hand drop to his side. "Look at you, look how much you want this. You got wide-on written all over your face, you whore."

Prostrating herself still further, she parted her skirts and kissed his feet, wetting his pale fine-boned insteps with her saliva and tears. She would do anything—she pleaded for mercy—anything, to save Ned.

"It's a little late," he said, as he took a handful of her hair and not without tenderness brought her head back up, "for all that, wouldn't you say?"

"I heard Doc speak for the first time tonight. Just before they took him. He said that he wanted to go home because his dad would be worried about him. He meant you."

She saw the look in his eyes, the fleeting haunted look that let her know she had reached him.

"He is home, Karen."

She felt the lethargic thud of fear. "What do you mean?" Her eyes wide.

Tom was smiling at her now.

A kindling of hope, as he took her wrists and gently raised her. "Come upstairs, I've something I want to show you."

The blue and white bedroom corridor at Edgewater ran with a break for the stairwell the full length of the house.

Its faded coir matting, the parade of identical louvered doors, the five ceiling fans with mahogany blades that paddled the dead air, belonged in her dreams to the cabin deck of an old Cunard liner: Karen would find herself creeping along here in the dark, feeling her way, trying brass door-handles that refused to turn, looking for an exit. The dream always ended with the discovery that she was too late, the ship had already put out to sea.

They descended on the master bedroom. Over their heads, rain hammered on the black skylights.

At every step the corridor seemed to grow narrower. The walls, hung with prints of aquatic birds and naval engagements, pressed in on her. The floor became an oily swell that heaved under her feet. It felt as if they were making no headway. But Tom was there at her side, leading her by the hand. At the end of the hall, Karen could see through the cracked double doors of their bedroom that the light on the balcony was still on, as she'd left it.

He stopped short, outside the entrance to the bathroom, which was also accessible from the master bedroom and Tom's dressing room. This third door on to the hall was usually kept locked. Tom pushed it open.

The room was full of steam. Karen gave a little exclamation, seeing nothing, hearing nothing. The hiss of the shower, even in this confined space, silenced by the rain outside.

"Funny, I could have sworn . . ." Tom began, picking up a towel from the floor, but didn't finish his sentence. He went in to turn off the water.

"It's like a goddamned sauna in here."

She looked down and saw between his legs what appeared to be a hand sticking out beyond the end of the tub.

And then, as Tom stepped aside, the steam cleared enough to show her the rest of Victor Serafim's body slumped against the birdcage showerstall. She saw the blood, oozing from under the loan shark's waterlogged jacket, being diluted by the run-off and carried away down the drain.

"Oh, my God!" Her hand flew to her mouth.

Tom must have showered with him lying there.

The tiles, the ceiling, the clouded mirror over the sink were speckled with his blood; everywhere, in places you wouldn't expect it to reach, inside the tub, on the soap, the bottles of Floris bath essence, an azalea plant in the high window, Ned's Captain Nemo submarine, a branch of South Sea coral, on their toothbrushes . . . there was blood.

A shiny gun had been buried in his chest, up to the trigger-guard, in the wound it had made.

"Oh, my God, my *God!*"

"Rather shocking, isn't it?" Tom said, folding the towel and draping it neatly over the heated rail. "I never killed anyone before. But this was self-defense. What did you expect?" Tom, returning to her side, put an arm around her shoulders and murmured in Karen's ear. "That you'd find *me* lying there? Or did you leave those kind of details to the others?"

"What d'you mean? I think I'm going to throw up." She pushed him away, collapsing on to her knees beside the tub, but retching brought no relief.

"Where's Ned? You said he was . . ." Looking up at him. "What others?"

"Just told them to make it look good."

"I didn't tell anyone anything," Karen said, shaking her head. "I don't understand. What happened? What have they done with my baby?"

"When you got home all you had to do was pick up the phone and call the police. Tell them there's been a tragic accident. Wasn't that the idea? You just walked in and found me lying there with my brains all over the carpet."

"No, *no*, you can't possibly think that."

"Suicide," Tom went on, "while of unsound mind, isn't that the phrase? I tie a string to the trigger and chew on my trusty 12-gauge. No note, but at the inquest the grieving widow—that's you, honey—testifies that her husband had just received some upsetting news. The household is naturally devastated."

"We have to call somebody, Tom, we can't just . . . we need to get help." She struggled to her feet, then suddenly, re-membering the girl, said, "My God, where's Hazel?"

Tom ignored the interruption.

"How did he know, Karen? How did Mr. Serafim know I keep my shotguns in the basement, if you didn't tell him? He knew an awful lot about our lives, about this place."

"He came over once," she said, raking her hair and holding it back off her face. In her left hand she was still clutching the jagged arm of the bronco rider. "Darlene left him alone in the hall. He had plenty of time to look around. Or else . . ." She hesitated, hearing the doubt in her own voice. "I dunno, maybe it was the detective. The one that you had follow me. They murdered him, Tom."

He shrugged. "No great loss."

"He was decent, he tried to help me escape."

"Escape?" Tom raised his eyebrows. "Look, you don't have to keep this up. Why not admit it? You'd feel a whole lot better, if you came clean. You always do. When I told your friend in the shower here to go screw himself, he said, well, gee that's too bad, we'll just have to turn this back around the way your wife wanted it in the first place—he meant the plan you all dreamed up in the back of his Lincoln."

"No, not true. It was his idea. He tricked us. He stole back the money out of the locker, I told you. He did it so he could turn up the heat. So we'd have no way out."

"What money, Karen?" Tom looked blank.

"The five hundred thousand. The loan, for Christ's sake."

"He didn't lend you five quarters."

"What?" she gasped. "What d'you mean?"

"What would have been the point? There was no money, was there? The money never existed."

"Stop playing games, Tom." Karen felt her mouth dry. She clutched at the edge of the sink and held on. Wherever she looked Serafim's dead eyes seemed to follow her.

"You say you left a suitcase in a locker?"

"Yes." She found it difficult to breathe. The heat in the bathroom was suffocating.

"There haven't been lockers in Grand Central Station for what, fifteen years? Everybody knows that."

"Tom, I can't take much more." Breathing hard through her open mouth. "You've got it all wrong. He forced us to agree. It was the only thing we could do to get away from him. He threatened to hurt Ned."

"Oh," Tom said. "No contest, then."

She turned suddenly to face him, still leaning on the sink. "But I came to you, didn't I? I confessed, I told you . . . not all of it maybe, but the only thing that really mattered. I warned you that your life was in danger."

"You did," Tom smiled, "and I'm honored. It was one of your finest performances. There you are one minute spilling your guts in the moonlight. Begging my forgiveness. Half an hour later, you're back with the boyfriend you swore never to see again and I come home to find Ned gone and a guy in the garden asking me for twenty million dollars.

"That was being a little greedy, don't you think? What was the split, babe? I'm curious."

"It's not true, none of this is true," Karen wailed. "I know how it must look, but I had nothing to do with taking Ned."

"Don't lie to me, you bitch."

She flinched, as if he'd hit her.

"You and Haynes wanted money to start a new life, so you made a plan to kidnap your own son and hold him for ransom." His voice had dropped to a hard murmur, still the voice of reasonableness, but with an edge to it now that frightened her. "You planned it together with Serafim and his crew, set this whole thing up—the fake loan, the meetings in Central Park, the talking me into having you tailed; then there was the detective and his dirty tapes—you gave it your all, babe, and all for my benefit—the carefully presented 'evidence' that you were about to run, taking the boy with you . . . even down to the offer of a contract on your Mr. Nobody's life. How could a jealous jealous guy like me resist?

"Of course, if the ransom plan looked like hitting a snag, you always had this murderous little scheme as an alternative, something to fall back on."

"You tried to have Joe killed."

Tom laughed harshly. "I wonder what went wrong."

"Where's Ned? What have they . . . what have you done to him?" said Karen in fresh alarm. "I've got to talk to Hazel."

"She left already. You fired her, remember?"

The glass shelf under the mirror lurched out of kilter, she reached out as if to stop things sliding off—then the room began to turn, gathering a sickening momentum.

"Tom, listen to me." She closed her eyes, opened them again and saw behind her in the mirror her husband's sweating face, the lower half still masked by condensation.

"Ned loves you. I never told him anything about Joe. All he knows is that you're his father. He needs you, we both need you. Tom, please, it's not too late."

"No, you listen," Tom said, turning his back, "you listen."

He was over by the showerstall, bending down to retrieve the gun from Serafim's chest. She heard the squelch of gristle and bone as he tugged it free.

"Things could have worked out for you," he said over his shoulder, "if Victor hadn't screwed up. He wasn't in full possession of the facts. You really should have told him about Ned. You should have told *me*."

He held the barrel of the gun under the faucet in the tub to wash off the blood.

"Then maybe this whole wretched business could have been avoided. He tried to make out that he knew, but it was obvious he was lying. When I told the fellow that I had no intention of coughing up twenty million for a kid that wasn't mine, he got mad. It made him careless."

Slipping the gun in the pocket of his robe.

"You know what he said? By now, don't forget, he's also getting to be a little desperate. He told me I wasn't leaving him any choice. If I forced him to take the second option, they'd have to kill Ned."

Backing away, she turned and tried to run out into the hall, but he caught her and held her in his arms.

"Karen, Karen. It's this way."

He led her into the bedroom.

His vision cleared gradually like fog that lifts for a moment only to swirl thicker again. A secondary explosion echoed at the base of his skull. Joe felt waves of nausea sweep over him as he sat up, his fingers exploring the lump on the side of his head. His right ear was sticky with blood. The mute had judged the blow perfectly, struck just hard enough to immobilize him while his partner spirited Ned ashore. Joe wasn't sure how long they'd been gone. The *Shark* was still tied up with her port side nudging the dock. He could hear the drone of the marine drive idling below decks and the occasional creak of the landing stage's half-rotted timbers.

He looked around carefully, nursing his throbbing head, and made out Roy Roy's bulky form standing motionless in the companionway; the tire iron hung from his wrist like a cane.

"Can I get a drink?" Joe mumbled, his mouth full of cotton. "A glass of water."

There was no response.

He remembered the cigarette Donut had offered him and wondered if a smoke would have been a more acceptable request. Just thinking it made him want one.

Joe closed his eyes. "Maybe later."

He should have known better than to trust them. Should have known that once he'd served his purpose, they wouldn't hesitate to screw him. What other reason could they have had for taking Ned off the boat? Unless they intended to hand him back to Welford . . . which could only mean cutting him out, reneging on the bargain he'd struck.

Killing him after all.

"Hey, Roy!" He needed to get on a basis with the gorilla.

Presently, Roy Roy sauntered across the saloon and sat on a chair opposite the couch. He pulled an outsize Adidas sneaker up on to his knee, rested his chin on the curve of the tire iron and stared at Joe with tawny eyes.

Joe smiled. "You got pen and paper?"

The mute shook his head.

"I'll speak slowly, then," Joe said, putting exaggerated emphasis on each syllable. "This is not how it was supposed to be. I was told no harm would come to the kid. The man said that as long as I played ball I could be with Ned at all times.

Until the negotiations were completed. Then we would be free to go. That was the deal. Now what the fuck's going on, man?"

Roy Roy shrugged his bull's shoulders.

"Something's wrong, and you know it. Where's Victor? He was meant to be here by now. We need to find him and talk." Joe rose unsteadily to his feet. The pain spasmed down his neck making him wince. "Well? What are we waiting for?"

Roy Roy yawned and reaching out suddenly with the tire iron jabbed its curved end in Joe's stomach.

The wind huffed out of him. He doubled up and sat down again, then slid off the couch on to his knees.

"I know," he gasped when he'd found enough breath, "I know you're just trying to make me mad"—he had to hunch over, hugging himself, the deck a few inches from his cheek— "but I ain't taking this shit. Here's where I make my stand, Roy, where I go the distance."

Something had caught his attention.

He had no idea yet what he was going to do. But staying bent over, he wheezed, "Now can I have that glass of water?"

Looking up into the yellow stare. "W-A-T-E-R."

Roy stood right over him. For a moment, Joe thought he was planning to use the iron on him some more. Finish the job there and then. But the big neatly laced sneakers next to his face backed up and squelched away in the direction of the galley. Joe stayed on the floor.

What he'd seen under the couch was a ten-foot boathook.

Tom had to drag her over to the windows.

"They're still out there," he said, "the other two, watching the house. They've got Ned on a boat tied up to the dock. One of them's probably ashore, some place around the Temple or maybe closer. Watching the light you left burning on the balcony. Did he tell you what it's for?"

"No," Karen whispered, "I must have left it on by mistake. You know what I'm like, you're always accusing me of wasting electricity."

"Serafim knew where to turn it off, honey. How do you explain that? 'I'll ask you this,' he kept saying, 'one last time.' He couldn't believe that I wasn't going to pay, that I was really prepared to let Ned go."

"Are you, Tom?" Her voice shook when she added, "I know you, you don't have it in your heart."

"He couldn't see that a man in my position might feel justified in wanting to get even. All he could talk about was what *he* would do to protect *his* sons. Then he began to lose patience, and suddenly it all changed."

With an arm around Karen's neck, Tom reached for the light switch behind the curtains. "The sonofabitch started counting. He had the gun on me, Karen. Like this."

She felt the cold snout of metal touch her neck.

"ONE . . . 'When I get to five,' he said, 'you're gonna shut the light. You're gonna give them the signal to pop the kid. It doesn't have to be this way, Tom, it really doesn't.' "

"Why are you doing this?" Karen whimpered.

"TWO . . . 'The boys will know how to handle it. The way it has to look now'—these are his exact words—'is like a fucking Greek tragedy. You know? The loser who just found out his wife loves somebody else and that his son isn't his. You came home from the party with vengeance in your heart, Tom, and you killed the boy in a fit of jealous rage—then blew your fucking brains out. That how you want to be remembered?' "

Karen said, "Tom, stop, this is insane. You know I couldn't have had anything to do with . . ."

" 'Leaving your wife sole beneficiary.' "

"I couldn't, I couldn't possibly hurt Ned."

"The moment you got involved with these people, you put him at risk. You must have seen that if push came to shove they wouldn't share your inhibitions. Or were you too besotted to even think that far?"

Karen didn't know how to answer. She looked down through the rain that was beginning to ease off. There was a light at the end of the dock that could have been a boat.

"But at this point," Tom continued, "Serafim was pretty much running on empty. He'd made a mistake. Holding a gun on me that he knows he can't use. It obviously had to be one of mine to look like suicide. Where did I get to? Two, three? Anyway he interrupted the count: now we have to go back downstairs and fetch a suitable weapon from the gun-rack in the basement.

"The key's in the bureau in my dressing room. On our way through, he lets himself be distracted. I see my chance and take it. You know what I did, honey? I saved Ned's life. Saved our little boy's life."

"You love him, Tom, as much as I do."

"*Unless . . .*" His mouth was on her ear. "Unless, of course, it was all just a game and they don't really mean to kill Ned. Maybe Serafim was bluffing. You know, pushing me, taking it to the absolute limit. I mean he had to be, didn't he, with you and Joe involved?

"What if I had cooperated? What was the plan? You'd stick around here at my side, the loyal wife, until the ransom was paid, then join him and the three of you disappear?"

"There was no plan."

"THREE . . . You ready to call that bluff, then?"

"No, Tom, wait!"

"The mutes naturally never heard the shot. If they're out there, they're still waiting for his signal."

"What do you *want?*" Karen howled.

"FOUR . . . Beyond the pleasure of seeing you suffer, I want you to know what real pain is. Not the kind you indulge in, not those tidy little cuts you inflict on your far too willing flesh, not the kind you can control. The smart wounds. I understand now why all that started up again. It was on one of the tapes: '*How could you let him* do *this to you?*' Was your Mister Man a little reluctant to get involved? Did he need coaxing? Did you have to show him the claw-marks of a cruel abusive husband before he'd come to your rescue?"

"If I were to say yes, I mean, admit that in a way you're right . . . please, please, I'll do anything."

"All I want is to share with you the loss of what you stole from me. The pain that I feel, Karen, there's nothing for it."

"Won't you at least give Ned a chance?"

"*You* didn't. Now reach out and cut that switch. I want you to keep me company in hell."

"Home," Karen pleaded. "Home, Tom."

"What do you mean?" he laughed at her. "You *are* home."

There were vents somewhere close to the floor, a continuous whisper of air being extracted and replaced. Joe felt his sweat turn cold as he waited on hands and knees for Roy Roy to come out of the galley. The mute's eyes never left his face while he filled the tumbler until the water spilled over.

Joe kept talking, telling him about his hopes for the future, telling him about Karen and the boy, how they planned to find the last unspoiled corner of America and start a new life together as an honest-to-God family . . . telling him anydamned-thing while his hands, hidden from view, worked to free the boathook from the clips that secured it to the mahogany baseboard. He heard it clank down underneath the couch.

"It's not too late, Roy," he said, raising his voice, as if he needed to drown the noise. "You can still walk away."

Roy Roy frowned. Whether he'd picked up the vibrations, or some slight change in Joe's expression, he put the glass down on the counter and came slouching back to investigate. Joe waited until he was in range, then, sliding the boathook out from under the couch, drove the unwieldy lance up between the mute's legs. At the same time, he rose to his feet and yanked back hard with the long brass hook as it tore into the fabric and flesh of Roy's baggy crotch.

He gave a high whistling scream, then made a frantic grab for the shaft with both hands, letting the tire iron clatter to the floor. Joe twisted his end of the boathook and, taking advantage of his superior height, jacked up the angle to gain more leverage. He managed to drive the mute back a few feet toward the galley, far enough so that he could trap the tire iron with his heel and send it skittering behind him. But he had nothing to match Roy Roy's strength. Face contorted with rage, the mute began pulling himself hand over hand along the wooden pole, using it like a rope, coming for him.

You fucking dildo, Joe grinned, high on his own fear. He could hear waves, the wash of another boat, breaking along the shore. A second later, the *Shark* made a pitching motion that would have thrown them both off balance, but Joe was braced and, in that same instant, he suddenly let go the shaft. Roy Roy took a sideways step to save himself and fell backward clutching the makeshift harpoon.

Joe ran for the ladderway and, stooping to snatch up the tire iron, scrambled out on deck. He slammed the door to the saloon behind him and turned the key in the lock: it would give him a couple of minutes, not longer.

As he stepped off the transom on to a yawing gangplank made slippery by the rain, he saw the lights of Edgewater dip down behind the headland, and leaped for shore.

Tom took his wife's hand and gently, firmly, guided it toward the curtains. She tried to resist, keeping her fist tightly shut on the jagged piece of bronze, waiting for a chance to use it. But Tom still had the gun at her throat, and he extended the slender arm linked with his as easily as if he were coaching her in a tennis stroke or a new dance.

"Stop! You have to stop now. You know what we agreed, Tom, the safe word . . . HOME!"

"What're you talking about? You're crazy. Open your hand."

Outside, through the rain, Karen heard the static of a short wave radio, the watery sputter of wheels on gravel.

"Listen!" she said, and immediately regretted that she hadn't screamed for help at the top of her lungs.

Tom clamped a hand over her mouth and, moving quietly but fast, half marched, half carried her across the room to the opposite windows. Standing close to the wall so that they couldn't be seen from below, he let her watch the Nassau

County police patrol car sweep slowly into the driveway and come to a halt outside the front door.

"It's all right," Tom whispered, as the driver got out and stood looking up at the house, "I know this guy, he's a friend."

4

In the hall mirror Tom took the time to straighten his robe, adjusting the collar to hide the reddish imprint Victor's fingers had left on his throat, then stepped up closer to check for anything in his face that shouldn't be there. His eyes steady while he turned his head this way, then that. He inspected his fingernails—a smear under one of them looked like blood—while he prepared what he was going to say if somebody had reported a gunshot.

Dried already to a dark rust.

The door bell rang again.

"All right, all *right!*" He cleaned the nail with his teeth, ran a hand through his still damp hair; then, ordering Bracken whom he could hear growling in the basement to hold it down, opened the front door.

"This better be good, Charlie," he said to the elder of the two uniformed police officers standing under the dripping canopy of wisteria. "You have any idea what time it is?"

"Sorry to bother you, Mr. Welford." The cop respectfully tipped his hat. "I'm sure it won't be for long."

He was almost glad to see Charlie Kawalski, who'd been on the Locust Valley force for as many years as Tom had lived at Edgewater. A grizzled, slab-faced Polack with sloping shoulders and a beer belly, close to retiring now, he'd once stopped a runaway gelding for him in Skunk Misery Road and Tom had made a generous donation to the PBA that put him in good standing with local law enforcement.

Officer Kawalski had remained particularly well disposed.

"We have a, ah, complainant." Weary eyebrows going up as

a squall of rowdy voices blew over from the grounds of Nonsuch. "That is, a concerned young lady back there in the car says she works for you." He flipped open his memo book. Tom's eyes went beyond him and saw Hazel's white blonde head framed in the rear window.

"I seen her around the village, but I need you to confirm that she is in fact your son's nanny. A Hazel Withers?"

"Why, yes, of course." Tom hesitated. "Hazel worked here nearly two years. Is there a problem?"

Kawalski frowned. "She came into the station house around one fifteen, acting pretty upset. Talked mostly to my ah partner . . . this is, by the way, Officer Talese." Tom nodded at a small unsmiling woman with dark hair scraped back in a bun, her summer uniform losing its crispness in the rain. "Told her she'd been babysitting—Ned must be what, four by now?—when you came back from the party and found the boy was missing. What time would that have been, Mr. Welford?"

"A little after midnight." Tom pulled the door wide. "Come in, for Pete's sake, you're getting soaked." All three moved inside the doorway, but no further.

"She's not still worried about that, is she?"

"You mean you found him?" Officer Talese said.

"This is my fault." Tom rubbed the back of his neck. "When I looked in on Ned earlier, and saw he wasn't there— the nanny had been asleep—I guess I overreacted. I'd had quite a bit to drink. But then I realized my wife must have come home before me and taken him into the city. I assured Hazel there was nothing to worry about and she went back to bed."

Officer Talese said, "Wouldn't your wife have told you she was planning to do that? I mean move the kid so late? Wasn't she with you at the party?"

"Yeah, well, I'm afraid that's just the point," Tom said ruefully, "we'd had an argument. I don't think we need go into it. Everything's fine now, I called my wife at the apartment and spoke to her and Ned. They're *both* fine. She plans to bring him back out here tomorrow. So there we are."

Tom folded his arms across his chest. "One way or another, it's been quite a night."

When nobody spoke, he made a slight gesture toward the door as if to show that as far as he was concerned the discussion was over. Case closed.

"We'll let you get some sleep, then, Mr. Welford," Kawalski said, yawning and rubbing his eyes as he turned away, "but you understand we had to check this one out. With kids you can never be too careful."

"Appreciate it, Charlie, I really do."

Officer Talese stood her ground. "Your nanny mentioned there was somebody else in the house. She heard a man's voice down in the library and became concerned that he might have been threatening you in some way. She said it was why she felt she had to get out. She was afraid."

Tom laughed. "A friend gave me a ride home and came in for a nightcap. I assure you we remained on the best of terms. He left about half an hour ago."

At that moment there was a faint crash from somewhere deep in the house. It sounded like it came from upstairs, which Tom knew really wasn't possible, but he'd heard it none the less—the unmistakable sound of breaking glass.

He saw that the others had heard it too.

Under the bridge of her thighs, skirts fallen back, she could see a green lake advancing slowly across the tiles from the shattered bottle of Caswell Massey bath essence. Paris green, the label had said; the bathroom stank of pine forest.

Karen let her head sink back, exhausted by her efforts, her nostrils dilating as she tried to control her breathing so that she could listen. She was only able to breathe through her nose; her mouth, stopped by Tom's handkerchief and the rubber ball-gag he'd taken, along with a piece of silk rope, from what he called "the toy box" at the back of his closet, was stretched like a suckling pig's over an apple.

There were voices in the hall below. But she couldn't tell whether the impact had attracted their attention. Even in the bathroom, it hadn't seemed that loud.

If they'd heard something, the cops would ask to look around, wouldn't they? They only needed to come up the stairs to find her, and then she'd be able to tell them about Ned. Tom would deny everything, of course, he'd say she was crazy, make up some story. But the way he'd left her here—the loan shark's splayed hand inches from her face—they'd see for themselves she didn't imagine things.

Drawing her knees up to her chin, avoiding the shards and splinters she couldn't see but knew were everywhere, Karen twisted over on to her side. Then she pulled herself back by her aching wrists, which Tom had tied tightly to one of the main struts of the showerstall. As the pressure on her arms eased, she was able to slide her rope handcuffs up the two-inch thick chromed shaft and get back into a squatting position.

Only this time facing forward, the dead man staring at her.

Tom had made her put her hands through her legs before tying them behind her, so that her back was to the shower. The knots were, as always, expertly tied; but he'd been in too much of a hurry to secure her ankles and failed to notice that there was nothing to prevent her putting her head down and flipping over. By stretching out on the floor to her fullest extent, Karen had managed, with the help of a luffa gripped between her feet, to knock the bottle off the edge of the tub.

The maneuver had taken time, though, precious minutes.

She waited, listening, but the voices below sounded muffled and distant again, as if they'd all moved back out on to the porch, into the rain.

Please, God, don't let them leave.

In her right hand, she still clutched the little piece of bronze that she'd tried using earlier without noticeable effect to fret the rope. Its jagged end barely proud of her bent fingers, she went back to work with a growing, ever more frantic sense that her task was hopeless.

Any moment now Tom would be coming back upstairs.

Then something caught her eye: a long sliver of glass that had landed up inside the cage between Serafim's fanned-out dress cowboy boots. Karen saw at once that if she could only reach it, fishing for the razor-sharp spike with her toes, she'd have a more efficient cutting tool.

"She's okay," Tom said as he ran back up the steps, closing his umbrella and shaking it. The two officers stood waiting for him under the porch. "I think nanny just got things a little mixed up, that's all."

"She coming in?" Kawalski asked. "I mean, she still lives here, doesn't she?"

"There's something I ought to explain," Tom said. It had been his idea to go out and have a word with Hazel, just to reassure her that all was well.

"The girl is in an emotional state. My wife had to fire her earlier this evening."

He replaced the dripping umbrella in the hat stand.

"She already mentioned that," Officer Talese said. "She also claims you reinstated her, said the job was hers long as she wants. Didn't you tell her that your son 'needed' her?"

"Wishful thinking, I'm afraid." Tom shook his head. "I try not to get involved in domestic issues. Leave all that kind of thing to my wife. But Hazel has many good qualities."

Like loyalty and devotion, he thought, wondering about Karen and whether she could possibly have loosened her bonds.

He was beginning to get impatient.

He turned to Kawalski. "Charlie, do me a favor and see she finds somewhere to spend the night. I'd have her back here, but in the circumstances . . . well, you know how it is."

He cleared his throat, giving him a look that excluded the woman police officer. "I told her to stop by tomorrow so she can pick up her things, and say goodbye to the family. She was genuinely fond of the boy."

"Before leaving the house," Officer Talese remarked

coldly, "your nanny said she called the apartment in New York, three times, and got the answering machine."

"So?" Tom looked perplexed. "My wife told me she was going straight to bed. What are you trying to say?"

"Would you object to our contacting the NYPD and asking them to send a squad car around to your building?"

"Why, yes, ma'am, I would," Tom replied, "strenuously."

"Just to make sure they're okay."

"You have any reason for doubting my word?"

"It's not that, Mr. Welford," Kawalski intervened, "but me and my partner were wondering, ah, about that noise we heard earlier. You said you were alone in the house. You quite *sure* everything's all right?"

"To tell you the truth," Tom laughed, "I wondered too. That was protest, Charlie. I clean forgot, I stuck the damned dog down in the basement as a punishment. Sounds like old Bracken's been getting his own back. If it's the Château Talbot we heard hitting the deck, he's in serious trouble."

The two police officers exchanged a glance.

Behind them, the sporadic crackle of cross-talk on the car radio was interrupted by a thin insistent beeping sound.

"South boy south charlie we have a Ten Thirteen at Community on Landing Road, Glen Cove. Shots fired. Emergency Services on the scene. All units respond."

"Do you want to come in and take a look around?" Tom said.

Officer Talese gave him a long hard look, then turned and trotted down the steps, sidearm and night-stick bouncing at her round hip. She reached in the window of the patrol car and pulled out the handset.

"Five Eddy to Central, we're on our way."

Tom shrugged. "Another time, maybe."

"You bet. I'm real sorry about all of this, Mr. Welford"— Kawalski's chagrined eyebrows went up—"believe me."

His partner had the engine running and was already starting to pull away when Kawalski jerked open the passenger door and clambered aboard. Tom caught a glimpse of Hazel through the window of the patrol car, sitting there, head bowed, her heavy shoulders hunched. He couldn't blame her. She'd behaved exactly as he'd predicted she would. Wanted her to. She'd done the sensible and right thing in bringing help.

It was just that they'd arrived too late . . . or too soon, depending on how one looked at it.

Tom was still watching when the car reached the end of his driveway. He waited to see the beam of its headlights turn right at the junction with Lattingtown Road, then he closed the front door. And locked it.

Inside the hall, he stood for a moment and listened.

Joe kept his eyes straight ahead as he climbed. He didn't trust himself to look down, or back. He leaned into the cliff, feeling his way in the teeming darkness with hands and feet.

The steps cut in the soft rock-face were worn smooth and treacherously overgrown with weeds and brush. In places, the stone risers had crumbled away altogether and the narrow track reverted to a forty-five-degree slope that funneled the run-off torrenting down from the headland. It took him longer than he'd expected to scramble to the top.

He waited a couple of minutes, squatting behind a boulder, the tire iron gripped in readiness as he listened for anyone coming up the track behind him. Far below he could see the deck lights of the *Shark* glimmering at the end of the dock; there was no sign of Roy Roy topsides, or any sound of pursuit, yet he doubted somehow that the mute was still aboard.

He plunged on through the rain.

The track widened and became a grass path that was mown short and easy to follow. He jogged along the edge of the wood heading in the direction of the mansion house.

The lights of a car swung out over the headland. Joe ducked down as they came stabbing at him through a stand of Scots pine, and then almost at once were swallowed up. He couldn't tell whether the car had driven away from Edgewater, or the party next door. He started to run.

After twenty yards the dull ache in his stomach, where Roy Roy had hit him, sharpened to a stitch, and he was forced to slow his pace. Realizing how exposed he must be to anyone following, he left the path and turned in among the trees.

The last strand of the rope gave way.

Karen pulled one hand, then the other free and quickly undid the gag's rubber straps at the back of her head. Conjuring Tom's endless silk handkerchief from her mouth, she wrapped it around her numb, bleeding fingers. The glass hack-saw cut both ways, but there was no pain, no loss of function. She struggled to her feet, tripped over Serafim's legs and only missed going down on top of him by grabbing the showerstall. She had to come back around the body to lock the door on to the hall.

Then she ran into her husband's dressing room.

She knew how little time was left. She'd heard the patrol car drive off and guessed that Tom must already be on his way up. If she waited, delayed even a second, Ned was lost.

She tore open the drawers in the bureau, looking for the key to the gun-rack in the basement. There were bunches of them, all neatly labeled, color-coded, for Christ's sake. She swept up the lot, hesitated before switching off the desk-light—then cracked the door to the bedroom hallway.

There was no one.

She slipped out, closing the door softly behind her, keeping her eyes on the landing at the head of the stairs. She started to move along the empty hall, between the louvered doors, her bare feet soundless on the worn matting. If she could just get to the far side of the stairwell, where the hall dipped and snaked around into the warren of the nursery wing, before Tom came back up, she had a chance. Only the landing kept stretching away from her; there wasn't going to be enough time.

Fear sapped her will, making her drowsy. She wanted to run, but would've just as soon lain down and slept . . . knowing that what lay ahead of her and she was looking at, as if through the wrong end of a telescope, was certain disaster.

Hearing him now. His slow, deliberate tread.

She wasn't even halfway there, when she saw the back of Tom's head clear the banister. She froze, holding up her tattered dress to stop its rustling, as he mounted the stairs. If he happened to look round, it was all over: another five steps, fewer seconds, he would turn and see her anyway.

She reached for the nearest door-knob and tried to ease it open. Twisting it one way, then the other. Nothing. It revolved freely between her bloody fingers. The hairs on the back of her neck stood up. She tried again—Mother of God help me, I beseech you—feeling the icy flails of panic.

There was a half-second delay before it dawned on her that this wasn't one of the guest rooms but the housemaid's closet. She pulled the door open, holding her thumb over the spring catch to muffle the noise, and stepped inside and closed it behind her.

In the wax-scented dark, she crouched down to wait.

Listening to his footsteps as they came along the hallway, her eyes fixed on the section of floor she could see through the door's angled slats. There were spots of blood on the matting. Oh, God, the door-knob must be covered in it! She bound her fingers tighter in the blood-soaked handkerchief, Tom's cologne making the cuts come to life.

He was very close now. She held her breath, praying that he wouldn't look down and notice the blood. She got a glimpse of her husband's slim, almost girlish ankle . . . a tapestry slipper that stayed in the frame a second too long. Her heart hammered in her chest. But he kept going.

She counted the seconds.

The moment he tried to open the bathroom door and found it locked, he would know. She imagined him now, the look on his face. But first he'd have to go around through the bedroom to make sure she'd gone.

It'd give her a headstart.

The trees were becoming more spread out, the undergrowth less dense, as he worked toward the light. Hazy silver beams filtered through the clearings. He moved swiftly across them, joining one black shadow, then another. Ahead, he could see an expanse of lawn with steam rising off it like the surface of a lake, and the dark mass of the house beyond.

At the corner of the wood Joe stopped for a rest, and to listen. He leaned heavily against the trunk of a conifer, trying to steady his breathing as he wiped the moisture from his face. A smell of wet piny rot rose from the earth. He was about forty yards now from the west wing of Edgewater— back in the same spot where, two hours earlier, he'd smoked a joint before entering the house to take his son.

He watched the windows of the hall and library for any sign of movement downstairs. Even a glimpse of Karen would let him know how things stood with her and Tom. A number of second-floor windows were also lit. He thought he saw a shadow flit across one of them, but couldn't be sure. Immediately above the library, the master bedroom was in darkness.

The lamp burning on the balcony had drawn a cloud of moths and other insects out of the rain, extending to them the shelter of the awning. Joe was beginning to have doubts. If that had been Victor he'd seen driving off in the car, if some kind of deal had been struck, and they already had Ned back safe—then there was really nothing left.

The house looked so peaceful.

He felt his pockets for the keys to the Suburban. It'd still be waiting for him down at the boat basin in Sea Cliff, where they'd boarded the cabin cruiser. A four-mile walk. He could do it inside an hour. The wagon was all packed, ready to roll.

Maybe Karen had made the right decision. And this was where she and Ned belonged. A gilded cage, after all, had its compensations. From across the bay came the watery sounds of poolside high jinks, a series of dull splashes followed by girlish shrieks and braying male laughter. Rich kids. Ned would grow up to be one of them. There were worse fates. Joe was suddenly filled with deep loathing for Tom Welford and his magic fiefdom, this sterile little paradise stockaded against the real world by money and dread.

He hesitated at the edge of the short grass.

Some instinct held him there. Some sense of a presence that he could neither see nor hear. What if he was wrong about what had gone down?

He couldn't leave without knowing that they were okay. Run out on them now . . . could he? Just in case they still needed him.

Then he heard, distinctly, a thin piping sound like a high frequency whistle coming from the woods behind.

She was waiting at the bottom of the basement steps.

Holding the gun loosely at her side, pointed at the floor, half hidden in the folds of her dress. Tom recognized the silver chasing on the dark walnut stock; it was one of a pair of Greener 12-gauge double-barreled shotguns he'd bought at a Christie's sale, thinking they'd do Ned when he was older.

Karen stood with her back to the claret bins, her bare feet planted well apart, her eyes steady. He could tell she was out of breath only from the rapid rise and fall of her chest. He watched her bring the gun to her hip, break it open, chamber a couple of rounds and snap the breech. One of her hands was bandaged, but she didn't fumble. He'd taught her how to handle a gun himself, shooting skeet over the Sound from a trap on the terrace. Karen had proved to be a natural.

"I'm impressed," he said quietly, knowing he was going to have to reason with her, talk her down from the ledge, as it were. "Don't get me wrong, babe, but you look magnificent."

At the sound of his master's voice, Bracken, who'd been milling around at her feet, came to the foot of the steps and gazed up at him longingly, wagging his tail.

Tom descended further into the basement.

"Hold it there!" She leveled the shotgun at his chest. "Any closer, you take one more fucking step," she said, "and I swear I'll shoot."

"Mind if I say hello to my dog? You didn't like being stuck down here on your own, did you, Brack?"

She must have come the other way, he figured, run like hell

along the nursery passage and down the back stairs. The basement at Edgewater was extensive enough to warrant two entrances. At the service end of the house, outside the kitchen, another flight of steps led down to the furnace room and a series of grimy brickbuilt stalls used in earlier days to store apples and root vegetables as well as fuel for the open fires. The door that connected them with the wine cellar was ajar. He could see a bare bulb hanging in the gloom back there.

Tom took another step. "What's happenin', buddy?"

"I'm warning you, Tom!" She brought the gun up to her shoulder. "Don't make me do this."

The old Lab started painfully up the narrow stone stairs. Keeping his eyes on Karen, Tom slowly squatted down and reached a hand out to stroke the dog's head.

"Why don't you put that thing away?" he said, working his free hand into the pocket of his robe, sliding it around the grip of Serafim's .38. "Then we can talk. What happened up there . . . I was just trying to teach you a lesson, make you see the error of your ways. But you know I would never, never do anything to hurt Doc."

He saw her finger curl in behind the trigger-guard. "I can't listen to you, there isn't time."

Tighten. Squeeze. Just like he'd shown her.

"Jesus, hon, you keep doing that it'll go off." Tom started to straighten up, worried now.

"I do still care about you," Karen said, drawing a bead on what he guessed was his heart.

He heard the tiny click as she slid off the safety catch.

"Then we can work something out, just put the gun down. We've been here before, remember? When we first knew each other? You were doing all those crazy, self-destructive things? Maybe I was a little harsh, just now, accusing you."

"It was wrong of you," she said flatly, pulling the stock tighter into her bare shoulder. "I have to go look for Ned now. If you're not coming, fine, but don't try to stop me."

She took a step backward.

"Yes, it was wrong."

"Let's just call it quits, Tom."

"I can't judge or blame you for something you have no control over. I've never judged you. You wanted me to protect you . . . 'be my strength and my redeemer,' you said. Isn't that why we belong together? You need help now, Karen. I called the people at Silverlake. They're ready to have you back. Trust me, babe. You ought to get some rest."

He turned his head away, looked back at her, then, letting her see the revolver in his hand, took the last step.

"I'm not going back, Tom. I'm perfectly well."

Tears streaming down her face.

"But you pull that trigger," he said, on level ground now, the dog by his feet, "you shoot me, and it'll just go to show, won't it? They'll say I was the fool who married a murdering little tramp. She killed him for his money. Who's going to *want* to believe anything different? Now give me the gun."

She'd begun to move away, backing slowly down the basement.

"Give me the gun, Karen."

He took another step and she shot him.

Saying something at the same time, something he'd just turned his head to catch but that was drowned by the buffeting roar of the shotgun in that enclosed space.

He saw Bracken cringe, the twin orange tongues of flame that sprang from both barrels flinging the dog's shadow back against the wall.

Then he fell, still not believing it.

5

Wading up the Temple path through the rain, the shotgun sloped over her shoulder, Karen doesn't bother to hide. In plain sight, she knows they're certain to have spotted her by now. From the moment she left the house even. She's not afraid for herself; her worry is that they'll realize something's wrong and take off with Ned.

There's no strategy, no other way of doing this that she can see making a difference. She recalls the detective's advice, when he was trying to help her escape from Overbeck—get up into the woods, use the only advantage you've got: sounds have more substance than objects in the dark. Imagining he meant that the mutes would make indiscriminate noise moving through undergrowth, whereas she didn't need to worry.

She can just make out the Temple's pale outline looming ahead of her and behind it the seam in the darkness where the rounded knee of the headland bends into the Sound. Relieved to see the boat's mooring light still gleaming at the end of the dock, she considers leaving the path and approaching the Temple stealthily through the sycamore grove. Only what would be the point? They could be anywhere. But if Tom was right and they've got Ned on the boat and one of them has stayed with him, she has at least a chance of evening the odds.

Soaked through, her hair plastered to her head, Karen doesn't notice. Her dress clings awkwardly to her legs as she walks. She feels nothing. Numbed by what she's done.

She saw the devastating effects of the blast before she turned away. She saw herself . . . calmly reloading the gun, and walking back through the basement and out of the house. The ringing in her ears won't stop, which heightens her sense of detachment, of being invulnerable. She knows now that she can do anything, whatever it'll take to get her baby back.

One foot on the lowest of the Temple steps, she stands with the shotgun ready and calls his name.

The rain hammering on the green copper roof.

She calls Ned again, louder now, letting him know it's her. A fearless shout that in her ears carries no distance at all.

Then stops to listen, wiping her eyes with the back of her wrist, trying to see into the pavilion that gapes before her like the black damp mouth of a cave.

This time there's no mistaking the frightened cry, more the

whimper of an animal than of a child. It cuts straight to her
heart. But the sound is so weak and indistinct she can't tell
whether it's coming from the pavilion or some place else.

Don't look round . . . not yet, Karen.

It's no stronger, this other voice, little above a whisper,
coming from inside her head.

At the back of the Temple she sees something flit across
one of the faintly outlined arches overlooking the water.

In the same instant, behind her, there's a rustle of leaves
and what sounds like a branch snapping underfoot. She slips
the safety catch and wheels around, stares into the hissing
woods.

There's nothing.

"Take it easy now. They're both up there. Ned too."

"Joe?" Her heart leaps.

"Not yet, I said."

From the surge of joy and hope she feels, she turns back
again to see a dark bundle detach itself from the entrance to
the pavilion and come rolling down the steps toward her. She
brings the gun up to her shoulder, hesitates, thinking it could
be Ned, her child, in there.

The bundle unfolds at her feet. She takes a step backward,
then sees her mistake as Donut, lunging up inside the reach
of the long-barreled shotgun, gets a hand to her throat. He
takes the gun away easily and, spinning it around like a baton,
uses it to put her in a choke hold.

"Joe!" she screams. She reaches behind her and claws at
Donut's face, which doesn't distract him in the least from lac-
ing his fingers behind her head and exerting forward pressure while he pulls back with his forearms on the gun.

Giving her his full attention.

He doesn't sense the rush of footsteps behind them, or
hear the whistle of the tire iron as it comes down on his skull.

The pressure on her throat eases suddenly, but Donut
takes her down with him and for a moment they roll together
in the mud before he lies still.

Joe retrieves the shotgun, then helps her up and holds her.

"What took you so long?" she says, as soon as she gets her breath.

When you're shot you don't feel pain.

Tom had always heard this, and comfortably doubted it, never imagining he'd get the chance to find out for himself.

She'd shot him in the legs. At the last second, lowering her aim. She could have missed, or simply lost her nerve, or maybe she didn't mean to shoot him at all and the gun had gone off accidentally. But both barrels? He was prepared to give Karen the benefit of the doubt.

Not that it really made any difference.

Below his knees that were no longer recognizable as such, he could see how the buckshot had stripped back the flesh and muscle, blowing most of it clean off. His calves looked like raw drumsticks that have been gnawed to the bone. And the bones themselves were burst and splintered, sharp white ends coming up through the skin in odd places. His slippers, still on his feet, were all blood.

If he could view this so calmly, Tom decided, there had to be no feeling. He wondered for how much longer.

He was having to rest more often now.

The table and chair he was trying to reach, less than ten feet from where he'd fallen, never seemed to get much closer; the snail-like trail he'd left behind him on the painted concrete floor didn't look halfway yet. Above the table a phone hung on the basement wall. Beside it, the control panel for the alarm system and the three boxes of circuit breakers that served the whole house.

Raised on one elbow, and using his other hand for leverage, he dragged himself forward inch by inch, like a swimmer practicing the sidestroke on dry land.

He lay his face against the cold floor for a minute and felt the blackness go over his head like a wave.

Bracken was licking his hand, whining continuously. The soft flap of one of his ears was wet with blood, but Tom couldn't tell whether the old dog had taken some of the buckshot or whether the blood came from his own wounds.

She'd never much liked Bracken, which was something he'd always held against her. Ned loved the dog as he did, but whatever happened he wasn't going to see him again.

He saw the Lab lift its gray muzzle and test the air, suddenly alert, listening. Spurred on by the thought that he might be too late, Tom reached for the leg of the chair and started to pull himself up. He got an arm over the edge of the seat but put too much weight on it and the chair slid out from under him. He heard the dog barking as he fell back. The blackness engulfed him; this time the wave was freezing cold and a long time going over.

She says Joe, quietly, Joe, for God's sake, because he hasn't seen him yet, standing at the top of the Temple steps in his pajamas, not moving, his head tilted at an unnatural angle. It's too dark to make out Ned's face, but she can hear him crying now, softly. Which reassures her a little. Roy Roy, squatting beside him, on the boy's left, has one arm around his shoulder and a knife or something that gleams like a fucking knife pressed to the hollow of his neck.

What Joe does is raise the shotgun. She cries out no, close enough to grab his elbow and push up the barrels, but there isn't any question of his being able to use it. Roy Roy starts slowly down the steps, holding Ned's small body before him as a shield he knows has the power to make his own bulk invisible. He's talking to them, throwing out quick fierce gestures with the hand that has the knife in it, telling them to back off.

They have no choice but to do as he says.

As they retreat from the path into the long grass at the edge of the woods, Karen keeps talking to Ned, telling him not to be afraid, everything's going to be all right. The kid can't answer with the knife at his throat or turn his head to look at her, but she sees his terrified eyes whiten her way.

There's maybe four or five yards distance between them.

If she stretched out her hand she feels she could touch him. As they come down the steps, Joe has the shotgun leveled at the mute's shaved bullet head.

When they reach the bottom, Roy Roy stops and gives Donut's body a tentative kick with the toe of his sneaker. Then pushes at him irritably with his foot until he rolls over. His impatience, which is like a refusal to accept the evidence of his own eyes, reminds Karen of the way some animals, hyenas or geese she thinks, behave when confronted by the loss of a partner.

Donut doesn't move.

"He isn't dead," Joe shouts, "but you leave him here, man, I swear he will be. Give us back the boy."

Ned seems so close she can almost smell him.

For a moment it looks as if something might come of this. Some kind of trade-off. Roy Roy produces a series of low sub-articulate sounds from the back of his throat, but then just shrugs and keeps going. Backing up now, still facing front, as he moves his hostage around the side of the Temple.

Taking the path that leads down to the water.

Joe walks quickly over to where Donut is lying and holds the shotgun to his head. "You sure about it?"

But Roy Roy and Ned have already faded, slipped away under a covered walk of dripping rhododendrons.

"Mr. Welford? Can you hear me? You're gonna be okay now. We'll get you an ambulance right away. Can you hear me? Make a sign if you can hear me."

A shadow from the surface far above floated over his eyes.

"I don't think he can hear me. Use the landline, for Christ's sake, right there over the table. He must have been trying to reach it. Jesus Christ, what a mess!"

Tom opened his eyes and saw the other swimmers.

Charlie Kawalski was kneeling beside him, spreading some kind of towel or blanket over his legs. The Italian girl with the hard face was talking on the phone over his head, one foot on the overturned chair.

"Thank you, God," Kawalski murmured. "Now stay with me, Mr. Welford. You just got to stay awake now until the medics get here. Can you talk?"

He answered yes, but nothing came. Tried again and achieved perfect clarity. "Good to see you, Charlie."

Kawalski was still looking at him.

"EMS say they got a bus on Forest Avenue. Be with us in less than five," Officer Talese said. "You think I should look around?"

"No, call for back-up." His voice changed key. "What happened here, Mr. Welford? Who did this to you?"

"It was an accident," he tried shouting this time and saw Kawalski's worried face lighten.

"You're doing good. You lost some blood, but you hang in there, you'll be all right. What kind of accident?"

"She didn't mean to do it. My wife loves me. A little off balance, that's all. She needs help."

"What about your kid? Is he with her?"

Tom closed his eyes. Nodded.

"Upstairs, in our bedroom."

Tom was shivering uncontrollably. "They're holed up in there. She turned all the goddamned lights out. You didn't notice . . . how dark it is?"

"I don't see anything different." Kawalski frowned.

"I'm afraid of her going right over this time."

"You're right, Mr. Welford, maybe it is a little dim."

Humoring him, for Pete's sake.

"You have to . . . she took the shotgun. Said she had nothing left to live for. You get Ned away from her."

Tom saw Kawalski turn to the female deputy and say, "Tell Central we got a possible EDP." He brought his head back close to Tom's. "Easy now, we'll take care of this . . . we'll get him back, he'll be okay."

The rain has stopped, leaving the cool air smelling of sage and freshly dug earth. Out over the Sound, high and bright behind the thinning cloud, a three-quarter moon casts hazy pools of light on the water. It allows Karen to make out the track that runs a hundred yards across the headland and forks at the top of the low cliff, one path leading to the old bath-house, the other down some stone steps to the shore and boat dock.

It's at the junction of the two paths that Roy Roy now stands, looking back over to Edgewater. He's put Ned up on his shoulders, the way Tom liked to do. Together, in the shifting light, they make a single grotesque figure.

On the water, below them, the dock with Victor's white cabin cruiser bumping softly at its mooring comes fully into view. Karen glances behind her and sees the house lights blazing out over the bay.

"They're heading for the boat," Joe says, as they steadily close the gap between them.

"No, he won't leave without the others," insists Karen, whose idea it was to give Roy Roy a little more space. "He has to be where he can watch the house."

She sees him turn then and, swinging Ned down off his neck, lead him by the hand over the brow of the headland toward the bath-house. They still have fifty yards on them. She starts to run, suddenly afraid that Roy Roy was given instructions neither of them knows about. "Hurry, Joe, for God's sake," she calls, regretting now that she let them out of their sight even for a minute.

Built into the side of the cliff, the bath-house, or what's left of it, can only be seen from the water. Its long terrace, where dancers once moved against each other to the rhythms of another age, and most of its supporting sea-wall have crumbled into the Sound. Unused since the late fifties, the building has a sign warning trespassers that they enter at their own risk. All that remains of the bath-house itself, the upper deck which forms the roof of a carved stone shell—Tom had a wooden balustrade put around it to protect anyone from the fall to the rocks below—lies glistening before them, a condemned belvedere, slick with rain.

She watches Roy Roy walk to the edge of the platform,

then lift Ned over the railing and hold him the other side by one arm while he clambers over and joins him on the narrow outer ledge, nothing now between them and the drop.

She can hear Ned whimpering.

"You know you can't hurt him," Karen says, as she advances slowly across the deck; Joe's at her side, holding the shotgun. "If you let anything happen to him, it's your life too. There's no point any more. Victor is dead. You understand, he's DEAD."

Accompanying her words with gestures and a few halting signs she learned in an unsuccessful attempt to get Ned to communicate after he lost his voice. "It's all over, Roy. Just give him back to us, then we'll walk away . . . *Please.*"

Roy Roy remains motionless, staring at her, his eyes dark slits in the broad impassive face. He gives no indication of having understood a word. Above his head the sky has opened up to reveal a vault of pale watery stars.

"You know what happened," Tom said, "I caught her down here doing something to the electrical . . . listen, I want to ask you a favor, Charlie."

"Sure, anything, Mr. Welford. What do you need?"

"See the circuit breakers on the wall up there?" He had to pause, his breathing was becoming shallow and rapid. "Third box from the left, one that says 'Master' on it. Flip the lever, make sure . . . she didn't tamper with the goddamned supply."

"What would she want to do that for?"

"How the hell do I know? She's crazy."

"I dunno," Kawalski said. "I'd feel better waiting till the back-up gets here. We don't want to start anything that might upset her. It could make the situation worse for the kid."

"It's Ned I'm thinking about." Tom felt the wave rising over his head again. "He's scared of the fucking dark. And you know something?"

"I dunno, Mr. Welford."

"So am I." There's still no pain.

He closed his eyes. "Just do it, Charlie."

He allows her and Joe to come on, until they're only a matter of yards from the balustrade, then he holds up a hand to show it's far enough.

He still has an arm around Ned's neck. But there's no sign of the knife: he doesn't need it any more.

She begs him to let Ned go.

Roy Roy turns his head in the direction of the house.

She sees his face darken for a moment as if the moon has gone behind a cloud. He seems to hesitate.

Karen knows what is coming. She yells at him to stand aside and, grabbing the shotgun from Joe, takes aim at the mute's chest, but he has foreseen this too.

Boosting Ned in the air, he places his bare feet carefully on the three-inch railing in front of them so that for a moment their heads are level, one silhouette against a dazzled patch of water far out on the Sound.

The next moment he's vanished.

She swings the gun, but he's already ducked down behind the balustrade, scuttled along the ledge a short way before swinging over the edge and dropping out of sight.

Leaving the boy standing.

"Ned," Karen screams, as she sees him turn his head, looking around for Roy Roy.

"Don't move, honey."

"Mom."

Sees him look down at the rocks below; then, reluctantly, as if he has to drag his eyes away, back at her.

"Mom, I'm scared."

What she has to do is keep calm, keep talking, say to him in an ordinary voice, You'll be okay, honey, if you stay where you are. Look at me, Ned . . . don't look down.

But she can't get the words out. She just stands, paralyzed by the fear that if she opens her mouth, if she takes another step or tries to reach out for him, he won't be there.

He glances down again at the sea, closes his eyes and begins to sway.

"Go ahead, you can do it, you can fly, Ned," she hears Joe softly cajoling him. "You don't have to be afraid"—moving up steadily, holding out his arms—"remember the story about the albatross? Remember Dumbo and the crows? If you believe enough, you can fly. All you do is lean forward . . ."

Making a game of it.

". . . reach out to me, then jump."

Hears Ned give a little cry.

"I won't let you fall."

"No!" Karen shrieks.

As suddenly he topples backward, windmilling his arms to save himself. She hurls herself at the rail, knowing it's too late to close the horrifying gulf between them; and gets a glimpse of taloned scaly wings flapping lazily up to claim her child for the darkness: not believing that Joe can possibly reach him in time to perform the miracle, which is somehow to catch Ned by a fleeing ankle—not believing, even as she watches him do it—and bring the boy back over the rail and down with him on to the hard hollow deck.

God, oh God.

She lets slip the shotgun she's still holding and, with a hoarse sob, kneeling beside them, folds Ned into her arms.

Everything else is forgotten. She barely notices Joe's hand on her shoulder, or hears him say gently, "There isn't time for this, Karen, not now."

Reaching for her gun with his foot, he kicks sideways and sends it spinning over the edge. In the same instant, coming from somewhere underneath them, she feels a low vibration. The platform begins to sway as they scramble to their feet and back away from the overhang. The rumbling grows louder before it suddenly stops. There's a moment of eerie stillness, which makes her think of Roy Roy and whether he's still down there.

Then the balustrade and part of the deck break off neatly into Long Island Sound and, after a split-second delay that feels like eternity, chunks of falling masonry hit the rocks and water below with a thunderous roar.

But there's no cry, or none that she can hear.

The silence surged softly backward.

"Let's go," Joe said, taking the boy from her and pulling him like a sack on to his shoulders. "I heard the shot, you can be damned sure somebody else heard it too. Next thing the whole place'll be crawling with cops."

Karen brought her head up slowly. "What am I supposed to do now, Joe?" she asked in a low voice. "What would you do?"

Behind her, a crack had appeared in the night sky; along the eastern horizon, the sea was already fading to gray.

"We had a plan, didn't we?"

She gave him a tired smile.

Joe had already considered and rejected the only viable alternative: the boat was their nearest means of escape. They could sail her back to Sea Cliff and pick up the Suburban. But he knew the difficulty of the cliff path that led down to the old dock: they'd never make it with Ned.

"Where did you leave your car?"

She laughed. "Where I always said I would."

They're halfway across the lower lawn, running for the Caprice, which she parked down by the stables, out of sight of the main house, when Karen stops and looks back at Edgewater.

Joe catches her arm and drags her forward.

"I didn't have any choice," she pants after him. "It was either that or . . . he tried to kill Ned. You saw what happened."

The lights in the west wing, and the lamp on the balcony outside their bedroom, are burning steadily. Surely she didn't imagine seeing them go down? What if Tom is still alive?

What if he's not?

"For God's sake, just keep going."

They circle around the long floodlit pool. She sees Ned

look back over Joe's shoulder and hold out a hand to Flipper, his inflatable dolphin, blown hither and thither by a breeze that barely ruffles the glowing blue water. Jostling the other aquatic creatures corraled at the shallow end, it keeps nodding and smiling, nodding and smiling.

In the distance she can hear sirens beating their way up the shore road from Glen Cove.

Karen hesitates. When ear and eye are in conflict, she remembers Tom telling her once, it's always the eye that wins.

And another thing Tom said, just before she shot him.

If she stays to explain, who will believe her story.

SOUTH

She was woken by the sun coming in the car window and warming the side of her face as they drove south.

Karen turned her head and saw Ned asleep on the back seat, clutching his security blanket, and knew it hadn't been a dream. She lay back and watched the horizon roll up ahead of them, the sky over the forested levees of the Interstate a different, deeper blue. In a minute she would ask Joe if he was getting tired and would like her to drive.

She closed her eyes, but the pain in her fingers would keep her awake now. Joe reached over and pulled her head on to his shoulder. She looked up at him with a smile. They didn't speak for another fifteen or twenty miles.

"You feeling hungry yet?" Joe asked, "I thought we'd stop for breakfast somewhere outside Raleigh. Then maybe see about trading the car."

It was what they'd always planned.

"Looking like this?" Under a man's seersucker jacket she'd found in the back of the Caprice, she still had on the damp rags of the ball-gown from last night. She put a bare muddy foot up on the dash.

"With not even a pair of shoes to my name."

"We'll find you something to wear," Joe laughed, "don't worry. And Ned too. What size does he take?"

The exchange felt a little strained, leaving her with a sense of *déjà vu* and a vague apprehension or sadness that she didn't want to analyze, but her mood didn't last.

The idea of having breakfast together for the first time as

a family pleased her, and she told him. An honest-to-God family, Joe proudly declared. He was playing a Van Morrison tape he'd discovered, with a whoop of delight, among Hendricks's mostly jazz and standards collection. When it got to a track that had been a favorite of theirs, "Cleaning Windows," he turned the stereo up high and sang along at the top of his voice to the rolling Celtic soul beat.

The music still sounded good; where Joe saw victory in a lyric that hymned the free and easy life, she heard irony; but nothing could take from the joyful spirit of an old song that fit the new morning just right.

Her eyes filled with tears.

To think that they had come full circle, back with hardly a dollar between them on the open road and just those odd wild surges of happiness because you never know where it can lead. She wasn't sure if she was capable of getting them now, or feeling that way again.

"You'll wake the boy," she said, but Ned slept on.

"Did I tell you he had a gun? Tom wouldn't have hesitated to use it." She spoke in a low, dull murmur that made Joe reach across and switch off the tape deck. "Sometimes I think he really meant to kill us all."

Ahead of them, he watched a yellow dog trotting along beside the highway in the hot sun.

Karen said, "That's what they came to do, you know. Tom paid to have you killed."

"Yeah?" He didn't look at her.

The dog getting nearer by the second.

"Then after they'd gone, when I didn't find you"—he heard the tremulous note in her voice—"I guess I thought it was because you were somehow involved. I thought they might have put pressure on you to take Ned. I'm sorry, Joe."

A speck in his rearview mirror now, the animal turned, ran across the highway and jumped the divider. Joe waited for a screech of brakes from the northbound lanes. But there was none. He rolled down the window to let some air circulate.

"Well, don't be," he said, "because it's the truth."

Last night, heading out on the New Jersey Turnpike, the fear of pursuit receding with the Manhattan skyline, Joe had begun to tell her his side of the story. She didn't want to hear it then. She only wanted to sleep.

"When you were at the beach yesterday afternoon," he went on, determined to have this out now, "Victor stopped by the cottage. He didn't stay long. What he had to say was, Either you help us, Mr. Haynes, or we honor the contract."

He told Karen the conditions of Serafim's irresistible Balkan offer. And then some of what happened.

"Why did you come back to Overbeck?" she asked.

"It was where they said to bring him."

"You didn't know I was there."

"What do you think? If I'd had the slightest idea, Jesus, I dunno, maybe it's a lucky thing I didn't."

He saw her frown. She'd made a statement, not asked a question. "You knew nothing . . . nothing about what they did to that poor man, the detective."

Joe shook his head.

"I could hear you moving about upstairs in the apartment, I tried to warn you, only they . . . prevented it."

Her hands were trembling. He wanted to comfort her, to tell her how much he loved her, but it wasn't the moment.

"We were supposed to wait in the wagon," he explained. "Ned wouldn't stop crying, he kept asking for you and, well, Tom. I'd forgotten his security blanket."

"Yes," she said softly, "I know."

"You realize it was the first time we'd ever been alone together?"

She touched his cheek. "You've got a lot to learn."

"I thought I'd lost you for good, kiddo."

For a moment neither of them spoke. Then Karen asked, "What would you have done? I mean if Victor had gotten the ransom money and let you keep Ned?"

"Sent you a postcard from Ritzville, Oregon, or some place back of beyond, saying wish you were here. It would have

been blackmail," Joe smiled at her in the mirror, "but I figured there was a chance you mightn't see it that way."

She waited for Joe in the mall parking lot, while he went shopping for clothes and a few basic needs at K-Mart. Ned was
still asleep in the back. She hung the detective's jacket over
the window to keep the strong Carolina sun off his face.

She played the radio dial, searching for the news bulletin
that would tell her whether or not she was wanted for murder. But it was too soon, the story hadn't broken yet.

Joe came back looking pleased with his purchases. He'd
got her what she'd asked for: sun-glasses, white jeans, some
extra-large white cotton T-shirts and a pair of Keds. He'd also
bought her some hydrogen peroxide for her hair and Band-
Aids for her cuts, and a toothbrush.

"Did you remember to get scissors?" Karen asked.

The truth can't hurt us, Joe had said.

She had made up her mind to tell him. Tell him about what
happened in the bedroom, the hell Tom had put her through,
the way he'd tried to twist things around, about the crazy ac-
cusations he'd made—they *were* completely crazy, and yet . . .
she could understand how it must have looked from her husband's warped perspective.

In cases of abuse, they say, it's the victim who becomes the
villain, and the villain . . . the victim.

You see what he tried to do to me.

But then she decided that really Joe didn't need to know.

She changed in the car, then, after dumping her ball-gown
in a trash can, went into the mall to look for a washroom.

"How much money do we have left?"

"Eighteen hundred, just under. We'll be lucky to see five
for this heap," Joe said. "We'd had the Suburban to trade, our
prospects right now might be looking a little brighter."

"Don't say anything about a nest egg, please. You think we
should take the time to clean it out?"

The floor of Hendricks's Chevy was a deep litter of waste

paper, empty cigarette packs, torn-up parking tickets, brown paper sandwich bags, Styrofoam coffee cups—the detritus of waiting. Joe shrugged.

They were sitting across the street from a used car dealer's called Peden's Auto; its forecourt, gaily decorated with flags and bunting, was lined with late models of all makes, prices drawn and slashed through in white chalk on their windshields. "Let's just get it over with," he said as he swung the battered Caprice out in to the traffic, made a U-turn and drove on to the lot.

Karen was to let Joe do the talking.

The salesman, whose name was Floyd Miller, had obviously sized them up before they got out of the car. In his mid-forties, tall with a long-jawed narrow face, perfectly coiffed chestnut hair and a slow easy grin, he stood and chatted with them for a while—the only questions Floyd asked were ones you had to answer yes to, just to get you in the mood—before leading Joe off to what Karen had no doubt would be slaughter.

All she'd asked was that it shouldn't be a Buick.

While the two men talked and looked at automobiles—in their price range, the twelve to fifteen hundred dollar bracket, they were mostly parked at the end of the lot—Karen got in the back of the Caprice with Ned, who had just woken. He stared at her in silent bewilderment. Afraid that last night's trauma might have stolen back his voice, she held him on her knee and comforted him, before she explained gently that they were taking a long trip with Joe: it would mean a lot of driving but they were going to have fun, the three of them.

"Mom," he interrupted her, "why do you have different hair? You look like Hazel with your hair like that. I'm hungry. When are we going to eat?"

She hugged him to her until he squawked, then dressed him in his new K-Mart clothes, which he claimed hurt him. Between his shoulder blades, Karen discovered a fiery red mark the size of a penny. She didn't ask about it, but promised

Ned that when they got their new car they would stop at a restaurant she'd seen on the strip and order up the biggest and best breakfast ever.

"What would you like, Doc?"

"Waffles and syrup," he said, "the way Darlene fixes 'em."

She packed their few things into a K-Mart shopping bag.

While she was going through the glove compartment, making a selection of Hendricks's tapes—there was nothing else in the car worth taking—her hand at the back came on a half-empty bottle of Pepto-Bismol and a small snub-nosed automatic with an extra ammunition clip taped to the grip.

She had the gun in her lap, wondering what she should do with it, when she saw Joe coming back toward the car. She pulled up her T-shirt and stuck it in the waist of her jeans.

Joe held open the door of the Caprice for her and took the shopping bag. "Leave the keys."

"Well? Did you cut a sweetheart deal?" she asked as they walked to the end of the lot.

Joe nodded. "You bet. An '85 Cutlass Sierra. The kind of car only a couple of fugitives would be seen dead in. Floyd said . . ." He saw the look she gave him. "Just kidding."

Floyd Miller had disappeared into his office. He came out as they passed under the windows to congratulate them on their excellent choice, and to hand Ned a balloon. Then, for the first time, he went over to look at the Caprice.

"What about papers and stuff?"

Joe said, "No problem. He told me they'll probably break it up for spares. I got two hundred for it."

"What does that leave us?"

"Four hundred dollars."

"God, Joe. What are we going to do?"

"It's enough to get us across the country, if we're careful. Out of Texas anyway."

They climbed into the gold Sierra, which had maroon plush upholstery and a cloying smell that reminded her of Juicy Fruit chewing gum. Karen opened all the windows.

Ned said, "Mama's got a gun."

"She may need it," Joe laughed as they drove down the ramp to rejoin the highway.

He had to hold for a gap in the slow but steady stream of Sunday traffic. In the side mirror Karen saw Floyd Miller step out from behind the Caprice, which had both the hood and trunk lids up now, and wave at them.

"Hey, wait a minute, wait!" he was shouting.

She turned to Joe and said, "He's on to us. I knew it. He was in his office too long . . . Keep going, Joe, drive."

"That might not be such a great idea." Joe tilted his eyes at a police patrol car that had appeared from nowhere and was parked the other side of the street. Watching them.

"Shit." She slipped a hand under her T-shirt, closing it over the grip of the detective's gun.

"Better see what he wants," Joe said.

Floyd Miller put his head in the window of the Sierra on the passenger side. A little short of breath, he grinned down lazily at Karen. "You folks sure do seem to be in a hurry. I didn't see you with any baggage, so I thought I'd take a look. You forgot this."

He held up the suitcase Karen had last seen in the locker at Grand Central Station.

Joe took both hands off the wheel and wiped them on his jeans. He cleared his throat. "Honey?"

"It was a mix-up," Karen said to the salesman, when she felt able to speak. "He thought I'd taken care of it"—she shot her partner a sideways glance—"and I thought he had. Thanks a lot, I mean, thanks for not . . . you know what I mean."

She leaned up impulsively and kissed Floyd on the cheek.

"If you can't be honest, ma'am, I always say what's the sense in doing anything? Where you folks headed?"

He looked over at Joe. "Should be a lever some place down there under the dash. Pull it to you, bud, and I'll be glad to throw this in the trunk."

"No, wait, that's okay," Karen said, watching the patrol car across the street move off. "It can go up front with me, there are some things I may need for the trip."

She gave a little sigh that had a prayer in it somewhere, and opened the door.

"Y'all take care now," Floyd Miller said as he handed her the heavy case. "Drive easy."

Joe raised a hand and, with a family man's proprietary smile, told him, "Disney World."

"All *right,*" Ned gave his blessing from the back of the gold Sierra as it glided forward.